A HOLLYWOOD ENDING

A HOLLYWOOD ENDING

ROBYN SISMAN

First published in Great Britain in 2008 by Orion Books,
an imprint of The Orion Publishing Group Ltd
Orion House, 5 Upper Saint Martin's Lane
London WC2H 9EA

An Hachette Livre UK Company

1 3 5 7 9 10 8 6 4 2

Th
aut as the
ce with
88.

A
re ay be
mitted
i nical,
t the
d the

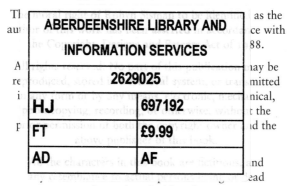

ABERDEENSHIRE LIBRARY AND INFORMATION SERVICES	
2629025	
HJ	697192
FT	£9.99
AD	AF

is purely coincidental.

A CIP catalogue record for this book
is available from the British Library.

ISBN (Hardback) 978 0 7528 9888 9
ISBN (Export Trade Paperback) 978 0 7528 9889 6

Typeset by Deltatype Ltd, Birkenhead, Merseyside

Printed in Great Britain by Clays Ltd, St Ives plc

The Orion Publishing Group's policy is to use papers that
are natural, renewable and recyclable products and made
from wood grown in sustainable forests. The logging and
manufacturing processes are expected to conform to the
environmental regulations of the country of origin.

www.orionbooks.co.uk

To Adam, Flora and Charlotte

PART I

HOLLYWOOD

CHAPTER 1

He was the man she'd been looking for all her life. Paige adored him: body and soul, heart and mind, today and for ever. Even though she'd known him barely twenty-four hours. Even though they could never be together.

They lay facing one another, each propped on a bare elbow dug into the scratchy sand: too exhausted to move and too enraptured to want to. Their clothes were ripped and filthy, their faces marked by the ordeal they had shared and survived against all odds. But that was unimportant now. What mattered was that at last they were truly alone, just the two of them in the empty desert, with no one watching and no need to pretend.

'How long before they find us?' His voice was deep and mellow as a bass drum. They were so close that she could feel it reverberate through her own body: an intimate invasion. Her eyelashes flickered in response.

'Maybe two hours, if the locator chip's still working.' Only two hours in which to pack a lifetime of loving. '... Sir,' she added, with a gulp. It was hard to keep her voice steady.

'Sir,' he echoed bitterly. He looked away, suddenly moody and distant, displaying his impossibly handsome profile lit by a fiery sunset glow. Paige gazed with longing at the tensed muscle of his jaw and golden gleam of his hair.

'Wasn't there some British king,' he said, still staring

across the sand, 'who gave up everything to marry the woman he loved?'

'King Edward,' she answered softly. 'The woman was an American. The Brits thought she wasn't good enough for him, just because she didn't have a title and a castle.' She paused. 'And because she was already married.'

'But you're not married.' His head snapped back to her in alarm, and he grabbed her shoulder so fiercely that she winced. '*Are you?*'

'No ... But you are.' Her face crumpled. Tears squeezed from the corners of her eyes.

'Don't!' He reached over to smudge her cheek dry with his thumb. Helplessly she melted towards him, tilting her head to caress his hand with her cheek. Any second now they'd be kissing. Her lips parted in anticipation as his hand slid to the nape of her neck and drew her towards him. 'Don't cry,' he murmured huskily. 'Please, Catherine, don't cry.'

For a moment time seemed to stand still. Expression drained from Paige's face. Her green-grey eyes darkened to flint. 'Catherine's your *wife*,' she told him.

'Aw, shit.'

'Cut!' called a voice.

'Sorry, guys.' Jackson Rolfe raked back his artfully tousled locks and swept the watching darkness with his naughty-boy smile. 'Guess I never could tell one woman from another.'

Sycophantic laughter rippled around the set. Jackson was currently the highest earning actor in Hollywood: if he cracked a joke, it was funny. Paige forced herself to smile along, as if she too found it a real gas that after six weeks of filming Jackson had 'forgotten' the name of his co-star's character (Sally, short for Salima: not too taxing). She knew perfectly well that Jackson's lapse had been intentional.

'Fifteen minutes, folks.' The assistant director's second assistant's assistant appeared at the edge of the brightly lit set, hugging her clipboard, walkie-talkie pressed to one ear, and started relaying instructions. The sand that had been artistically strewn among polystyrene boulders needed to be brushed smooth for the next take. Greens wanted to check that the olive tree was secure. The cinematographer was worried about shadows, and wanted to test different filters on the stand-ins.

Paige stood up, brushing sand from her combat trousers. She heard the insect whine of a Polaroid camera as someone took a snapshot record of how she looked. Hair, probably, or maybe Wardrobe: both were obsessed with continuity.

'Help me up, will you, angel?' Jackson, still sprawled on the sand, reached out his hand to her. Paige glanced down at him. 'Angel' was not what he called her in private. But the crew were watching. She did as he asked, but he leapt up at the same time, so that inadvertently she pulled too hard and he toppled against her, momentarily bouncing off her breasts. He leered down at her as if she had deliberately engineered this. 'Whoa there, Salima.'

Paige disengaged her hand, determined not to react. 'Could I get a glass of water here?' she called into the shadows.

'Sure thing, Miss Carson.' Almost at once there was the sound of crushed ice rattling into a paper cup.

She stepped off the raised set onto the concrete floor.

'Careful, Miss Carson. Watch out for the dolly track,' warned a voice.

It took a moment for her eyes to adjust after the brilliance of the set. Then the familiar scene came into focus: not sunset in the desert, but a sound stage on a Hollywood lot, where the sun never penetrated and the air was strictly temperature-controlled. It was a huge, windowless aircraft hangar of a building, with fat rubber cables taped to the floor, plywood walls that ended in mid-air, and steel gantries stretching overhead like the tracks of some vast floating railroad station. There was the usual clutter of ladders, tripods, reflector boards, and metal tables covered with focus tape, screwdrivers, batteries, spare lenses and stained Styrofoam cups. People stood or lounged in apparently aimless groups, dwarfed by their surroundings. Two cameras were poised on the set, like empty-eyed robots waiting to attack.

As usual between takes, Jackson had hurried over to Video Village to check his performance on the monitor. Paige could see him bending over the director's shoulder as they both peered at the screen on the steel trolley table. Lester sat hunched in his wood and canvas chair, sneakered feet tucked on the footrest, wearing his usual director's outfit of sloppy black T-shirt, headphones and straggly beard. It was part of the Lester Legend that he grew a beard while shooting a movie, then shaved it off for the wrap party. Next to him sat the script editor, the shooting script open in front of her amid the usual clutter of water bottles, megaphone, highlighter pens and coils of coloured cabling. The assistant director and cinematographer were there too, looking like Tweedledum and Tweedledee in their matching *Code Red* baseball caps as they consulted the stopwatch that recorded the duration of each take. Behind them stood various assistants, dressed as though for the beach in shorts and tennis shoes. Everyone was staring at the monitor. Paige hated seeing herself on screen, but for a moment she couldn't resist watching the watchers, trying to gauge how things were going from their expressions. Lester frowned as Jackson pointed at the screen and murmured persuasively into his ear. What was it this time? Did Jackson have yet another 'suggestion' that would result in more camera time for him and less for her?

'Miss Carson?' Someone was holding out a cup to her.

'Is this my special water?' she demanded.

'Kabbalah mineral, right?' The boy was ridiculously cute, and looked so anxious that Paige regretted her snappy tone. It wasn't his fault that she was so wound up.

'Thanks.' She smiled, taking the cup. There were two crates of this stuff in her trailer, a gift from her friend and total lifesaver, Gaby, who'd told her that the wisdom of centuries was distilled in every drop – though it tasted pretty much like ordinary water. Paige drained the cup and crushed it her hand. If Lester was unhappy with her performance, he could tell her to her face. Meanwhile, she needed to keep focused. She went over to her chair, found her iPod and plugged herself in. Her eyes closed. *Stay in character.*

OK. She was Salima, one quarter Palestinian by birth, one hundred per cent American by upbringing, a top CIA field agent whose tough exterior hid a failed marriage and a dead child. Because she spoke fluent Arabic she'd been one of the team parachuted into Lebanon to rescue the US President (played by Jackson), who was being held hostage by an Islamic militant group after Air Force One had crashed.

No one had wanted Salima on the 'Code Red' mission. Firstly, she was a woman. Secondly, there were doubts about her loyalty: Salima's grandmother had been expelled by Israeli forces from her home in Palestine and had nearly died in a refugee camp before fleeing to America. In the movie's second-act climax, when Salima revealed herself as a double-agent in cahoots with the kidnappers, these doubts seemed shockingly justified. Of course this turned out to be a clever double bluff, as well as a total rip-off from *Where Eagles Dare* – or *hommage*, as Hollywood liked to call it. 'For the first two-thirds of the movie Salima is a beautiful enigma,' Lester had told her, sculpting his words out of the air with a pudgy hand. 'Is she a patriot, or the enemy? A closed-down fighting machine, or a real woman? Then she releases her inner passion: emotionally, politically – and of course sexually.'

Of course. Paige counted deep breaths in and out, trying to will herself into a passionate yet enigmatic state. But all she felt was the same knot of anxiety and mounting rage that had lodged behind her breastbone for weeks.

It was hard to remember how ecstatic she'd been to land this part. After an inexplicable run of flops her position on the A-list had been looking a teensy bit precarious, and she'd needed a bankable project. Obviously, she also owed it to herself to choose a role that would stretch her as an artist. *Code Red* had seemed perfect on both counts. It was a thriller, but it was 'edgy' (Hollywood's latest buzzword), thanks to on-screen Presidential adultery and the daring portrayal of an Arab woman as liberated, empowered, and pledged to America's democratic values. Lester was the king of action movies; Jackson had just won a Golden Globe for his title role in the King Arthur blockbuster, and was nominated for Best Actor in the upcoming Academy Awards. Here was a huge opportunity for Paige to show the world her acting range which did, yes, actually, go beyond taking off her clothes.

Consequently, she'd pulled every string in town, hassled her agent, put out for the studio execs, and made sure that she was seen looking super-fit and sexy in running shorts and crop top. Fortunately, she was what Hollywood called 'the exotic type', which basically meant you weren't blonde. For once she'd had the edge over the favoured golden ones. There'd been a bad moment when it seemed that the part might go to a rival, but then it turned out that the shooting schedule clashed with the other actress's plan to travel to China and pick out a baby girl to adopt. *Quel* relief!

Paige had totally knocked herself out on the preparation: three weeks training with the Marines (her thighs were like rock); hours in the firing range (even though she hated loud noises); late-night sessions with her acting coach, mapping out the inner journey of her character. The studio had hired a dialect coach for her too. Arabic had a wonderful snarling sound to it. Paige had loved sitting out on her patio at night with her earplugs in, gazing over the lights of Los Angeles and repeating the breathy phrases to any eavesdropping coyote. Her coach said she was one of the quickest students he'd ever had. Ha! Tell that to the Principal of Pacific High, where she'd majorly flunked out. Though maybe the coach was just flattering her because of who she was. Last week she'd learned, just by chance, that a real Arabic speaker had been hired to loop in her Arabic words in post-production. All that practising had simply been to ensure that her mouth made or less the right shapes on screen. Unconsciously Paige bent her head and pressed her palms cross-wise to her chest.

'Hey, babe. You OK?' Lester had lumbered up behind her and laid his hands on her shoulders, bending close to her ear so that his beard grazed her neck.

'Sure.' Paige snapped her eyes open and sat up perkily. 'Just getting a little, you know, head space.' She turned to give him her best good-sport smile, which tightened as she saw Jackson beside him.

Lester pulled a chair close, and gestured to Jackson to do the same, so that the three of them were huddled in a tight, secret circle. Oh God: group hug time. Sure enough, Lester draped his arms around Paige and Jackson and pulled them close.

'Remember the scene at the airport when Ilsa and Rick say goodbye?' he began.

Paige nodded. She knew what was coming. In practically every picture she'd made, from comedy to costume drama, there was always a moment when the director invoked *Casablanca*. 'That's the kind of intensity we need here,' Lester continued. 'This is *the* emotional climax. A four-handkerchief scene. I want audiences all over the world sobbing into their popcorn. This is real love. This is real tragedy. You're not President and agent any more, just Hart and Sally, a man and a woman wanting what they can never have. I need you to give me all you've got. And you've got plenty: I know that. Now let me see it.' With a final squeeze of their shoulders he let them go, stood up, and clapped his hands. 'Let's get this show on the road.'

Instantly all was bustle and efficiency. Jackson was swept off to have his tan retouched. Paige hardly had time to put her iPod away before she was pounced on. Hands kneaded gel into her hair to reinstate the mussed-up, escaped-from-death look. She offered her lips for more gloss, her cheek for a dab of purple bruising. The layers of putty that gave her nose that authentic Arab look (so Lester said) were checked for cracks, and repowdered. The putty took forever to apply, and itched like hell. There were fingers at her shirt, undoing another button – 'Lester wants more cleavage' – and smearing the tops of her breasts with something to make them look slick with sweat. She climbed back onto the set, where Jackson was holding a tiny spray can to his mouth. 'You'd better have some of this, too,' he told her, angling it towards her. Paige dug her nails into her palms, suppressing a rude retort, then opened her mouth obediently so he could give her a squirt of minty breath-freshener before tossing the can to one of the crew.

Lester and the cinematographer took one last look through the view-finder. Paige and Jackson got into position, in front of the blank blue screen onto which SFX would later project the desert background that was already in the can.

'Final touches!'

'Rolling. Quiet, please!'

'Speed.'

'Action.'

The clapper board snapped its jaws, and here they were again. *Scene 34. Exterior. Lebanese desert. Hart and Salima confess their love.* Paige gazed rapturously into Jackson's square, handsome, hateful face, focusing on his startlingly blue eyes (tinted contacts). Close up, his cheeks looked puffy under the make-up. Too much junk food, booze, partying, et cetera. Especially et cetera.

Concentrate! This was the man she loved – admired – desired, just like ... well, like no one she knew, actually, or might ever meet, the way things were going. 'Paige Carson, twenty-nine and currently single', as the movie columnists loved to describe her.

Jackson was holding his head higher this time, as he gazed out across the non-existent desert and ruminated about King

Edward: he must have noticed his double chin on the monitor. The studio had hired a full-time nutritionist to stock his fridge with wheatgrass juice and yoghurt and accompany him to every meal, but it would take an FBI surveillance team to keep him away from the bagels, cherry pies and giant subs provided in truckloads by the caterers, plus the other substances smuggled in by his entourage. It was so unfair that guys could always get away with a couple of inches on their gut, as if beefy was macho, while everyone freaked if a female actor gained a single pound. The reason so many actresses adopted babies was that they'd wrecked their ovulation by being forced to lose weight. Paige couldn't help the way she was built. Thanks to her dad she was tall and big boned; from her mother she'd inherited an exuberant bust that refused to shrink below a C cup, however much she dieted. Right now she'd kill for just one sugar-coated, fat-drenched doughnut.

Concentrate! Here was the part where she had to cry. Time for Skipper. Paige's face began to crumple as she pictured the beloved dachshund of her childhood, run over by a car on her tenth birthday. Darling Skipper ... Limp. Lifeless. His cute little paws still for ever. That time after he'd died, when she'd found the rubber ball that still bore his teeth marks. Tears welled in her eyes.

This time Jackson remembered to call her Salima. Now they were about to kiss. Paige did her droopy, swoony thing and fluttered her eyelids shut. Ew, his face was scratchy. Forget it! This was the man she loved. Rick and Ilsa. Inner passion. Now slide your hand up to his hair. But remember the camera. Don't hide his face.

His hands tightened round her neck and ribs. His mouth pressed against hers. She pictured the way the camera would capture the surrendering curve of her neck and the red-gold sparks in her dark hair as it swung free. But something was wrong. This wasn't the way they'd rehearsed it. Jackson was holding her way too tight. She couldn't breathe! She tried to ease away without ruining the shot. He must have felt her move, but he just grabbed her tighter. Bastard! The blood was thrumming in her temples. Sweat prickled her skin. In a moment she was going to pass out. She yanked herself free, let out her breath in an explosive hiss and gasped in fresh air.

'*Cut!*'

'Sorry, Lester,' Paige panted, fanning her face. 'Couldn't breathe.'

'Yeah, OK. Let's go again.' Was there a tinge of exasperation in his voice?

'It's not my fault,' she couldn't help saying. 'It's just that in rehearsal we—'

'It's nobody's fault.' Lester cut her short.

Paige twisted round to the camera crew, looking for confirmation. It must be obvious that Jackson had deliberately sabotaged the shot. The focus-puller, an old pal, raised his eyebrows at her in sympathy, but no one dared say anything.

Then Jackson's mellifluous voice rolled out across the sound stage, low and regretful.

'No, she's right. Lester. It's my fault. I was so in the role. I just, you know, *went there.*'

Yeah, right. Was Lester going to swallow this shit?

'That's what we want, Jacko,' Lester crooned back. 'Don't apologise. It was looking great until … Anyway, you OK now, Paige?'

She nodded. What else could she do? As they eased into position again Jackson shot her a triumphant smirk.

It had been like this right from the beginning. Before this movie Paige had never met Jackson, apart from exchanging a casual 'hi' at parties and awards ceremonies. He had a reputation for being difficult, but the best actors often did – herself included. Their first encounter had been at the so-called chemistry reading, when the studio suits checked that there was enough sizzle between the co-stars. It was humiliating to recall how eager she had been, how flattered and flattering, with every polished tooth on show, every nail buffed, every extraneous hair removed, and an outfit that had been painstakingly devised by her manager and acting coach to strike the perfect balance between credible CIA competence and screen sexiness. Jackson, by contrast, had slobbed unshaven into the meeting, wearing jeans, T-shirt and flip-flops. The first thing he had done was to apologise loudly for not having seen her work – 'except *Biker Boys*, of course', he'd added with a lecherous grin. 'My son's got the poster on his bedroom wall.' Paige hadn't been sure how to react to this. Jackson was Australian: maybe he thought this was a compliment. She'd giggled inanely, wanting him to like her.

But he didn't. Usually actors helped each other out at these readings; they were on the same side. Jackson had mumbled his lines as though half asleep, deliberately giving her no help, insultingly casual. She'd practically faked an orgasm to get him to react. It was even worse than those early auditions when you had to go in cold and then suddenly 'be' a hilarious waitress or the terrified victim of a serial killer. When the reading was finally over he'd taken a piece of gum out of his mouth and stuck it to the table.

But somehow she'd persuaded the suits. She was an actor, after all. And maybe it had been an off-day for Jackson, who was in mid-divorce following several well-publicised affairs. So when location shooting started in the Nevada desert (the insurers wouldn't cover Lebanon), she'd flown off feeling optimistic. Even if Jackson didn't like her (and why the hell not? she'd like to know), he would surely behave like a professional. His fee was about four times the size of hers; he could afford to be nice. But no. He ignored Paige except in their scenes together, where he constantly found subtle ways to upstage or wrong-foot her. He insisted on shooting scenes over and over until his performance was perfect, while for her the first take was usually the best, after which energy leaked out of her like steam from an espresso machine. Most nights he spent in a men-only huddle with his coaches and Lester, which resulted in his part getting bigger, and hers whittled down to a two-dimensional sidekick. This wasn't an ego thing – well, not *just* a ego thing. Jackson was unbalancing the picture. Its pitch-line was: 'She rescues him from the valley of death – he restores her soul.' But Jackson's re-writes meant that President Hartman pretty much rescued himself via manly courage, self-reliance, painful insights into his own heart of darkness, blah blah, while Salima looked on admiringly and gave him someone decorative to emote at.

Almost worse, Jackson cut her out of the camaraderie that developed between actors and crew on location, which she'd always found one of the best parts about making a movie. Jackson was always the one who got to organise treats for the crew: a Ben & Jerry's ice cream truck, or a bunch of Mexican chefs flown in from LA to make everyone tacos. One weekend, Paige ordered in some crates of beer: nothing too ostentatious or competitive, just a way to get a good vibe going. Somehow Jackson found out about her simple plan and trumped it by having his Harley Davidsons shipped out so he could race them over the sand with Lester and the 'boys'. They drank her beer and toasted Jackson.

Eventually, egged on by Gaby, who'd reminded Paige that she was a uniquely talented human being and must not allow this situation to fester, Paige had confronted him one evening alone in his trailer. It was the latest luxury model, with Jacuzzi, plasma screen and all the techno trimmings, overlaid with a personal litter of clothes, CD cases and empty potato-chip bags; and stank of pot. Jackson was sprawled in a leather chair, wearing a towelling robe and smoking. He showed neither pleasure nor surprise at her appearance. Standing tall and dignified, Paige came out with the speech she had rehearsed with Gaby. She respected Jackson so much. It was an honour to be working with him. But she felt there were issues between them. Was there a problem he wanted to share? Was it personal, or perhaps to do with her style of acting?

He'd looked at her with eyes narrowed against the smoke. 'What acting?'

'Excuse me?'

'I'm sorry, I wasn't aware you were an "actor".' He loaded the word with sarcasm. 'Did you, for example, go to drama school?'

'Of course!' OK, not *school* exactly, but she'd had the best coaches and taken classes, dozens of them, even stunt horsemanship and sword-fighting. Anyway, acting was instinctive. It was just something she could do.

'Did you sweat and slave to scrape the money together, wondering every single week if you'd have to drop out?'

'Well, not exactly. But I don't see—'

'Have you taken Shakespeare out into the bush, putting up the set every night and taking it down again just so you could say "Yes, my lord" in Act Two, Scene Three? Did you live four to a room with no air-conditioning in downtown LA, and work in Home of the Pancake for eight hours straight every night, so you could go to auditions during the day? Did you pawn your grandfather's watch so you could turn up to those auditions without holes in your shoes?' He jabbed his joint into an ashtray and leaned forward, forearms on knees. 'No, you did not! You just got bored with parties and shopping and maybe a little light modelling work, and sailed straight into Hollywood on a wave of privilege and Daddy's money.'

'That is so not true!'

'The reality is that ten years ago you made one movie that hit the spot for reasons we both know – and it isn't what I call acting. Since then, what?'

Paige could not believe what she was hearing. She punched her fists into her hip-bones. 'Only one of the highest-grossing movies of all time. Have you forgotten *Journey to Mount Doom?*'

'You played an elf. For about three minutes.'

'It beats saying "Yes, my lord" to two sheep shearers and a kangaroo.'

'That's where you're wrong. Acting's about experience. Acting is a craft. It comes from here.' He tapped a forefinger to his temple, then raised his eyebrows at her. 'Hello-o, anyone upstairs?'

The arrogant bastard was calling her stupid!

'There's a lot more to acting than hitting your mark, or looking pretty. Which I admit you are.' He relaxed back into the chair, and clasped his hands behind his head. His towelling robe gaped. 'Fancy a fuck?'

'What?' Paige stared at him in disgust. 'You cannot speak to me like this. I am a p-p-professional person!' Shit. Her brain was starting to lock in that familiar, dreaded way. She'd rather die than stutter in front of him.

'Oh, come on,' he drawled. 'You need me. I'm your ticket back to the big time. We're stuck out here in the great bugger-all. Might as well have some fun.'

She turned her back on him and yanked open the trailer door, using the time to pull in a series of quick breaths so she could get a run at the next consonant. 'Wait 'til my agent hears about this. And Lester.'

He laughed. 'Do what you want. You think anybody's going to fire me off this picture because Princess Paige has her nosey out of joint?'

She was so angry that, ignoring the steps, she jumped straight out of the trailer, misjudged the distance and sprawled ignominiously on her hands and knees in the dirt. Scrambling to her feet, she marched into the chill desert darkness, bruised and bewildered. She *was* a good actress. She was a star. She was Paige Carson. (Shit, where was her trailer? Oh, it was back that way.) How shocked Lester would be when he heard how Jackson had spoken to her!

Lester would make him apologise. The crew would find out about it, as they always did, and take her side. *Code Red* would be a smash hit. She and Jackson would both be nominated for Academy Awards, but only she would win. She would not even mention him in her acceptance speech.

This fantasy sustained her until she was back in her own trailer, and cold reality set in. Princess Paige ... that's what the celeb garbage press had called her when she'd pulled out of *Prime Rib* the day before filming started. They didn't say why she had quit – because she'd discovered that her part had been totally changed in the latest re-write, and that she was going to have to play the *mother* of a twenty-year-old boy. The actor was twenty-two, she was twenty-nine. Go figure. But naturally, this was never reported, and she was stuck with the 'diva' label. It might not look good if she walked off another picture. Jackson obviously had some weird hang-up about her, and was deliberately goading her, hoping she'd quit or be fired. Well, she would not give him that satisfaction. She'd tough it out.

The location work had been just about bearable. They'd mainly concentrated on the action scenes, which involved her running with Jackson through a hail of bullet fire and shouting things like 'Make for the wadi! Go, go, go!', or being drenched repeatedly in water as they emerged from faked marshland in take after take. Even then, she'd had to keep her lip buttoned. Before one scene Jackson asked her, 'Do you know your lines?' Of course, she'd answered. Then he said, 'Do you know *my* lines?' Yes, those too. Then he'd had the nerve to make her feed them to him, as if she were some eager-to-please bit-part actor instead of his co-star.

But being on the lot was even worse. Their scenes together were developing the romantic sub-plot between Salima and President 'Hart' Hartman in close-up. Hart's wife, Catherine, had been confined to a wheelchair after her tragic water-skiing accident; there were certain needs she couldn't satisfy.

Would Salima step into the breach? Would Hart leave his wife? *Code Red* was not just another action movie, but a multi-layered, bittersweet human drama that would keep the audience guessing until the end. That's what Lester said, anyway.

Paige thought it would be so much easier if Salima had turned out to be a baddie after all, and could just shoot Hart dead. Following his Oscars nomination, Jackson was more impossible and more fawned-over than ever. His lamest joke was hilarious, his most casual 'thanks, doll' received like an honour. Even his daily arrival on the lot was treated like breaking news. 'Mr Rolfe's car is on its way.' 'Mr Rolfe's car has arrived.' 'Mr Rolfe has exited his car.' Finally he'd appear in person, pumped up for action, flanked by his acting coach and personal publicist like a mafia don with his hoods, and send the whole place scurrying. Paige had to admit that he was a fine actor, but the heat of his ego scorched everything in its path and devoured every last atom of her creative oxygen.

Today was his birthday. She'd forgotten this until, at the end of one take, Lester called a break and summoned everyone over to the snack table. The usual calorie-fest of cookies, candy, and bagels had been pushed to each end, and in the middle of the table sat a giant cake in the shape of a motorbike, with marshmallow handlebars, chocolate tyres, and wheels of spun sugar spiked with forty-five candles.

Everyone sang 'Happy Birthday'. Lester gave a speech. Jackson cut into the cake, receiving a huge round of applause when he pretended the cake-knife was stuck and reprised his lines from the King Arthur movie before triumphantly extracting the knife and waving it aloft. A camera assistant got the whole thing on video: one for the gag reel that would be shown at the wrap party. Paige smiled until her face hurt, and gave him the present that her assistant had bought gift-wrapped for the occasion. It turned out to be a fancy Italian aftershave. 'My co-star thinks I stink,' Jackson quipped through a mouthful of cake crumbs. Cue for thigh-slapping guffaws.

Finally they got back to work. Paige glanced at the big digital clock on the wall that flashed up the ticking seconds: almost eleven o'clock. Today's call-sheet had shown her due on the set and ready to go at 7.30 a.m. Her day had started with a wake-up call at four-thirty. She'd been living on the lot for three weeks now, in her trailer parked in its designated bay outside the sound stage. By five-thirty she had done her yoga, showered, eaten her fruit-and-wholegrain breakfast, and given herself over to Hair and Make-up. One hour later she was ready for Wardrobe. Then she'd hung around while the lighting was adjusted using stand-ins, and a further half hour waiting for Jackson to finish a promo interview. So far she'd done twelve takes of this scene. Would it be lucky thirteen?

Scene 34. Ext. Lebanese desert. Again. Paige stood on the set, arms folded, while she waited for Jackson to return from his bathroom break. She was tired and hot. She hadn't been off the lot for five days. She wanted her break, her massage, her pomegranate juice, and the sushi lunch that was specially prepared for her and helicoptered over to the lot each day. (She suppressed a stab of eco-guilt about the helicopter: plenty of actors demanded this service for their *pets*.) During the happy birthday break the grips must have slid the huge side-doors of the sound stage briefly open, for Paige saw that the camel was now in its pen, ready to be led on set by the animal wrangler dressed in Arab costume. This was an encouraging sign that Lester was at least thinking of moving on; the camel part was in the next scene. Paige resolved to make this the best and final take. Ten out of the eleven scheduled weeks of filming were behind her. There were only a couple more scenes with Jackson. If she kept her cool, and did her job, she'd soon be free of him for ever.

Maybe it was this thought that gave her a surge of energy.

For as she spoke the familiar words for the umpteenth time she suddenly felt inspired – transported – overtaken. She *was* Salima, hungry for passion, desperate for love, a real woman whose heart was breaking. At the same time, the critical side of her brain told her everything was right: timing, voice, expression. She knew in her bones that the emotion would transfer to the screen and burn a hole in the hearts of the audience. Such moments were rare, but exhilarating when they came. It was like magic, like flying, and this man wiping away her tears so tenderly was part of it. She forgot it was Jackson. Her eyes closed. She swooned into his embrace and waited for his kiss. His lips were almost on hers when he stopped short and let out a thunderous burp in her face.

'Oops, too much cake,' Jackson chuckled.

The whole sound stage exploded with laughter. Paige even heard some appreciative hand-claps. Jackson was laughing too, though as soon as he caught her looking at him he instantly rearranged his features into a pantomime of contrition. 'Sorry, Paige,' he said in a sing-song, little-boy voice. This too was apparently hilarious.

She jumped to her feet. 'That's *it*! I'm out of here.'

Hardly anyone heard her to begin with, except a cameraman who pulled his face from the viewfinder to gape at her in consternation as she strode across the set. For a moment she hesitated blindly at the edge of lights, where the animal wrangler was waiting, then began to climb off the set.

'What's going on?' someone asked.

'I am leaving. I do not have to put up with this. And screw you, too!' she told the camel, whose long-lashed eyes were regarding her with disdain.

People were hurrying over to see what was happening, even the catering guys. She stomped past them to collect her bag. Lester had left Video Village and was coming across to meet her. 'What's the problem, Paige?'

'The problem is I am getting absolutely no support here! I will not be treated like this!'

She couldn't believe it: someone was sitting in her chair! 'Get your butt out of there,' she yelled. A scared-looking blonde with her tits on display – one of the many Debralees and Ashlees and Infinitees who were only here because they'd slept with someone – jumped out of the way. Paige snatched up her bag.

She felt Lester's hand on her arm. 'Now, Paige. Calm down. What are you doing?'

She shook him off. 'What's it look like I'm doing? I am leaving.'

'But, sweetheart, why?'

'I have had enough. I am releasing my inner fucking passion.' Her eyes raked the sound stage. 'Where's my golf cart?' she demanded of no one in particular.

There was a gratifying flurry of activity. *Yes, Miss Carson. At once, Miss Carson. Hurry it up, guys! Miss Carson's golf cart!*

'Paige, your trailer's right outside,' Lester reminded her. 'You can't go off the lot now.'

'I will if I want to.'

'Wait. We can discuss this. Jacko couldn't help it. Could you, Jacko?'

Paige saw that Jackson had followed her off the set and was standing next to Lester, pretending to be deeply concerned. He shook his head gravely. 'It just slipped out.'

'Oh, ha ha ha.' The very sight of him made her scalp prickle with fury. 'Get yourself another Salima,' she told Lester, scything one arm through the air. 'Get Meryl Streep, why not? Or Dame Judi Dench? Maybe they'd be good enough for him.'

She started scraping at her face. There was an anguished wail. 'No, Miss Carson. Please. Not the nose!'

Paige flicked the putty onto the floor and ground it flat with her heel.

'Told you she'd be trouble,' Jackson murmured to Lester.

'I am not trouble!' She stamped her combat boot. 'I am an Artist.'

Her ears were roaring. She couldn't stand the sight of Jackson for a single second longer. Turning away, she headed for the red light above the exit door. The two men followed. Lester was talking to her, but she could no longer hear. Faces blurred as she passed. They looked shocked. Didn't they understand?

'I want my sushi!' she heard herself shout. 'I want my pomegranate juice. I want some respect!'

Here was the door. She grabbed the metal handle. With all the sound-proofing it was heavier than she expected. As she pulled, the weight swung her round and she caught sight of Jackson. His eyes gleamed with satisfaction. This was what he had wanted all along.

'Get lost, c-cake-face!' She yanked her sunglasses from her bag, jammed them in place, and strode into the dazzling sunshine. The door slammed shut behind her.

CHAPTER 2

The first thing Paige saw, when she stormed into the trailer, was herself.

'Sure, it's hard work, but you know what?' Her pixellated twin was leaning forward to offer an off-screen interviewer an equal dose of sincerity and cleavage. 'It's just such a privilege working with so many talented individuals.' Now she opened her eyes wide and smiled coyly. 'Especially, of course, a gentleman like Jackson Rolfe.'

'Turn that thing off!' Paige roared.

Akira, her tiny half-Japanese assistant, jumped from the couch in fright and scrambled for the remote. The TV died, then coughed out a gleaming disk which Akira hastily replaced in its package, labelled 'Code Red/Electronic Press Kit'.

The very sight of it added fuel to Paige's fury. 'Get me Nathan on the phone, *this instant*! Then get me Gaby, then get me Mom. And get me some sushi too. I'll be in the shower.'

Banging the cubicle door behind her, she tore off her costume and flung it in a heap on the floor. *Goodbye, Salima.* She gave the heap a karate kick, then trampled it for good measure. To think of all the time she had wasted on this stupid part – all the lines learned, all the hours in Make-up and Wardrobe. From the mirror above the sink a madwoman with wild hair and smudged bruises scowled back. The remains of the prosthetic nose made her look like the victim of botched cosmetic surgery.

Sand gathered in the shower tray as she stood under the high-pressure spray and lathered herself from head to toe in 'Grumpy Cow', the fancy body wash that her friend Davina sent all the way from England. Orange and lavender scents rose in a haze of steam as Paige rehearsed the humiliations she had suffered. Anyone would have walked out, she told herself. There could be no excuse for burping in the middle of a screen kiss. She owed it to herself – to her dignity as a woman, no, as a human being – to the whole acting profession, in fact – to put her foot down.

It was extra humiliating to be reminded of the garbage she had spouted about Jackson in the interview that she'd caught Akira watching. The EPK 'concept', as the studio publicists like to say, was to put together stills, behind-the-scenes footage, and interviews with both cast and crew, and send them out to every magazine and TV show on disk, so that when the movie opened there was a clip or a sound-bite ready to run. The so-called 'talent' interviews with the actors were invariably positive. Everything was 'fun'. Everyone 'loved' everyone else. If there was any kind of on-screen romance, the studio tried to suggest that the stars had the hots for each other off screen, too. That was the kind of rumour that the media lapped up, and the media sold movies. Paige hadn't watched the EPK yet; it must have just been sent over for her approval. But she remembered being asked what it was like 'to smooch one of the planet's biggest stars', and answering, 'Nice work if you can get it' with a suggestive lift of her eyebrows. She tipped her head back, eyes closed, to rinse the shampoo out of her hair. It was bad enough that actors wrecked their marriages and families by sleeping with their co-stars; but almost worse to have to pretend to do so. Sometimes she wondered whether the whole business wasn't rotten to the core.

There was a tentative knock on the door, which then

opened a crack. 'I have Mr Gold's assistant for you,' Akira said nervously.

'I don't want to speak to his assistant. Where's Nathan?'

'She says he's taking a meeting right now. Do you want to speak to her, or shall I—?'

For crying out loud, did she have to do everything herself? Paige stepped out of the shower, pushed the door open and grabbed the phone, careless of her nakedness and of the water dribbling onto the carpet. 'Listen: it's Paige Carson speaking. I have a major major emergency here. You need to get Nathan out of lunch, or off the golf course or wherever he is, and have him call me back immediately. This is a crisis!' She handed the phone back without listening for a reply, shut the door and returned to her shower.

She would tell Nathan that she simply could not continue. They would have to get another Salima. So what if it blew the budget? So what if the studio pulled the plug on the whole project? *Not my problemo*, she told herself, vigorously massaging her thighs with her anti-cellulite glove.

Half an hour later, dressed in leggings, T-shirt and her red high-tops, she was feeling marginally more human. She'd taken a couple of Xanex to calm her nerves. Nathan had called back, listened to her story with appropriate murmurs of sympathy and outrage, and assured her he was on the case. She wasn't to worry. He'd handle everything and report back within the hour. Best of all, Gaby was coming over right away to whisk her off the lot and talk through the whole situation.

The conversation with her mother had not gone so well, but that was fairly typical. Paige visualised their exchange like a film script. She wasn't sure if it was comedy or tragedy.

Scene. Interior: Pacific Palisades mansion
Hell-oo, Melanie Moon speaking.
'*Hi, Mom, it's me.*' [sniff]

Be quiet, Darcy! Mommy can't hear if you bark like that. I'm sorry, who is this?

'*It's me. Paige.*'

Sweetheart! I'm so glad you called. You haven't forgotten about Saturday, now, have you?

'*What?*'

Everyone is so excited that you're coming to our special day. They all want to hear about Jackson Rolfe. Isn't it thrilling that he's up for an Oscar?

'*Oh God, Mom [sob], you have no idea. He's the reason I'm calling. I didn't want to tell you before because—*'

Save it for Saturday. Then you can tell us every fabulous detail. It's like a madhouse here – manicurists, landscapers, caterers. There's so much to get ready.

'*But, Mom—*'

[Ding dong] There goes the doorbell. I think it's the cake stylist. Shush, Darcy! Catch you later, sweetie. Remember: two o'clock Saturday. Don't be late. And wear something special. [yap, yap, yap. CUT!]

Paige sighed. It had never been easy to get Mom's attention. 'How do you hold a moonbeam in your hand?' as some poet had written. She wondered what was happening on Saturday. Manicures? Cakes? Surely her mother wasn't getting married again?

Feeling depressed, she opened her laptop and scanned the inbox. Ooh, here was a message from Davina, one of her closest LA girlfriends, who'd stunned everyone by marrying a British film producer and moving to a sumptuous-looking mansion in the English countryside. Paige hadn't visited yet, but she'd seen pictures of it.

Davina was of course *the* Davina, rock goddess. Her New Year's Day wedding on a private island in the Caribbean had been a huge deal in the press and the most fun non-stop party Paige had ever attended. She missed her crazy friend, and loved being updated on Davina's new life as Mrs Trevor

Lovett of The Manor, Upper Titsworth, which was in a part of England called Wilshire – just like the Boulevard!

Guess what? I've just been HUNTING! Don't worry, nothing got killed except my back – 6 hours in the saddle. I love the outfit – boots, whip, white collar thing like a Catholic priest. Very dominatrix.

England is totally adorable. <u>You have to visit</u>. The men are so smart and witty and NORMAL. I'd love to introduce you to some diamond geezers, as they say over here.

Marriage is wonderful. I knew right from the start that Trevor was my destiny. Have just discovered via an awesome mystic that we first fell in love in Rome almost 2000 years ago but couldn't get together because he was a senator and I was a slave girl!!! Can't believe how lucky I am to have found him again.

Miss you, sweet P

X D

The email made Paige smile. It might be fun to take up Davina's invitation one day. But right now she needed some me-time. It was comforting to sit here cross-legged on her ottoman, eating sushi while Akira blow-dried her hair and massaged her shoulders. Paige had worked hard with her decorator to achieve the right atmosphere for her trailer, and she was happy with the minimalist, Zen feel they had achieved: everything very simple and soothing in muted earth tones, with just a couple of crystals hanging by the window to balance her psychic energies. It was a far cry from Jackson's testosterone-and-pot-infused pigsty.

She frowned. Wasn't it about time she heard from Lester? Wasn't he *sorry* she'd left the set? She'd been in her trailer almost forty minutes, and you'd think—

There was a knock at the trailer door. 'Delivery for Miss Carson.'

Paige flapped a hand at Akira, who answered the door and reappeared bent almost double under the weight of an enormous fruit basket sheathed in cellophane. She placed it at Paige's feet with a grunt of effort. There was a note. Paige ripped it from its staple and read, '*To the one and only Salima. We love you, Paige. From Lester and the gang.*' She peered through the wrapping at a cornucopia of pineapples, grapes, papaya and bananas. What was she – a monkey? The stuff was probably loaded with pesticides. Still ... it was something. They loved her. They wanted her back. Naturally.

'Oh, how beautiful! May I open it for you?' Akira already held a large pair of kitchen scissors poised. Her little face glowed with delight. Paige felt a flash of shame for the way she'd shouted at her. The poor woman was a single mother struggling to raise her kids. 'Tell you what,' Paige said, jumping to her feet, '*you* have it. Go on, take it home tonight. Fruit is such a healthy option for children.'

Akira appeared scandalised by the suggestion. The two of them acted out a little pantomime of insistence, demurral, hesitation and eventual, deeply grateful, capitulation, which Paige found thoroughly pleasurable. That was one good thing about being a movie star: you had so many wonderful opportunities to *give*.

Her hair was pretty much dry now, so Paige instructed Akira to take the weight off her feet and sit on the ottoman, while she lay on her yoga mat and loosened her back with some spine curls. They could run through her messages together, while waiting for Nathan to get back to her, and Gaby to arrive. Many of the calls were enquiries about what Paige was planning to wear at the upcoming Academy Awards ceremony, now only ten days away. The whole town went crazy at this time of year, as designers and jewellers scrambled over themselves to get their products photographed on the red carpet, and practically every female actor lay awake at night agonising about black or colour, short or long, established designer or hot newcomer? Everyone forgot that what really mattered was that other people in the industry admired your work enough to nominate you – even to vote you into a winning position. Paige knew how it felt to stand in front of that cheering crowd, filled to bursting with confidence and joy like a bright balloon soaring to the sun. *Biker Boys* had been her very first full-length feature film, when she was so young, and so excited by the part itself, that the possibility of an Oscar had not even occurred to her. Yet she'd won – at nineteen years old. That had been ten years ago. Ten *years* ...

There was a rustle as Akira turned a page on her short-hand pad. Paige tuned back in to her sing-song voice. An appointment with her acting coach had been confirmed, Akira reported. The termite treatment on her house had been completed, though she should allow another twenty-four hours for the fumigant to clear. Her waxer, always booked solid at this time of year, had looked again at her calendar and discovered that the very slot that Paige wanted was, in fact, miraculously free. Harry Winston's had called yet again to check that she would be borrowing the diamond choker for Oscar Night.

'Is that it?' Paige asked.

Apparently it was. Despite having left about a trillion messages on his phone, there was still no word from Dad. Paige lay on her mat in the silence, counting her breaths in and out. When you were filming, there was no time for family and friends; sometimes it felt as though they'd forgotten you. But if you weren't filming, the public forgot you. Either way, life could get lonely.

At that moment the telephone rang. Akira picked it up, listened, and looked at Paige. 'Can you speak to Mr Gold?'

Paige sat up and grabbed the phone eagerly. Darling Nathan ... She pictured him in his spooky old panelled office in Beverly Hills, half-moon spectacles perched on his nose. Confidence flowed back into her veins as she listened to his calm voice explaining that he'd now spoken with Lester, who totally agreed that Paige had been working very hard and needed a break. The shooting schedule had been rearranged. There were no scenes that required her presence for the next twenty-four hours.

'Or ever!' Paige chipped in defiantly.

In the meantime, Nathan continued, they would discuss the situation and decide what was to be done. He hoped very much that Paige would honour him with her presence for breakfast the next morning.

'Sure.' Paige smiled at his courtly manner and smacked a goodbye kiss down the line to give the old sobersides a thrill.

She'd barely closed off the call when there was another knock on the trailer door. 'Delivery for Miss Carson.'

Paige exchanged a gleeful look with Akira. 'Maybe it's another present,' she said. 'But don't carry it, Akira, if it's another great big heavy thing.' She wagged her finger playfully. 'You let the delivery boy bring it in.'

It was another great big heavy thing. Akira held the door open while a young man whom Paige vaguely recognised from the *Code Red* crew carried in a large pot, its upper portion completely swathed in expensive-looking gold paper.

'Oh, I *love* flowers. Quick, Akira, take the paper off. No, wait. Let's read the note first.'

Paige slid a piece of card from the cute little envelope. It was from Jackson!

'He wrote that himself,' the delivery boy told her in an awed voice, 'in his own handwriting!'

She bent over the note, trying to decipher the scrawled words. *Thinking of you ... With all my heart, Jackson.*

Well, well. The wild Australian dog had been brought to heel at last. Paige felt a spurt of triumph. No doubt Lester had forced him to make this gesture, but that in itself showed how highly she was esteemed. Obviously it was going to take a lot more than a bunch of orchids or whatever for

Jackson to wipe the slate clean, but she could afford to be gracious. She would show him, by example, how civilised people behaved.

'Tell him that I – I appreciate his gift,' she said in a queenly manner.

When the delivery boy had gone, Akira knelt on the carpet and carefully snipped at the gold paper. 'It's so big,' she marvelled. A moment later she suddenly winced, and snatched her hand away with a yelp of pain.

'What's the matter?' Paige started to say, but the words died on her lips as the wrapping fell free. A cactus! A huge, disgusting cactus, its bulbous trunk covered in prickles, with a pullulating red bud bursting out of the top like an engorged penis.

'*Thinking of you ...*' the note had said. Paige flushed with fury. It was all a great big joke. This wasn't an apology, but an insult; and Jackson had fooled her into actually thanking him for it. Her eyes narrowed. She couldn't allow him to get away with this.

It seemed that Akira had recovered from her prick. Now she was positively crooning over the cactus. It was so tall, so straight, so healthy! Did Paige know how long they took to grow this big? How many hundreds of dollars this one would have cost? 'Somebody must love you very much,' she said, with a fond smile.

Paige tossed her head in disgust. The hideous object dominated the trailer, polluting the atmosphere of calm and purity so essential to her inner serenity.

'Outside!' she commanded. 'Come on, I'll help you.'

She opened the trailer door, and together the two women dragged the pot across the carpet, arms outstretched and faces averted to avoid the spines. Akira was looking bewildered. 'But, Miss Paige, it's too cold outside. The cactus will die.'

'Good,' said Paige.

They had just manoeuvred it down the trailer steps and

dumped it on the tarmac when a familiar voice behind them gasped, 'My goodness! What is *that*?'

Paige spun round, her face lighting up. 'Gaby! You came!'

'Of course I came. Don't I always?'

As usual Gaby was dressed head to toe in white, like a diminutive angel, with touches of gold at neck and wrists, wearing a radiant smile. Paige could not resist throwing both arms around her. Here at last was someone who really cared.

Gaby patted her back soothingly. 'Poor baby. I can feel those tension knots. Let's get you out of here. My car's just a step away.'

Paige nodded. 'I'll grab my stuff.'

She returned to the trailer and got Akira to find her an outfit that would disguise her from all but the most rabid fan. In a few moments she reappeared wearing an unremark-able black zip-up fleece, hair crammed under a beret and outsize sunglasses in place. As she tripped down the steps, her eye fell on the cactus. If she left it there, the whole *Code Red* team would see it as they left work. Jackson might even point to it and make some boastful, crude comment. She imagined the sly jokes and secret smiles.

'Wait a sec,' she told Gaby, then shouted, 'Akira, I need you.'

As soon as she had what she wanted, Paige bent over the cactus. This should fix the smug bastard. There was a flash of silver as scissor-blades sliced into the fleshy plant. The glistening red bud quivered, then toppled to the ground and rolled to a stop in the dirt.

CHAPTER 3

'Thing is, Jackson's Aquarius, you're a Leo. That's a karmic disaster waiting to happen.'

Gaby swung her Mercedes around a corner, and cruised through the eerily traffic-free streets of the lot at the regulation ten miles an hour.

'Why does he hate me so much?' Paige wailed. 'I've given everything to this part, and he's blocked me all the way. What's wrong with me? I feel so ... empty. So lost. Sometimes I feel like I can't even act any more.'

'Don't say that. Don't even think it.' Gaby reached over to pat Paige briskly on the knees, beaming encouragement. 'You are a wonderful, multi-talented human being. An Oscar winner. A beautiful woman. A star.'

Paige slumped into the beige leather upholstery. That wasn't how she felt. But Gaby looked so positive and sparkling, from her huge brown eyes to her tiny Prada-shod feet which barely reached the car pedals, that Paige managed a wan smile. They passed a New York brownstone, a classically pillared court house, and a Western town complete with saloon and hitching rail. Visitors were forbidden to drive on the lot, but Gaby could sweet talk her way anywhere.

'Where are we going, anyway?' Paige asked.

'You'll see. Somewhere to clear the negativity out of your system and get that oxygen pumping. There's a bag of raw veggies in the glove compartment, if you need a vitamin boost.'

Paige gnawed at a celery stick. She hoped they weren't going to the gym. That's where she and Gaby had first met, a couple of years ago. It was hard to make new friends when you were famous; everyone always wanted something from you: an introduction, a phone number, support for a charity, the cheap thrill of saying 'my friend Paige Carson'. But Gaby was such a giving person, and so respectful of Paige's private space, that it had been impossible not to warm to her. Gaby had been an actor herself once – Mom had vaguely recognised the name Gabrielle Himmelfahrt from her TV soap days – so she could really relate to the pressures on creative artists. She'd just started up her life-coaching business when Paige met her. Now it was doing so well that she'd recently hired two more consultants and opened a branch in Silver Lake. Of course, Paige always saw Gaby herself. In fact, she'd put her on a retainer to cover both the weekly sessions and emergency calls. But their relationship went so much deeper than client/coach or employer/employee. Gaby was a dear and trusted friend. She was never too busy, never too tired, never at a loss. Whatever the crisis Paige was suffering – career, relationships, hairstyle – Gaby was always there for her.

At last the gates of the lot were in sight. The monochrome scene of beige sound stages rising from grey tarmac brightened to technicolour as they reached the reception area. Palm trees cast foreshortened shadows on brilliant green grass. Bougainvillea hung from an archway in magenta swags. Sunlight gleamed on the lustrous leaves of orange trees, and turned spray from a decorative fountain to rainbow crystals. Overhead, the sky was a clear, cloudless blue. Paige realised that it was a beautiful day.

The guard on the gate reclaimed Gaby's lot pass, tipped his cap to Paige, and waved them out into the real world of traffic snarl-ups, Taco Bells, Filet-o-Fish diners, street vendors under their gaudy parasols, and ordinary people doing ordinary things. But even here the movie industry was dominant. Oscar banners hung from the street lamps. On every news-stand, stars smiled or smouldered from magazine covers. There was a poster at every bus stop, a giant billboard on every corner. Paige stiffened at the sight of a forty-foot-tall Jackson Rolfe, brandishing Excalibur.

'All set for the big night?' Gaby asked, gesturing at the banners.

'Not really.' Paige sighed. 'It all seems such a circus when I'm not nominated for anything. I'm not even presenting an award.'

'All the more reason to get yourself noticed. I'm so glad I was able to get you onto the books of that new stylist everyone's been after. How did you like the Valentino dress she sent over?'

'Great,' said Paige enthusiastically, though she hadn't had a chance to try it on yet, and frankly found the stylist awfully pushy. She'd insisted on lining up not one, not two, but *three* alternative outfits, supposedly so that Paige could pick the one to 'suit your mood on the day', though this was bullshit. The stylist just wanted triple kickbacks from the fashion houses.

'Did you know that dress is made from one hundred per cent chemical-free, fairly traded cloth?' Gaby continued. 'Ethical fashion is *the* big trend right now. They say Angelina's going to be wearing shoes made from recycled Pakistani quilts.'

'*And* diamonds?' Paige enquired mischievously.

'Why not? Diamonds are organic, after all. Which reminds me, Paige honey, I've had the most *inspirational* idea for you. What do you say to wearing a tiara?'

Paige blinked. An image of Princess Diana rose in her mind. 'You don't think that's a little ... show-offy? I mean, I'm not royalty or anything.'

'But, darling, that's exactly what you are. We don't have any kings and queens, there's no "society" any more, and we certainly don't admire our politicians. Little people need someone to look up to. Who is there, apart from the beautiful, talented princes and princesses they see on the big screen? They worship you. They need you to be different – to be superior. It's your duty to live up to those expectations.'

Paige pursed her lips consideringly. She could look kind of amazing in a tiara, but wouldn't she feel ridiculous?

'Even when you're not wearing a real tiara, Paige, you should always visualise yourself as wearing a spiritual one. Think of it as a natural part of your aura.'

They left the main boulevard and climbed through one of the canyons into the hills. Dazzling sunshine softened to dappled shade as the bare trunks and pineapple-leaf topknots of palms gave way to the denser foliage of banana plants, pepper trees and mimosa. Instead of car fumes Paige could smell pine and eucalyptus. She knew these twisting roads well; her own house was only a couple of miles away. She felt a sudden longing to go home, wind herself in a comforter and sleep for a year. But she couldn't. 'Twenty-four hours' the termite company had said – and anyway, she was too professional to go home before the *Code Red* situation was dealt with. She'd give it one more night in the trailer and see what Nathan had to say tomorrow.

'And who's the lucky man that gets to escort you to the Oscars?' Gaby asked.

'Oh. Well.' Paiged blushed. 'Do you ever watch *Hippocratic Oath*?'

Gaby turned to her with widening eyes. 'Not Dr Goodman? Calvin Banks? The one you met on the talk show? Oh, I'm so jealous! Just thinking about him gives me goosebumps.'

'Whoa, nothing's definite yet. Let's just say I'm consider-ing it.'

'What's to consider?'

Paige couldn't answer. Calvin was the teensiest bit younger than her – three years at most, or maybe four – and far less famous, of course, but that hadn't seemed to matter once they'd got talking in the green room. Even after all her years of experience she was often nervous before a live show, but Calvin had been so charming and entertaining that the whole event had passed in a delightful whirl. He'd been interviewed first (they usually saved the most important person, i.e. her, until last) and was still in his seat when she'd walked onto the set in a storm of applause. It gave her a buzz to remember his smile as he'd jumped up to greet her with a kiss. They were still chatting long after they'd gone off air, and agreed it would be great to meet again. Naturally he'd been too respectful to invite her on a date straight out, but their publicists had spoken, schedules had been checked, and the idea had been floated that they might even attend the Oscar ceremony together. First, though, they were going on a date. The only slot available was Sunday evening – the day after tomorrow!

'Calvin wants us to go out to dinner somewhere,' she explained to Gaby, 'but I don't know – especially with the *Code Red* situation. It's so irritating when you're trying to have a private moment, and someone sticks a camera in your face. I really felt a spark with Calvin. If this is the beginning of a relationship I don't want anything to spoil the romance.'

'Hmmm ...' Gaby was thoughtful. 'Paige, you know that I'm not one of those people who likes to tell others what they should do, but here's a suggestion. Why not invite him over to your house? He'd love to see you in your natural surroundings – the view and the swimming-pools and everything. Let him see the real you: your taste in books, music, decor. Show him that underneath the trappings of stardom you're just a simple, home-loving girl who likes to cook for her man.'

'Cook?' Paige yelped in alarm.

'Of course, I'm not expecting *you* to cook, Paige darling. What are maids for?' Gaby laughed. 'I'm sure Concepcion can rustle up something for you to toss in the microwave. Or get a caterer. You know what they say: the way to a man's heart is through his stomach. And if you're already in the privacy of your own home, well, who knows what might develop?'

Sex on the first date? Paige wasn't sure about that. But she felt a pleasurable flip of excitement.

Up and up they drove, through a maze of roads that offered occasional glimpses of opulent mansions sheltered by lush gardens and security fencing. By this time Paige had guessed where they were going. Sure enough, Gaby slowed to a halt at an unmarked entrance, so discreet that even people who were looking for it often drove straight past. She pulled the hand-brake tight. 'When the city gets on top of you, it's time for you to get on top of the city. Come on, Paige, let's walk.'

Paige stepped out of the car and waited while Gaby changed her shoes. A warm breeze brushed her cheek as she gazed across the scrubby hillsides and down to the nebulous sprawl of Los Angeles. Skyscrapers and water-towers poked out of the smog, which stretched as far as the eye could see and obliterated the ocean on all but the clearest days. But up here the air was fresh. There was space to move, and peace to think. As usual, Gaby knew what was best for her.

Linking arms, the two women set off down the well-worn trail. Paige did a quick scout-around, wondering if she dared take off her concealing sunglasses so that she could enjoy the view properly. There were a couple of dog-walkers, a distant jogger in a sun-visor, maybe some lurking riders: she caught the acrid tang of fresh horse-droppings. Still, it seemed safe enough. She stuffed her beret into a pocket, and pushed the glasses onto her head.

Her senses opened to the beauty around her. Purple grasses and yellow flowers sprang out of the brown hills. The castle-like walls and domes of the Griffith Observatory winked back at her in the sunlight. She could even hear birdsong, when it wasn't drowned by the buzz of helicopters criss-crossing the skies. She'd always liked being out of doors. With no one to play with at home, half her childhood had been spent skateboarding, surfing, fooling around on her bike, or playing beach volleyball with the neighbourhood kids.

As they strolled, Paige gave vent to her frustrations with *Code Red*. Having kept the lid on her emotions for so long (except on screen, of course), it was a luxury to talk about herself. Gaby was wonderfully sympathetic, exclaiming 'no!' and 'how dare he?' at appropriate intervals.

'And what made it especially humiliating,' Paige confessed, 'was that I started stuttering again.'

Strangely enough, it had been Paige's stutter that had propelled her into acting in the first place. She must have been about twelve when her mother decided she needed speech therapy – not to mention orthodontics, hair highlights, hypnosis treatment to stop her nail-biting habit, and a nose job. Of course, Paige had absolutely refused. At that time she was in an almost perpetual state of pubertal rage, relieved by brief moments of equally passionate affection, usually misplaced and unwelcomed by the recipient – except by darling Skipper. Her dad had left years ago and was deep into his bombed-out phase. From time to time he would send a plane to bring her to one of his gigs, but if she'd had three heads he probably wouldn't have noticed. Her mom was obviously disappointed at the way Paige was turning out. She particularly disliked the fact that her daughter was already taller than she was. 'Is she ever going to stop growing?' she wailed to her friends – or simply: 'Meet my daughter, the incredible hulk.'

Paige had not wanted to be like her mother. She *liked* stuttering, she told herself defiantly; it made her different. Mom got her way, naturally, and it turned out that Paige adored Jeannie, who was a voice coach as well as a therapist. Together they had discovered that Paige rarely stuttered when she'd learned something by heart. If she knew the dangerous consonants were coming, she could deal with them.

It was like catching a wave just right and surfing all the way to dry land. Paige recited poems and speeches from plays, increasing in confidence and ability until one day Jeannie asked her if she'd ever thought of acting. The idea terrified her, but one summer Jeannie persuaded her to sign up for a youth theatre camp, centred on an open-air amphitheatre in one of the canyons. The atmosphere was laid-back and hippyish. It was fun doing warm-ups and rehearsals with other kids and crazy directors in beards and sandals. The first time she stepped into the lights in front of an audience Paige almost threw up with nerves, but once she was there – saying her lines, being someone else, even getting a laugh, and not stuttering once – she thought, *Wow, this is easy*. More than that: she loved it. She wanted do to it again.

For the next four summers she'd attended the summer camp, and taken all sorts of film-acting classes in between. By this time she had been 'fixed'. Mom was almost proud of her. Then she was spotted in an MTV video for her dad's band and asked to take a screen test, and the next thing she knew – bingo! – she'd been offered a part in a TV pilot. It never aired, but a casting agent saw the pilot and asked her to test for *Biker Boys*. No one thought the movie would be big, but it had hit the jackpot and catapulted Paige to stardom. Everyone had wanted her, and she'd assumed that they always would. Until recently. Now she had the sickening feeling that she was on the slide – in 'movie jail'. *Code Red* was supposed to have been her lucky throw of the dice, not a career-killer.

'How did I get myself into this situation?' she now moaned to Gaby. 'What if I make another bad choice?'

'There are no wrong choices,' Gaby reminded her, 'only opportunities for positive change.'

'Yeah, but a change to what? I feel like I'm spinning round. What am I doing? Where am I going?'

'Always go forward. Never go back.'

'But go *where*? You know what it's like in this business,

Gaby. You're too young, you're too old, you're too tall.' She mimicked a carping voice. 'Change your hair, lose some weight, get some surgery. Why can't you be more like Scarlett, or Drew, or Julia?'

'Sweetheart, you can only be the unique human being you are. That's why we're working to de-tox your mind – to eliminate the old falsehoods that block your creative channels, and replace them with the yeast of new productive beliefs! Remember your positive affirmation exercises: "I am beautiful." "I am confident." "Men love me." "I attract all the acting parts I want." As soon as you truly accept these thoughts into your heart, the essential you-ness of you will be revealed in all its glory. Your spirit will soar, free and unfettered, just like that beautiful bird.' Gaby pointed to a common warbler.

Paige scuffed the ground. 'I just feel I don't know who I am any more.'

'What nonsense!' Gaby was shocked. 'You're Paige Carson, world-famous movie star, daughter of Melanie Moon and Ty Carson. Everybody in the universe knows that. Accept it. Embrace it. *Be* it.'

'I'm trying. I mean, I know I'm a good actress – but am I *really* good? What if I've somehow lost my talent?'

Gaby took her hand and patted it. 'Talent can never be lost, Paige; it can only be hidden, or blocked. Think of a cloud going across the moon. We think the moon has vanished, but it's still there, as bright as ever. All we have to do is to remove that cloud of self-doubt.'

The trail had now brought them to a point directly below the Hollywood sign, set just under the crest of the hill in a thicket of scratchy scrub. Each letter was almost fifty feet high and over thirty wide, made of solid, white-painted steel secured to a metal cross-structure; together, they dominated the landscape. Paige paused to look up, remembering the failed actress of the 1930s, reduced to topless modelling, who had committed suicide by throwing herself off the letter 'H'.

'I always feel this is a very spiritual place, don't you?' said Gaby. 'I'd like you to think of our little walk today as a pilgrimage. I am hoping that, if you concentrate on who you truly are and what you want, you will be able to experience a moment of revelation. That will be the key that will unlock the door to your happiness, and show you your secret desire.'

Paige nodded. She felt so inadequate. No matter how often Gaby explained things to her, or how many goal-charts Paige filled in with the coloured pens and highlighters Gaby had given her, she still felt confused. What if she couldn't find the key to unlock that door? What if she wasn't a moon, or even a star, but a tiny flame that had flickered out? Nevertheless she gazed up solemnly at the sign. *Who am I? What do I want?*

She heard a deep, unearthly humming, as if a pagan spirit was answering her from bowels of the earth itself. 'Mmmmmm ... Mmmmmm.'

'What's that?' She clutched Gaby's arm.

Gaby drew a cell phone from her pocket. 'That's my new "om" ring tone. Isn't it fun?' She checked the tiny screen, then killed the call with her thumb. 'No one important.'

She stooped to pick up a pebble, and folded it solemnly into Paige's hands. 'As I was saying, today is a pilgrimage. You've been carrying a heavy burden, and now we're going to get rid of it. I want you to close your eyes a moment, and make a mental list of the reasons why Jackson treated you the way he did.'

Bright spots danced behind Paige's eyelids while she concentrated. She wasn't a good enough actress – not famous enough – too famous? – not blonde. Her eyes opened wide. 'You're right, Gaby! I'm not blaming him for being rude and arrogant. I'm blaming *myself.*'

'And now you have to forgive yourself. Let go of resentment and guilt. What do we always say?'

'I am a unique individual. I love myself.'

'Good girl. Now I want you to pour all that wasteful self-blame into the pebble and throw it away, as far as you can.'

Paige brought her fist back to her ear, then punched it into the air. But her aim was wayward. The pebble shot straight up and then began to drop back towards them. She dodged out of the way just in time.

'Excuse me, but aren't you Paige Carson?' called a voice.

Instantly Paige was on the alert. Her fingernails scrabbled at her sunglasses and raked them down her forehead. She glanced round quickly to see two women of late middle-age, one holding her dog on a leash and looking embarrassed, the other gazing rapturously at Paige as if she was the Virgin Mary. The first was an Angeleno, Paige diagnosed, the second her out-of-town friend. They looked harmless enough, but you could never be sure. Only last month, one of her actress friends had been stabbed in the neck by a 'fan'. Paige gave the women her usual pleasant but dismissive smile, grabbed onto Gaby, and started walking.

'Wait!' The out-of-towner panted alongside her. 'I have to tell you, I just *love* your movies. I've got them all on DVD. I watch them over and over again. Don't I, Lois?' she called back over her shoulder.

'You do,' agreed a long-suffering voice.

'Thank you so much.' Paige inclined her head, polite but final. She felt Gaby squeeze her arm in sympathy.

'Just one more moment of your precious time. I would be so honoured if ...'

Here it came: the autograph request. Paige could hear the two women scuffling and whispering behind her. They didn't have a pen – yes they did. What about something to write on?

Into Paige's peripheral vision edged a cautiously proffered piece of torn cardboard, bearing the image of a cute Dalmatian and the words 'Doggie Poop sacks: Handipak of 10 – 99c'.

'If you could just sign it on the back ... ? I apologise for not having anything else. I'll neaten up the edges and frame it when I get home.'

Gaby snatched the cardboard fragment from Paige's hands and waved it reprovingly at the women. 'Now, really. This is not respectful.'

'It's OK, Gaby.' Paige took the offered pen, scribbled her signature, and handed everything back. 'Have a nice day.'

'Oh, you too! I am so deeply, *deeply* grateful.' The woman was almost bowing as she backed away.

That night, as she got ready for bed in the trailer, Paige reflected how strange it was that, in the course of a single day, she could be made to feel like shit by her co-star, and greeted like a goddess by a total stranger, when she was just a girl like any other, smoothing night-cream onto her face in front of the mirror, worrying about her career, and about getting older and being alone.

Raindrops pinged on the metal roof as she flossed her teeth and drank another ration of Kabbalah water, rubbed in hand-cream and put on the special gloves, combed her eyebrows, dabbed on eye gel and found her padded eye-mask. Finally she snuggled into bed and slipped the mask into place. But sleep would not come. Gaby's words went round and round her head. *What do you want?* The answer eluded her. Finally she turned the light back on and found her iPod. She scrolled through the playlist and chose 'Dad', a compilation her father had made especially for her. This was one way she could feel close to him. All the songs came from the bands of his youth: Fleetwood Mac, Jefferson Airplane, The Doors. What an old rocker he was! The music washed over her, familiar and comforting. Her body relaxed. She drifted down into a shadowy limbo of jumbled thoughts and dreamy fragments. A witchy voice sang into her ear, repeating the same words over and over. *Somebody to love* ... For a split second she was roused to sharp, unclouded consciousness. That was it! That was what she couldn't see when she stood beneath the Hollywood sign, straining for a glimpse of her secret desire. *I want someone to love.* Then she plummeted into sleep, and the thought was lost.

CHAPTER 4

As the car rocked to a halt, Paige sat up from the deep leather cushioning and glanced out of the smoked-glass window. 'Not here,' she told the driver.

He swivelled round to fix her with his mournful bandit eyes. 'Farmers' Market. This is place.'

'No, this is not place. I want the little entrance, further up.' She pointed, and flicked her fingers to urge him forwards. He came from one of the Stans – Uzbekistan, Kazakhstan, wherever. It drove her crazy that she had to do everything in sign language. Once they were as close to the entrance as possible she mimed the passage of thirty minutes on the car's digital clock, then stabbed her forefinger downwards. 'Here. You wait.' She buttoned her trench-coat to the neck and turned up the collar while waiting for him to open the door, then stepped out.

The smell of doughnuts hit her right away, wafting her back twenty years or more to the time when she and Mom, temporarily single, were living in the Beverly Hills house, and one of her favourite childhood treats was to be taken to breakfast at the Farmers' Market. The higgledy-piggledy cluster of white clapboard buildings, with their green roofs, brown shutters, and cute old clock-tower poking out the top, really did look like a storybook version of a little farming town, even though it was smack in the middle of LA and surrounded by car parks instead of wheat fields.

She used to love exploring the maze of alleyways, packed with food stalls and tiny restaurants, while Mom and her girlfriends lounged under parasols in the open-air courtyard and yackety-yacked about men, hairstyles and the torture of Jane Fonda workouts. At home, food came hygienically packaged from the grocery store; it seemed exotic to see steaming loaves of bread emerging from the oven, real nuts being ground into oily peanut butter, silvery fish with their heads still on, and crabs waving their claws at her. Each turn in the maze brought cross-currents of tantalising smells: cinnamon doughnuts, spicy Korean chicken, and the honeyed perfume of ripe melons. Best of all was the breakfast itself: a tall glass of freshly squeezed orange juice that gave her a frothy moustache to be luxuriously licked off ('use your napkin, Paige!'), blueberry pancakes stacked high in a lake of maple syrup, and hot chocolate with marshmallows.

But the days had long gone when she could linger unnoticed, or indulge in calorie-fests. This morning she stalked past these delights, head down, hands dug into her pockets, and made for the rickety staircase that led to a small eating area where tourists rarely penetrated, especially at this early hour. Nathan was already seated at a corner table with a cup of coffee and a stack of the trades. Wearing a camel-coloured jacket to match his suntan, dark trousers to minimise his expanding waistline, and a tie as conservative as his politics, he might almost be mistaken for any old Vice-President (Paperclips Division), but for the aura of power and prosperity that marked him out as a movie mogul. At the sight of him Paige felt her tension ease. She'd known Nathan and his wife Martha as neighbours since childhood, and he'd been her agent right from the beginning. Although hardly a week went by without an approach from a hopeful rival – invariably 'a huge fan' of her work who 'would love to facilitate an exchange of ideas with Steven (Spielberg) or Bob (de Niro)' – Paige had never wavered. Nathan returned her calls, was neither a hood nor a cokehead, had never tried to get her into bed, and had a hotline to every big-name director, actor and producer in town. At fifty-five he was still at the top of the tree, and if his hair colour was a highly suspect bronze without a speck of grey, so what? He was a survivor, a fixer, a magician. One wave of his wand, and all her problems would disappear.

He had seen her now and, courteous as always, stood up to greet her. He was barely her own height, but then she was taller than average. Anyway, the most successful agents tended to be short: no movie star wanted to look up to their own agent.

'Mmm, you smell wonderful,' he said, as Paige put her hands lightly on his shoulders and pressed alternate cheeks to him. 'You *look* wonderful.'

'Hey, do I feel biceps there?' Paige squeezed her thumbs deeper into his jacket and gave him a teasing smile. 'Don't tell me you've been working out.'

'Personal trainer.' He grimaced. 'Martha's idea. She says I spend too much time on my ass.'

'Poor Nathan.' She patted him fondly. 'Thanks for meeting me here. I thought we could be more relaxed than in the office.' What she really meant was that she hated the possibility of running into his other clients. She preferred the fantasy that Nathan was exclusively hers.

'It's my pleasure and privilege.' He pulled out a chair for her, eased it into position with her back to the room, the way she liked it, and sat down opposite her. 'Now, what can I tempt you with?'

In the end she settled for an apricot and blueberry juice, fresh mint tea and, at his insistence, the teensiest corner of Nathan's apple doughnut which he had bought on the way in. 'They should be arrested for making these,' Paige moaned, dabbing the last delicious grain of sugar from her lips.

They gossiped companionably about the usual stuff. Why had so-and-so left his agent? What was going to win Best

Picture? How about the married agent and his A-list client who'd been papped in Venice in a far from professional position? And why, Paige would like to know, was a guy who'd cheated on his wife always portrayed as a victim of temptation, while archives were ransacked for the sexiest, preferably naked photo of the girl, which was splashed across the tabs under the headline 'Whore'? This business was so sexist! Then they got onto the studios. What was with the new penny-pinching regime? It was so outrageous the way they were pleading poverty, tightening up on perk points, and claiming that actors had become too demanding.

'They don't seem to realise that without the talent there would *be* no studios,' said Nathan, shaking his head at this stupidity. 'Have those bean-counters and tail-chasers ever bared their souls to the camera? Have they ever written a script? Do they have any idea what it's like not to have a pay check hitting the account every month – no bonuses, medical insurance, car, expenses, annuities? No, they don't. They're parasites, mostly uneducated ones too. They never read a book. Half the time they don't even watch the movies they make. They have no creativity themselves, and no concept of the toll it takes. If they want to exploit people with true talent, *of course* they must pay for it.'

'You're so right.' Paige nodded vigorously, thinking of herself. 'Although *some* actors,' she added with a frown, 'can go way too far. I have to tell you, Nathan, that no one has ever treated me so insultingly, with such disrespect, as – you know who.' She lowered her voice and glanced suspiciously over her shoulder for eavesdroppers, but could only see two women sharing a breakfast platter, so engrossed in conversation they hadn't even noticed that a major movie star was in their midst. She turned back to Nathan and began to undo her coat-buttons in irritated jerks. 'You know me, Nathan: I'm a pro. I wouldn't complain without reason. But he behaves like this is *his* movie. He's the cake and I'm the pink bimbo icing. I hate that. It's not fair. It's not who I am. And pardon me for saying so, but who's got the Oscar here?' She flapped her lapels to cool herself down.

Nathan smiled sympathetically. 'Paige, I'm with you one hundred per cent. We all know his reputation. In fact, I believe we discussed this at some length when you were so eager to get in on this project.'

'Well, yes, but—'

'But it's been far, far worse than we imagined. I'm amazed – really almost speechless with admiration – at the way you've dealt with the situation for as long as you have.'

Paige tossed her hair, conceding the point.

'Nevertheless, we have a problem here, and it has got to be solved.' He reached down to pull a sheaf of papers from his briefcase. 'I've made some calls, and I've had the lawyers take a look at your contract.'

Lawyers? Contract? Paige's eyes flew to his face. Surely she wasn't going to be held to some petty sub-clause?

Nathan was taking a pen from his inside breast pocket. He put on his glasses, and began to leaf through his papers. He looked serious and formidable. Paige felt her heart begin to thump.

'I'm not going back, 'she said stubbornly. 'I'm not shooting another single scene with him. And I want a full apology, and ...'

Her voice trailed into silence as he reached over and gently patted her arm. His eyes were kind. 'Just listen to what I have to say. Then we'll talk it through.'

Nathan had been busy. He'd spoken with Jackson's agent and 'people', with Lester, the producer, the studio. Although he didn't say as much, it gradually dawned on Paige that some of these conversations had been far from easy and that Nathan had had to deploy every ounce of his considerable influence. Of course, that was his job. He had his percentage. And none of this was her fault. Guilt was a negative emotion that sapped your energies, Gaby said.

'So as I see it, there are two ways we can go,' Nathan was saying. 'Option one is that you quit the picture for good. Now, you're a smart girl, Paige, and you've been in the business a while. I don't need to tell you that the studio would sue you for all costs to this point. That's maybe twenty million dollars.'

'But it's *Jackson* they should be suing,' she protested. 'He drove me to it. Ask anyone.'

'I have no doubt you're right. But let's be realistic. Jackson has just won a Globe, and he's up for the Best Actor Oscar. No studio on earth is going to sue him for bad manners on set. But they could very easily sue *you* for loss of revenue from a potential blockbuster starring Jackson – we're looking at fifty million, easy.'

'I could afford that,' she said defiantly, wondering if it was true.

'It's not just the money I'm worried about. There would also be a good deal of unpleasant gossip, some of which would inevitably stick to you.'

'But that's not fair!'

'No, it isn't. However, a couple of people mentioned the fact that you pulled out of *Prime Rib* last year – for very good reasons,' he added hastily. 'And we all know you're an impulsive girl: that's what makes you so fresh on screen. Still, we don't want you getting the wrong reputation.' He paused to give her a piercing look over the top of his glasses. 'Not if you want to go on working in Hollywood.'

Paige suddenly felt frightened. Nathan was serious. She was in danger of blowing her career for good. 'So what's option two?'

'As I understand it, you've only got three more scenes to shoot, and only one involving you and Jackson together in close-up. For that, Lester's figured out a way to shoot you and Jackson separately, using stand-ins, then put the footage together with CGI. It won't be easy, and it'll mean a lot of extra crew-time, but he thinks he can make it work. Jackson has agreed. The studio is not at all happy about the extra expense, but they'll wear it – with conditions.'

Paige folded her arms, and waited.

'Firstly, Jackson has agreed not to bad-mouth you—'

'Bad-mouth *me*? That's just so backwards!'

'And you will agree the same. You will also fulfil your publicity obligations, attend all the junkets, and generally deny any rumours of conflict on the set.'

Nathan looked up at her from his notes. His face softened. 'It's your choice, kid, but this is the course I'd very much recommend. When the going gets tough, the tough get tougher, right? Show them you're a pro. Finish the picture. You don't have to see Jackson, you don't have to talk to him, you don't have to touch him. How do you feel about that?'

Truthfully, Paige felt like a wild horse that had been lassoed, forced into a pen, and made to gallop round and round until all the fight had gone out of her. Deep down, she'd known all along that she'd have to go back. 'I want approval of Jackson's stand-in,' she told him.

'You got it.' Nathan looked relieved. 'And you need some more tea, am I right?'

While he busied himself with getting her a fresh pot Paige stared out at the grey morning sky, still covered with the layer of marine mist that rarely lifted before noon. What a place: sunny California with no sun. A farmers' market with no farmers. The dream factory that was more like a nightmare. Pretend people making pretend love. But it was the only world she knew. She was an actress; that was what fired her, made her feel most alive. She craved the tingling excitement of being under the lights, her imagination at full stretch as she lived and breathed, spoke and felt, like a completely different person. Even when the hours were long and the director pulled the guts out of her, she loved her job; it was the industry that was such a struggle.

Every time you got to your feet it knocked you down

again. There was the time, pre-*Biker Boys*, when she'd won a part and turned up on the first day of shooting, put her purse in the dressing-room and went to find the director, only to be told that he'd hired his new girlfriend instead – plus when she returned to the dressing-room, her purse had been stolen. And what about that Russian millionaire she'd been told to schmooze because he was financing the picture? He'd pushed her into a back room at a party and threatened to pull the plug if she didn't join him in a threesome with a porn star and a stash of sex toys. And the weirdo who'd parked outside her driveway every night until the security firm finally dealt with him? Why couldn't she just be left alone to do what she was good at?

Whoa, negative vibes! Look forward, not back. Nathan was bound to have lots of exciting projects for her up his sleeve.

'Have you heard anything about the Spanish Project?' she asked, as he poured out her tea for her. That was the code name for a bio-pic about this amazing woman called La Passionaria who had fought in Spain against – well, Paige couldn't quite remember whom; it was one of those funny little European wars – but she was brave and intelligent, and it was an extraordinary story scripted by a brilliant British director whose movies had won many awards. Paige hadn't seen the whole script yet, but Nathan had managed to get her some 'sides' – just a few pages – and she could tell it was a wonderful part, complex and demanding and definitely non-blonde, that would really test her.

'Nothing definite. They know you're interested, and they're very, very excited about that, no question. I've told them I've got to know within the next two weeks because we're closing out your calendar for the next couple of years and if they want a window they'll have to grab it.'

'Go, Nathan! That's not the truth, though, is it?'

'Since when do we tell the truth? You've got the serial killer comedy shooting in the fall. There are at least two TV guest spots on the table. I've got enquiries coming in all the time.'

'Like what?'

'Well, first let's get the no-gos out of the way.' He thumbed through his papers and tapped his pen against the pad as he frowned at a handwritten list. 'The usual openings and disease parties, a TV pilot – I don't know why they even ask. A couple of promising indies, but they're still in development so we won't hold our breath. Oh, there's a very attractive offer for a commercial—'

'A commercial?' Paige wrinkled her nose.

'—to be shown exclusively in Japan. That's the point: no one sees it so it doesn't devalue your image. Harrison's doing cigarettes in Japan, Clooney does suits in Spain. Trust me, it's kosher. And the money's great.'

Paige considered. If George was doing it, then it must be a good thing. But she knew how it would be: a foreign hotel with no one to talk to, hours in Hair and Make-up, days under hot lights repeating the same dumb words, being shepherded from press call to tourist site by smiling, besuited clones.

'What's the commercial for, anyway?'

'Underwear.'

'How original. Next.'

Nathan wrote a cross on his list and moved on to the next item. 'Ah, now this could be very exciting.' He leaned conspiratorially across the table and lowered his voice. 'This is just a whisper, but Jake, Skid and Al are in talks about a really big-ass movie: great idea, fabulous script, budget no problem, at least one major name already attached.'

Intrigued, Paige too leaned forward, eyes widening, until they were practically nose to nose. 'What's it about?' she mouthed.

'It's about Jesus. Well, Pontius Pilate really. He's African-American. Apparently lots of Romans were. He helps Jesus escape from the cross; they put up some other guy. It's kind of a buddy movie slash historical epic slash Da Vinci Code thing. They were going to call it *Pilate's Lesson* until they realised that could get confused with an exercise video. I'm thinking of you for Mary Magdalen.'

For a moment Paige couldn't think of anything to say. Wasn't this the same old crapola: adventure and soul-searching for the boys, emoting and cleavage for the girl? If she was Mary Magdalen, she bet it wasn't just Jesus's feet that she'd get to kiss. But Nathan was smart; he probably knew better than her. 'Wow. Sounds really interesting. Keep me in the loop.' She took a sip of tea. 'Anything else?'

He checked his pad. 'Here's a new one. I got a call from a British stage director the other day. Really smart guy, a total fan of your work, thinks you'd be perfect for a Shakespeare play opening in London in April.' He let out a chuckle.

Paige bridled. 'What's so funny? You think I couldn't do Shakespeare?'

'Paige, dear, I think you can do anything you want. I was laughing at the pay. Maybe I lost a zero somewhere, but my notes seem to say two-fifty.'

'Two hundred and fifty thousand dollars? Nathan, that's really good for theatre work.'

'Two hundred and fifty British pounds – that's about five hundred dollars. Per week.'

Paige's brain practically fused as she tried to comprehend this. 'Are you telling me that's for a main part?'

'*The* main part. In fact, I think he said it's the biggest female role in the whole of Shakespeare. She's called Rosalind, and for most of the play she's dressed as a boy.'

That would be a change. But most trans-gender dramas ended badly. 'Does she get raped? Murdered?'

'Quite the contrary. She falls in love.'

At that moment Nathan's face underwent an extraordinary transformation. His face flushed pink, his mouth collapsed into a foolish smile. He whipped off his glasses to reveal eyes alight with appreciation. But it wasn't Paige he was looking at.

Behind her, an uninhibited voice rippled out, 'Nathan! My God, it *is* you. What are you doing here?'

Paige turned around to see a girl sashaying towards them, smile at full wattage. Her hair was Marilyn Monroe blonde. She wore a short leather jacket, long black boots, and scarlet lipstick to match the low-cut dress in which her breasts jiggled like two tennis balls in a champion's palm. The women with the breakfast platter noticed her, all right; their forks were suspended midway between bacon and gaping mouths. But then who wouldn't recognise Brooklyn Blanck: nineteen years old, the screen's current darling, and Nathan's latest client?

Brushing past Paige in a cloud of musky perfume she swooped on Nathan, still struggling to rise from his chair, and smooched the air somewhere behind his left ear. 'Don't get up. I just came over to say "hi". This is so incredible,' she announced to the world at large, gaily swinging a fancy store bag. 'I'm just walking along, and I look up, and there you are!'

'Here I am,' Nathan agreed helplessly.

Paige reached for her tea-pot and clinked the spout against the rim of her still-full cup. Nathan jerked into life. 'Yes, uh, Brooklyn, you know Paige, of course.'

Brooklyn's somewhat bulbous blue eyes eventually found their way to Paige's and, after a second's vacancy, sparked into recognition. 'Of course,' she echoed. 'Well, we've not exactly met. This is such a pleasure.' She stretched out her hand for Paige to shake. It was as soft and boneless as a kitten's paw. 'Are you with Nathan too?' she enquired artlessly.

Paige gave a gracious nod. Only for ten years, you little upstart.

'Isn't he like the most incredible agent ever?'

'I think so.' Paige tried to give Nathan a proprietary smile, but his attention was elsewhere.

'I am so looking forward to seeing *Red Code*,' Brooklyn

prattled on. 'Jackson Rolfe is just the most incredible actor. I'm totally in awe of his talent.'

'*Code Red*, actually.'

'Sure. Whatever.' Brooklyn continued to radiate her all-embracing smile; she was the glowing sun of her own wonderful universe. 'Listen, I won't disturb you guys. My boyfriend's waiting in a tow zone outside, so I've got to run. Oh – and thanks for the script, Nathan. Those writers are such geniuses. What an incredible, challenging role. I just pray that there's a slot left in my schedule. Anyway, call me next week and we'll talk. *Ciao*!' With a waggle of her red-tipped fingers she was gone.

Nathan stroked his tie as he gazed after her. His face still wore the expression of a kid who'd just had his first taste of chocolate. He caught Paige's eye. 'Talented girl,' he pronounced judiciously.

'Truly incredible.'

'So where were we?' Nathan fumbled for his glasses.

'Just a minute.' Paige leaned her forearms on the table. 'What's the script, Nathan? The one she was talking about?'

He hesitated. 'Nothing you'd be interested in, Paige. Trust me.'

She stared him down. 'I want to know. Tell me.'

'Well … OK. There's no big secret. It's an original script by the Levin Brothers, black comedy slash family drama, set in the South. They'll direct, of course. Holly Hunter's already signed to play the mother who had her baby adopted. Teenage pregnancy, dark secrets etcetera. Brooklyn's a possibility for the long-lost daughter, just a possibility. It's early days.'

Paige was stabbed with vicious, searing envy. The Levin Brothers were indeed geniuses. She *loved* Holly Hunter – funny, smart, original, opinionated, scared of nothing and nobody, a chameleon talent. Paige would have done anything to work with her. *Why not me?* Why that pert little airhead? It hurt that Nathan hadn't suggest her. Maybe it was time to fire him. Her fingernails played a drum-roll on the table. 'W-why didn't you think of me?'

Nathan took a breath, let it out again, studied the ceiling for inspiration, and then gave up. 'Paige, I did think of you,' he said gently. 'I knew you'd like the script, and in my opinion, you'd do great.'

'But?' she prompted.

'Bottom line?'

She nodded. Her teeth were too tightly clenched to speak.

'They're only looking at actors under twenty-five. I know it's crazy – Holly must be fifty and you could easily be the daughter. You look way under twenty-five anyway. But what can I do? It's their decision.'

Paige slumped back in her chair. 'Under twenty-five': there wasn't much she could do about that. Her birth had been a front-page headline, in *Variety* anyway; it wasn't something she could lie about.

'All right,' she said. 'Give me something else, then.'

'Well, we've talked before about the legal drama, and I really—'

'No.' Paige cut him off dead. 'Remember what Goldie says about the three phases of an actress's career? Babe, District Attorney and *Driving Miss Daisy*. I'm not going there.'

'OK, OK. All I'm saying is, maybe it's time to consolidate. Not every part is perfect, I admit, but if you keep acting you build up a body of work. Talent is like a diamond: it has to be honed; then it will sparkle even in the dirt. Your talent is always going to shine through, Paige, I'm sure of that.'

Something in his voice made her suddenly want to cry. She had to get out of here. 'Nathan, I've got to go.' She began buttoning her coat. 'I need to get back to my house and check everything's OK. Then there's this party Mom wants me to show up for this afternoon and – well, a million other things. You know how it is.' Oh, shoot. In her haste she'd put the buttons in the wrong holes, and had to start again. Nathan had stood up and was saying something about Martha and telling her mom 'hello', but Paige could barely hear through the clamour of thoughts in her head. 'If you keep acting' ... 'We don't want you getting the wrong reputation' ... 'Only under twenty-five'. Nathan had signalled for the check and was taking out his wallet. She couldn't wait. Somehow she made the right noises, smiled the appropriate goodbye smiles, and got herself to the stairs. Halfway down, her ballet pump skidded on the worn step and she had to make an undignified grab for the rail. *I'm slipping. I'm going down the friggin' tube.* Disoriented, she zig-zagged through the alleyways, dodging herds of tourists. How could she act if no one offered her a part? What if Nathan fired *her*?

No, that was nonsense. She steadied herself by a voluptuous tumble of oranges with their leaves still attached. She was Paige Carson. People loved her. 'I watch your movies over and over again.'

On impulse she turned into the doorway of the Doggie Bakery, picturing her mother's delight at receiving a present for her beloved poodle. It would have been nice to get him a cake (bone-shaped, kitty-shaped, low-fat option) with his name written in organic beef-flavoured frosting, but these had to be pre-ordered. She drifted round the shelves and tables displaying leashes and toys, and eventually settled on a cute red T-shirt, with the slogan 'Spoilt Rotten'.

It was only when she was at the counter, holding out her hand for the gift-wrapped package, that she realised she didn't have any money. 'Cash or credit card?' the assistant was saying, for the second time. Paige looked round vaguely; usually someone else took care of that. But there was only a line of shoppers building up behind her, wearing expressions of curiosity or impatience. Automatically Paige reached for the phone in her coat-pocket: Akira could bring some money down. Then she remembered that she'd sent

Akira to the house to supervise the staff for Paige's return. With Calvin coming over tomorrow night she wanted everything to be perfect.

She looked back at the assistant in her phoney baker's hat. This was so stupid. Obviously the girl knew who she was. 'Can't you just put it on an account or something?' she asked.

'If you have an account, sure.'

Paige did not care for her tone of voice. Embarrassment and frustration suddenly fused into anger, and she slapped her hand on the counter. 'You know what? Forget it. I don't need your asshole store.' Turning her back on the assistant she pushed her way through the gaping shoppers and out into the open air. Her cheeks were flushed. Tears stung her eyes. All she'd wanted to do was buy a present for her mom. Was that so difficult?

A car horn tooted at her. God, she hated that! It was like people whistling at animals in the zoo, so they could get a good picture. She teetered on the kerb, gazing blindly across the spreading wasteland of parked Toyotas, SUVs and tour buses. There was another toot. Panic gripped her. She had no money. She couldn't remember what her car looked like. When she felt a hand on her elbow she almost screamed. Then she recognised her driver. 'Come,' he said gently.

With overwhelming relief Paige saw that her car was only a few feet away, the rear door already open to receive her. She scuttled inside. It wasn't until they were back on Sunset that she realised she'd forgotten something. She leaned towards the driver's seat, waiting for him to notice her. 'Thank you,' she enunciated carefully.

He smiled his yellow smile. 'You're welcome.'

CHAPTER 5

Paige decided to drive herself to her mom's house. She'd been cooped up for so long on the lot, at other people's beck and call, that it was with an exhilarating sense of freedom that she strolled out of her own house, climbed into her own little sports car, gunned it down the driveway, and swung onto the curving canyon road to a rocking soundtrack from her speaker system. Her hair had been styled into a simple but chic up-do that should please her mother. She was wearing her new lime-green dress with the wide belt that flattered her hourglass figure, teamed with a little fur jacket (humanely sourced) to lend the required touch of understated glamour. Actually, now that the sun had appeared, she was rather warm – the outside temperature according to her car dial was sixty-eight degrees – but if you couldn't wear fur in February, when could you? She turned up the air-con.

Oh look, a yard sale! Paige wished she could stop. She loved snooping around someone's cast-offs, picking up an antique mirror or an interesting carving or more patio furniture. Thanks to real-estate prices, the craze for remodelling, and couple split-ups, the turnover of both residents and possessions in this district was high. Sometimes items hadn't even been unpacked from their boxes, which was sort of sad. Paige had often found herself speculating on the human dramas that lay behind matching sets of monogrammed bath towels, never used, or a Tiffany wall-lamp that looked perfect except for the exposed wires where it had been ripped out of the plaster. As soon as this movie was over, she promised herself that she would do normal things like yard sales and lunches with her friends. She might even go on vacation, Aspen or the Caribbean – perhaps with Calvin if things worked out.

At the thought of tomorrow's date Paige's felt a flutter of anticipation. With his smiling charm and lean, dark looks, Calvin was such a contrast to Jackson. She'd checked him out on the net and he seemed to tick all the right boxes. He'd even been to college (on a tennis scholarship, but still). There were no mentions of rehab. It was pretty clear he wasn't gay, judging by the stories that had linked him with various minor actresses, a hot producer, his personal trainer and – well, you couldn't believe the lies that passed for gossip on the celeb sites. Plus, he was successful enough not to be too jealous of her superior fame, but not such a star that he'd be tripping on his own ego. On the whole it was good that he was in the biz, since that meant he was cool with the media attention that tended to freak out civilians. But they probably wouldn't even talk about acting; being college-educated, he was bound to have a fascinating range of subjects at his command.

She had taken Gaby's advice and invited him over to the house tomorrow night. It would all be very chilled, very natural, no pressure: a simple meal, a glass of champagne, conversation round the fireplace or in the hot tub. She'd dress casually, to indicate it was no big deal. She might even greet him absent-mindedly wearing glasses (a prop from the environmental disaster movie she'd shot last year: the lenses were clear but they made her look intelligent), as if she'd been deeply absorbed in ... what?

Paige had been stop-starting through the West Hollywood traffic, and was now waiting at a light, idly watching people cross back and forth between the stores that lined the road.

A sign caught her eye, abruptly shattering her daydreams. She knew she'd forgotten something. Quick! Where was her phone earpiece? Turn down the music – no, that was the air-con. What jerk was honking at her? Oh, the light had turned green. Finally she got Akira on speed dial. 'Hi, it's me,' she said. 'Listen, I need you to get down to Book Soup and buy some books ... Yes, right now, I need them for to-morrow night ... Well, can't you pick up your son later? Or take him with you? Tell you what, you can buy him a book too, present from me ... *Which* books? I don't know, ask the store – whatever's hot and in hardcover. About twenty. See if you can get a discount. Tell them you're choosing for Paige Carson – no, don't! Say it's for a very intellectual ... um ... intellectual.'

She cut the call. Now she was worrying. Maybe her CD collection needed upgrading, too. Should she buy some Mozart? Inviting a man to your house was so exposing. She almost called Gaby for advice, but stopped herself in time. She could handle this.

She was just reaching to turn the music back up when her phone buzzed. A flurried voice cascaded into her ear. Paige rolled her eyes and waited until the voice paused for breath. 'No, Mom, of course I haven't forgotten ... Yes, Mom, I'm in the car right now ... No, I'm not wearing jeans ... It will be perfect, Mom, as always. Love you, too.'

Paige shook her head, but she couldn't help smiling. Her mother thrived on drama, and still conducted her life with the rollercoaster intensity of the TV soap character she'd played when Paige was growing up. *Inheritance* had been a prime-time series typical of the glitzy, shoulder-padded eight-ies, in which two powerful families feuded for supremacy, employing such unscrupulous methods (and wearing such extraordinary outfits) that viewers were agog. No week passed without a kidnapping, miscarriage, incestuous seduc-tion, boardroom punch-out or the discovery of Nazi gold. Melanie Moon had become a household name in her role as the gorgeously wild and wilful heiress, Jade Parkhurst. Paige could still remember the excitement when she made the front cover of *TV Guide*. The high-profile divorce from Ty Carson in real life, and exotic but brief re-marriages (Argentinian polo-player, three months; plastic surgeon, nine months; lifeguard, ten days) only added to her glamour. Nowadays her volatile energy was invested in tamer activities: renovating houses, playing club tennis, organising a slew of charitable events, and retaining the face and figure of a thirty-five-year-old. But she still behaved as if the camera was pointed at her, recording the continuing drama of her life.

Paige was not looking forward to this afternoon's event, but it would be good to see Mom. She might have some career advice to offer; or at least a sympathetic ear. They were mother and daughter, after all.

For a while now she'd been catching glimpses of the ocean, deep turquoise against the brighter blue of the sky. Leaving the highway, she revved the car up steep twisting roads and finally turned into an unobtrusive driveway guarded by twin eucalyptus trees. Wow, Mom had really gone to town on the decorations. Bunches of bright balloons twirled in the wind, tethered to any available tree, pillar, or balustrade. There was a banner across the front door and a string of coloured pennants fluttering over the porch. A sign directed guests round the side of the house to the yard. Paige changed out of her driving shoes into strappy high-heeled sandals, found her purse, and picked a fancy gold box tied with ribbon off the passenger seat. OK: deep breath.

She teetered round to the back lawn. This, too, had been transformed into a festive scene, with more balloons, tables and chairs grouped on either side of a long red-carpeted platform, and a striped circus-style tent with the flaps down. It was clear from the noise that this was where the stars of the show were gathered. She found an entrance and stepped into an atmosphere of backstage frenzy that took her right back to her brief modelling days. Bright clothing hung from rails, dangled over chairs and littered the trampled grass. The air smelled of hair spray and nail varnish, with more basic animal undertones. Urgent voices rose above the general din.

'Who's got the blow-drier?'

'Are the buttons supposed to go at the front or the back?'

'Stand *still*, you crazy bitch.'

There were at least thirty dogs in the tent, of every conceivable shape, size and colour – in cages, on laps, tethered to tent poles, or forcibly held on table-tops while a fleet of young girls in matching overalls clipped their nails, styled their coats and coaxed them into their clothes.

'Paige! Thank goodness. You're here at last.' Her mother emerged from the chaos, flushed and wide-eyed, and grabbed Paige's arm. She wore a silky Gucci-print tunic over slim white trousers; her blonde hair was swept into its usual peekaboo style. 'Yoo-hoo, everyone, my movie star daughter has arrived!' Paige found herself propelled towards a group of smiling women, evidently the officials of the proceedings. There seemed to be no time for a hello hug, or the presentation of the gold box as she had planned. 'Paige, darling, you remember Patsy, don't you, our Vice-President? And Nancy?'

'Of course.' Paige shook hands with a tall woman wearing a full-length Dalmatian suit, including cap with lolloping ears on which a tiny cardboard party hat was jauntily perched. The others wore matching white sweatshirts with 'Waggy Tail Animal Shelter' picked out in rhinestones. 'How wonderful to see you again!' Paige chirped. 'I'm so happy to be here.' Around her the dogs yapped, whined, growled, strained to thrust their noses into each other's private parts, and tried to rip off their finery. 'So what can I do?' Paige asked brightly. 'Give me a job.'

'You can come up to the house with me, and check on the caterers,' replied her mother. 'The guests will be arriving any minute. We'll never be ready! And you can take off that coat,' she hissed privately to Paige, as they crossed the lawn. 'What were thinking of, wearing fur? Some of our boys and girls are still recovering from mange. How do you think they'll feel?'

The house was Mom's latest project, recently built in the Cape Cod style, which meant shingle cladding, turrets, and a covered veranda that ran right along the back of the house, offering sensational views of both the ocean and the Santa Monica Mountains. But there was no time to enjoy it now. Mom had already disappeared through the French doors into the huge, bustling kitchen and pounced on one of the catering team. There appeared to be a crisis with the sugar tongs. Paige saw that the twenty-foot Brazilian walnut table in the centre of the room was covered with porcelain cups, tiered serving platters, lacy napkins, and silver cutlery winking in the light from the chandelier. Mom told her how, after much agonising, she had decided to serve a classic English afternoon tea of finger sandwiches, scones with lemon curd and clotted cream, chocolate-covered strawberries, and Earl Grey tea; plus fruit sorbets for the picky eater and any seniors with dental problems.

'You don't think it's too warm for tea, do you?' she asked anxiously. 'I don't want my butter curls to melt.'

'Mom, everyone will love it.' Paige placed the gold box conspicuously on the table while she took off the offending jacket.

'And, Esperanza, I want that tea hot, hot, hot! Make sure your staff refill the pots.'

'Yes, Miss Moon. Every ten minutes, like you said.'

'No, Darcy, this isn't for you.' Mom's grey standard poodle was eyeing the food longingly from behind a dog-gate into the hallway. 'OK, just one for my precious baby.' She popped a salmon sandwich into his jaws.

Paige picked up the gold box again. 'Mom, I've brought you a present. Just come into the dining-room a minute, and open it, will you?'

'For me? You sweet thing. Now I don't want to hear any more of that whining, Darcy.'

Paige hung her jacket and purse from one of the dining-chairs and watched her mother slide the ribbon from the box, remove the lid and prise open the tissue paper wrapping. She had beautiful hands – far more elegant than Paige's, as Mom had often pointed out.

'Sweetheart, this is gorgeous. I love it!'

'Really?' Paige had been so pleased to find a present after all, an Italian hand-dyed scarf bought for herself but never worn. The material was as fine and featherlight as a spider's web, washed through with cloudy greys in which silvery threads shimmered.

Her mother wound it round her neck, swept her hair free, and turned to admire herself in the Louis Quinze mirror above the inglenook fireplace. 'You've definitely inherited my fashion sense,' she told Paige, patting it into place.

'You look beautiful,' Paige said truthfully. 'You can keep it on if you want.'

The next moment they were interrupted by someone asking about parking arrangements. It proved impossible to talk further as Mom flew from one disaster-in-the-making to the next, until the first guests began to trickle across the lawn and take their places at the tables. Classical music drifted from loudspeakers camouflaged by giant pots of azaleas. Nancy puffed up from the tent, to report that everything was as ready as it would ever be and the dogs were getting antsy. Thanks to one or two unforeseen accidents, some adjustments had been made to the running order, and she apologised for the handwritten corrections on Paige's script.

'Don't worry, I'm used to that.' Paige took the script and skimmed through it quickly. This was a dog adoption party she was compering, not the Oscars. But she wanted to do it well, so that her mother would be proud of her. As soon as Mom took Nancy into the kitchen to approve her tea arrangements, Paige used the pocket mirror from her purse to slick on a fresh coat of lipstick, examine her teeth for foreign bodies and check her hair.

'Come *on*, Paige! Everyone's waiting.'

Grabbing the script, she joined her mother on the veranda and switched on her smile. Showtime!

Mom spoke first. She made an appealing, heroic figure standing alone on the wooden platform under an 'Adoption – the Loving Option' banner while she outlined the plight of stray dogs: lonely, starving, diseased, unloved and un-wanted, through no fault of their own. Her voice throbbed with passion as she revealed the shocking truth that, even in a democracy like America, these poor creatures were often simply euthanised. Waggy Tail's mission was to rescue such animals from Death Row and to care of them until they were adopted into a 'forever home'.

'Some of these dogs may not be pedigrees; they may not look beautiful; they may have suffered physical impairment or emotional trauma: but remember they are *people*, just like you and I. Their souls are beautiful, and I guarantee that they will bring beauty into your lives. I urge you from the bottom of my heart to give them a second chance.' She paused, too choked up to continue. Her audience filled the silence with warm applause. 'And here to introduce today's doggie friends is my beautiful and talented daughter, Paige Carson, whom all of you will know from her many ...'

Blah blah blah. This was her cue. Paige mounted the make-shift stairs onto the platform, and finally got the hug she'd been trying for all afternoon. More applause. Eventually her mother relinquished the stage, kissing her hand to the crowd as if taking an encore at the Met, and sat down at one of the tables.

Paige stepped to the microphone. 'I know what you're thinking,' she told the audience. 'You're thinking that she's too beautiful – and way too young – to be my Mom. But she is. And I'm proud of her.' More clapping, some cheers: she'd got them. She read some introductory remarks from her script, then ad-libbed a couple more until Little Richard's voice burst from the loudspeakers with 'You Ain't Nothing but a Hound Dog'. Out of the tent shot a large spotted dog dragging one of the uniformed girls behind him on a leash.

'And first up on the red *cur*pet' – Paige waited for the joke to sink in – 'is ... Baby Boy! Baby's a pointer, about two years old, and a real gentle giant. Today's he's wearing a pure wool jump suit with genuine leather buckles and, of course, his party hat!' With difficulty the dog was restrained from living up to his outfit and jumping right off the end of the platform, his keen nose having picked up the scent of scones. The girl managed to steer him round, and the pair of them passed Paige at a fast trot and disappeared into the tent. Next came Leonardo the Labrador in a striped sailor suit, Sandy the Chihuahua in a swansdown tutu, and a three-legged basset hound in a cowboy outfit. His name was Rocky.

Trying to read the script, check on what the dogs were up to, and stay in touch with her audience all at the same time was not easy, Paige discovered. Her eye had to skip ahead so she that wasn't caught out by changes of tone in the script. One minute there'd be a wise-cracking line like: 'They call him Max-a-Million because his devotion will make you feel like a million bucks!' The next she'd be reading out: 'Precious has diabetes and impaired vision.' Several of the dogs found her microphone stand of intense interest, so she also needed to remain alert to the threat of a cocked leg. On top of all that she had to appear charming, composed, and alluring, with just a hint of aloof mystery. These people could walk into the dog shelter for free any day of the week; they'd paid to see her.

Now the Rolling Stones were belting out 'Walking the Dog', and she was into evening wear. Caesar the mastiff strutted his stuff in a tux while Paige reported that he was doing very well with his house training. MacDougal did his own version of the Highland Fling in kilt and tam o'shanter. A pair of overexcited Pekineses frisked up the carpet and back in matching pink chenille evening coats and slightly askew tiaras, like a couple of Florida matrons who'd hit the gin. Just as Paige read out a reminder to potential adopters that all the animals had been spayed and neutered, the music changed abruptly to the wedding march. For a while nothing happened. Paige could hear frantic behind-the-scenes whispering and a series of high-pitched yaps. 'Last-minute nerves,' she quipped, and got a laugh. Finally two dogs yoked together on a double leash wandered uncertainly onto the red carpet. Patches the beagle looked so miserable in his wedding suit and striped waistcoat that Paige's heart was stirred for the first time. You couldn't tell about his sausage-shaped bride, Lulu, since she was pretty much invisible under her veil. Cheered on by the audience, the unwilling couple made it to the end of the runway and back, and were led into the tent, bewildered. Paige couldn't bring herself to read out the line about the wedding 'ruff-ception'.

This was the grand finale. All that remained was to congratulate the dog handlers, thank the Waggy Tail supporters for their tireless efforts, and invite the audience to go backstage and get to know 'that special somebody'. For her own part it had been 'a privilege – in fact, an absolute joy' – to contribute to this unique event. She stepped back from the microphone, smiling in acknowledgement of the generous applause. Mom was looking happy – though she'd taken off the scarf. Well, it was a warm day ... She was turning to leave when a retriever in a flounced sundress emerged beside her, holding a florist's bouquet in its mouth. It was accompanied by Patsy, still in her Dalmatian suit, who interpreted the dog's wish to say a big woof of thanks.

Paige patted the dog's head and accepted the flowers with a mime of delighted surprise, trying not to get dog slobber on her dress.

Finally she was allowed off the platform, though her duties were not yet over. There were photographs to be taken (by the 'puparazzi'), autographs to be signed, and hands to be shaken. Several people wanted to confide that they'd found 'their' dog. A flagrantly gay fashionisto, dressed entirely in black with a silver crucifix, rhapsodised about the panting pug cradled in his arms. 'What a little munchkin! I think I'm in love! I'm going to get married!'

Paige was pleased to see that Patches the beagle had been snapped up by a nice-looking family, and was looking a lot happier unclothed. A little girl petted him tenderly while her parents watched with fond approval. Maybe *she* should get a dog. There'd been no one since Skipper. It would be lovely to be welcomed home – though of course she was hardly ever there. Even if she hired a personal groom and dog-chef while on location (and Nathan could surely get that written into her movie contracts), it wouldn't be fair to disrupt the life of a creature who had already been traumatised by adoption and needed a stable and loving home. She sighed, and instead, when no one was looking, filled out one of the Waggy Tail donation forms, pledging herself to a four-digit sum per year.

'Paige! I need you right away up at the house.' Mom's voice was shrill with worry. She'd forgotten to stuff the party bags.

'For the guests?'

'For the dogs, silly.'

Several of the local pet stores had been persuaded to donate treats for the occasion, which were laid out in piles on the dining table. Paige and her mother sat side by side apportioning the loot.

'Mom, you haven't heard from Dad recently, have you?' Paige asked, reaching for a squeaky rat. 'I've been calling him, but either he doesn't pick up, or he doesn't call back, or he's in a hurry and can't talk. I'm worried. You don't think he's … ?'

'Zonked out of his brains again? Who could blame him, stuck out in Arizona with a bunch of horses and the saintly Lindsay?'

'Mom, that's not fair. Remember how wrecked he was after the farewell tour? He was practically a zombie when he met Lindsay. She's really turned him round.'

'Maybe.' Her mother shrugged, and dropped a dog-anklet into a pink Poochpak. 'All I know is that when I was married to Ty he never wanted to be pinned down. He'd do anything he could think of to avoid making a decision or facing up to reality. Whenever I wanted him I had to track him down myself, in whatever dive – or bed – he happened to be in at the time. We had some good times, though,' she admitted with a sudden rich chuckle. 'He used to pick me up from the studio on his Harley and off we'd zoom to a gig or a party, or just hit the road and wind up sleeping on the beach or at some crazy Norman Bates motel.'

Paige loved these stories. She loved their evocation of an earlier, golden time of barefoot freedom, when Mom and Dad had been wild about each other. OK, they'd split up. But they'd been in love once, and out of that love they'd created her. That must mean something. She wished Dad would contact her. It would be so great if she could go out to the ranch and spend some quality time with him. Even if she could only get away for a day, it might give her some perspective on her life. She wondered if she could persuade him to send the jet.

'Sit up straight, Paige. You're hunching. My Pilates instructor says that good posture can take ten years off your age.'

'Sorry.' She straightened. 'It's just that I'm, well, worrying about things.'

'You're not pregnant?' Mom looked at her in horror. Becoming a grandmother was her worst nightmare.

'Of course not. But I'm feeling ...' Paige hesitated, unable to articulate her unease that her career – her life – she herself – had gone off the rails and was stuck in a dark tunnel. Yesterday's conversation with Nathan still troubled her. What if her work dried up? What if no one wanted her? Mom should have some insight on that. After all, she'd been pretty brutally dropped from *Inheritance* and had hardly worked again. She tried to put this tactfully. 'I wanted to ask, do you ever miss acting?'

'Goodness, Paige, what a question! I never think about it. I'm so busy.'

'Yeah, but – I mean, what happened when you ... left *Inheritance*?'

'Everyone knows what happened. That episode got the highest ratings of the whole series.' Her mother paused, rubber bone in hand, gazing dreamily out of the window. 'It was my wedding night, and I'd discovered that my husband was a bigamist. Years before, he'd married my half-sister Desiree in a secret ceremony. Of course I was out of my mind. I *hated* Desiree. I ran out of the mansion, jumped in the car and fled into the night. Next morning they found the wreck at the bottom of a cliff. But they never found Jade Parkhurst's body,' she added, with a strange kind of triumph. 'It remains a mystery to this day.'

Paige could only nod, and pack another box of organic dog chocs. After a decent interval, she tried again. 'And what about you? What did you do?'

Her mother frowned, trying to remember. Then her face cleared. 'You know, I think that's when I had my first surgery.'

Paige left soon afterwards, having turned down an invitation to join Mom and 'the girls' for dinner. It would only be another performance, telling a lot of lies about Jackson Rolfe and all those exciting projects in the pipeline; being grilled about her dress and her date for the Oscars. No one wanted to hear the truth, and she couldn't face telling it. As she slipped through the garden everyone else was absorbed in rounding up several of the dogs who'd got loose and were popping balloons and cavorting across the lawn in various stages of undress. Caesar and Leonardo were playing tug-o'-war with one of the discarded items of clothing. Was it the wedding veil? They jerked their heads from side to side, teeth clamped, legs braced, until the material suddenly parted, leaving each of them standing foolishly with the severed ends dangling from their jaws. Paige peered more closely. With a sick feeling she recognised shreds of the grey scarf she'd given to her mother.

CHAPTER 6

Calvin wasn't coming. She'd invited him for seven-thirty; it was already seven-thirty-three. If he was coming, he'd have been here by now. Or maybe he didn't care about arriving late? That was so typical of men. So what if the dinner that your cook had been slaving over for hours was ruined? So what if you'd been standing in this poky back room staring at the CCTV screen, watching for headlights to stop at the security gate, when you could have been doing something productive?

Such as?

Did she have time to rush upstairs and brush her teeth again?

Come on, people were always getting lost on these canyon roads ... or killed! Think of all those makeshift crosses and bunches of wilting flowers marking the sites of fatal accidents. Calvin could even now be trapped upside-down in his car, the steering-wheel lethally rammed into his chest. In fact, was that a siren she could hear? OK, it was a coyote. *Calm down, Paige!*

So what was keeping him? It was now seven-thirty-four. Maybe he'd forgotten. No, that was impossible, given the flurry of communications between their two publicists about directions, timing, and dietary requirements. She didn't eat red meat and tried to avoid dairy; he was wheat-intolerant, allergic to nuts, and could eat only those vegetables that grew above ground. (She and Concepcion had held a heated debate about whether squashes, which generally lay *on* the ground, fell into the 'above' or 'below' category.) Neither of them liked tofu, thank God. Even in the interests of the body beautiful, Paige had never seen the attraction of chewing what was basically bathroom sealant.

Maybe he'd had a better offer: a hot party, a premiere, someone prettier – younger – than herself. *Stop it, Paige!* Dragging her eyes from the CCTV screen she walked swiftly down the hallway, took the stairs two at a time and burst into her bedroom to check herself out in the full-length triple mirror. Frankly, she looked great: hair loose and shiny, slim jeans, cashmere sweater that was casual but discreetly sexy, fabulous underwear underneath – though they wouldn't get to that tonight ... probably not anyway. She'd had fresh linen sheets put on her enormous Cal-king-sized bed just in case.

The sight of her bed induced a wave of depression. It was so ... neat, so unrumpled, so ridiculously big for one person, that it seemed to shout her single status. Despite the fancy headboard and colour-coordinated scatter cushions it had a bleak, impersonal look, as if – well, as if everything had been chosen by a professional decorator, which it had. Filming schedules didn't allow too much time for shopping, and she'd bought this house in a rush, after the split with Aaron. Just as she'd bought her previous house in a rush, after the split with Pete. Her face softened. Pete had been her first real boyfriend. He was a great guy, loyal and straight – too straight to handle the razzmatazz of her stardom. They still kept in touch, though he'd moved outside the city. In fact, he'd called twice in the past few days. She must get back to him when she had the chance. But not tonight.

Paige seized her hairbrush and vigorously brushed her hair upside-down before tossing it back into a thick and wanton mane. Calvin, unlike Pete, was used to the spotlight. It wouldn't faze him. She pouted at the mirror. *Come and get me, Doc.*

The sound of a car outside drew her to the window, where she peered through the drapes, but the headlights had only paused for a moment before moving on: false alarm. OK, back down to the living-room for a final check. The drapes here were pulled back, revealing the fabulous view over the city, as if from an aircraft coming in to land; the glass doors leading out onto the deck were invitingly ajar. Here were the vases of fresh flowers, hand-delivered by Bloomz. There was the stack of serious magazines, topped by *Newsweek*; Paige had skimmed its contents in case they came up in conversation. The books picked up by Akira from Book Soup were scattered on tables and windowsills in artistically random piles. A selection of CDs was stacked by the music system. Yes, everything seemed in order. Next door the table was laid for two, the candles ready to be lit: check. In the kitchen, the quietly ticking timer showed that the *tarte aux abricots* (French for apricot pie) needed to be put in the oven in twenty minutes time: check. Two portions of pre-seared tuna with fingerling potatoes and a *ragout* of pink peppers and teardrop tomatoes lay in their microwave-able containers in the ice-box: check.

Chill, Paige! So he was a few minutes late – so what? Her problem was that she'd forgotten how men and women behaved. It was so long since she'd been in a real relation-ship ... OK, once or twice she might have clinched a deal via the bedroom, but that was just business. She wasn't proud of it, but she wasn't going to beat herself up about it either. And of course there'd been the occasional escapade with some cute guy on a crew or cast. These things were under-standable when you were thrown together on location, but everyone knew the rules: you stoked up the passion by day, let off steam at night, and forgot the whole thing as soon as the movie wrapped. Looking at things objectively – she loved the sound of that; it sounded so mature and consid-ered – looking at things objectively, she'd really had barely half a dozen major relationships since her teenage days. No wonder she was het up about Calvin: *she'd forgotten how to date.*

Back in the living-room, Paige opened the doors of the antique armoire that concealed the TV and zapped the screen into life. Calvin's blue eyes gazed down at her with an expression of compassionate concern, a stethoscope hanging casually around his neck. He looked so cute with the collar of his white coat turned up at the back. Over the past twenty-four hours, she'd watched both series of *Hippocratic Oath* available on DVD: this was her favourite moment. She pressed another button, and the frozen image melted and began speaking, while an insidious soundtrack plucked at the heart-strings. 'It was touch and go in there for a while,' said Calvin, his chiselled features breaking into a smile, 'but I think your little girl is going to be OK.' The music rose to a crescendo as the camera panned away from Calvin and focused on an African-American couple, their eyes shining with gratitude. 'Doctor, how can we ever repay you?' stammered the father. 'Only one way,' replied Calvin with a grin. 'When she graduates from college, I want an invite to the ceremony.'

Paige's heart swelled as she killed the screen with another press of the button. He was such a great guy, so caring and so thoughtful. She loved his dishevelled look as he strode masterfully down the white-painted corridors, his coat streaming out behind him and his wavy hair bouncing, an everyday hero striving tirelessly on behalf of his fellow human beings. She imagined him striding towards her, his expression of noble concern melting to warmth as he ...

The buzzer sounded. Was that him? Of course it was. She scampered to the CCTV screen and saw Calvin sitting behind the wheel, patting his hair. She lifted the phone. 'Hi!' she trilled girlishly, as she buzzed him in. He smiled up at her, the same smile he had flashed on her TV. A few moments later he was standing at the door, dressed in an expensive jacket over an immaculate white T-shirt, drainpipe trousers and sneakers. She was slightly disappointed to notice that he wasn't wearing a white coat. But he was even more ridiculously handsome than she'd remembered. 'So you found me at last?' she murmured coyly.

'Wow!' he exclaimed, 'you look fabulous.' He leaned forward and kissed her cheek, squeezing her shoulder as he did so. Paige was used to compliments, but still she simpered a little as she ushered him inside and led him into the living-room. 'Wow!' he exclaimed again, 'Great view!' He squeezed through the opening out onto the deck.

'Can I fix you a drink?' she asked, raising her voice.

'Ah, no,' he replied over his shoulder, 'I'm off the booze.'

'Oh.' Paige felt crushed, as if she'd suggested something improper. So much for that bottle in the ice-box, then.

'Just kidding.' He stepped back in from the patio, smiling that devastating smile. Relief surged through Paige. It was going to be OK.

'The stuff of life for me now is, literally, to perfect my back-hand.'

It was an hour and a half later. They were seated at the dining-table, plates pushed to one side, and Calvin was talking about his game, as he had been for the past ten minutes. It was fun to be with someone who was so enthusiastic, Paige decided, as she leaned forward on her elbows, hands clasped. And so nicely muscled – he'd taken off his jacket to show her his new serving style. The evening had been a success, all things considered. He had admired her *Poisson à la* whatever it was – even asking her how she'd cooked it – but she'd wisely anticipated this question and had an answer prepared: 'my little secret'. There had been a crisis when she hadn't been able to open the microwave door. She'd spun various dials, with the result that the buzzer kept sounding. Then she hadn't been able to find any serving spoons: why hadn't the cook left them out? How was Paige supposed to know where the friggin' things were kept? She'd opened one drawer after another, slamming each shut in frustration. Meanwhile Calvin sat next door at the dining-table, drumming with his cutlery and singing along to the mood music. Finally she'd leaned round the door, muttered some excuse and locked herself in the bathroom to call Concepcion in secret.

Another difficult moment had come earlier, when they were still in the living-room, drinking wine and eating nibbles. Paige had been mid-olive when Calvin had suddenly leaned towards the coffee-table with an animated expression. 'Wow, books!' he said, 'I love books.' He picked up something called *The God Delusion* and started leafing through it. 'What's this one about?'

Paige choked on the olive pit, trying not to panic. 'It's … um … about God, and – and how deluded He can be.'

'Neat,' said Calvin, snapping the book shut.

She'd been embarrassed when she'd come back into the living room from pretending to 'whip up the sauce' in the kitchen to find him watching *Hippocratic Oath* on DVD. 'You like my stuff, uh?' But he hadn't teased her about it – on the contrary, he seemed gratified. The rest of the evening had been fine. They'd talked – well, he'd talked most of the time, but that was OK – and she felt that they were really relaxed together, just like a normal couple.

'It's truly one of the most disgusting things I have ever seen happen to anyone, much less myself,' Calvin was now saying in an outraged tone. He'd moved on from tennis, and was telling her about how clips from the forthcoming series of *Hippocratic Oath* had appeared on an unauthorised website. The way he described it, this was an invasion of his personal privacy. It seemed no big deal to Paige, but she adopted what she hoped was a sympathetic expression. 'I'm trying to live under the radar,' he said gloomily. 'I guess you know all about that, right?'

Paige tried not to feel piqued. It didn't seem right for him to compare his experience with hers. She was the A-lister, after all. He was hot – well, warm anyway – but he wasn't a star like she was. *Don't think like that, Paige!* This was the kind of attitude that had kept her single, putting up barriers between her and the men she liked. OK, so she was more famous than he was, but they were just people, weren't they?

'Yeah, I do,' she said, with only a slight effort. 'Shall we move next door?'

As she walked ahead of him out of the dining-room, Paige wondered for the umpteenth time that evening whether she should have worn a skirt. She had wanted to look casual – but maybe jeans were too casual? She had summoned Gaby earlier in the day for a consultation, and tried on a variety of skirts. She hadn't wanted to look middle-aged, especially on a date with a younger man – but she didn't want to look cheap either. Life was so difficult! She perched beside him on the couch while he bobbed up and down, re-enacting the audition he'd just done for a part in a World War Two action movie (working title: *Shoulder to Shoulder*), as a USAF ace during the Battle of England.

'Peeow! Peeow! Akkakak! Akakakakakak ...' Calvin jumped up and started swooping around the room, his hands clutching an imaginary joystick. Paige clapped her hands, laughing. He was now imitating the whining noise of an aeroplane falling out of the sky. He had slipped off his shoes and, balanced on the arm of the couch, he mimed escaping from the cockpit and then bailing out, landing unsteadily on the living-room floor after a short but intense parachute drop.

He held his heroic pose for a moment, then grinned up at her from the carpet. 'So what do you think? Did I get the part?'

'You were totally fabulous.'

'That's what my coach says. He thinks it's in the bag.'

Calvin flopped beside her. 'You know, I'm just so ready to show the world that my repertoire extends way beyond a TV doctor.'

'Of course it does. Anyone can see that you're incredibly talented. I – I think you're great,' she added shyly.

He looked deep into her eyes. His face was suddenly very close to hers. 'You don't mean that.'

'I do, I do,' Paige squeaked happily, wondering if he was going to kiss her. But he turned away.

'So,' he said meaningfully, after a pause: 'What about Jackson Rolfe?'

'What about him?'

'The word is you two are an item.'

'Oh, no.' She was quick to reassure him. 'That's the usual studio bullshit. Truth is, I can't stand him and he can't stand me.'

'No kidding? But whatever, what are you going to do about him?'

'Do I need to do anything?'

'It's going to look kinda weird if I take you to the Oscars while you're still supposed to be with him. Though maybe ...' He broke off, obviously deep in thought.

'Who cares what it looks like?' Why didn't he shut up and kiss her?

'... if people think there's some kind of rivalry, they'll be more interested in us as a couple ...'

'So?' She wasn't sure where this conversation was leading.

'So we'll get more publicity, right?' He was nodding now.

'Well, maybe ...'

'I get it.'

Did he? Personally, Paige was confused. 'Do we really want to attract attention?' Very tentatively, she reached out and started stroking his fingers. 'Just when we're getting to know each other ... ?' She felt him tense.

'What are you doing?'

'What I'm trying to say is, can't we just be ourselves and forget about the media for once?'

He stared at her uncomprehendingly, and then pulled his hand away from hers. Something was very wrong. 'Let me get this straight,' he said at last. 'This *is* a PR set-up, right?'

Paige felt dizzy. 'I – I – I …'

'I mean, we both know what we're doing here, don't we? I heard you couldn't get an Oscar date. My publicist suggested I did you a favour, and got myself some coverage at the same time. Wasn't that the deal?'

She couldn't speak.

'Don't tell me you thought I really wanted to go out with you?' He spoke as if the idea was absurd. 'Let me tell you, I'm covered in that department. Anyway, aren't you, like, *thirty* or something? It's OK to have our picture taken, but … whew, no way.' He shrank away, his blue eyes no longer warm, but scornful.

Paige felt sick. She stood up, summoning what was left of her dignity. 'I think you'd better leave.'

'Don't worry, I'm out of here.' He jumped to his feet, picked up his jacket and slung it over his shoulder. 'Guess it's past your bed-time,' he sneered. 'I'll see myself out.'

She heard his sneakered tread on the tiles, waited for the slam of the front door, then collapsed onto the couch with a groan, face buried in her hands. *You idiot! Pathetic, stupid, simpering idiot!* He was doing her a favour! He'd never even liked her. She thought back over tonight, and their first meeting on TV. Phoney, phoney, phoney. How had she, of all people, forgotten that he was that most self-absorbed species on earth: an actor?

The sound of his car engine faded into the distance. She rose unsteadily to her feet and stumbled to the front door to set the alarm code. Then she made her way back into the living-room. The sliding patio door was still open. The night is young, she thought bitterly. For a moment she peered out over the twinkling lights of the city below. Tinsel town. So much on the surface, so little underneath. She thought of her image on a million magazines and posters, and her empty bed upstairs.

The patio door jammed when she tried to close it. *Story of my life.* She jinxed everything she touched. Nothing worked. By the time the door finally clicked shut, she was in tears. Something had to change.

CHAPTER 7

A fierce wind was blowing at Bob Hope airport as Paige scuttled across the tarmac, head bent, hair whipped into tangles. At her side loped a stocky figure in a checked shirt, one hand gripping her overnight bag, the other jamming his cowboy hat in place. Duey was Dad's usual pilot, who doubled as a ranch hand these days. Planes and horses were alike, he always said. You rode one through the air and the other over the ground, but both gave you speed and freedom. He gestured ahead towards a row of small jets, and she squinted through the shimmering fumes of aircraft fuel to pick out the name 'Paige 5' on one of the tail-fins. Dad had called all of his planes after her. Underneath the lettering was the Scrap Metal logo, a black guitar licked by orange flames. But she was cool with that. She didn't mind sharing him with the band.

Duey unlocked the door – 'security', he explained, with the scorn of a rugged individualist for petty officialdom – then unfolded the stairs and stood aside to let her enter first. It was a relief to be inside, breathing in a pleasant smell of leather and air-freshener. Paige blinked away the airport dust, and tried to smooth her hair back in place. 'Some wind!' she exclaimed to Duey as he stowed her bag in one of the closets.

'Yep. There's a mean downdraft this morning. Gonna have to ask you to strap yourself in for take-off. She'll be buckin' like a filly in the breaking pen.'

'What about Arizona?' she asked. 'How's the weather there?'

His craggy features melted into a grin. 'Like the first morning of Creation.'

'Well, the sooner we're out of here the better. I have had the week from hell.'

It was six days now since the disastrous evening with Calvin – or the Hippocratic Oaf, as she now called him. The memory was still painful, but there'd been no time to mope. By six a.m. the following morning she'd been back on the *Code Red* set and hadn't stopped since. On her orders Concepcion had burned the *Hippocratic Oath* boxed set.

Duey had now secured the door and ducked through to the cockpit, where she could hear him talking to the tower as he started up the engines. Paige hung up her jacket, kicked off her shoes and padded back to the galley to check out the drinks situation. The fridge held an impressive stock of champagne, Californian chablis and Dad's alcohol-free beer, as well as low-cal salads and forbidden munchies. At eight-thirty in the morning it was way too early for alcohol, but she pounced on a Diet Coke. She'd been craving soda for weeks, and now that filming was finally over she could let rip. She popped the tab and drank it straight down. Yum. Feel those chemicals a-whizzing and a-fizzing through her body! Watch that tooth-enamel dissolve! She wiped her mouth, gave a discreet burp, and dropped the empty can in the trash. Now what? She riffled through the lockers, wondering whether to read a magazine, watch a DVD on the forty-inch screen bolted to the floor, or catch up on her emails. But every magazine had the picture of some movie star on the cover, with a banner headline about her beauty secrets, his Oscar hopes, their hot romance – or even fierier split. The very first DVD she spied in the rack starred – guess who? – Jackson Rolfe. Paige slammed the lockers shut. She was sick of actors, sick of movies, sick of make-believe. Just for one day she wanted to forget about Hollywood, breathe some honest-to-goodness fresh air, and hang out with her dad.

Paige had invited herself to the ranch for a day and a night, squeezed between the final shooting of *Code Red*, which had wrapped last night, and Oscar weekend. Dad had seemed slightly taken aback when she'd phoned, but after humming and hawing and consulting with Lindsay he said sure, he'd send Duey down in the Cessna; in fact, of the two of them Lindsay had seemed the more enthusiastic. Paige couldn't explain even to herself why she wanted to see him so badly. By conventional standards he'd been a crap father. He'd left home before she could even walk, and she didn't see him again until she was ten. But then it was love at first sight, on both sides. They had the same eyes, the same smile, the same gestures. Sure, he was unreliable: he forgot her birthday even though she was his only child, went AWOL for months on end, cancelled arrangements at the last minute. But how many other fathers flew their daughter to Hawaii for a weekend, or took her onstage at Shea Stadium, or bankrolled her first movie? Right now Paige felt that her life was spinning and she'd lost the compass. She needed to touch base.

The jet was beginning to taxi out to the runway. Duey's voice announced over the intercom that they'd be taking off in two shakes of a lamb's tail. Paige sank into one of the soft leather seats by a window, fastened her seat belt and idly watched the view slide past. There wasn't much to be said for the flat, smog-ridden suburb of Burbank apart from the convenience of this airport, a short hop over the Hollywood Hills – and the film studios, of course. She felt an increasingly familiar flutter of panic and crossed her fingers, thinking of the Spanish Project. Somewhere nearby her fate was being debated: was she too young, too old, too big a star, too small – or just right? Everything would be OK if she could land the part of La Passionaria. She'd have work, recognition, a goal. She might even meet someone. *Please let them choose me.*

Flat roofs and curving freeways receded beneath her as the little jet left the runway and lifted its nose to the sky. For a few uncomfortable moments they kangarooed through the air currents. The far-away glitter of the ocean bounced briefly into view, then the plane banked and a ridge of brown mountains reared perilously close, like a dinosaur's horny spine. Finally they pulled clear into smooth, clear blue. Paige unclasped her belt, tilted back her seat until it was almost horizontal, and closed her eyes.

She felt drained. Because she and Jackson were filming separately, their working hours had effectively doubled. Paige could hardly believe the call-sheet that had been emailed to her, and honestly didn't think she could have survived without the masseuse and dietician recommended by Gaby. Sixteen-hour days started with Hair and Make-up at dawn, and ended with late-night sessions talking through scenes with her stand-in. In between were concentrated bouts of work on set and tedious hours on call in her trailer or dressing-room, twiddling her thumbs while she waited for Jackson to finish. Typically, he overran his allotted time in order to ensure the perfection of his own performance. Paige thought it was the hardest thing she'd ever done to go to set when finally called, banish her seething frustrations, and produce the emotional intensity required at the snap of the clapper-board – especially when the lines she was re-sponding to were being read out in a monotone by Jackson's stand-in. 'You're going to make it,' he told her with all the poignancy of a train station announcement, as she lay dying in his arms. (Naturally, Salima had to die. The love-interest always died in such movies, having first performed an act of selfless heroism. In the case of *Code Red*, to do otherwise would be to countenance Presidential adultery – unthink-able!)

A small consolation was that the crew, though unhappy about their extra workload, did not seem to blame her. The senior make-up artist whispered to Paige that her whole team had cheered when Paige had walked out – silently, of course; they didn't want to lose their jobs. She also received a few discreet chuckles about the emasculated cactus. But the atmosphere had been tense. Late yesterday evening, when Lester had finally announced 'it's a wrap', there had been none of the usual euphoria, just a weary acknowledgement of an ordeal successfully endured.

The wrap party was taking place tonight – without her, thank God – at a Moroccan restaurant somewhere in West Hollywood. Paige had heard rumours of its fabulous harem atmosphere, awesome belly-dancing show, and the *pièce de résistance* dessert of exotic fruits and honeyed pastries, served on a gigantic platter carried in by loin-clothed slaves, and eaten off the gradually uncovered body of a naked 'actress'. She could exactly predict the progress of the evening, from sentimentality to hilarity to debauchery. After the gag reel Lester would be presented with a gift of spectacular opulence or vulgarity. *Code Red* cocktails would be on tap all night, suitably coloured with something lethal like sloe gin or cherry schnapps. There would be a cabaret involving a girl in a thong, who would later turn out to be a guy. During the dancing the stunt men would start a drunken mock-fight in which someone would get hurt. A minor starlet would be papped falling into or out of a car with her skirt round her waist. All the people who'd been itching to sleep with each other would finally do so. On one of the ottomans the still-sticky actress would get fucked in return for the promise of an introduction to a casting director. Around dawn an army of cleaners would appear to deal with the broken glasses, vomit, used condoms and cocaine residue, glad of the double pay they received for seeing, hearing and reporting nothing.

The images in her mind were so distasteful that Paige had to open her eyes for a few moments and reassure herself that she was here in the familiar barrel-shaped interior of the jet, with its pale carpets, polished walnut detailing, and small works of art. It did not suit her to remember those wrap parties where she herself had danced topless, insisted on singing 'Hey, Big Spender' before passing out, and on one occasion had sex in a hot tub with a best boy. Instead, she congratulated herself on her escape, negotiated via Nathan at the cost of a personal present for everyone on the picture (organised by her publicist), and a special message (written by her publicist) that would be read out at the party, apologising for her absence due to 'urgent family business'. Paige stretched out her legs and wriggled her bare toes on the soft leather footrest, smugly picturing herself at the ranch, slumped on a couch with Dad in front of a real fire, while far away the *Code Red* orgy raged. Lindsay would be at the ranch too, presumably, but she would surely have the tact to give father and daughter some time alone.

Lindsay wasn't all bad. At least she wasn't a druggie, a gold-digger or popping out of her clothes like most of Dad's previous girlfriends, and at fortyish was of a much more suitable age. She'd been working in an art museum when Dad met her at a private dinner while promoting his last album. Paige didn't exactly like Lindsay, and scowled if anyone referred to her 'step-mom', but conceded that she was pleasant enough in her dull way and seemed to make Dad happy.

A change in the engine noise impelled Paige to haul herself into a sitting position so that she could look out of the window. Yes, the plane was already descending towards a monochrome moonscape of desert and wrinkled mountains, with daubs of lush greenery and the occasional cobalt splash of a lake. Soon she was able to pick out roads with tiny cars winking in the sun, and the silvery snake of the river. And there was the ranch! She could see the barns, then the adobe outbuildings, then the roof of the house itself, its sprinkler-green lawn and blue swimming-pool strip. A group of horses, spooked into flight by the shadow of the jet, sprinted and wheeled over the pasture, their tails flying like banners. She heard the wheels unlock, then Duey's laconic voice suggesting that she might want to buckle up. It wasn't necessary, though. He set the plane down on the landing strip as lightly as a leaf. An open-topped jeep was waiting. When the figure at the wheel waved, Paige whooped aloud to see that Dad had come to meet her himself. Hurriedly she shoved her feet back into her shoes. As soon as the plane had come to a stop she struggled to release the door lock, too impatient to wait for Duey.

'Baby!' Dad called up to her with a grin. He looked tanned and fit, and somehow younger. He'd cut his hair! Gone were the straggly rock-star locks to which he'd clung for decades, and the harsh black dye that made his skin look dead (along with a few million other chemicals). It was a little startling to see his real salt-and-pepper hair colour, still long enough to curl onto his forehead and collar, but he looked OK, in fact pretty good, as he jumped out of the jeep revealing battered jeans and cowboy boots. She was reassured to spot the single earring, though. Lindsay hadn't yet turned him into Mr Middle-aged Golf Bore.

He folded down the steps, and Paige tripped down them eagerly and into his arms.

'Hey, beautiful.' He hugged her to his warm shirt. Tall as she was, her head just fitted under his chin.

'Hey, yourself. I like the new look.'

'Yeah, well ... it's cooler like this. Don't be fooled, though. I'm still the same crazy bastard.'

'I'll bet you are.' The earring, she saw, was in the shape of a skull.

They climbed into the jeep together, where Duey had already deposited Paige's suitcase and jacket, and set off at a cracking pace along the dusty track to the house. The weather was perfection: breezy sunshine without a speck of humidity, clear skies sliced by the outline of the mountains, pure air with the faintest tang of pines, horses and woodsmoke. Bright tufts of wildflowers sprang out of the rocky terrain. Birds flew in and out of the giant cactuses that held their prickly arms up to the sun. Paige's spirits rose.

'So what's the plan? What shall we do? How's Lindsay?' she added as an afterthought.

'Oh, fine, fine. We can do whatever you want, babe. Hang out, take a sauna, listen to some sounds, eat, drink.'

'Dad, it's ten o'clock in the morning!'

'Eleven. You're on Mountain Time now.' He slowed the jeep as the house came into view, a genuine old wooden homestead with a wide porch to keep the sun out. There were hammocks slung between the posts, and benches set on the mellow brick floor, invitingly scattered with pillows and Navajo blankets. Paige pictured herself lying out here this evening, sipping chilled white wine and admiring the sunset while she waited for dinner. But now she was full of energy. And Dad revealed that he did have a plan, after all – well, Lindsay's plan, he admitted, as pushed open the screen door into the hallway. She'd organised a picnic. If Paige wanted, the two of them could take a ride along the trails and eat lunch up in the mountains.

'Sounds great. Doesn't Lindsay want to come, too?' Paige looked around, half-expecting her to materialise from the shadows. But the house was silent.

'She's kinda busy.' Dad tugged off his hat and used it to whisk sand from his jeans. 'Doing stuff, you know?'

'You mean, the gallery idea?' Paige remembered that Lindsay was an expert in native American art. 'Is she still planning on converting one of the barns?'

'Well, yeah … maybe,' he added evasively.

Paige let it go. Maybe they'd had a fight. It was none of her business, and she didn't care anyway.

She changed into jeans, found some boots to fit her, slathered on sun cream, and before long was loping along a dry gully on the back on an Appaloosa cross called Buckwheat.

'You ride like shit,' Dad called from behind as she bounced in the saddle.

'I'm not retired,' she shot back over her shoulder.

There was a roar of outrage, and he flashed past her, startling Buckwheat into a gallop with a thwack on the rump. Paige screamed, lurched backwards in the saddle, almost fell off, then clung to the pommel as Buckwheat took up the race and thundered after Dad's horse, a huge black thing named Demon. Sand sprayed into her eyes. She'd lost a stirrup and could hear it clanking uselessly. Hauling on the reins had no effect. Buckwheat's hooves slithered on bare rock as they charged up a mountain trail that seemed to Paige to be barely a foot wide, with a sheer drop on one side. Dad was out of his friggin' mind. She closed her eyes and prayed.

When she opened them again she had sweat trickling down her back and a mouthful of mane, but the world was mercifully still.

Dad was grinning. 'You show some respect, girl. I may not be doing the gigs any more, but I'm still hangin' in there.' He paused, adding, 'In fact, in some ways you could say I'm still a pretty hot dude.'

For a moment Paige wondered what he was talking about. Then she remembered. 'Oh, I heard! Scrap Metal's going to be in the Rock and Roll Hall of Fame.'

'Yeah, well ...' He twiddled his skull earring. 'That's not so special compared to – to ... some things,' he finished lamely.

'Of course it is!' Paige felt she hadn't been sufficiently enthusiastic. 'I mean, Hall of Fame, that's like winning the Oscars. Better, probably. At least you don't have to dress up like a Christmas turkey and get carved up by the media – which is what I'll be doing tomorrow, by the way.'

'You going with that dickhead director?'

'If you mean Aaron, we broke up a year ago, Dad. I told you all about it.'

'Oh, yeah.' He pushed back his hat and scratched his head. 'Remind me.'

'He told me I was his "muse" and we would be together for ever. I accepted a tiny fee to play a dying artist in what he said would be a cinematic masterpiece. Instead he laid an egg, a great big stinky one. They booed us in Cannes. Then I caught him in bed with a Brit-with-no-tits. She is currently starring in his new movie.'

'Bummer.'

'Actually, I'm taking Pete to the ceremony.'

'Who's Pete? ... Oh, *Pete*. Good guy. Fuckin' A.'

It was thanks to Dad that Paige had met Pete in the first place. He'd been working as a sound engineer for Scrap Metal when she flew in for a gig. Gangling, boyish, obsessed by sound techniques, worshipful of her but utterly uninterested in celebrity, he was exactly what Paige had needed when *Biker Boys* shot her into the stratosphere. They had moved together into that great apartment in Santa Monica, and while Paige was whirled into parties, casting sessions and talks with big-ass directors, Pete had steadily worked towards his ambition to become a Foley artist. These were the specialists who created the background sounds to movies – soldiers marching, glass breaking, cartoon cats purring – and matched it to the actions on screen. Foleys were notorious perfectionists, inventive to the brink of sanity and usually way beyond. When Julia Roberts and Hugh Grant kissed, the sound you heard could be Peter slobbering on his forearm. The echoing footsteps of a giant monster in a kids' animation film might be Pete's as he clonked around on a metal sheet in ski boots. It used to drive her crazy the way he stopped concentrating on her to listen to the exact noise of her swishing stocking as she pulled it up her bare thigh, or attached weird objects to the blades of their fan to see what whirring/clanging/rasping effects could be achieved. But she'd been faithful to him for four years (not counting the hot tub episode) and still felt bad about the way she'd finally left him after falling madly in love, so she'd thought, with one of her co-stars.

'You're not back together with old Pete, are you?' Dad was looking puzzled again.

'Of course not. He just wants to see me, and I'm so busy that tomorrow night is my only slot.'

This was not strictly true, but when she'd finally got round to returning Pete's calls, post-Calvin, the brilliant idea had popped into her mind that he could be her Oscar date. He hadn't seemed crazy about the notion. Now that he was a successful freelance he lived outside of LA, alone with his subwoofer or whatever it was, and he'd never been one for dressing up and going on the razzle. But he wanted to meet – she had a sinking feeling that he had a favour to ask – so it hadn't been too hard to persuade him.

'Chill, Dad. We're just friends.'

They rode on to the picnic place – a slab of rock with a scrubby tree for shade and a fabulous view across the ranch – and ate guacamole, cold chicken and strawberries while Paige poured out her frustrations with *Code Red* and her career in general. Dad was a great listener. He hardly interrupted at all, just watched her face or frowned thoughtfully into space. When he did speak, he was awesome.

'You're paying your dues, babe. It ain't easy but it's got to be done. Don't let the dollar men mess with your head. Keep working, keep thinking, try new things. Don't let the flame go out. As long as you've got the flame you'll be OK. Know what I mean?'

Paige nodded solemnly. He was, of course, the perfect person to advise her, Reinvention Man himself, having sunk into the abyss and climbed out again. There'd been the motorbike crash, then the break-up of the band and the lost years in New Mexico. But the band had got back together. They'd forced Dad back into rehab because his hands were shaking so badly he couldn't play guitar, and they were nothing without him. This time it had worked. There'd been the comeback tour, the album that went platinum. Out of the wreckage of addiction Dad created 'Nightmare Days', which outsold anything the band had recorded in the seventies. Now he had success, a new partner, a great home, even his own brand of wisdom. Right now he looked almost like a guru, sitting cross-legged and still, his face carved with the lines of experience.

A bold idea thrilled through her. Why didn't she just forget about acting for a couple of months, shut up her empty, echoing house, and come and live with Dad? He could teach her so many things: how to be creative, how to ride, how to live. They could picnic like this every day, or swim when it got too hot. He could work on his music and she could, well, rekindle her flame. They'd be together, like a real family. There would be peace and beauty and space to think, far away from the Hollywood hoop-la.

The thought had barely taken hold when he took a deep breath and turned to her. 'There's been something I've been meaning to say. Uh ... you're my daughter, right, and that's a big deal for me. I know I messed up at the beginning. I should've been there more when you were a kid. But you never laid a heavy trip on me, and we're OK now, you and me. Thing is ...' He paused, fumbling for words, then tried again. 'The ranch, see, it's like my home but it's your home too, and I want you to know you can come here whenever, wherever, however ... whatever happens.'

God, this was incredible. He was asking her to live with him. They were telepathic! She must tell Gaby.

'And things do happen,' he meandered on, 'crazy, wonderful things you never expected, like fireballs in the sky ... or flowers in the fuckin' desert or ...'

Paige stopped him with a gentle touch on his arm. 'Dad, you don't have to say any more. I understand.'

'You do?' He looked amazed.

'Of course I do. I'm your daughter. We have such communion. It blows my mind, to tell you the truth.'

He was still looking perplexed, but men were always mystified by women's intuition. Men liked everything to be spelled out. Paige smiled at him affectionately. 'We'll talk it through tonight. But thanks, Dad.' She started gathering up the picnic things to relieve him of the stress of further speech. He'd never been very fluent, except on bass guitar.

They rode back in companionable silence. Dad led the way, his broad shoulders seesawing in easy rhythm with the horse's gait. There was no reckless galloping this time. He looked commanding and in control. He even pointed out a rattler basking on a rock and told her to be careful. There was birdsong in the air, sun on her face. Paige could hardly contain the bubble of happiness that swelled inside her.

They unsaddled the horses and let them loose in the corral, then took a detour to admire Dad's new recording studio in one of the outbuildings, where she let him play her a few riffs from a new song he was working on. By the time they returned to the house it was a relief to enter the cool sanctuary of the living-room and fling herself full-length onto one of the big couches.

'I am going to be so stiff tomorrow,' she announced to the beamed ceiling. 'And I'm dying of thirst.'

'I'll get us some water.'

'At least a gallon. With ice.'

She heard the scuff of his boots across the wooden floor, then a sharper rat-tat of heels as he entered the tiled kitchen next door. Glasses clinked. The refrigerator hummed briefly and fell silent. There was another sound, too, a soft rustle which she couldn't identify. But as Dad came back into view she heard Lindsay's voice behind her saying, 'Did you tell her?'

'Tell me what?' Paige struggled into a sitting position and popped her head over the back of the couch.

But the answer was obvious as soon as she glimpsed Lindsay. 'You're pregnant!'

'Oh, Ty ...' Lindsay cast a brief, reproachful glance at him over Paige's head.

'I know, I know. I tried to tell her, but ...'

Paige was on her feet, mouth open as her head swivelled

from Lindsay to Dad and back again. 'You're pregnant,' she repeated stupidly.

'Yes, I am,' Lindsay came towards Paige with a tentative smile. 'I'm so sorry you had to find out this way.'

Paige recoiled, staring in disbelief at the swollen belly under Lindsay's loose shirt. 'But you're huge! What are you – five months, six months? Why didn't anyone tell me?'

'I wanted to tell you much earlier.' Lindsay's blue eyes pleaded for understanding. 'But first we wanted to be sure the baby was OK...'

The baby. Everything in Paige revolted against these words. *She* was Dad's baby.

'... and then you were busy filming. We didn't want to interrupt your work.'

'And Lindsay thought – I mean, I wanted to tell you my-self, in person,' Dad added.

'Except you didn't.' Paige turned on him accusingly. 'You funked it. As usual.'

'Hey, I thought we were on the same vibe. You said you understood.'

'What was all the crap about the ranch being my home? How could you say that when all the time – when you knew ...' Her voice was trembling. She swallowed away the tell-tale prickle of tears in her nose and drew herself up tall. 'This isn't my home. I'm never coming here again. I want to leave now.'

Both of them started talking at her in consternation. Paige clapped her hands over her ears. She didn't want to listen. She didn't want to see Dad walk over to stand next to Lindsay, or the way their hands instinctively reached for each other. Mommy, Daddy, Baby.

'Hey, c'mon,' Dad said coaxingly, 'it could be fun to have a little brother.'

Paige tore her hands from her ears in fury. 'I don't want a little brother!'

'OK, a little sister—'

'Shut up, Ty,' said Lindsay.

Paige could feel her heart hammering. Visions crowded her mind: Dad rocking a baby in his arms, Dad reading bedtime stories, Dad teaching a little mophead to ride horses and play guitar – *everything he'd never done for her*. She felt consumed with jealousy. 'It's grotesque – disgusting!' she shouted at him. 'By the time it's my age you'll be eighty-something. You'll probably be dead!'

Lindsay drew in a shocked breath and clasped her hands protectively over her bump. Dad shook his head, lips tight. Paige couldn't stand the way they were both looking at her, with regretful sympathy, as if she had a terminal illness. She had to get out of here.

Dad caught her by the arm as she pushed past to the door. 'Please, baby, wait.'

'Don't call me that!' She yanked herself free, eyes blazing, and stabbed a finger at Lindsay's stomach. '*There's* your precious baby. From now on it's the only one you've got!'

CHAPTER 8

Paige's fingers jabbed at the keyboard as the jet flew west towards the setting sun. She was emailing Davina, desperate to find a sympathetic ear for her cataclysmic news. Tears of self-pity blurred her vision as she typed: *Can you believe it? How could they do this to me? How come Dad's so gooey about a baby he hasn't even seen, when he never noticed ME until I was ten? Lindsay's already got Dad and the ranch – isn't that enough for her? Why does she need to...* Paige paused. Somehow this wasn't coming out right.

It had all seemed so clear when she'd spoken to Gaby on her cell phone, while waiting at the landing strip. As always, Gaby had totally understood where she was coming from. 'Lindsay must have known how hurtful this would be for you. These forty-something women are just plain selfish. I'll bet she didn't even consult your Dad about a baby. She just wants to keep hold of him – and his money. You're going to need a smart lawyer. Poor Paige, of course you're right to leave. This has been a terrible, terrible shock. And right before the Oscar ceremony, too. How could they be so thoughtless?'

That's right, Paige told herself, her indignation sparking again into life. So why couldn't she convey her feelings to Davina? She reached for her can of soda, and sipped reflectively. It dawned on her that Davina might not share her indignation since Davina herself was dying to get pregnant.

How could Paige say that Lindsay's desire for a baby was unreasonable without implying that the same was true of Davina? The truth was, it was natural to want a baby. Even Paige wanted one, some day. She couldn't exactly blame Lindsay – though she did! Nor did she really believe that Lindsay was after Dad's money – though Gaby was a life coach and knew about this stuff; she must be right. Oh, it was all so confusing. Paige deleted the unfinished email and slumped in front of the screen, chin in her hands.

It was Dad she was mad at, she realised. It hurt that he'd missed most of her childhood, preferring to fry his brains. It made her angry that he'd been avoiding her calls, delaying the moment when she'd have to know about the baby, letting her think that he wanted her on the ranch when he was preparing for a brand-new family. A lump knotted her throat. Despite everything, she loved him. Why couldn't he love her back?

Her face burned as she remembered the cruel things she'd shouted and pictured his bewildered expression. But she couldn't forgive him – not yet. Gaby said it would take many sessions, even years, to work through her feelings of rejection. What a depressing thought …

Her computer screen had timed-out on her, switching to inky black. Paige fiddled idly with the mouse. She needed colour. She needed distraction. She needed to feel good about herself. Guiltily she went to Google and typed in her own name, skimming through the dross for something to boost her ego. Here was a promising-looking fanblog. *Paige Carson is my favourite actress ever!* That was more like it. *Why dint they pik her insted of Renee? She'd of been way better.* Nice, if untrue. *This avid fan confesses to a particular fascination with her hot butt …* Yuk!

OK, try another. *Paige Carson, one of Hollywood's biggest stars* – uh huh – *currently shooting a big new movie with Jackson Rolfe* – huh! – *has been nominated in the Worst Actress category in this year's Golden Raspberry Awards for*

her performance in the title role of the re-make of Cleopatra
*– Oh God! – also nominated in the Worst Re-Make, Worst
Director, and Worst Screenplay categories, and nominated
for a special award: Worst Toga.* Paige chuckled. At least
she hadn't been wearing a toga. In fact, much of the time
she hadn't been wearing very much at all. When she queried
whether an Egyptian queen would have spent most of her
time lolling about dressed in little more than a gold bikini,
the director had explained that it was 'very hot over there'.

*... Ever since its release the film has figured prominently
on the 'Rotten Tomatoes' website, achieving a record score
as measured by their trusty 'Tomatometer'. Insiders predict
that the new* Cleopatra *may out-perform the record-holding
turkey* Basic Instinct 2, *commonly dubbed* Basically Stinks
2.

Paige took a sip of her drink, feeling just a little aggrieved:
the clunking script hadn't been her fault. What could you do
with lines like: 'It is said that Caesar is wise. But no matter
how wise a man may be, he is still a man.' She blushed to
recall how she'd been directed to stare pointedly at Caesar's
crotch as she said this.

... Cleopatra *is a hot favourite for the 'Mouldy Tomato'
award for being the worst-reviewed film of the year. Sample:
'in trying to appear as enigmatic as a sphinx, Miss Carson
acts as lively as a statue ...'*

She read on, half appalled and half amused. *The annual
Golden Raspberies – affectionately known within the business as 'The Razzies' – are presented at a mock-glittering
ceremony, held each year at the spruced up New Ivar Theater
in Hollywood on the eve of the Academy Awards. Paige's
admirers will have their fingers crossed for her, though un-
doubtedly she will be 'too busy' (read 'embarrassed') to pick
up the award in person ...*

Oh really? Paige bristled. Why should she be embarrassed?
She'd been the innocent victim of a lousy script and a crap
director, that was all. It was part of being a professional to

take the rough with the smooth. Sir Laurence Olivier had once won a Razzie, for God's sake. You could look at it as a kind of honour. And how dared the writer presume to know what she might do on any given evening? Tonight, for example – well, obviously after the showdown with Dad she had no plans other than to go home and be miserable. Saturday night and nowhere to go ... Then it hit her. *The eve of the Oscars*: that was tonight! Suddenly animated, she scrolled down the screen to check the time of the ceremony, then consulted her watch. It was just possible.

Duey announced over the intercom that they'd be landing in five minutes. Paige closed down her notebook and packed it away. She looked out of the window to see that it was almost dark outside. The city glittered invitingly. As they skimmed the mountains and swooped towards the airport, she buckled herself tight and leaned back in her seat with a smile. *Fasten your seatbelts. It's going to be a bumpy night.*

Two hours later she stepped out of a limousine, dressed in a gold halter-necked evening dress that plunged practically to her waist. 'Oh my God, it's Paige Carson!' someone screamed. Head high, she pushed her way through the goggling crowd towards the theatre entrance. Above it a banner proclaimed: 'Razzie Awards: Celebrating Cinematic Crap for over 25 Years'. Inside, a geeky guy in an ill-fitting suit stumbled up to her, looking shocked and thrilled. This was such an honour – he'd never expected – no one had told him .... He seemed completely overwhelmed, poor thing, by the presence of a real-live star. Paige patted his shoulder kindly and told him to relax.

They entered the darkened theatre, where the warm-up act had already started. Onstage a trio of men wearing gravity-defying wigs and squeezed into cocktail dresses were swaying in approximate co-ordination, miming to the theme tune of a recent girl-band biopic. The audience was young and wildly enthusiastic. A gasp of excitement greeted Paige's appearance: heads turned and fingers pointed. The geeky guy consulted a girl standing in the aisle, who was wearing a T-shirt printed with 'Human Searchlight' and waving two torches in apparent homage to the famous Twentieth-Century Fox logo. She showed the two of them to a row of empty seats right at the front, each one marked 'Reserved for –'. Paige noted with amusement some familiar names as they searched for her seat. No one else, of course, had had the nerve to show up.

The girl/boy band finished their number and wiggled offstage. A large man in a light-up bow tie entered from the opposite wing, accompanied by a raucous soundtrack punctuated with rude 'raspberry' noises from a trumpet. He reached a lectern and launched into a witty introduction. Paige found herself chuckling along with everyone else at his denunciation of Hollywood's follies. Cocooned by the good humour and energised by an audience, she could even laugh at his introduction to *Cleopatra* as 'not so much a re-make as a regurgitation of an original and award-winning artifact into a pile of puke'. It had already won three awards by the time a drum roll announced the Worst Actress category. The winner was ... Paige Carson! A surge of applause propelled her to her feet and up onto the stage. The large man turned from the lectern to greet her. In one hand he held the award, a gold, spray-painted raspberry the size of a golf-ball, on top of a mangled reel of Super 8 film. Paige kissed him on both cheeks and accepted the trophy, made of one hundred per cent Styrofoam, while the crowd whooped and whistled. She dipped her head to the microphone.

'I don't know what to say,' she said, smiling bravely as if almost overcome. 'I never dreamed I'd be standing here.' More applause. She adopted a mock-serious expression. 'But, you know, I don't deserve this.' The audience fell silent, unsure of her mood. 'It's just not fair to take all the credit for such a total piece of shit.' There was a roar of relieved laughter. 'There are so many people I need to thank. First of all, the studio for their inspired decision to re-make this movie. Then, the director for what I can only call his unique talent. I mustn't forget the writer, who penned such an unforgettable script. All these guys deserve the recognition you have so kindly bestowed on me tonight.' She waved the trophy triumphantly above her head. 'Thank you so much!' She turned to leave the stage, but they wouldn't let her go. Everyone was clapping. Below her was a sea of smiling faces. These people loved her.

'You are beautiful,' she added as an afterthought into the microphone. Most of the audience were standing now, applauding and whistling. Paige smiled her million-dollar smile and floated into the wings on a tide of rapturous applause. There was no doubt about it: she was a star.

CHAPTER 9

The next morning Paige was woken up by her publicist sobbing down the phone.

'How could you do this to me? I thought we had a relationship. Haven't I always been there for you?'

'Huh? Wha ... ?' Paige scrabbled at her eye-mask with gloved hands and squinted at her alarm clock. 'It's six o'clock in the morning,' she croaked disbelievingly. 'What's going on, Heather?'

Duh, the Razzies. News of her performance last night had hit the headlines – in the celeb media, anyway. Poor Heather, a control freak just short of insanity, was convinced that the whole thing had been a publicity stunt, stage-managed by a fancy new image consultant to whom Paige had switched loyalty, without warning or explanation. 'My email alert system's gone crazy, my voice mail is backed up with messages, and *I know nothing about it!*'

It took some time to talk Heather down from the parapet, to explain that the Razzie thing had been an act of pure impulse, and to apologise for not keeping her informed. (Apologise to her own publicist! What were things coming to?)

Once back on firm ground, Heather was off with the ball and running. 'Fortunately the coverage seems mainly upbeat.' Paige could hear her clicking dementedly through the web pages. '"Good sport" ... "funny" ... "refreshing". I think I can spin this for a home run.'

'What's to spin? I was great. They *loved* me.'

'Of course they did, Paige. I really wish I'd been there. But you know how it is; there are always skunks out there who want to negativise everything.'

'Like who? Like what? What are they saying?'

'Don't go there. You don't want to know.'

Paige did want to know. Eventually she bullied Heather into reading out one report – 'nowhere important' – depicting her Razzie appearance as a pathetic PR attempt to grab her some much-needed limelight. There was also an accusation on one of the regrettably popular 'bitchblogs' that she was developing bingo wings.

'The usual garbage, nothing I can't handle,' Heather assured her. 'But today of all days the world's eyes are upon us. My very strong advice would be to go for the black dress tonight. I'm thinking classic, refined, dignified. That should counteract any Razzie downside, and will also send out a positive subliminal message: versatility – an actress who can play any role – comic, tragic – one night kidding around at the Razzies, the next an undisputed Oscar queen. Yes! I'm really feeling my creative juices flowing. Are you on board with this? ... Paige, are you receiving me?'

'Hm?' Paige had climbed out of bed and was standing naked in front of the mirror, elbow crooked to hold her water bottle behind her head. She raised it high into the air and down again, one-two, one-two, admiring the taut musculature of her triceps. No wobbles, no sag, absolutely no bingo wings. So there. Reassured, she returned to bed and tuned back in to Heather's checklist.

'And finally, can I get this Pete thing nailed down? Old friends, absolutely no romance: is that right?'

'Correct.'

As soon as Heather had finished, Paige buzzed Concepcion to bring up a tray with wheat-germ, egg white omelette and carrot juice. She was going to need every ounce of energy to carry her through an insanely packed day, starting with the appointment with her waxer at ten, continuing non-stop with Oscar prep until the limo picked her up at four, then the actual awards and finally the parties. Paige sighed aloud at the marathon that lay ahead.

All morning the congratulations flowed in. Every time she tried to get into the shower or zip up her skirt, her cell phone rang yet again. Nathan told her she was the wild card in his pack, and he adored her, though he was thankful that she had not dragged him along: 'I'm too old for transvestites.' No, he couldn't tell her anything new about the Spanish Project except that things were hotting up and he was doing his best for her. He hoped to catch a glimpse of her tonight in the scrum.

Gaby called, of course. 'I'm so proud of you, Paige. I knew something positive would come out of our work together. Incidentally, I gather from one of my clients that you can expect a *very* favourable response in *Daily Variety* ... No, nothing to do with me. Well, I may have dropped the teensiest hint ...' She was sure Paige would look beautiful in whichever dress she wore: black was certainly very striking, though she knew that many people found blue more serene. Either way, she'd be glued to her TV set hoping to catch a glimpse of Paige and 'your Pete'.

'He's not mine, Gaby,' Paige laughed.

'But you said he was single.'

'Yeah, but—'

'Now don't close your mind to possibilities. You've both had time to mature. Who knows what surprises tonight may spring?'

The only irritant in these otherwise gratifying conversations was everyone's assumption that her Razzie appearance was the result of some behind-the-scenes mastermind. One of her friends even asked for the phone number of whoever had scripted her speech, and was really quite snippy when Paige denied that there was any such person. Why couldn't anyone accept that she could do something *by herself*?

By the time Paige dashed downstairs she was already running late. Concepcion told her that there'd been even more messages on the house phone, and earlier on she'd seen some 'strange guys' on the CCTV monitor, fiddling around by the entrance gate.

'Reporters? How many? Never mind, call Security and get rid of them. I *cannot* have my personal space invaded in this manner!'

She gave instructions to her driver not to stop, whatever happened, and armed herself with sunglasses and a scowl against camera flashes and impertinent questions. It was faintly disappointing when the gates swung open to reveal two members of the neighbourhood clean-up crew, hefting the carcase of a dead deer onto their truck.

'Brazilians are so yesterday,' Lola was saying. 'Everyone wants personalised designs now – flowers, hearts, a dollar sign, their boyfriend's initials. I knew Laura and Scott were an item way before they went public, when she asked me to shave the Scientology logo into her muff. Boy, that was tricky.'

Paige crossed her legs as she lay flat on the couch, grateful that at present she was suffering nothing worse than eyebrow-shaping.

'Young girls still want the bare-all, of course,' Lola continued. 'I don't personally think it's hygienic to racket around town with no underpants on, but at least if they do happen to flash it's not embarrassing because they're groomed.'

'Mm,' murmured Paige. Lola was the best beauty therapist in town, but she sure loved to talk. Paige craved some peace, so that she could prepare mentally for tonight. A lot of things could go wrong on the red carpet. The media vultures would be hungry. She needed total confidence to retain her poise and handle any tricky questions.

'But get this.' Now Lola was telling her about some accountant guy who'd rented out his palatial home in the valley as a location for a film. 'He tells his wife – that's my client, a lovely woman – that they're making an exercise video, and sends her off to the in-laws with the kids while he stays behind to "supervise". But it's really a porno movie, and he's doing a lot more than supervising. He doesn't even take the family portraits off the piano before getting down and dirty on the bear rugs.'

'Oof.' Paige grimaced. 'What a sleazebag!'

Lola sighed. 'Sometimes I wonder about men.'

Me too, thought Paige. In particular, she dreaded meeting Jackson tonight – strutting, snide, rude, insufferable. It would be the last straw if he won Best Actor.

Lola straightened to admire her handiwork. 'Perfect. Now let's fix that nail. I don't know what you were thinking of, going horseback riding right before Oscar night. Meantime, I'm going to give you one of my Euphoria facials, just to plump up your skin and give it a lift.'

'Whatever you think,' Paige said meekly – and then with alarm, 'You think I need lifting?'

'Goodness, no! Not yet, anyway. Everyone's skin starts decaying around the age of twenty, but there are so many fabulous treatments nowadays. They don't cut any more; they just put in these little screws that dissolve.'

Twenty! She'd been decaying for nine years already. Her spirits sank a notch lower.

'So tell me about the dress,' said Lola, applying green gunk. 'Who's doing your make-up? Are you seeing any other aestheticians? Who's your date?'

Paige answered as best she could, given the gradual numbness spreading from forehead to bust like frostbite. A great friend – well, a really nice make-up girl she'd met on set and hired regularly – was coming to the house to get her ready. They'd decide together on the dress. And the jewels. And the shoes, the bag, the underwear, the hairstyle …

Her nerves began to knot. Suddenly the whole thing seemed crazy. What was she doing, going to an awards ceremony where she wasn't going to win an award, wearing a dress that someone else had chosen and jewels that weren't hers, with a man she hadn't even seen for a year or more? Why subject herself to all the questions and cameras and sly looks? Why line herself up on the red carpet to be picked over and compared to every other actress?

Because that was the way it was. She was on the treadmill and she couldn't get off.

CHAPTER 10

'Over here, Paige!'
'Did you vote for Jackson?'
'Oscar or Razzie – which is better?'
'Are you and Pete back together?'

Paige stood on the red-carpeted sidewalk, straight-backed, chin up, smiling into the glare of TV lights and the barrage of reporters in their roped-off pen. Behind them, tiers of spectators were packed into bleachers emblazoned with an Academy Awards banner. The air reeked of gas fumes from the limos and SUVs that crawled down Hollywood Boulevard. Her hand tightened on Pete's arm. 'Don't let go,' she told him through locked teeth. 'Look happy! ... OK, you can let go now.' She allowed one of the Oscar greeters in his navy blazer and red tie to lead her to an unoccupied patch of carpet, and offered the cameras her best three-quarter profile (the right side) and a good view of the diamond bracelet which she had elected to wear, warrior-like, round the slim upper curve of her biceps instead of on her wrist. That should fix the bingo wing brigade. Though it was a little chilly out here on the sidewalk late on a February afternoon.

There was a flurry of activity behind her. She heard the crackle and gargled speech of a walkie-talkie as a muscled security guy in blackout sunglasses rushed past. Then the entire bank of cameras panned away from her to the next arrival, and she was politely hustled into the crowd that swarmed towards the theatre entrance. *Over and out, Miss Carson.*

'This is worse than a Macy's sale,' Pete said as she rejoined him, and Paige threw back her head theatrically and laughed as if this was the funniest joke she'd heard all year. (She'd popped a couple of pills before leaving the house, just to keep her afloat.) The next moment she was being rapturously greeted by a girl dressed in a billowing ball gown made of shredded white feathers. Paige squealed back with equal excitement, and fairly shortly thereafter recognised an actress friend under a rainbow array of cosmetics, and a hairstyle which suggested that she had just been plugged into the LA grid.

'You look wonderful!' Paige exclaimed.

'So do you!'

Truthfully, everyone looked like a waxwork crudely crafted by an overenthusiastic apprentice. Looking good in real life ran a very poor second to looking good on television, especially now that HiDef picked up every line and blemish. Paige herself was larded with make-up, as well as sprayed, buffed, polished, pulled in, pushed up, and held together with yards of body tape. At the last moment she had ignored the advice of both Heather and Gaby, and chosen the skin-tight sheath in deep rose, held up by a single strap wound diagonally from left breast to right shoulder-blade. She looked sensational from the front, but was already regretting the massive taffeta bow on her butt, which kept getting snagged on women's bracelets, and whacked guys in the balls if she turned round too quickly.

They edged towards the broad walkway that led to the theatre. In real life this was part of a shopping mall, aggrandised by a huge arch framing the distant Hollywood sign (eclipsed, as usual, by smog) and decorated with vaguely Assyrian motifs. Stylised birds were etched into its massive entrance gateway. An elephant – half Disney, half ancient

Babylon – reared over one of the plazas. But on Oscar night the storefronts and tourist eateries were concealed by swathes of gold and red curtaining. Troughs of hothouse flowers replaced the usual garbage receptacles. Acres of red carpet led the privileged many past the sightless eyes of giant sprayed-gold Oscar replicas.

Paige had never figured out why the trophy for the Academy of Motion Picture Arts and Sciences had to be male, let alone a naked crusading knight with an enormous and very erect sword positioned over its privates. The atmosphere of Oscar Night was more ancient-Rome gladiatorial than mediaeval chivalrous. Who would triumph before the baying crowd? Who would be tossed to the lions? Which battle-scarred survivor, hitherto overlooked, would secure the Honorary Award for a lifetime's achievement in the nick of time, before pegging out from natural causes? The thumbs-up or thumbs-down decisions were already sealed into envelopes – two sets locked into two briefcases and handcuffed to two executives, who took two separate routes to the theatre in case one of them got shot or kidnapped. (The executives also memorised the winners in the event that both briefcases were stolen.) But everyone still flocked to witness the kill. Or as Pete now said, more prosaically, 'It's sort of like finding your gate at the airport.'

She glanced up at him with fond exasperation. Same old Pete. He'd always hated 'that black tie crap', and even at the height of their romance refused to go to industry parties with her. Yet he looked good in his tux: not quite at ease, perhaps, but handsome in a serious, almost professorial way that compared favourably with many of the other men present, who looked either hyped to the eyeballs or as if they'd dived headfirst into a vat of fake tan. His wavy brown hair was intact, and he was still as lean as a greyhound. Pete looked what he was: intelligent. She'd always loved the way he told her about science and history and stuff, and listened to her, too, as if her comments counted for something. She felt a tug of nostalgia for the old days, when they'd gone bicycling in the hills, or nosed around junkyards looking for weird items to produce Pete's sound effects, or just stayed at home entwined on the couch; and wondered if he was thinking the same.

'Why did you agree to come tonight?' she asked.

He took a moment or two to formulate his answer, then said simply, 'I wanted to see you.'

She didn't press him further. Anyway, the decibel level had suddenly shot up as they entered the theatre lobby, an Art Deco confection of creams and browns adorned with backlit portraits of famous Oscar winners. Stray voices rose above the babble.

'You're gonna have to add two zeros to his fee if he wins ...'

'... but Sundance is so commercial these days!'

'We've got a first-look deal with Sony ...'

'Fuck! Somebody stepped on my train.'

Everyone was here. She exchanged air kisses with Hilary and Jen, Tom, Jake – ooh! there was gorgeous Georgeous raising his devilish eyebrow at her and pointing towards the bar. She waved back her assent, redirected Pete, and they were edging their way across the flow when the crowd parted and she came face to face with Jackson. Surrounded by a jostling all-male entourage, he was already sweaty and dishevelled, and clearly drunk. He squinted down her cleavage, then ran his eyes over her dress. 'Raspberry pink. How appropriate.'

One of Jackson's posse sniggered. There was a murmur of shock from the immediate bystanders, who stopped to gape. A flush rose to Paige's cheeks. She bowed her head very slightly, as if accepting a compliment, and started to turn away.

'Aren't you going to wish me luck?' he demanded loudly. 'After all, you've got so many trophies for your ... performances.'

She stared into his scornful, bloodshot eyes and felt her veins fill with hatred. 'Good luck, Jackson,' she said coolly. Then she wheeled Pete about and headed for the auditorium. 'Let's forget the bar. I need to sit down.' He started to protest but she shook her head, lips pursed, burningly aware of the whispers and sidelong glances that pursued them.

'What was that all about?' Pete murmured into her ear, once they had safely left Jackson and the onlookers behind.

'Didn't you see the news this morning?' she hissed.

'What, the Iran thing?'

'*Me!* The Razzies. I told you in the car. I told you about Jackson. That was a deliberate insult. You should have hit him.'

'But—'

'Shh. We're coming into camera range. I don't want anyone lip-reading us.'

Automatically Paige smiled and greeted people as they made their way down the aisle towards the front stalls, but her mind raced and stumbled on a completely different track. *How could he?* How could Jackson humiliate her so publicly, and in this of all places? He might as well have taken out an ad in one of the trades: 'For your consideration: Paige Carson stinks. Do not hire her.' The rumour tom-toms would already be drumming. She might never be offered a good part again.

Somehow she was in her seat (row eight – not too bad) with the stiff, embossed programme in her hand. The stupid bow on her dress meant that she had to sit up even taller than usual; she felt as conspicuous as a giraffe. Pete was huffily silent. Paige bent her head and flicked through the programme, noting that the paper had been 'selected with a sensitivity toward reducing the threat of global warming', whatever that meant. The Oscar ceremony always liked to have a theme: war, a social issue, the contribution of one or other ethnic group; she had a feeling that tonight's was going to be the environment.

'How's your mom?' Pete asked eventually.

'In love with her dog. Apparently it calls her "Mommy".'

'And your dad?' he persisted.

'Having a baby. Lindsay's pregnant.'

'That's great!'

'Is it?'

Paige switched her glance to a peculiar-looking woman who was making her way towards a middle seat in the row in front. Her face had clearly been rearranged in the bad old days of cutting. Even under all the make-up you could see the scars at her hairline – no, it was a wig! Her gold lamé dress was at least twenty years too young for her, as was her escort, a bling-encrusted stud who might as well have had 'gigolo' printed on his breast pocket. But the woman's voice was girlish, even flirtatious, as she thanked the people who stood up to let her pass. With horror Paige realised that this was a once-luscious actress, an Oscar winner, whose career had plummeted to rock-bottom via on-set tantrums, broken relationships and barbiturate addiction. *Poor woman,* she thought, then: *That could be me!* If the parts didn't come in, if the right man didn't show up, she too would be a pathetic has-been. For several morbid seconds she conjured up an image of herself in a gloomy mansion, alone and unwanted, waiting for the offer of a character role in a low-budget TV cop drama, while tiny screws dissolved in her skull. She felt an impulse to leap up from her seat and run screaming out of the theatre. Her eyes swept round the auditorium, taking in the acres of plum plush, wraparound balconies and tiered boxes, now packed to capacity; the TV cameras on standby, the spotlights ready to pounce.

'This theatre is hideous,' she burst out to Pete. 'I thought it was supposed to be modelled on an old-fashioned European opera house, not a brothel. Why do we need that gold arch over the stage? What's with the porno-blue lighting and the TV screens all over the ceiling?'

He seemed surprised, even amused, by her vehemence.

She glared back. 'It's so tacky, so phoney.'

Even as she spoke, there was an apocalyptic drum-roll. The on-stage TV screens exploded into animation. Blinding spotlights criss-crossed the stage and audience. The orchestra materialised from a cloud of dry ice on a crescendo of feel-good music.

'Welcome to Hollywood,' murmured Pete.

I was right, Paige congratulated herself: tonight's theme was green. First there was a montage of clips from *Mad Max*, *The China Syndrome*, *The Day After Tomorrow* and the like, affording the fun of comparing the youthful on-screen stars with their real-life counterparts, smiling bravely in tonight's audience as the cameras zeroed in on their wrinkles. The compere arrived in a bicycle rickshaw, and quipped that he had saved energy tonight by getting someone else to write his script. There were several in-jokes about recycling (movies, partners, body-parts) and the usual digs at the White House: 'The President has a plan. He says that if we need to, we can lower the temperature dramatically just by switching from Fahrenheit to Centigrade.' *Boom boom*. A screen icon gave a speech about the magic of movies and the power of artists not only to entertain, not only to move hearts, but to change minds and triumph over ignorance and bigotry. He was cheered to the roof. Finally they got around to the first award: first for visual effects, then for an animated film about the rain forest. The ceremony always began with the least interesting, building up to a climax at the end. Paige suppressed a yawn. It would be fatal if a camera zoomed in and caught her with her mouth wide open. Anyway, there was always the drama of the envelope-opening, plus the excitement of the winners as they flourished their trophies, gabbled incoherent thanks to colleagues and family before their forty-five seconds were up, and when in doubt yelled 'God bless America!'

It seemed that they had barely got going when, with a few suave words, the compere left the stage for the first ad break and there was a mass-stampede to the bars and toilets. The seat-fillers, hired by the network to ensure that the theatre looked full at all times, emerged from their holding pen and hovered in the aisles, ready to cover the still-warm imprint of any departing ass. Paige decided to stay put, to avoid the danger of running into Jackson again.

'Enjoying it?' she asked Pete.

'Actually, yes. I feel bad now that I wasn't willing to come to these things with you. Just pride, I guess. I wanted to be my own man, not an appendage to someone else.'

'You could never be that,' Paige said warmly, temporarily forgetting that this was exactly why she had invited him tonight. 'And look at you now, so successful, with your own little house out in the wilds, as you always wanted.' She thought back to the time when they had confided, even shared their dreams for the future. 'Isn't it funny the way things change ... and yet in some ways, deep-down, they don't?'

'Mm,' he said absently. 'I wonder how they got that squishing noise – you know, when the boa constrictor crushed the logger?'

The show resumed with a live rendering of one of the contenders for Best Original Song, always something of a penance and not improved by dancers 'interpreting' the lyrics in the background. They ground on through Costume, Make-up, and the technical stuff that no amount of montages and compere jokes could make interesting except to the nominees – and Pete. But despite the tedium Paige felt the tension rise within her as Best Actor inexorably approached. Scanning the audience, she had finally pinpointed Jackson in the second row of the stalls, on the opposite side of the theatre to herself, right on the aisle.

Here were the clips of the five nominees. Jackson was last on screen, wielding mighty Excalibur as he embarked on King Arthur's heroically doomed quest. A ravishing actress in yellow silk sashayed on stage to present the award. She opened the envelope, favoured the audience with a teasing smile, and finally drew out a card. 'And the award goes to …'

No, no, no, no, no! Paige prayed silently.

'… Jackson Rolfe!'

The audience erupted in applause, which Paige felt bound to mimic as the TV cameras panned back and forth, scooping the reaction shots. She saw Jackson jump to his feet, pumping his fist in the air, then charge onto the stage like a fighting bull entering the ring. He grabbed the presenter, bent her backwards in a full-blown smooch and, while she was still staggering from this assault, snatched the Oscar from her hand.

'I am the king!' he bellowed into the microphone, to wild cheers. 'And you know what? I'm not going to thank anybody. I deserve this. Me! It's bloody mine! America's a wonderful country' – whoops and whistles went into overdrive – 'but let me tell you there's another great big beautiful continent on this planet beginning with A, and that's Australia!' He began to strut round the stage singing '"Australians all, let us rejoice, for we are young and free. We've golden soil and—"' He broke off as the presenter linked her arm into his with a very passable imitation of gaiety and attempted to lead him away from the microphone. 'I'm not bloody finished,' he yelled, whipping his arm free. '"We've golden s—"' Now the orchestra struck up jauntily to drown him out, and when that didn't work two men in dark suits emerged from the wings and jostled him offstage with implacable bonhomie. Everyone seemed to find this hilarious.

'Jackson's such a trip,' chuckled a voice from the seat behind Paige.

'And a brilliant, *brilliant* actor,' added his companion in reverent tones.

Paige found her hands were sticky with sweat. She couldn't believe the way everyone else was laughing and clapping as if Jackson were an adorable wayward child instead of a loathsome boor. 'I'm going to the john,' she told Pete at the next ad break, standing up abruptly. She heard something rip. That bow of her dress must have got pinched between her seat and backrest, and was now hanging half off. She felt mortified as she minced her way to the ladies' room while trying to hold it in place. The attendant offered to pin it back on for her, but Paige was sick of the damned thing. 'Do you have any scissors?' she asked.

By the time she emerged, bowless, from the cubicle, everyone else had returned to the auditorium and she was alone in the ladies' room, apart from the still-shocked attendant. Or almost alone, for as she was washing her hands she heard a door lock disengage and a voice gushed, 'Oh my God! What an incredible coincidence!'

In the mirror Paige saw a girl with blonde hair, scarlet lips and an ecstatic smile, draped in vestal-virgin white. Only someone as dumb as Brooklyn Blanck would think it 'incredible' for two actresses to meet at the Oscars. 'Hello, Brooklyn,' she said coolly, flicking water from her fingertips. 'Are you enjoying the show?'

'I love it! This is the best night of the year. In fact, I think this is the best night of my entire life.'

Paige raised her eyebrows. 'That's pretty enthusiastic. Did someone special win?'

'I don't really know,' Brooklyn confessed with a ripple of laughter. 'Actually, I've been in the bar for the last half hour with this incredible director. And guess what, he's offered me a part!'

'Congratulations.'

'It's supposed to be a secret, but I'm so excited I have to tell someone. Nathan will totally kill me when he finds out I've said yes without even consulting him, but the director is such a genius I'd literally work for nothing.' Taking a tiny vial from her purse she dabbed perfume behind her ears and between her opulent breasts. 'Plus we get to film in Spain,' she chirped. 'That's so romantic.'

Paige turned slowly from Brooklyn's mirror-image to look at her in the flesh: pale, milky, incontrovertibly Scandinavian flesh, with eyes and hair to match. 'What's the part?' she asked casually. But she knew. Cold certainty settled in her stomach like a stone. She barely heard Brooklyn's prattlings about how the role was really going to stretch her. All she knew was that Brooklyn Blanck had got the part of La Passionaria and she hadn't. Another door had slammed in her face.

'By the way,' said Brooklyn, as she turned to leave, 'I hope you don't mind me mentioning it, but your dress is coming apart at the back. See ya!'

Shrieks of excitement echoed from the auditorium as Paige emerged from the ladies' room, wringing her hands as if they were still wet. The ceremony was reaching its climax: Best Screenplay, Best Director, Best Haircut, Best Breasts ... She veered abruptly to the bar, ordered a bourbon on the rocks and hoisted herself onto a stool. So what if her dress was unravelling? Her whole life was unravelling. Anyway, there was only one guy in here apart from the bartenders, sitting on the far side of the curving counter, back hunched to the hectoring TV screens; and he looked too drunk and despondent to care if she was stark naked. They sat in silence, deep in their own separate pools of misery.

'Bloody farce,' he muttered into his drink.

Paige ignored him.

'They fly you all the way from London, put you up in a poncey hotel ... car, prezzies ... "Oh I just *love* your work, we must have breakfast."'

He spoke such satiric venom that Paige couldn't resist a tug of amusement. She looked up, recognising the bony, sardonic face of Harry Keenan, the British actor who'd just lost out to Jackson. He ought to be in the interview room being grilled on how it felt to lose, but who could blame him for slipping his leash?

'Apparently, the "rootability quotient" of my character was inadequate. What do you say to that?'

Paige said nothing.

'Do you know that they're taking the car off me *tonight*?' he demanded, eyebrows leaping comically to his hairline. 'I've done their sodding interviews, eaten their disgusting food, now it's goodbye Mr I'm-Sorry-I've-Forgotten-Your-Name, you can pay for your own taxi to the airport.'

Paige knocked back a slug of bourbon. 'Hollywood likes winners. You lost. If it's any consolation, I voted for you.'

'Ah ha! The gorgeous creature speaks.' He raised his sharp nose like a hound sniffing the wind. 'Dare one approach?' Unwinding long rubbery limbs he paced across to her, weaving only slightly, and leaned an elbow on the bar to gaze down appreciatively into her face. Fifty-something, with hair swept back from a receding hairline, he was still stealthily attractive. 'I suppose you're an actress,' he said. 'Everyone seems to be. Well, take a tip from a sad old man and stick to the theatre. The theatre's real. In the theatre you have chums. They love you even when you're crap. They don't keep asking you how it feels to be crap, or make you go to the Governor's Ball to celebrate your crappity crappiness ... And why does he have only one, I'd like to know?'

Paige giggled.

'That's better. Always look on the bright side. Mustn't grumble. Christ! You're not Julia Roberts or Cameron Diabolo, one of that lot? Thing is, I don't actually watch moo-vees, I only act in them. When they ask me. Which they probably never will again.'

Still smiling, Paige slid from her stool. 'They're winding up now. I have to go.' She held out her hand. 'It's been a pleasure meeting you – in fact, the high spot.'

He slid his palm against hers and held on. 'Back to the boyfriend, I suppose. Or husband, is it?'

'Neither.'

'That's what I mean! This is a totally fucked-up place.' He raised her hand to his lips and kissed it with an actor's grace. 'Don't let the buggers get you down.'

'Have a safe trip back to London.'

'If I make it out of the bar it'll be a bleeding miracle.'

Hysterical fanfares were already signalling the ceremony's end as Paige hurried down the curving hallways. People began to surge from the exits in an avalanche of bright colours and glittering jewels, their voices rising in head-splitting cacophony. They looked strangely at Paige as she pushed by in the opposite direction, one fist behind her back to keep her dress closed. 'See you at the party, Paige!' someone called. Her anxieties came rushing back. No way was she going to some party to be sneered at by Jackson. She did not want another encounter with Miss Perkitits Blanck, Spanish revolutionary. Nor could she face Nathan's sympathy as he broke the bad news to her.

But at least there was Pete. She could see him now, standing loyally by his seat, looking this way and that in the maelstrom. Her heart flooded with relief and affection. He might be a little geeky but he was a decent guy.

His face cleared as she approached. 'There you are. I was getting worried. I thought you must be sick.'

'I am, a little,' she said, seizing on the excuse. 'Would you mind terribly if we skipped the party and went home?'

'Of course not.' He looked relieved. 'I mean, with all this craziness going on it's hard to talk. That is, about anything personal.'

Aw, he was blushing.

'One more thing.' She swung round to show him the hole in her dress. 'Could you possibly put your arm around me while leave? And keep your hand on my butt to cover the rip?'

'Sure, if you don't mind the wagging tongues. I've already been asked about twelve times if we're back together again.'

'Oh, who cares? Let them talk.'

It was comforting to have a man to lean against. No one looked at her oddly now. She even saw other women giving Pete the eye. Hands off! She began to think about getting home, inviting him in, maybe settling down on the couch for a long talk. Should she call Concepcion and get her to turn on the fireplace?

It took an age to shuffle their way out to Hollywood Boulevard and find their car, since nearly everybody else had the identical thought and the identical vehicle. Pete surveyed the lines of nose-to-tail limos. 'Did you know that there's still a city law that no one's got round to repealing, which states that no more than two thousand sheep may be driven down Hollywood Boulevard?'

'Baa-aa-aa,' said Paige.

They laughed. It felt good.

When at last she sank side by side with Pete into the leather seat and eased off her shoes, she gave a sigh of relief. Who needed booze and dancing? Who needed a bow on her dress? Who needed a job? She was warm and comfortable and going home with a nice man. Pete hadn't seen this latest house of hers. It would be fun showing it to him. His voice would fill up the empty space. He could admire her Razzie award. *Come up and see my trophies ...*

He had turned to speak to her now – was he thanking her? That was so sweet. He'd really enjoyed the show, he said, especially a clip that happened to include one of the sounds he had created (when the alien ate the Mormon). 'But the real reason I wanted to see you ...' He hesitated.

Don't close your mind to possibilities, Gaby had said.

'Yes?' Paige murmured encouragingly.

'Well, you know how some things can be right under your nose but you can't see them? A person, say. You know them, you like them, but you kind of take them for granted. Then one day, wham! Everything changes. Maybe it's something to do with maturity, with finally recognising what you want, but suddenly you realise that she is *the* person.'

'She?' Paige echoed. Was Pete talking about her?

'Elinor!' His face burst into a radiant smile. 'The Foley editor I've been working with for two years. We're getting married!'

Paige shot bolt upright. For several seconds she stared at him, open-mouthed. 'You're getting married,' she repeated.

'I've been dying to tell you all night. Of course, I had to tell you in person. The thing is, Elinor and I really want you to be at the wedding, but I know what your schedule's like. If I hadn't come to the Oscars tonight I probably wouldn't have seen you for another six months, and unless I book you right now Elinor and I will be rockin' up the aisle on our zimmers.'

Elinor, Elinor, Elinor. He loved her name. He loved saying it. He loved *her*. Paige marvelled at how far off the truth she had been. Shame ripped through her. She took his hand and reached forward to kiss him lightly on the cheek. 'I'm so happy for you. This is wonderful, wonderful news.'

'Yep.' He was grinning like a schoolboy. 'It's the real deal.'

They talked about Elinor. Her hair was sort of brown, she was tall but not too tall, she was way smarter than him. She could cook! He couldn't explain: Paige would have to see for herself. Paige said she couldn't wait.

But weariness seeped into her bones. Wrong again. Stupid again. Wherever she turned she met rejection and failure, and she was trapped in the one place in the world where winning was everything. She had to get out.

'I have to get out!' she called suddenly.

Pete looked alarmed.

'I – I feel nauseous. I need fresh air. Look, there's the Whatsit Hotel. I can get a cab there. You take the limo home. No, really, I insist.'

Pete protested – he couldn't possibly let her go home

alone. But she stabbed the intercom button and told the driver to pull over. She squeezed her feet painfully back into her shoes and gripped the door-handle, waiting until the limo halted obediently. 'I'll be fine,' she said, stepping out onto the kerb.

Even so, he leapt out after her, looking troubled.

'Please, Pete, let me go. ' She pressed her palm briefly to his cheek. 'Go on, get back to Elinor. I'll email you my schedule.'

He knew her too well to argue. Baffled and unhappy, he climbed back into the limo. But first he took out his wallet and stuffed dollar bills into her hand for the cab, remembering how she always forgot to carry cash. His thoughtfulness was almost the hardest thing to bear about the whole evening.

The limo slid down the street and at last she was alone, clicking her way towards the hotel forecourt and a free cab. *I have to get out, I have to get out*, she repeated under her breath to the rhythm of her footsteps, and wondered if she was going crazy. Ahead of her, a stationary truck at the roadside flashed warning lights. There were two workmen on the hoist, systematically pasting over a movie poster. Paige just had time to read the words 'Nominated for Best Picture' before they were obliterated by an ad for tanning lotion.

Bloody farce. She wondered if all Englishmen were like Harry Keenan: funny and rude. And smart, witty and 'normal', according to Davina.

Paige stopped dead. Stray fragments from the past few days suddenly clicked together and resolved themselves into an electrifying idea. She prised her cell phone from her bag and thumbed the touch pad with a trembling hand. After interminable rings she heard blasting music, the roar of a party in full swing, then Nathan's voice.

'Paige! I've been all round the party looking for you. Where are you?'

'I'm not coming. Listen, you know that Shakespeare thing? I want you to call them up and tell them yes.'

'Are you out of your mind?'

'No. And I'm not drunk either.'

'Paige, I really think we should discuss—'

'No!' She stamped her foot, desperate to act before her nerve seeped away. 'Call them now.'

'But the time change – they'll be asleep—'

'Then wake them up! Right this minute, Nathan. I mean it.'

She closed off the call, aghast and elated at what she'd done. Then she twirled round once, a lone girl in diamonds and pink silk on the brashly lit city street, and ran on. Goodbye, Hollywood. Hello, London.

PART II

LONDON

CHAPTER 11

Ed Hawkshead stood in front of his bedroom mirror, eyes narrowed. Was the pink shirt too arty-farty? He'd already discarded the white one (too dull) and the electric blue (too flash). The suit was no problem: newish, Italian-made, thrillingly expensive, and in fact the only decent one he possessed. But its unusual shade of pigeon-wing grey produced different effects according to the colours it was teamed with. Today's lunchtime meeting could change his life; he didn't want to mess up by wearing the wrong thing. For the third time he slid the jacket onto his lean frame and fastened the top two buttons only, in unconscious obedience to the long-ago girlfriend who'd crushingly remarked that only oicks did up all three.

What the hell? Pink shirt, no tie: stop arsing around. Other people could think what they liked. He wasn't kow-towing to some number-crunching exec just for the sake of a million pounds or so. *A million pounds!* Ed was gripped by simultaneous panic and excitement, which he quelled by walking through the flat's narrow hallway to his sitting-room/study next door, where his computer screen glowed awaitingly. The meeting that would decide his fate was still three hours away. He'd told his office that he would be working from home this morning, partly to avoid speculation about the unusual sight of the boss wearing a suit, partly to keep his head clear and his nerve steady – and partly because a prospective tenant would be arriving any minute to view the upstairs flat. Undoing his jacket once again he hung it on the back of a chair, sat down at the screen and jiggled the mouse.

A pale blue chart sprang into life, listing the viewing figures for last-night's TV programmes – 'the overnights' – rated according to channel and popularity by the implacable goddess Barb, otherwise known as the Broadcaster's Audience Research Board. Needless to say, his documentary on Arthur Miller's trial in the 1950s did not appear at number one, nor even at number one hundred and one. Archive footage of a dead, white, male playwright could not compete with the nation's favourite soap, let alone with the suspense of which contestant on *Fattie!* would slim down sufficiently to win the modelling-contract prize. It would not have been commissioned at all if he had not cunningly entitled it *Miller and Monroe*. Marilyn Monroe had little relevance beyond being married to Miller at the time, but Ed knew the publicity value of a shot of a Hollywood actress with her dress billowing up around her waist. Such were the compromises that had to be made in this culturally heathen age.

The viewing figures weren't bad, considering that the programme had been aired on one of those BBC digital channels watched by a minuscule fraction of the population. It was no good expecting quantity when quality was your unique selling point. Still, this was bread-and-butter stuff. The big projects were what he loved – the three-hour story of the Berlin Wall which he was currently editing, and the major series on West Indian immigration to Britain which would be brilliant if only he could get the money together.

Money, money, money ... Ed thrust a hand into his hair and tugged at a thick, dark fistful. Sometimes he thought he'd been mad to start his own production company. The overheads of his Soho office were terrifying. He was at the mercy of commissioning editors who – with noble exceptions – ripped off his ideas or watered them down to pap. Even when he got the green light he had to fight all the way to the final edit, and pray that his show wouldn't be bumped to a graveyard slot by 'major news' about a footballer's injury or the engagement of a celebrity. Then came the final insult – the ignominious battle for payment that barely covered his expenditure. The only way to make real money was to sell an idea or a film internationally, which usually meant the Americans. Ed scowled. Not one of the US networks would touch his award-winning series *The End of Reason*, despite the rave reviews it had received in Britain. It was judged 'too controversial', i.e. insufficiently reverential about lunacies such as Creationism – which meant that Ed was currently looking at a gaping hole in his company finances.

But it was thrilling to be his own boss (with Maddy, of course), after ten years as a mere employee. He did not have to conform to the School of the Bleeding Obvious, but could let his creativity rip. Ed's speciality was to combine news footage, pop cultural references, academic interviews, fragments of *film noir*, cartoons, and images of all kinds to ambush the viewer into looking at the world in a new way. Nothing made him happier than sitting in darkened room looking for the right clips, making connections, weaving together politics and culture, science, history, society. A shot of the Prime Minister at the dispatch box with the soundtrack from *Psycho*: why not? 'Stoppard on speed', one reviewer had called him, a compliment Ed cherished.

So was he about to give all that up? To sell out? Anxiety drove him from his chair and into the kitchen to make himself a double espresso, his drug of choice. He switched on the machine and went through the automatic routine of measuring out coffee, tamping it down, and swivelling the holder into place while his mind raced on a now familiar switchback course. The letter from Alex Wolfe, CEO of the media conglomerate Grapevine, had arrived out of the blue last week, crisp and to the point. Ed's work was the best in the business: would he be interested in discussing the sale of his company? For the first few dizzying moments Ed had felt triumphant. Somebody out there valued what he was doing. He would be rich! To sell his own company (and Maddy's, of course) at the age of only thirty-six must mean that he was a success, something he often doubted.

The age felt significant. It was at thirty-six that his father had been killed, while driving home over the fells in treacherous fog. Ed had been five years old. He remembered a tall man, full of energy and laughter, who used to stand Ed on the kitchen table to polish his school shoes, and pushed him round the garden in a wheelbarrow at delirious speed. He remembered the desolating sound of his mother trying to stifle her sobs in a suddenly silent house. It was wholly irrational to fear that his own life would be cut similarly short. Nevertheless, in recent months he had sensed the urgency of this internal deadline, like an approaching drumbeat. Something important needed to happen this year – but what? Ed placed a cup under the twin spouts of the espresso machine, pressed another switch and watched the coffee splutter and flow. Perhaps the sale of Hawkshead Barry was the significant marker he was looking for. Was it too fanciful to think of it as a kind of gift, or at least an acknowledgement, from his father?

Christ, Ed, engage brain! This touchy-feely drivel was unworthy of the creator of *The End of Reason*. He snapped off the machine and drank down his coffee in a single heartjolting, mind-clearing gulp. Right: Hawkshead Barry, sale of. Once again he reviewed the list of questions and doubts that had flooded in after that first explosion of euphoria. How *much* money, exactly? Would he be pegged down to 'targets', in the vile management jargon? Could he keep his staff and his office? Most importantly, what about his artistic integrity?

As if in response to this barrage of questions his telephone began to ring. Ed slammed down his cup and raced back to his desk. He knew that it would be Maddy, as nervous and confused as he was about their forthcoming meeting. For obviously she would be there too, with all the facts and figures and projections and whatnot. If Ed was the aerial stuntman of the company, Maddy Barry was mission control. They'd been a team since the very beginning – and would be, as they often reminded each other, 'to infinity – and beyond!'

Sure enough, when Ed snatched up the phone on the third ring he heard Maddy's voice, breathy with anxiety. 'It's me.'

'Are you in the office?' he asked. 'Does anyone suspect? God! Isn't this waiting a nightmare? I can't concentrate on a thing.'

'Me neither. That is ...'

Ed was dismayed to hear an uncharacteristic hesitancy in her voice. His grip tightened on the phone. 'Everything's OK, isn't it? You've got the reels? The blue folder?'

'Yes, it's all fine here, Ed. Don't panic.'

'So what's the matter? I know you, Maddy. Something's wrong.'

Eventually she admitted that someone from the primary school had just rung to say that Lilly had been taken ill. Lilly was Maddy's daughter, aged six, father unknown – unknown to Ed, anyway. Maddy had always been so determined not to be typecast as a sad single mother that he had not even known that she had a child, until several months after they'd met. Then all she would reveal was that Lilly was the result of a one-night stand, and she'd kept the baby because this might be her last chance of motherhood. Ed was full of admiration for the way Maddy managed childcare without disrupting her work, via nannies, neighbours and a baffling network of kiddy groups which he sometimes overheard her co-ordinating from the office. (The names Gymboree and Creschendo floated up from his unconscious.)

'She seemed OK this morning,' Maddy was saying. 'Lilly's hardly ever ill. But she's lying down in the head teacher's room now, and – and moaning. They think she should see a doctor.'

'Oh.' Ed scratched his head, uncertain what to suggest. Maddy lived in deepest unfashionable Acton, miles out of central London. There obviously wasn't time for her to go all the way home and take Lilly to a doctor before the Grapevine meeting. Equally obviously, this meeting was way too important to cancel. There were no other alternatives unless ... Ed's whole body tensed in alarm. He couldn't go to the meeting alone – not without Maddy, without her voluble charm to smooth over awkward moments, without the facts and figures and whatnot – without the blue folder!

'I'm sure she'll be fine,' he said with brisk certainty. 'Can't the nanny deal with it?'

'Yes. Yes, of course. I've already rung Verushka.'

Phew! That was all right, then. But something in Maddy's voice still made Ed feel uncomfortable. 'What's wrong with Lilly anyway?' he demanded.

'Apparently she has a headache ... and a stiff neck and – and her eyes hurt when she looks at the light.' There was the smallest tremor in Maddy's voice, swiftly masked. 'I'm sure it's nothing.'

Ed was silent. The unmentionable word rose between them: meningitis. All the different possible outcomes of the situation flashed through his mind, plunging him into a turmoil of conflicting emotions. Why did this have to happen today? If Maddy wanted to go home why couldn't she just say so? Would insisting that she came to the meeting make him a shit, and if so why couldn't he just be a shit without feeling a shit? The unfairness of his position made him writhe. He realised that he would have to choose for Maddy: between himself, aged thirty-six, and Lilly, six.

'Right, Maddy. Go home now. Call the cab service. I'll ring Alex Wolfe and cancel the meeting.'

'No! Ed, you mustn't.'

'We'll postpone it until next week. It's only lunch. No big deal.'

'Don't talk crap. It's a huge deal. I'm not going to be the one to muck it up. If you're going to cancel, then I'm coming.'

'No, you're not. Lilly needs you.'

'Yes, but she needs me solvent, with a job and a future. I'm thirty-nine, Ed. I want this deal.'

Ed paced from window to wall and back again, listening to Maddy assure him that he would be brilliant without her, that she would arrange for everything he needed to be sent round to the club where the lunch was booked – yes, including the blue folder. He must ring her afterwards and tell her every detail. He could even come over this evening, depending on Lilly. She'd cook him supper. 'Please, Ed. For me.'

Twisting indecisively, Ed caught sight of a pair of extravagantly buckled boots descending the stone steps down to his basement front door, followed by an eye-popping expanse of brown thigh, a tiny flounced skirt, and a leather jacket with studs. Shit! He'd forgotten about his prospective tenant. There was no more time for shilly-shallying.

'You're right, Maddy. I'll be fine on my own. Got to go – someone at the door. Speak later. Love to Lilly!'

Tossing the phone onto his desk, he rootled about in a drawer for the keys to the upstairs flat, then grabbed his jacket. His door-knocker banged. Yes, all right!

His first thought on opening the door was that there'd been a mistake. Normally he let the upstairs to sleek City-bonus couples while they looked to buy their own house, or to the occasional overseas businessman adventurous enough to prefer Islington to Mayfair. This girl, five-foot nothing with sparky brown eyes and a big grin, looked like a cheeky teenager. 'I'm Fizz,' she announced. 'I've come to look at the flat. Are you Ed?'

Her voice was upfront Cockney, though her caramel skin

and glossy black hair, styled into a pixie cut, suggested a remoter heritage (India? Pakistan?). Ed revised her age upwards to early twenties on the basis of a general air of no-nonsense competence, which extended to a clipboard held to her chest. He rather liked the look of her, but wondered if she'd been told the stupendous rent he charged. Almost certainly this would be a time-wasting exercise; but thanks to the dramatic departure of his previous lodger (a Belgian businessman who'd installed a boyfriend during the week, while returning to the bosom of his family every weekend – until the wife found out), Ed was desperate to find a new tenant. He ushered the girl back up the steps and pulled his own front door closed behind him. 'Come on, then. I'll show you round.'

The house was Ed's great romantic folly. Set towards one end of a classic flat-fronted Georgian terrace, it was built of grey (once yellow) brick punctuated by elegantly proportioned sash windows, with a fanlight over the front door, twin wrought-iron window-boxes on the floor above, currently sprouting daffodil shoots, and black railings with an acanthus-leaf design guarding the basement area. To the front it overlooked a broad flag-stoned pavement and a quiet road; to the back was a small oasis of garden shaded by next-door's plane tree. The neighbourhood was indisputably metropolitan: bars, theatres, shops and restaurants were only a few minutes' walk away; yet in the same space of time you could access secret steps leading down to the Regent's Canal, which wound its way from Paddington to Limehouse, and be among birdsong, buddleia and boats.

Such attractions had not gone unnoticed, and property hereabouts was fabulously expensive. Ed had fallen in love with the area when he first arrived in London and was living nearby in grotty King's Cross. On weekends he would escape the noisy chaos of his shared flat and stroll up here, fantasising about the gracious, spacious lifestyle of an admired and successful documentary-maker. When his Nazis film had sold to TV companies around the world, and the tie-in book had thrillingly crept into the *New York Times* bestseller list for two whole weeks, he'd blown the lot on this house. Even then the money wasn't nearly enough, so he'd also taken out a gigantic mortgage whose monthly repayments virtually wiped out his income and could wake him up sweating at night. The only way to make financial sense of his impetuous purchase was to rent out three-quarters of the house, and the only way to maximise the rent was to refurbish it to the highest standard. The result was that he was too poor to live in his own house, and was still confined to a cramped basement flat while others wallowed in luxury on the three floors above his head.

Luxury was the word. As always, Ed felt a glow of pride as he opened the front door and showed ... 'Fizz, did you say?' (ridiculous name) into the kitchen/dining area which ran the whole depth of the ground floor. He opened and closed a couple of drawers, pointing out their cunning compartments and the way they automatically shut themselves tight, and was in the middle of explaining the harmony he'd achieved between the old (cornicing and marble fire surround) and the contemporary (stainless steel and halogen) when she asked abruptly, 'Do you have a juicer?' Mildly irritated, he opened a cupboard and pointed. She made a little tick on her list. 'And an ice-maker?' He showed her that, too.

And so it went on. She seemed utterly uninterested in his story about the Regency newel post he'd been able to match from an architectural salvage yard; and simply murmured, 'Cool,' when he explained the state-of-the-art sound system that operated throughout the house. She seemed a little disappointed when he explained that there was no video entry-phone. 'I prefer a door-knocker,' he retorted: 'functional, reliable and authentic.' When he showed her the stunning double drawing-room upstairs, with working fireplace and original folding doors, her only utterance was a query about air-conditioning. Ed cast a withering glance at the ice-grey March sky outside and confessed that the flat was lacking in this regard, but he'd always found opening a window to be an excellent solution. In an attempt to impress her he waxed more and more eloquent about the house, flinging open cupboard doors which lit up miraculously from within, pointing out the sleek TV screens, and urging her to try out the bounciness of the bed. No, he did not know the thread-count of the sheets. Yes, of course there was a cleaner. It was probably a mistake to demonstrate the water-pressure of the side jets in the upstairs shower, and he was still anxiously blotting an embarrassing wet patch on his trousers with toilet paper when she asked, 'You don't have like a gym or anything?'

'No, I do not. Nor a badminton court, or a ballroom.'

That cracked her up, and for a moment he liked her again. But he couldn't figure out what she was after. Sometimes it seemed that she was more interested in him than in the flat. What did he do? Who else lived downstairs? Did he entertain a lot? Did he personally fix anything that went wrong in the flat? He almost wondered if she fancied him, which made him consider if he fancied her. Too young, he decided. No: either she was a very unlikely and eccentric millionairess, or she was having a laugh. Ed did not enjoy being the butt of someone else's not-very-amusing joke and suggested that she had seen enough to judge whether the flat was up to her standards.

On the way downstairs she paused on a landing, consulted her clipboard again, and peered out of the window.

'What's in the garden?'

'Plants,' he answered stonily.

'Right. So ... no hot tub?' She took one look at his face and wrote a cross on her list.

But once they were out on the pavement again Fizz underwent a mystifying transformation. 'I love your place, Ed. It's fantastic.'

'Really?' Belatedly he tried to re-inject landlordly charm into his features. 'Does that mean … ?'

'I'll call you as soon as I can, OK? Maybe later today. Will you be at home?'

Christ! The meeting! Distractedly Ed gave Fizz his mobile number and uttered the usual polite phrases, though as he watched her swing jauntily down the street, boot buckles clinking, he had little expectation of seeing or hearing from her again. His thoughts were gloomy as he trotted down the basement steps. No tenant. No Maddy. Damp trousers. He caught sight of his watch and groaned. On top of everything else he was going to be late.

CHAPTER 12

In fact Ed arrived half an hour early for his meeting, thanks to an unprecedented run of luck on the tube. The club at which he had arranged to meet the CEO from Grapevine occupied a large corner house in the heart of Soho. It existed to serve the overlapping worlds of film, television and advertising: here agents and actors rubbed shoulders with producers, copywriters and creative directors. This was where the men with money met the boys and girls with talent. The club had been established for about ten years. Ed was a founder member, his fee frozen at the joining price; he was pretty sure he wouldn't be able to afford to continue with it otherwise.

As always, he'd forgotten the card you were supposed to swipe at the entrance. He pressed the doorbell instead, and waited for the usual unintelligible burst of static from the entryphone. Long convinced that no one could hear any better at the other end, he sometimes amused himself by giving whatever name came into his head. Today he shouted, 'Winston Churchill!', and was instantly admitted.

Bounding up the stairs, Ed handed his coat to the startlingly pretty girl on reception and told her that he would wait for Mr Wolfe in the bar. A stiff drink would set him up, though he would need to be careful to resist the temptation to have more than one. He was trying to decide whether to order a beer or splash out on an extortionately priced, but delicious, Bloody Mary when a familiar voice sent a chill deep into his heart. 'Are you buying, Ted?'

Phil Glover was the only person who called him Ted. They had met at Oxford, more than fifteen years before. Both had read history: Ed at Merton, Phil at Balliol – which he referred to as Ball Oil. Because they were both Northerners, Phil had assumed a tribal familiarity. Ed had been trying to shake him off ever since, without success. He squirmed when Phil tried to claim him as a member of the fraternity of beer-drinking, plain-speaking 'real men', as opposed to effete southern 'poofters'. Phil's northern accent had actually become more pronounced over the years he'd spent in the south. During the same period he had developed the podgy torso of the terminally unathletic. His baby-blond curls had darkened and were now slipping over the horizon of his forehead. In a mood of resignation Ed acknowledged his loose-lipped grin and ordered two beers from the barman.

'So,' said Phil with awful finality, 'are you still making films that nobody watches?'

Phil was a television person too, only infinitely more successful: in fact he was fast becoming a TV tycoon. After coming down from Oxford both of them had gone into the Beeb, but while Ed had struggled to make serious programmes, Phil had moved swiftly into entertainment before setting up on his own. Ed was grudgingly forced to admit that Phil had a sound commercial instinct. Though he didn't have many ideas, he was quick to pick up other people's. He had specialised in 'Factent', the hideous abbreviation for Factual Entertainment, referred to by the media as Reality TV, and by Ed as total garbage. But garbage was popular, and it was making Phil rich. Each time they met, his material success was more and more obvious. Ed listened sullenly to his sly boasts about expensive sports cars ('liked the first one so much I put my name down for another'), second homes ('just an investment – I've never actually spent a night there'), chartered yachts ('gets you to all those beaches you can't reach otherwise'), exclusive safaris ('so remote they had to bring in ice for the G&Ts by plane') and holidays in places like Dubai ('flew first-class, of course, thanks to my air miles'). Ed had to remind himself how much he hated dumbing down, triviality, the Hollywood-isation of everything; and how lucky he was not to be working on *Celebrity Barbecue*.

'At least I'm not making *Celebrity Barbecue*,' he said aloud.

'All right, sneer if you like. Hug your Bafta if it keeps you warm at night. Which of your programmes has *eight million* prime-time viewers?' Phil stroked his burgeoning paunch complacently.

'Call them "viewers"? They just want a bit of background noise while they snog on the sofa.'

'Welcome to the real world, chuck,' said Phil cheerfully. 'Eight million viewers can't be wrong.'

'They can if they're morons.'

'Come on, you know the broadcasters only take your stuff as window-dressing, to look good when it comes to franchise time. Us now, we're in the hits business.'

'Mm. Have you ever noticed that hits is an anagram of shit?'

'Nice one.' Phil thumped him on the shoulder, making him spill his drink on his shoe. 'Well, you go on making Goggle with Granny and living in a basement if it makes you happy. But I'm telling you, the eighteen- to thirty-four-year-olds is where it's at, and they like a bit of entertainment. Presenters with cleavage, reconstructions of historic bonks. Phone-ins. Prizes. That's what the punters want. No one wants to think.'

'I do,' Ed said.

'You're a snob. You know in your heart of hearts that nobody's really interested in your type of TV. Your viewing figures are so low that they're hardly measurable. Television isn't art any more; it's pantomime.' Phil grabbed a handful of smoked almonds from the bar and funnelled them into his mouth.

Ed was still formulating his riposte when his mobile bleeped. He flipped it open. 'Hello?'

'Hiya, Ed. Fizz here.'

For a moment Ed couldn't think who Fizz was. 'Yes?' he answered cautiously.

'I came to see your flat this morning.'

'Oh, right. Yes. Hello.' Ed came to attention. This could be good news.

'I would have explained, but it's sort of confidential. You see, I work at the Old Fire Station Theatre.'

Ed knew the place well: tiny space, huge reputation and some of the most uncomfortable seating in London. He sometimes popped in for a last-minute ticket as it was only a few minutes' walk from his house.

'... and we sometimes need accommodation for visiting actors. To get to the point, we'd like to rent your place for two months, starting next weekend, on behalf of Paige Carson.'

A vague image rose in Ed's mind: motorbike, bare flesh, green eyes. But she couldn't mean ... '*The* Paige Carson?' he asked incredulously. He noticed that Phil's pudgy hand was suddenly arrested halfway to the nut bowl.

'Yes, isn't it exciting? We'd almost given up hope, then her agent rang and said she was coming. I know you'd prefer a longer rental, but it's only a short run – though she might extend the lease if the show transfers into the West End.'

'You want my place for the Hollywood actress Paige Carson?' Ed repeated, largely for Phil's benefit.

'Yes, that's right. We'll pay the rent in advance for the whole period – so long as you haven't got a problem with the short lease.'

Ed stared at Phil, who was looking impressed. 'No problem at all.'

'Good. I'll call you in a day or two to make arrangements to pick up the keys.'

'Right.' He snapped the phone shut.

'Phwoar!' roared Phil. 'Paige Carson! *Biker Boys*! Best wank film ever!'

Ed winced at Phil's vulgarity, but he couldn't resist an inner glow of satisfaction that came from so comprehensively trumping this boastful plonker. Game, set, and match!

'Well, well,' said Phil, a lecherous grin contorting his features: 'You'll have to invite Jess and me for a foursome, eh?'

'Very funny,' Ed answered. Jess was Phil's equally thrusting and loud-mouthed partner, the brutally spelt Jessika Diamond, who wrote for the *Evening News* (generally known as the *Evening Screws*). The idea of a foursome with this pair made him distinctly queasy.

'You'll be well in there.' Phil winked. 'Going to have to pop up and check her gas meter, are you?'

'Sorry, Phil, can't stop,' Ed said loftily, looking at his watch. 'Important meeting.'

'On your bike, then, Ted.' Phil prodded him in the ribs.

Ed left the bar and made his way downstairs. His good mood had returned. Not only had he secured a new tenant, he'd out-boxed Phil. Fleetingly his mind dwelt on one of Phil's most recent so-called 'documentaries' called *Gynaecologists from Hell*. Were there no depths that Glover Productions would not plumb?

He reached the reception area just in time to hear his own name. The man enquiring for him was in his mid-fifties, sleek and immaculate in a pin-striped suit – and a *tie*. Shit. This must be Alex Wolfe. Ed stepped forward to introduce himself. Wolfe by name, wolf by nature? He had a feeling that he was about to be gobbled up. He wished Maddy were here. He wished he hadn't worn the pink shirt.

CHAPTER 13

'So, how did it go?' Maddy demanded, almost before she'd opened her front door. 'I thought you'd never get here. I've already started on the wine. Come in and I'll find you a glass. Hey, nice shirt!'

They kissed cheeks. Ed followed her into the small front living-room, picking his way round furniture, pot plants, knick-knacks and children's toys, and collapsed into the comfortable saggy sofa. He felt exhausted. The meeting with Wolfe had continued until after three. Then he'd walked up to the office in order to ring Maddy from the privacy of his own cubby-hole, only to find the whole place in uproar. The American co-producers were threatening to pull out of the Berlin Wall project, which they complained was 'too German'. The BBC had rung in a flap to say that one of the 'blood chits' – the release document requiring signature by anyone appearing on film – was missing for *The Day Fleet Street Died*, and unless it was produced within the next twenty-four hours the programme could not be aired as scheduled.

Consequently, there'd been no time for Ed to do more than exchange brief headlines with Maddy. Yes, Grapevine had made an offer – of sorts. No, Lilly did not, thank God, have meningitis. By the time he had dealt with the office emergencies it was almost seven. Ed would have liked nothing better than to go home and cook himself something pure and simple with lots of ginger and go to bed early. But in the circumstances the very least he could do was to trek out to Acton and tell Maddy in person as much as he could, especially as she'd offered to cook him supper. He sniffed the air, hoping it wasn't going to be tagliatelle again.

'You can have red or red,' she announced, reappearing from the back kitchen and flourishing a glass.

'I'll have red, then.' Despite his weariness Ed couldn't help smiling back at her. Maddy was always so upbeat and expectant. She radiated an enthusiasm for life that was almost schoolgirlish, an impression reinforced by her short-bob-with-fringe hairstyle and plump but athletic figure, and by the bright blue eyes and lightly freckled skin that hinted at distant Celtic ancestry. She loved parties and chat, and was interested in other people in a way that he was not – unless, of course, they actually were interesting. It amused him that her terrier-like efficiency at work dropped from her like a cloak the minute she stepped over the threshold of her own home, where genial chaos reigned. The house was tiny and miles off Ed's geographical radar, but Maddy had always been determined to have a 'proper' home with a garden near 'nice' schools for Lilly, and this was the best she could afford on a single salary, most of which seemed to go to the live-out nanny.

He watched her pour out his wine from a bottle that was, he noticed, nearly empty already, and remembered to ask about Lilly.

'The doctor said it was a virus. That's what they always say, don't they? "It's a virus. Plenty of fluids and bed rest. Next, please." But no, she's fine. And asleep, you'll be glad to hear.'

'Come on, Maddy, I never—'

'Oh, I know. You love children; you just couldn't eat a whole one.' She chuckled gaily at this old joke, plopped herself down on a big cushion on the floor and picked up her glass from the coffee-table between them. 'So what about the big bad Wolfe? Are we going to be rich? Did he really say *seven* figures?'

'Possibly,' Ed answered cautiously. 'As I told you, he wants to study the figures in the blue folder, look at the backlist and our forward programme, et cetera.'

'That's at least half a mil *each*. I can't believe it!'

'Minus tax, remember. And we wouldn't get it all at once. He talked about staged payments relating to productivity and profitability – all the usual guff.'

'That's only reasonable, Ed. Stop being such a grump.'

'And he says our overheads are too high. We need to cut down on office space, or even move, when the lease comes up for renewal.'

'Well, that's not impossible, is it?' Bit between her teeth, she began to outline the ways in which they might rearrange the office, and to weigh up the merits of other, cheaper areas, until interrupted by the ping of the kitchen timer. 'The tagliatelle!' She gave a start and jumped to her feet. 'Come and help me serve it up, Ed. Bring the wine.'

Once the laundry basket had been removed from the table in the steamy kitchen, and Ed had uncorked another bottle and lit a candle ('for atmosphere,' Maddy insisted), they sat down to eat.

'But first, a toast to the brilliant Hawkshead and Barry duo.' Maddy scooped up her glass and raised it high. 'To us!'

'To us,' Ed agreed, clinking glasses. 'I could never have done it without you.'

Over dinner he gave Maddy an (almost) blow-by-blow account of the meeting. Ed had wanted to despise Alex Wolfe as a crass money man, but in fact he had found him frighteningly clever – not intellectually, of course, but in terms of business sense: balance sheets, contracts, how to exploit new technologies and markets. Or as Alex had put it, 'Grapevine is looking hard at how multi-platform, 360-degree content creation and distribution can exploit the underlying value – both more widely across platforms and more systematically over time – and at how it can drive new revenue streams.' Why could these people never speak English? 'Soon the entire media will be online with multi-portal access, including mobile phones. The old business models are outdated, Ed. Grapevine is rolling out a whole raft of new strategies and synergies whereby film can be monetised.'

Ed had nodded sagely while chewing his crusted cod loin. As the meal continued he felt increasingly like a schoolboy having 'a chat' with the headmaster. Hawkshead Barry wasn't productive enough, Alex suggested; they took too long making films without a corresponding financial return. 'Take *The End of Reason*, for example. Brilliant, of course, but you spent six months on it and haven't even got an American buyer. Quite frankly, that's too slow – and a little self-indulgent, if I may say so.' Alex dabbed Chilean merlot from his thin lips. 'Grapevine values quality, of course, but at the end of the day we're in the profits business. For your company to be optimally attractive to us we'd need to put in place some financial disciplines, and introduce a slightly more popular dimension.'

Ed had stabbed at his organic lentils. *Make a bloody film yourself, mate. Try churning out crap in a couple of weeks and see how many Baftas you win.*

'The films we make are good *because* we spend time on them,' he now burst out to Maddy. 'The man's got to have faith in us. You can't do history the same way you do *How Clean is Your Nose?* or whatever it is. It's all very well him cherry-picking profitable projects while he sits in his fancy office with his salary rolling in like clockwork. If he wants us, he's got to value what we do, and give us the time in which to do it – and support us when things don't go according to plan.'

'Quite right,' Maddy said staunchly. 'Have another drink.'

'He says we should cast our net wider, not deeper: what the hell does that mean? Hawkshead Barry stands for originality – intelligence – quality. We don't want to dilute that by making programmes about the royal family or sperm donors, for Christ's sake.'

'A's'lutely,' Maddy agreed, before adding, 'though maybe we could compromise a wee bit, if it means a secure future for the company. And believe it or not, Ed, there are people who are interested in sperm donors *and* history.' She flushed a little – or was it the wine?

He came off his high horse with a wry smile. 'You think I'm a pompous prig, don't you?'

'Only sometimes.' She leaned forward to place a warm hand over his. 'I love you really.'

Ed tensed under her ardent gaze, and withdrew his hand to pull back one cuff and check the time.

'Don't go yet,' Maddy protested. 'You haven't had your coffee. You always like your coffee.' She stood up and started bustling about, opening cupboards.

Ed stood up too. 'Thanks, but I think I'd better head home. It's after eleven. I'm completely knackered.'

With her back still turned to him she said, 'You could always stay here ... if you like.' When he didn't answer she looked round. 'I mean, on the sofa or – or wherever.'

Ed fastened the buttons of his jacket, avoiding her eyes. 'That's really nice of you, Maddy. But we both need a bit of space to think this through. Besdies, I'm beginning to rant. We'll go out for a boozy lunch tomorrow and talk everything over, OK?'

Maddy closed the cupboard. 'Yeah, sure. That'd be great.'

At the front door he put a hand on her shoulder and kissed her lightly on the cheek. 'Thanks for a delicious supper. It really was ... delicious. And love to Lilly!'

'I'll tell her.'

Ed strode to the front gate with self-conscious briskness,

and waved at Maddy who was still watching him from the lighted doorway. She fluttered her fingers in reply. After a few paces he heard the door bang, and let out his breath.

You're a shit, he told himself. *No, I'm not*. It wasn't his fault that Maddy was lonely and sometimes drank too much. No, but it was his fault that he'd slept with her – only once, mind, and well over a year ago, after seeing her home from an awards bash. He'd been drunk and tired – and stupid. Afterwards, it had been a bit awkward in the office. He'd apologised. She'd said it was just one of those things: not to worry. But he did worry, from time to time. Maddy was his best friend and collaborator. She buoyed him up and tethered him down. He liked and admired her, even loved her in the platonic sense, but he wasn't *in love* with her, any more than she was in love with him. At least, he hoped she wasn't.

Here was the tube station. Ed skimmed his travel card over the yellow electronic eye, then stood on the escalator, watching advertisements for underwear and online dating services cruise past his shoulder. What did 'in love' mean, anyway? He was prepared to acknowledge that there appeared to be such a thing as true love between a man and a woman; he had observed it for himself in rare couples. But 'in love' was no more than a phoney chicklit fantasy, a mirage that evaporated to reveal a viper's nest of egotistical needs – money, status, security, sex, babies – and provided an excuse for commercial nonsense such as eternity rings and Valentine's Day cards. He'd been 'in love' himself once, a long time ago. Long dark hair and creamy skin flashed into his mind. He remembered the way she'd wrapped her naked legs and arms around him and vowed never to let go. But she had. The experience had made him so unhappy he'd wanted to die. But as someone once said, 'Men have died from time to time and worms have eaten them, but not for love.' He had not died. The experience had simply taught him to be more rational and clear-sighted, a lesson for which he was grateful. Women as friends, women as colleagues, women for sex: yes. A wife: yes, in theory, when he met the right person and had had time to observe her in all moods and circumstances – say, two years?

You're still a shit, he told his ghostly reflection in the tube window as the train rocked through tunnels. Doubly so, since he'd held back from Maddy one vital element of the potential Grapevine deal, which he couldn't yet bear to tell her: Grapevine did not want Maddy. They wanted to be rid of her. Or, as Alex Wolfe put it, 'There are synergies within the Grapevine structure which indicate a streamlining of Hawkshead Barry's current human resource levels.' Ed had been aghast. Maddy was his right hand: she organised the office, contracts, budgets, sales – everything! He needed her. Shock was swiftly followed by anger. He didn't care if Grapevine had some Obergruppenführer who managed such things centrally. Maddy was not a 'resource'; she was a person – a single mother who needed a job. On the other hand ... Was he going to turn down half a million, just for her sake?

He emerged from the tube and steered a course through the gusting litter and lounging teenage boys, still deep in thought. If Maddy felt rejected tonight, by him, imagine what Grapevine's rejection would do for her self-esteem. How and when would he tell her? Was there any chance that he could change Alex Wolfe's mind?

His spirits lifted, as they always did, as he turned the corner into his street. Traffic noise and careering headlamps receded. He could smell spring in the rain-soaked earth. The street lamps emitted a soft glow, turning the trees to silver. His own house came into view, its upper windows shuttered and dark.

At that moment he remembered Paige Carson. Christ! What had he let himself in for? Sixty days of sharing his house with a self-obsessed birdbrain with a daft name, just because he couldn't resist getting one up on Philistine Phil.

No doubt she would be doing weird yoga stuff on his carpets, sniffing coke from his designer coffee-table, hopping in and out of stretch limos, and expecting constant attention. Well, she wouldn't be getting it from Ed Hawkshead. Celebrities did not interest him. He had far more important things to think about.

CHAPTER 14

Paige stood by the window, looking out at the street for the umpteenth time that morning. The sky above was grey and depressing. It was ten o'clock on her first Monday in London; she was due at the rehearsal room in half an hour. Already the frantic bustle of people leaving their homes for work had diminished, to be replaced by the more leisurely pace of mothers, wheeling their toddlers in strollers along the sidewalk. *Where was her car?*

Shivering, she hugged her cashmere sweater more tightly to her body. The apartment was freezing, even though the peculiar metal radiators were warm to the touch. She probably should have had breakfast. Her last meal had been the vegetarian option on the plane yesterday. (Or was it the day before? Her body clock was all messed up.) But she was too nervous to eat, and anyway there was nothing to eat here except bread, butter, cereal, eggs and bacon. No fruit! She did find a carton of orange juice in the surprisingly large and modern fridge, but just as she was about to pour it out she noticed the words 'With Bits'. Bits of what? Earlier this morning she'd decided to throw caution to the winds and imbibe some caffeine – except that for some time she couldn't figure out how the stove worked, and when she did finally get it going she couldn't find the tea kettle, and when she found the tea kettle it turned out to be some electrical gizmo. No way was she even touching it. Everyone in LA had warned her about British electricity, which had twice as many volts, or amp things, as American electricity, and could blow up your appliances just like that. For this reason she hadn't brought her hair-straighteners, or hair-curlers, or even a hair-dryer, which meant that she'd be turning up on her first day looking like a freak. Maybe one of the Hair crew at the theatre could give her a quick fix-up before she met the other actors.

Other actors. She shivered again. While she was still in LA, the idea of playing Shakespeare in London had possessed an exciting, fairytale quality. Her friends had been impressed. Davina was thrilled she was coming over, and had already invited her for a country weekend. 'I'll be sure to invite some cute English guys to keep you company,' she'd promised. Julian Seabrook, the British theatre director, had flown over from London specially to take a meeting with Paige, and had been charming and respectful. 'You remind me of the young Vanessa Redgrave, whom I had the privilege of seeing as Rosalind in 1961, when I was still in short trousers. You have a Light, my darling. It shines through, even on the screen. But how much more brightly will you glow in the veritable flesh, on the stage of the Old Fire Station.' And he had stroked his pointy beard and twinkled at her so reassuringly that Paige had pretty much glowed there and then. Vanessa Redgrave! Wasn't she a dame or something?

A further plus was that Harry Keenan, the old but dishy guy she'd met in the bar on Oscar night, was signed up to play the part of Jacques. (Paige had pronounced it Jakes until a friend told her that the name was French and should be pronounced more like Jock. Thank goodness she hadn't said it the wrong way in front of Julian.) Nathan had been outraged by the terms of the contract Julian brought with him. Apparently the Old Fire Station, though one of the most elite theatres in London, was also very poor. Julian admitted that he could not, alas, offer Paige the luxuries she was used to. But Paige had overridden both men's doubts.

'I'm not a diva, for crying out loud.' They'd all laughed.

By the time everything had been agreed, rehearsals were only a couple of weeks away. Her days had been busy learning her lines and practising her accent ('Peace, I say! Good even to you, friend'), buying essential clothes for the trip, and getting her teeth checked so that she wouldn't have to risk an English dentist. Before she knew it, she was in the VIP lounge at LAX. Doubts began to set in somewhere over Nova Scotia. She'd found it difficult to sleep on the so-called 'lie down' bed, and had stayed awake most of the night, worrying about what she had impulsively let herself in for. All those lines, all that old language. Everyone would laugh at her accent. She knew nobody in London. Its newspapers were said to be the most vicious in the world, its paparazzi the most intrusive.

So she was tired and nervous by the time the plane had landed in London yesterday afternoon. The priority line for Immigration had seemed just as slow as the regular line, and fewer than half the desks were manned. (The British were famous for their unwillingness to work.) The Immigration officer didn't even smile when he said, 'Welcome to England, Miss Carson,' and stamped her passport. Was it possible that he hadn't recognised her? Then she'd had to load her own suitcases onto the baggage cart, or 'trolley', and push it herself, trying to ignore the nudgings and pointings of ordinary passengers. As she came through Customs she'd been relieved to see a uniformed driver holding a placard reading 'Rosalind', though his first remark – 'traffic's murder' – had been alarming. Even more so was her discovery that she'd been confusing Islington with Kensington, and they were not at all alike. 'Kensington's yer posh people, Islington's more yer meeja types and City boys.' Islington certainly did not look 'posh', as they crawled along a scruffy, traffic-choked street. 'City boys' conjured up an image of drug-crazed teenage gangs with knives. The Mercedes had pulled up outside a long row of tall, narrow houses of dirty brick, vaguely reminiscent of New York brownstones. The driver had unloaded the car, and opened the front door with a set of keys which he then presented to her, before carrying her bags inside, along the hall and up two flights of winding stairs. When she'd given him a handful of those crisp, purply banknotes Akira had got for her, and told him that she hoped he'd be driving her again, she'd been rewarded by her first English smile. By that time it had been early evening, and she'd done no more than shower and unpack before crashing out.

Of course she'd woken in the middle of the night, but she didn't dare take a sleeping pill in case she was too zonked in the morning. By six o'clock she was dressed, exercised, and had filled in the goal-chart that Gaby had given her to tide her over the next two months. Today she'd decided her goals were: 1. Give the best you can. 2. Listen to others ... She'd chewed her pencil over the third one, and finally written, 'Be happy.' By seven-thirty she had been through all her lines once more. Since then she'd been exploring the apartment that would be her home for the next few weeks.

It was weirdly vertical, occupying three floors of a four-floor house. The rooms were tiny, but with high ceilings that gave a sense of space even if they were not very practical. Outside at the front was a stairwell, with steps leading down to a separate entrance on the basement floor. Maybe the maid lived there. On the top floor were two bedrooms and a bathroom; on each of the floors below one room ran right through the house; on the middle floor was a room with comfortable furniture which could be divided by folding doors, and on the floor where she was standing now, there was a kitchen and a dining-room, with a narrow balcony and spiral steps leading down to the back garden.

Where was her car? It was now ten-fifteen. To be late as well as American was too embarrassing to contemplate. She turned back to the kitchen table and hunted for the hand-written welcome note that she'd found on the hall table.

There was a telephone number underneath the signature, 'Fizz (Felicity Rahman)'. In a moment she'd punched it into her cell phone. The phone rang twice and then she heard a voice answer: 'Hiya. Fizz here.'

Paige explained her problem, making an effort to appear gracious in the face of this gross inefficiency. She didn't want to pull the Hollywood star number – not yet, anyway. It was therefore disconcerting when Fizz burst out laughing. 'But we're just round the corner, Paige. Only five minutes' walk. Didn't you see my map in the envelope?'

Paige was totally freaking when she put away her phone. Walk! It was completely outside her experience. What should she wear? Where would she find an umbrella? What if she got attacked – or worse still, recognised? She rushed up and down those stupid stairs about seventeen times to collect everything she might need, and at ten-twenty-five emerged cautiously onto the doorstep, wearing sunglasses, baseball cap, and raincoat. In the leather knapsack on her back were keys, phone, English money, two extra sweaters, tranquillisers, four thousand dollars in American Express travellers' cheques, the play script, beeswax lip balm, a cute little pad-and-pen set from the Getty Museum, gargle fluid, and her passport – just in case. Fizz's map and instructions were in her hand, but she couldn't read them, thanks to the gloomy sky and her sunglasses. Eventually she made out the words, 'Turn left.' She turned left.

It's OK, I can do this, she told herself. Nobody walked on the LA streets except poor people and weirdos, but of course it was different here. England was really small and there was nowhere to park. Surreptitiously she scanned the faces of people she passed, telling herself that these were just normal human beings. One or two of them gave her a funny look, and she tucked her chin into the collar of her raincoat to make it apparent that she was *not* in an autograph-signing mood. Oh my God! A huge busy street: what was she supposed to do here? 'Cross road.' Paige looked left, and was just about to step off the kerb when a red bus sailed past her nose from the other direction. She jumped back, then scowled at its retreating rear end. Wrong side of the street, buster! Or maybe not. She noticed a traffic-controlled crossing, and joined some other people and followed them until she had safely reached the other side. She consulted her map again, and turned right. The wide sidewalk was filthy. Visible dirt skittered round her ankles in a cold, brisk breeze. Old crates and cardboard boxes were piled up outside grocery and clothing stores. There were pigeons and pigeon crap everywhere. This was not the London she remembered from a few years ago when she'd stayed at Claridge's on a movie junket. Where was Big Ben? Harrods? Where was the beautiful wide river you always saw in British films like *Bridget Jones* and *Love, Actually?*

Oh, no. A man was standing right in her path, waving a newspaper around and talking to himself – something about a shoe. His trainers were certainly very dirty and torn: obviously a beggar. She veered sharply. He turned towards her. Heart hammering, she broke into a run. Two women in saris stared at her in alarm. This was terrible. She was going to be robbed – knifed – left for dead among these foreigners. She was ... Oh, she was here, at the address Fizz had written down. Finally! She pressed a buzzer by the beaten-up door, pulled off her sunglasses, then checked her watch. It was ten-thirty.

Julian Seabrook clapped his hands. 'Ladies and gentlemen, boys and girls, settle down please!'

Paige was already seated next to Harry Keenan, on one of the metal stacking chairs that had been placed in a rough circle. Her script and notepad were on her lap, her pen poised. The place was so down at heel that she hadn't even enquired if someone was available to fix her hair, but since no one else seemed to have paid any attention to their appearance, perhaps it didn't matter. There were about twenty other people here, none of whom (apart from Harry) she'd recognised, who grumbled and joked as they took their seats. The room was high and square like a church hall, with three large windows above eye-level, and a scuffed linoleum floor on which the stage area had been marked out with tape.

Julian surveyed them from his position on the opposite side of the circle to Paige. His sleek girth and perpetual smile, genial yet enigmatic, reminded her of a porpoise. He waited for silence. 'Are we all met? ... Then let us begin.

'Take a young man, let us call him Orlando – handsome, brave and well-born, yet treated as a peasant by his vicious elder brother, who controls the purse-strings and wants him dead.' He gestured towards an actor in a grey T-shirt, who did look kind of cute in a blond, floppy-haired way. She wondered if she'd get to kiss him.

'Now take a young woman, let us call her Rosalind – witty, wilful and lovely' – Julian indicated a blushing Paige – 'whose father has been banished from court, leaving her alone and friendless apart from her dear cousin Celia.' That must be the girl with all the eye make-up, who was text-messaging under the cover of her script. Paige tried to smile at her, but she didn't look up.

'One day at court Rosalind watches Orlando win a wrestling match, and the two fall in love at first sight. But Orlando has been warned that his life is in danger and he flees into the forest. Immediately thereafter, Rosalind is banished from court, like her father. She too flees into the forest, disguised as a boy and accompanied by her cousin.'

'And me, mate,' interrupted a short fat guy, who looked like Danny DeVito and spoke in what Paige guessed was the English version of a Noo Joisey accent. 'Them two wouldn't have got nowhere without Touchstone the clown. Though why he's called a clown is a ruddy mystery. I'm not laughing, I can tell you. You've got to cut the verbals, Jool. No one's gonna have a clue what's going on, know what I'm saying?'

'Shut up, Sid,' said Julian imperturbably. 'In the forest Rosalind, dressed as a boy, meets Orlando, who does not recognise her even though he claims to be unable to think of anything else. Desperate for an excuse to stay near him, Rosalind persuades him to pretend that she/he is Rosalind. For the rest of the play she teases him, scolds him, and teaches him how to love her, while he alternately woos her as a woman and opens his heart to her, man to man. When the time is right she reveals her true identity, and they fall into each other's arms – one in body as they have already become one in soul, mind and heart.' He paused for a moment, looking down at his steepled fingers while he summoned up further thoughts.

'Is this realism? Is it even a story? No. It is an enchantment. It is the very gossamer breath of love. And that, my darling loves, is what we are going to create together over the next four weeks.' He beamed a benign smile. Paige wrote the word 'enchantment' on her pad and underlined it three times.

'But first we're going to concentrate on the language.' Julian was suddenly brisk. 'Language is always the key in Shakespeare. I want it audible, I want it accurate. I want you to absorb its rhythms into your bloodstream so that you speak the lines as if they've just entered your head for the first time. The thought is the word, the word is the thought. And I want laughter! Laughter in the play, and laughter among the company. No point in getting paid a pittance if we're not having fun. So remember the three Ls: love, language, laughter.'

He spoke next about the themes of the play: the court versus the country, corruption versus innocence, age versus youth, and Shakespeare's extensive use of prose as well as verse. Paige, at first terrified that she wouldn't understand anything, found it fascinating. She could hardly believe that more than an hour had passed before he said, 'Now let's take a break. We'll start our exercises in fifteen.'

Paige looked up in a daze of thoughts, then hastily closed her notebook, before anyone could see how she'd spelled iambic pentameter.

'Usual load of old bollocks.' Sid had come round to chat to Harry. 'The three Ls, I ask you. Language, laughter … I've forgotten the third one already.'

'Loony,' said Harry. 'Come on, let's take Paige for some so-called refreshment.'

Paige saw that everyone was gathering in the corner of the room, where there must be a snack table. It was probably too much to hope that they would have Kabbalah water here, but maybe a fresh fruit juice or –

'Tea or coffee?' asked Sid.

'Whatever,' she answered weakly.

The Celia girl was standing nearby. In an attempt to be friendly Paige asked if she had acted in many Shakespeare plays.

'Loads. I did *The Dream* last summer.'

Paige looked blank.

'Like, *A Midsummer Night's Dream?*' The girl raised her eyebrows, as if incredulous that anyone could not know this.

'How's it going, lovey?' Julian surged out of the scrum and gave Paige's shoulder a squeeze.

'Fine. Great. I loved what you said about the play. It's given me real inspiration.'

'Excellent, excellent.'

'And it's such a treat to be working with Harry.' She turned to give him a special smile. 'I was so thrilled when I heard he was going to be playing Jock.'

She knew at once that she had said something wrong. There was a hiccough of silence. Julian's smile took on a frozen quality. The Celia girl looked round and smirked.

'Actually,' drawled Harry, 'our William seemed to think it was pronounced Jay-queeze. God knows why.'

'Silly old fart,' Sid chipped in. He winked at Paige and

handed her a mug of pale brown liquid. Mortified, she bent her head, and without thinking took a sip. *Bleagh!* It took all her acting skills to hide her disgust.

At lunchtime Fizz appeared from the office upstairs and offered to take Paige up the road to see the theatre. 'Afterwards we can grab a bite to eat in the café, if you fancy it.'

Paige cautiously agreed. She was taken aback by the breezy manner and kooky clothes of this young girl. It was on the tip of her tongue to inform Fizz, tactfully of course, that she was accustomed to being addressed as 'Miss Carson', but something stopped her. 'Oh, you have the new Chanel bag,' she observed instead. 'I'm still on the waiting list for mine.'

'Cool, isn't it?' Fizz remarked complacently. 'Five quid in the market. Fake, of course, but who gives a shit?'

Nonplussed by this response, Paige changed the subject. 'What exactly is your job here?' she asked, as they stepped outside. She hastily turned up the collar of her raincoat and clapped on her sunglasses, though the sky remained uniformly grey.

'Everything,' answered Fizz with a laugh. 'I mean, they call me Stage Manager, but I do all sorts – publicity, buying tea-bags, answering the phone, even replacing the bog roll in the toilets. We're so small, see, that everyone has to muck in. I love it,' she added.

Paige stuck close to Fizz for fear of getting lost. She was still nervous of being recognised, but the other people out on the street ignored them both.

'We're assuming that you'll be happy to publicise the show?' Fizz asked. 'It's very important to us.'

'In principle, yes,' said Paige cautiously, 'but I'll have to refer specific requests to my publicist.'

'Fair enough. We're hoping to get you on the top TV chat show. The presenter's a bit of a sleazeball, but you can handle them, right?'

'Oh yes. We have plenty of those in the US.'

The theatre was an old red-brick building with a wide arched entrance and a turret sprouting from the roof. Inside, the decoration was stark and functional, with plain wooden seats and a narrow balcony running round three sides of the auditorium. Paige had lowered her expectations – but not this low. It would be hard to imagine anything more different from the theatre where she had watched the Oscars: no gold, no red plush, only three hundred seats instead of six thousand. The stage was tiny and exposed. There would be little scenery to distract attention, no hiding behind lights. This was the ultimate test. She would stand or fall depending on how closely she drew the audience to her character. 'An enchantment,' Julian had said.

Fizz took her down to the basement to see the dressing-room that she would be using. It was small and shabby. Bare pipes ran around the walls. There was a narrow bed, a tiny closet, and a mirror bordered with spotlights.

'Not much, is it?' said Fizz. 'But have a look at this.' She opened the closet and pointed out the rows of initials carved on the inside of the door. 'It's sort of a tradition for the actors,' she explained. 'IM – that's Ian McKellen. Then you've got Helen Mirren, Kevin Spacey, Maggie Smith ... and in a few weeks' time, Paige Carson!'

Paige felt moved by these rough scratchings. It was awesome to follow in such footsteps, yet strangely heartening. 'I don't know if I'm quite in this league,' she said to Fizz with a small laugh.

'Rubbish! You'll be great. By the way, Julian's asked me to set up some sessions with a dialect coach. She's a bit of an old bat, but bloody good. Take along a nice bottle of gin and she'll love you for ever.'

Gin! Toilet rolls. Chanel bags for ten dollars. Maggie Smith. This was a new world, all right. By the time they'd gone back upstairs to the glassed-in café Paige was ravenous, and recklessly ordered an omelette from a young waiter with vertical bright-red hair.

'Cheese, ham, or mushroom?'

'Uh, just egg.'

'Chips or new potatoes?'

Horrified, Paige chose a salad – 'no dressing'.

'So, is the flat OK?' Fizz asked, when the waiter had disappeared with their order.

'The flat?'

'You know, the place where you're staying? I checked it out myself and it seemed to have most things on your list.'

'Oh, the apartment. It's ... it's fine.' Paige decided not to mention the complete absence of walk-in closets.

'Sorry about the mix-up over the car this morning. But we can't afford one. And it's daft, anyway. Much quicker to walk.'

'The traffic's murder?' Paige said experimentally, and was rather thrilled when Fizz just nodded.

'Two omelettes, one ham with chips, one plain with salad,' announced the waiter. 'No dressing,' he added triumphantly. They began eating.

'So, what do you think of Ed?' Fizz asked, raising one eyebrow suggestively.

'Who?' Paige tried to remember which actor that could be. 'You don't mean Orlando?'

'No,' giggled Fizz. 'You must have twigged that he's gay. No, I mean the guy in your house. Lives downstairs.'

'Oh.' No maid, then. Paige shrugged. 'I don't know. I haven't met him yet.'

'He's really sweet – and fit, as well.'

Paige wrinked her nose. 'I don't go for those muscly guys.'

'Nah,' Fizz laughed. '*Fit* – handsome, sexy, nice bum. Reminds me of John Cusack. You know, sort of smouldering but makes you laugh.'

Paige looked at her with interest.

'Yeah, I was almost tempted myself,' Fizz admitted, 'except he's too old.'

'How old?'

'Thirty-five, maybe.'

Paige speared a lettuce leaf. 'And does he, um, live there all by himself?'

'Apparently so.'

Paige looked up to find Fizz grinning at her. She couldn't help smiling back. Things were looking up.

CHAPTER 15

Ed stared gloomily at his computer screen. Outside it was beginning to get dark. Soon he would get up and trudge through to the kitchen to fix something to eat. He'd come home from work earlier than usual this evening, in order to write a proposal for a new three-part series provisionally entitled *The American Empire*. A promising idea – and surely guaranteed to sell to the Americans, even if they gave it some absurd title like *The Triumph of Democracy*. But he'd forgotten about his new tenant, who'd moved in yesterday. He hadn't seen her yet, but he'd certainly heard her. It seemed that every time he began to feel inspired, fingers poised over the keyboard, there would be a rat-a-tat on the front door, the sound of footsteps on the floor above, then girly squeaks of delight. Surely there couldn't be any more stuff to come? By now the three floors above must be crammed with flowers, fruit baskets, champagne, glossy boxes of designer goodies, and trinkets of the sort that only people with more money than sense purchased and had delivered to their friends. Even her food arrived in a Harrods van. If this was what life was going to be like for the next two months, he wasn't sure that he could stand it.

She was obviously your typical Hollywood airhead. Take the 'house healing' exercise, for example. Ten days ago he'd been asked 'as a matter of urgency' for a floor plan of the upstairs flat. Ed had told the girl from the theatre that no, funnily enough he didn't happen to have such a thing as a floor plan – so she'd sent in a surveyor to make one *that same day*. This had been emailed to some female guru in Los Angeles, who apparently 'studied' the plan, and then 'healed' the flat over the phone, by a process as yet unknown to science.

It was difficult enough to concentrate when the future of Hawkshead Barry was up in the air. Since the lunch with Wolfe two weeks earlier, Ed had found it hard to motivate himself. What was the point of working up proposals for films on serious subjects if that wasn't what Grapevine would want? He clicked the mouse to save the work he had done so far, though to be honest it was barely worth saving. Not for the first time, he succumbed to bitterness. He was a first-class film-maker, he told himself. What was he doing, prostituting his talent for corporate profit? On the desk beside him was a folder marked 'Private and Confidential' containing Grapevine's offer for Hawkshead Barry. It meant a lot of money for him – a lot of money in his terms, anyway – but he would be bound by 'golden handcuffs', committed to work for Grapevine for five years after the deal went through. Was that really what he wanted? He dreaded being sucked into the world of 'emotainment'. He remembered Phil's tasteless suggestions for sexing up his programmes. Oh God, was this the future?

He logged on to his email. Here was a message from his mother. He frowned as he scanned its contents. The tone was breezy enough – too breezy. Ed was her only child, and she was his only parent: there wasn't much they could hide from each other. He could tell that she was anxious. His mother had been a schoolteacher all her life, and a headmistress for the past twenty years. Teaching was central to her life. Recently she'd been asked to take 'early retirement'. Ed knew what a blow that was, and how hard she was trying to conceal this fact from him. They were so alike, preferring to slink off and lick their wounds than admit hurt.

He wondered how to cheer her up. If only she didn't live so far away ...

Once again he was distracted by footfalls overhead. Should he go up and introduce himself? That's what he usually did when a new tenant arrived. He felt slightly ashamed that he hadn't done so already. But he'd never had anyone famous living there before. She might think he was sucking up. Ed despised people who were impressed by fame: the pathetic rubber-neckers who thought that someone was interesting just because they happened to be on television, or featured in a magazine. He couldn't bear to be thought one of them; it was too humiliating. He'd already been mercilessly teased at the office, where his views on popular culture were well known. *Ooh, Ed, could you get us her autograph?* No, he bloody well could not.

What would she make of England, he wondered? Of course, she would see it as a succession of theme-park clichés. Probably she'd do no more than make the regulation pilgrimages to 'Nodding Hill' and 'Ass-cot' with her glitzy friends. Absolutely typical! He was already irritated by her patronising attitude to the country of his birth. Patriotic hackles that he barely knew he possessed rose in indignation. This was a real place with real people doing real jobs – a country with a real culture of its own. Did the English honestly need someone from Hollywood to show them how to perform Shakespeare? Still, it might be good for a laugh: he must remember to book himself a ringside seat. These movie people thought they ruled the world when they were simply clogging the channels with dross. It would be satisfying to see one of them put in their place by good old, fuddy-duddy, genius-of-the-fucking-universe, William Shakespeare.

He tried to remember which films of hers he'd seen, and idly Googled her name. Here was a biography, illustrated with a recent 'red carpet' shot of her attending the Oscars. Hmph. What a ridiculous dress with that enormous bow thing on the back. *Born Los Angeles, only child of rock star Ty Carson* (oh God, Scrap Metal! – 'cock rock' at its least subtle) *and actress and model Melanie 'Melons' Moon, Playmate of Month, October 1973* ... He scrolled down the list of films, most of which he'd never seen, though the sheer number of them was impressive. But so what, if they were all crap? Ed clicked on the heading marked 'Personal Quotes' and began chortling almost immediately. *You either walk with a straight head or you don't ... All that really matters is that I control my journey and my destination ... This is where my soul is at right now.* Just as he thought: a ditzy, self-absorbed birdbrain.

Under 'Paige's Faves' he learned that her favourite book was *Gone with the Wind* (at least she could read); favourite film, *Angel in the Dirt* (one of her own – so modest!); favourite artist, Henri Matisse; favourite ice cream – no, this was absurd. He clicked randomly through the news stories. *Is Paige Carson Pregnant?* demanded a headline from three years back. Apparently not. *'Paige is my muse, my other half – we will never be parted,'* said arthouse director Aaron Grosknopf ... *Paige and Aaron split! ... Paige Carson finds love at last with Jackson Rolfe!*

Paige Carson's Breasts, judged by size and pertness, rated number three in the Hollywood Top Ten. There was a link marked 'See nude pictures here' which Ed avoided after only a moment's hesitation, deciding instead to read what a reputable critic had written about *Biker Boys*. The iconic poster came up first. A pouting young girl sat astride a huge motorbike, wearing leather boots, cut-off denim shorts and a white singlet sliding off one shoulder. She stared straight at the camera, nose raised defiantly. Ed had to admit that she was very attractive in an annoying way. He moved on to the serious stuff : '... *but what could have been a sex-ploitation movie about teenage gangs in Nowheresville is turned into a classic by the young actors, then unknown, in particular Paige Carson, whose freshness offsets the darker sexuality—*'

What was that? Ed looked up, startled. It was the upstairs front door banging shut. Now he could hear footsteps coming down his stone steps. Shit! Hastily he lowered the lid of his laptop, just as his door-knocker sounded. Was it her? Despite himself, he couldn't help passing a hand over his hair as he went to answer the door.

Pearly skin, hair the colour of new conkers, green eyes that sparkled into his: she was even more gorgeous in the flesh than on screen. In fact, she looked like a different species. She *shone,* as if she'd been polished. He disliked her on sight.

'Hi, I'm your new neighbour.' She shot him a dazzling smile, each tooth a flawless gem. 'Paige Carson.'

'Yeah. I know. I'm – ' Something had gone wrong with his vocal chords. He cleared his throat. 'I'm Ed. Ed Hawkshead.' He shook her outstretched hand. It was smooth and warm. They stared at each other in silence for a moment, then both began to speak at once.

'I – no, you go ahead – sorry.' He cleared his throat again. 'Er, look, why don't you come in?'

Why did he say that?

She slipped past him in a flowery waft, and he closed the door behind her.

'In there,' he said, indicating his living-room/study. He was suddenly embarrassed by its messiness: papers everywhere, a dirty coffee-cup, his jacket slung on the back of a chair. But why should he apologise? He prickled with resentment. What was she doing here? Had she come to complain about something?

'I hope you're comfortable upstairs?' he enquired pointedly. *Bloody well better be.*

'Oh yes, very comfortable. It's an awesome apartment.' She stood serene and poised in the centre of the room, glancing round at his possessions. Her white shirt was immaculate, worn over black jeans and fancy red trainers.

'I must apologise for not coming up to greet you earlier.

I've been very busy,' Ed explained gruffly, gesturing towards his computer to indicate his preoccupation with more serious matters.

'That's OK.' She was moving around the room now, looking at his things. 'Oh wow! You've got a Bafta! Are you in the movie business too?' She strode excitedly to the bookshelf where he had perched his trophy, in the shape of a golden theatrical mask. He'd thought that the sunglasses over its hollow eyes added an ironic touch, until she gushed, 'I love the cute shades.'

'Yes,' he scowled, 'I'm in the film business too – at a very different level from you, of course. I write and produce television documentaries.'

'How wonderful! Would I have seen any of your films?'

'I very much doubt it. The Americans don't seem to like what I do.' Ed realised that he was sounding grumpy, but he couldn't help it. Her enthusiasm was patronising; he didn't need her approval. It was irritating that someone so obviously silly should be so attractive. He, of all people, should be immune to surface glamour. And that's all it was. *Of course* she looked nice: that was the whole point of her. For years she'd been primped and pampered and probably surgically reassembled to produce this very effect. Well, he wasn't falling for it.

She took a step towards him. 'I wanted to ask, would it bother you if I used the back yard? I noticed there's a stairway from my apartment, and I sometimes like to jump-rope.'

He frowned. 'You like to what?'

'You know, for exercise?' She jumped up and down a few times and twirled her arms in a daft girly manner.

He pressed his lips severely together. 'We call it skipping. Of course you can do what you like in the *garden*. I'm sorry there's no hot tub,' he added.

'Oh, right. OK. Good.' She seemed reluctant to leave. What was she doing, poking around in his life? 'Hey! You've written a book!' She pulled out a copy of *Nazis,* the tie-in book that had enabled him to buy the house, and started leafing through it. After a moment, two wide green eyes appeared over the swastika'd dust-jacket. 'Isn't it spooky the way those guys all had names beginning with either G or H? I bet I'd get them all mixed up!'

He eyed her coldly. 'Himmler wore glasses, Goering didn't. Goebbels had a limp, Hitler had a moustache. It's really quite simple.'

She gave a nervous laugh, and put the book back. He wondered if he'd been unnecessarily brusque. She came from Hollywood: obviously she couldn't be expected to know anything about history, especially in what she probably called 'Yurp'. He mustered a politer tone. 'What brings you to England?' he asked, though he knew the answer already. '... Shakespeare! That must be very different from what you're used to.'

'It's a challenge, sure. But in the end it's just acting. That's what I do.' She shrugged. Any minute she'd be telling him it wasn't rocket science. 'It's not rocket science, you know.'

'No, indeed.' Ed glared at her. 'It seems to be all the rage now to get a Hollywood star on the London stage. Good box office, I suppose,' he added nastily.

'I guess ...' She lifted her chin. 'Um, well, why I called by was to ask if you have any vases I could borrow?'

She pronounced it 'vaces'. No doubt she said 'bay-zil' as well, and ''erbs'.

'I have more flowers than I can handle,' she continued, by way of explanation. 'I'd be glad to give you some, if you want.'

'No, thank you very much,' he replied. 'I'm not big on vases, but I'll see what I can find.' He pronounced the word 'vahzes', which to his annoyance sounded ludicrously pretentious in his ears.

'A pitcher would do just as well.'

'A picture?'

'A pitcher – you know, for pouring?'

'Oh, you mean a jug. In English the word "pitcher" is archaic.' He was sounding pompous again. 'English English, I mean, as opposed to American English,' he clarified, making it worse. 'Hang on a minute while I go and look.' He left her with a sense of relief and retreated to the kitchen, where he banged the cupboard doors with unnecessary vigour. Vases! What else was she going to demand? He had an image of himself as a servant in his own house, running up and down the steps to do the bidding of this spoilt American diva.

'Afraid this is the best I can do,' he said shortly, returning to the living-room with a vase in one hand and a chipped jug in the other. She was already hovering by the door, ready to leave now that she'd got what she'd come for. Typical! No time for further pleasantries with a lowly documentary-maker.

'Thanks. I'll drop these back in a few days,' she said. 'Guess I'd better let you get on with your ... work.'

Ed showed her down the hall and opened the front door for her. On the threshold she paused and added, 'I'll try not to bother you again,' before turning and disappearing up the steps.

Good, thought Ed, as he closed the door on her. She'd got the message. There'd be no more wandering about and fiddling with his stuff and – and *smiling* in that ghastly, false manner. With luck, he'd never have to speak to her again. Except when she returned the vaces, pitchers, whatever. He wondered when that might be. How long did flowers last, exactly ... ?

Back to work! He returned to his desk, rubbing his hands briskly, then stopped in horror. *She'd opened his laptop!* Displayed on the screen was the infamous poster for *Biker Boys*. Paige sat astride the motorbike, legs bare, hair wild, green eyes narrowed in contempt.

CHAPTER 16

'"Come woo me, woo me,"' said Paige, '"for now I am in a holiday humour, and like enough to consent."'

'Did you say something, madam?' asked the driver.

'Oh, ignore me.' Paige leaned forward, raising her voice: 'I'm just rehearsing.' She sighed, and sank back in her seat. What, exactly, did 'woo' mean? How would the twenty-first century wooer go about his business? She remembered another line from the play: 'Men are April when they woo.' It was April now – was that significant? She wondered who the 'cute English guys' were that Davina had lined up for her.

They had left London behind and were speeding along a freeway. It was so thoughtful of Davina to have sent a limo. A weekend in the country was just what she needed, after the stress of the past week. She had totally freaked when a picture of her walking to the theatre had appeared in one of the sleazy British tabloids – especially as it was a highly unflattering shot that gave her a double chin. She'd called Heather, to see if she could kill it before the bitchblogs filled up with stories about her 'weight problem'. Gaby had suggested she should quit the play unless they gave her a more upscale address and a car with a driver. But Fizz had just laughed and said it was publicity for the show, and any fool could tell it was a shadow and not her actual chin.

Then there was the play itself: even with *Brodie's Notes* she still didn't understand half of her lines. How could you make a joke funny when *you* didn't get it? Also, Julian had insisted that she stuff a pair of socks down her trousers so that she could imitate a man's walk. This was (a) totally unhygienic, and (b) meant she had to wear saggy sweatpants, which was hardly an attractive look – always assuming that there was someone worth attracting.

Not for the first time, she reflected on her encounter with the guy downstairs. It didn't really bother her that he'd looked her up online. Everyone did it, herself included. But why the snotty attitude? She'd tried to take an intelligent interest in his book, congratulated him on his Bafta even though it was hardly an Oscar – and he'd practically snapped her head off. She'd gone out of her way not to act the big movie star, and he couldn't respond with even normal politeness. How Fizz could call him 'sweet', she couldn't imagine. OK, he was sort of good-looking, in a brooding, gypsyish way. Big deal. Practically everyone in Hollywood was good-looking. As an actress she'd kissed some of the most gorgeous men on the planet. What counted was how people behaved, and Ed Whatshisname had been plain rude. What gave him the right to act so superior? He was as bad as Jackson – and not even famous! Fortunately she hadn't spoken to him or even seen him since – apart from that one time, when she'd looked out of a back window to see him throwing stones at a cat crapping in the yard.

The car had left the freeway and was twisting and turning through increasingly narrow roads. Once they had to back up to let a tractor trundle past. It seemed very strange that the English hadn't built their roads wide enough for two cars to pass each other; surely that was pretty obvious. When the car turned into an entrance and stopped in front of high decorative gates, Paige sat up to peer expectantly through the windshield. It would be fun to see Davina's country place, and even better to see Davina herself. After a week among strangers she needed a dose of normality.

The gates swung open and they drove for a mile or so

through woodland. How green everything was – not the bright emerald of California lawns, but a soft yellowy-green, as if the landscape glowed from within. Then the trees ended abruptly, to reveal a wide sweep of lawn and an old stone house with a fancy pillared porchway. A figure on the front steps waved frantically. It was Davina! – but a Davina Paige hardly recognised. Gone were the indecently low-cut jeans, chain belts, and plunging necklines, teamed with four-inch heels and wanton blonde locks. Here instead was a demure-looking woman in grey wool slacks and cream cashmere sweater. Her hair was drawn back in soft waves and caught in a clip. On her feet were plain black ballet pumps.

'Son of a bitch!' she yelled as soon as Paige opened the car door. 'I finally got you here. Yippee!' Paige smiled with relief: different outfit, same Davina. In a moment she was enveloped in a cloud of familiar perfume. She hugged Davina back. It was so good to have a friend.

Rock music was playing throughout the house as Davina led her into a hallway and up a curving staircase to her room. The driver, meanwhile, had been dispatched with Paige's bags via 'the back stairs' – very *Gosford Park*, thought Paige.

'I so adore this house,' Davina exclaimed. 'You have to see everything.' She flung open doors as they walked along a wide corridor: Davina's bedroom, decorated in scarlet and black, with a huge Buddha in the corner; a mirrored bathroom with a round bath; a dressing-room which had been papered with the iconic image of Davina wearing nothing but strategically placed jewellery and blood-red lipstick. 'That's Trev's, of course.' Paige's room had zebra stripes and a four-poster bed draped in shocking-pink silk, somewhat strangely positioned in the centre of the room. 'I had the whole place feng-shuied,' Davina told her. 'It's so important to have a harmonious atmosphere.'

'It's wonderful,' said Paige. 'I love it.' She didn't, exactly, but she loved Davina and wanted to make her happy.

'Now don't worry about unpacking. Someone will do that for you. Oh – and all the remotes are in the top drawer of that little table: TV, DVD, music, and the drapes. They're all marked.

'I can't wait to show you the rest. But we'll do that after lunch. Trev likes to have his meals on time.' She glanced at her watch. 'In fact, I'd better check what's happening with the lunch. Come down when you're ready. There's just the three of us for now. I wanted you to myself, and I'm so dying for you to get to know Trev. Later on, all kinds of fabulous people will be showing up. It's going to be just super dooper.'

'More salad, Trev, darling?'

'I'm not a rabbit, am I?'

Davina burst out laughing. 'Trevor's such a gas. I think it's his sense of humour that made me fall in love with him, even more than his gorgeous good looks.'

Paige glanced at Trevor, who was cutting up his game pie with precision. He was certainly very masculine-looking, tall and muscled with dark close-cropped hair. But she found him somewhat inscrutable.

'And what about you, Trevor?' she asked him brightly, trying to make contact. 'What made you fall in love with Davina?'

'Her money,' he answered, smearing mustard on his pie. 'Joke,' he added with a deadpan expression.

Davina rolled her eyes at Paige, delighted by this witticism. 'Wait until you see him with his mates – that's what the guys call their friends over here. Vince and Clifford will be staying overnight, of course, and so will Lulu – you know, the model? – and this darling English boy called Tudor. Then we'll have some of the neighbours over for dinner. It's taken a while, but we're sort of in with the gentry now.'

'Load of tossers,' Trevor muttered. He wiped his mouth

carefully and threw down his napkin. 'Right. I'm off to see about tomorrow's shoot.'

'Is someone making a movie?' Paige asked in surprise.

'He means guns,' Davina explained. 'If it moves, Trev likes to shoot it, don't you, my hunky-dunk?'

'And what exactly will be, uh, moving tomorrow?' Paige couldn't bear it if she was made to kill a peacock or something.

'Only clay pigeons,' Davina reassured her. 'The game season's closed right now, but we like to have shooting parties anyway. They're such a wonderful old English tradition, and the clothes are to die for. You know how I love to dress up.' She gave her earthy laugh. 'Mom always said I came out of the womb posing. I can lend you one of my outfits, sweetpea.'

After lunch Davina got Paige to put on some green rubber boots and showed her the stables, the barns (one a gym and one a recording studio), her chickens in the orchard, and her walled vegetable garden. There wasn't much growing yet apart from a few onion shoots, but Davina's eyes lit up as she described the incredible thrill of eating her own produce. 'Everything's organic and natural. I even get the gardeners to collect the snails by hand instead of poisoning them. We put them in a pail, then the chauffeur drives them to some nice, leafy spot a few miles away.' She took a rapturous breath of fresh air, eyes closed, then turned to Paige, suddenly serious. 'You know, I had *nothing* when I was a kid. Life was hard and mean and ugly. I always swore that my own children would have everything they could want.' She saw Paige's eyes widen with speculation, and wagged a finger. 'Not yet,' she laughed, 'but we're trying. *All* the time, if you know what I mean. But you can't wear out Trev. If it's a boy, I'm going to call him Casanova; Babylon, if it's a girl. What do you think?'

Poor kids, thought Paige. 'Perfect,' she said.

And everything here *was* perfect, in a way, especially

when Davina had settled her in a comfortable armchair by a crackling fire in the living-room, with a cup of special herb tea at her elbow. But she couldn't understand what Davina saw in unsmiling, monosyllabic Trevor. If he was a 'real' man, she'd rather have an unreal one. 'A dreamboat', as her mother used to say. Someone gentle and kind, whom she could love ... someone to give her lots of babies ... someone who ...

Who was that? Paige sat up, startled. Had she been asleep?

'I'm most terribly sorry,' said a voice. 'I didn't know anyone was in here. Please forgive me.'

Paige peered dopily round the wing of the chair to see a tall, broad-shouldered man standing by the window. The dying sun made a halo of his blond hair which flopped attractively over his forehead. She guessed him to be about thirty.

'That's OK.' She smiled.

'In that case ...' He stepped forward and held out his hand for her to shake. 'I'm Tudor Shaftsbury – great friend of Davina's. I know who you are, of course. In fact,' he went on conspiratorially, 'don't tell anyone, but you're the reason I'm here. *Angel in the Dirt* is my favourite film of all time.'

'You're kidding!' Paige said delightedly. 'That's *my* favourite of all the movies I've made, but it never really got distributed. You must be one of the few people in the whole world who's seen it.'

'Then this is indeed a most marvellous and magical encounter. Do you mind if I sit down?'

'Of course not. It's not my bedroom or anything.' Now what had made her say that? Paige straightened up and smoothed her hair. 'I mean—'

'I understand perfectly. You mean to say that this is a public room which anyone may enter.'

'Yes.' Paige was smiling again.

'And do you think anyone may also put some more logs

on the fire? I'm afraid that you've allowed it to die right down.' He frowned teasingly. 'That's a cardinal sin in English country houses.'

'Is it?'

'Except for those houses where it's a cardinal sin if one *does* put logs on the fire.'

'And how do you know which is which?'

'Ah ha. You need a guide to the strange and unfathomable ways of the English.'

They looked at each other for a moment.

'You?' she suggested.

'I hoped you'd say that. In fact, I've already bagged the seat next to you at dinner.'

'Bloody ramblers. They've got no business traipsing about on other people's land, specially wearing those hideous plastic garments.' The old man's bleary eyes hunted round the table. 'Is there any more of that rather decent wine I brought?'

Davina flapped a hand at the butler, who ignored her for a few insolent seconds, then pushed himself off the wall where he'd been lounging and slunk round the table to top up the wine glasses. They had reached the cheese course, and Paige still didn't know the old man's name; Davina had simply referred to him as 'the squire'. Paige was beginning to wonder if her friend was a little too in love with England.

'I absolutely agree with you,' Davina now told him warmly. 'We have one of those Public Footpaths that comes right by the house. Anyone can just stand there and take pictures of me in my garden, and I can't do a thing about it. It's totally outrageous!'

'Father's having the same problem on the estate in Scotland,' Tudor chipped in. 'Half the grouse moor's been listed as open land. We're contesting it, of course. Otherwise the place will be heaving with grockles.' Grockles, he explained privately to Paige, sitting beside him, were the rubber-necking tourists who cluttered up the beauty spots of England.

'Funny word,' she murmured, pulling the strap of her dress back onto her shoulder. She was feeling so sleepy she could hardly keep her eyes open and longed to loll against Tudor's dinner-jacketed arm.

The squire had started up again, this time on the troubles of cattle farmers like himself. 'You can buy cheaper beef, of course – if you don't mind that some Argie has widdled and piddled all over it.'

'Davina darling, mind if I step outside for a fag?' That was the squire's dissolute-looking son Cosmo, who stood up without waiting for Davina's reply. 'Coming, Sabs?' he asked his wife Sabina, and she rose eagerly. Paige was pretty sure they were going outside for something a lot stronger than a cigarette.

'I thought England was a free country,' Davina continued. She'd transformed herself from lady of the manor to supervamp, and was looking magnificent in a long dress of Chinese red, slashed almost to the waist and revealing the Sanskrit tattoos on her toned biceps. 'But there seems to be a law about everything. We were right in the middle of converting the library into a panic room when some guy from your Council came over and told us we had to put everything back the way it was, even all the old, split panelling.'

'That's because the house is listed. You see, in order to protect our historic buildings we British introduced a law in about 1950 – or was it earlier than that, perhaps '49 or even '48 … ?'

Paige suppressed a yawn. Jonty, one of the 'nice' neighbours though not apparently 'gentry', was one of the biggest bores she'd ever met. Over drinks he'd sidled up to her and said, 'Do you remember Mexico, and that little place on the beach where we'd just lie in the sun and catch fish all day?'

'Excuse me?' Paige had asked blankly.

'No.' He'd tutted impatiently. 'You're supposed to say, "But we never made it to Mexico, Jeff. And now we never will." Then you sort of sigh – you're dying, of course – and say, "Do you think there's a Mexico in heaven?"' He'd looked at her with disappointment. 'Don't you remember your own films?'

'Not really,' she'd answered apologetically, and he'd looked affronted, as if she must be lying.

Apparently Tudor had been listening to this exchange, for he'd chipped in, 'How about *Angel in the Dirt*? I'm sure you can give us a quote from that, can't you, Jonty?'

'Er, well I'm not quite … What did you say it was called?'

'My dear chap, come with me and I'll tell you all about it.' And Tudor had led him away, looking back to give Paige a wink. There goes a true gentleman, she'd thought, and blown him a kiss.

Jonty's wife, Caro, brittle-blonde with one of those on-off smiles, was not much better. 'Now do tell me,' she'd murmured confidentially, having manoeuvered Paige onto the couch, 'have you had any plastic surgery? I'm thinking of having a face-lift.'

It was amazing the questions people asked. Because they saw you on screen, or in magazines, they felt they knew you, and could trample across your privacy. But Paige was used to this by now. She'd answered politely that she really couldn't comment and Caro must make her own decision.

Then there were Trevor's two 'mates'. Sitting across the table from Paige, Vince clearly had his eyes on the gorgeous Lulu, six foot tall with rippling red hair and skin as white as chalk. Paige hadn't heard her say a word all evening; she'd just toyed, blank-eyed, with a spear of broccoli, while Vince murmured in her ear and ran a finger up and down the prominent vertebrae of her bare back. Clifford was Paige's other dinner partner besides Tudor, and as different from him as he could be: dark, unsmiling, and pushy. Gradually he'd worked the conversation round to investments, and told her he could put her onto 'a nice little earner'. Paige had had to tell him rather firmly that she left all that kind of thing to her portfolio manager. At the opposite end of the table to Davina, Trevor was listening to Caro's pleas for a contribution to the village church restoration fund. Wearing a black jacket, black tie and black shirt, he presented a dramatic contrast to the framed photograph of Davina hanging on the wall at his back: a still from her notorious 'Losing my Head' video, in which she posed on a guillotine wearing an elaborate Marie Antoinette wig and very little else. 'You'll have to ask the missus,' he told Caro, and flashed his wife a smile of dark desire.

Somehow the rest of the evening passed. Vince and Lulu disappeared shortly after dinner. Cosmo and Sabs reappeared, giggling and glazed. Paige was swaying with tiredness by the time Davina re-entered the living-room after waving goodbye to the last guest, and gave a sigh of satisfaction. 'I think that was a big success, don't you?'

'It's been a lovely evening,' said Tudor. 'Delicious food. Everything perfect.'

'Mmm,' agreed Paige.

'It's so nice to feel accepted into real English society.' Davina beamed. Then her expression sharpened. 'Where's Trev?'

'He's just toddled off with Clifford,' Tudor offered. 'I think they said something about playing pool.'

'No way.' Davina's eyes glinted. 'I need him in the bedroom. I'm ovulating like crazy,' she confided. 'Good night, you two. Sweet dreams.' She kissed them both, then swept out of the room.

'Quite a lady,' Tudor remarked.

'She kicks ass, as we say in America.' Paige attempted a smile.

He put an arm around her shoulders. 'And what about you?' he murmured into her hair. 'Do you need anyone in your bedroom?'

Paige sank against him, but shook her head. 'What I need is sleep.'

'Then I shall escort you to your chamber. I promise not to quote from any of your films.'

Paige giggled.

'And tomorrow,' he said, drawing her gently up the stairs, 'I shall teach you how to shoot. I happen to be a crack shot.'

'I'll bet you are.'

Crack!
   'Pull!'
Crack!
   'Pull!'
Crack! Ker-boom! Ker-ping!

Paige stood behind the firing line with her hands over her ears, even though she was already wearing earmuffs, wincing at each shot. This had been going on for almost three hours now. Her head ached, and her shoulder felt sore. She was bored. Even with Tudor's patient instruction she had not made a single 'kill', probably because every time she pulled the trigger she also squeezed her eyes shut. She'd only ever shot fake guns with pretend bullets. The first time she fired the real thing, the recoil had knocked her flat on her back.

A proper English shooting party had sounded such a romantic prospect. This morning a watery sun had emerged through mist to give the landscape a luminous, ethereal quality. Paige had woken to birdsong, refreshed and expectant, picturing herself wandering through dappled woods with Tudor and toying with something delicious from a picnic basket. Davina had bustled into her bedroom, having already spent an hour exercising on her Power Plate, wearing an extraordinary outfit of mid-calf tweed skirt, long tweed jacket over a high-buttoned shirt, and thick socks protruding above lace-up boots. 'My God, you look like the Queen of England,' Paige had exclaimed. 'A lot better-looking,'

186

she'd added hastily. Together they had chosen an outfit for Paige in olive and russet, and decided to wear matching deerstalker hats.

After breakfast they had all piled into a Land Rover – minus Lulu, who was 'resting' – and driven along rough tracks to a small, tranquil valley, with woods rising steeply on one side of a meandering stream, and a soft slope of green on the other. The air smelled sweet. At their approach rabbits scampered for refuge in a flurry of white powder-puff tails. Alongside the stream was a line of three-sided wooden cages where you were supposed to stand to shoot. Apparently this was what was called 'sporting shooting' and their pretend prey was 'high pheasant'. In practice this meant that discs of clay were released from a 'trap' up in the trees and flew over their heads at top speed, to be blasted to smithereens in a barrage of gunfire.

Paige could not see the point of this. Soon the dewy grass was littered with spent cartridges. Noise ricocheted up and down the valley. What about the poor birds and animals who lived here, who didn't have earmuffs to put on? She felt stupid and uncomfortable in her borrowed clothes, dressed for a part she could not play. 'Tweed is such wonderful camouflage,' Davina had enthused. But those clay things couldn't see, could they? Tudor had turned boring and manly, discussing shotguns and trajectories with the other guys, instead of paying attention to her – though to be fair it was she who'd cried off the shooting after the first couple of rounds, and said she'd rather watch.

Someone was prodding her in the back. She looked up to see Davina, whose lips were moving although Paige couldn't hear a thing. She lowered her hands and removed her earmuffs. For a moment there was blissful silence. 'I said, Trev won,' Davina repeated. 'Isn't that wonderful?'

'Fantastic.' Paige looked over to where all the men were passing round a hip flask.

'And now we're off to the Titsworth Arms – the local

pub,' she added when Paige looked blank. 'That's what you do after a shoot. It's only about a mile away. And it's completely unspoilt – sawdust on the floor, a real fireplace, old-fashioned beer pumps. It used to be a dump, which is why we decided to buy it. All the food is organic now. There are vegan and macrobiotic options. We've banned those huge platters of greasy chips. Afterwards we can play darts, or even skittles!'

'Great,' said Paige faintly.

Davina pulled a cell phone from her game bag. 'I'm just calling someone to come and pick up the guns, then Trev will drive us over.'

Paige felt a pang of disappointment. All weekend she'd been hearing about these special footpaths; all morning she'd been wondering what lay beyond the valley and over the hill. 'Couldn't we walk?' she suggested boldly.

'You can if you want. But there will be, you know, people on the paths. It's more private in the car.'

'So who's walking?' asked Tudor, joining them.

'Me,' Paige answered promptly. Tudor, she thought, looked more like an authentic hunter in worn cords and a dark waxed jacket than Trev and his mates in their checked shirts, waistcoats and cravats. He'd removed the ugly flat cap that seemed to be an essential part of shooting equipment, revealing his noble brow and cutely curling hair. When Davina wasn't looking, Paige had also ditched her unflattering deerstalker. Now, while Tudor enquired if anyone else was joining the walking party, she surreptitiously rolled over the waistband of her skirt to shorten it and undid a few shirt-buttons.

In fact, there were just the two of them heading for the stile at the top of the hill. Paige had a feeling that Tudor had engineered this, and was flattered.

'I hear you lost,' she said provocatively.

'I came second.'

'Very diplomatic.'

'Of course, it isn't proper shooting.' Though Tudor didn't say as much, Paige had the feeling that he disapproved of Trev. Well, that was OK; so did she. It seemed that they shared the same tastes and sensitivities. When she remarked on the pretty white flowers growing among gnarled tree roots, he picked some for her, telling her they were wood anemones.

At the top of the hill they paused to admire the sweeping view of woods and fields, rising to meet high, flat grasslands which, despite being up, were apparently known as 'downs'. Below were the slate and terracotta roofs of Upper Titsworth. A square, stone church tower poked though inky trees.

Tudor cleared his throat. 'There's a sort of party next week. Birthday bash. I was wondering if you'd like to trot along.'

Paige gave him a look. 'Trot?'

'I'll pick you up.'

A party. Did she dare? There would be the usual stares and the usual stupid questions. She didn't want her picture taken. Nor did she want Tudor to be scared off by one of those silly newspaper stories about 'Paige Carson's new beau'.

On the other hand, why shouldn't she? Wouldn't it be fun to be a normal person at a normal party?

'Who's going to be there?' she asked.

'Me.'

She gave him a playful shove. 'I mean who else?'

'Only nice people. I expect I'll know them all. Went to school with half of them.'

'No grockles?'

He turned to smile down into her eyes. 'Not one. I promise.'

'All right, then. Thank you. I accept.'

CHAPTER 17

Ed paused at the top of the stone steps leading down to his flat, bent double, hands on bare knees, breathing heavily. Sweat stained his T-shirt. It was Sunday evening, and he had just returned from a run.

Normally it lifted his spirits and freed his mind to take the five-mile jog down the canal tow-path to Regent's Park, round the Outer Circle and back again, passing fishermen, lovers, people rowing boats, playing rounders, doing Tai Chi, or pursuing other innocent activities. Sometimes he could hear an elephant trumpeting as he ran past the zoo, or the wail of a mullah from the mosque. But today, as he straightened slowly and clung to one of the iron railings, he felt as wired as when he'd started. The deadline for a response to the Grapevine offer was fast approaching, and he was still no nearer a decision. Nor had he yet told Maddy that she wasn't wanted. In fact, he was in a funk about the whole thing. And then there was that wretched woman in his flat.

Her presence bothered him in a way he'd never experienced with other tenants. He heard her all the time, prattling on the phone, singing, practising her lines and, well, *moving about* in that entitled, Hollywood manner. It was *his* house. She wasn't even paying the rent; the theatre took care of that, though she must be a million times richer. Only yesterday, he'd seen her prance down the front steps and sail into a limo! The amount of luggage stowed by the driver suggested that she was off somewhere smart for the weekend. She'd been wearing a swishy little skirt and boots. Once again, he'd felt annoyed by her ability to look so stunning. But why? Film stars were film stars because they were watchable. QED, Ed: don't watch them. He trudged wearily down the steps to his basement.

Unlocking his front door, he stumbled inside and headed for the shower. He was still dripping with sweat. Was he that unfit?

Drip, drip. Something else was dripping. Puzzled, Ed back-tracked to his sitting-room. There was a wet patch on the carpet. He walked over to examine it, then looked up just in time to receive a drop of water in the eye. Blinking it away, he squinted up again. A line of droplets ran along the ceiling, from a bulge of sagging plaster. Bugger!

Turning on his heel, he dashed out of his flat and back up the steps into the street, then up again to the front door of the upstairs flat. He hammered urgently. There was no immediate answer, so he tried again, more vigorously this time. The door opened a crack and Paige peered through, holding a phone to her ear. A towel was wrapped around her head, turban-style, and she appeared to be wearing some flimsy dressing-gown thing. One bare foot could be seen, with fresh-painted toenails and pads of cotton wool between each toe. She frowned at him suspiciously. 'What is it? I'm on the phone.'

'You're flooding the house, you stupid woman!'

'What? I'm sorry, Gaby, I didn't catch what you said.'

'Listen to me! There's water coming though my ceiling!' He pushed past her into the hall, ignoring her squawked objections, and strode through to the kitchen, where water was spilling over the rim of the sink onto the floor. A bunch of wilting wildflowers bobbed around the sink. Christ! Ed pulled out the plug and wrenched the tap closed. Water gurgled down the drain. Paige appeared behind him, still talking on the phone. 'Just a sec, Gaby. There seems to be some sort of problem.'

'Too bloody right there is. Do you realise what you've done?'

'Oh dear,' she said vaguely. 'What happened?'

'Were you brought up in a swimming-pool?'

'Of course not!'

'I suppose where you come from, it's normal practice to leave the water running?'

'No ... but this would never happen in the United States. We always have efficient overflow systems,' she told him primly. 'It's the stupid landlord's fault if he failed to install one here.'

'I'm the stupid landlord!'

'You?' Her perfect forehead wrinkled slightly, as if she were a Disney fawn in the forest, hearing about hunters for the first time. 'So why don't you live here, instead of that poky little place down in the basement?'

'Because I'm too poor, you cretin!'

'*Paige? Paige? Paige?*' A woman's voice could be heard calling agitatedly from the phone.

'Oh, for God's sake!' Ed grabbed it from her hand, pressed the off button, and thrust it back.

Her eyes widened with outrage. 'Excuse me, I was having a very important conversation.'

'Tough. Now help me clear this up.'

She looked flummoxed. 'Shouldn't we, like, call some-one?'

'Brilliant idea. A flood on Sunday evening. By the time anyone arrives my ceiling will have collapsed.' He rushed out of the kitchen, kicking up sprays of water from the flooded floor.

'Oh no!' she shrieked, 'my nail varnish!'

She was wearing Wellington boots when Ed reappeared with a mop and a bucket. 'You get cracking with these,' he ordered brusquely. 'I'll be back in a minute.' He dashed back downstairs, grabbed another bucket and placed it under the sagging part of the ceiling. Somewhere he'd read that water causes the most damage when it accumulates above plaster: the thing to do is to make a hole and let it pour through. He found a screwdriver and, climbing onto a chair, shoved it deep into the centre of damp patch. A jet of water poured down his arm and inside his T-shirt. He uttered a series of curses, hoping that she could hear him through the hole in the ceiling.

Jumping off the chair, he pulled it to one side to allow the stream of water to flow into the bucket. Then he sprinted upstairs again, pausing only to grab the pile of newspapers waiting by the door for the recycling collection. He found Paige vaguely swishing water this way and that with the mop, making it spread even further.

'What the hell do you think you're doing?' demanded Ed. He grabbed the mop and squeezed it out against the inside of the bucket. Then he slapped it onto the floor to collect more water, and repeated the action. 'I suppose you've never mopped a floor before,' he said bitterly. 'In fact I suppose you've never done any housework of any kind.'

'I so have!' she protested, moving out of range. 'Maybe not mopped the floor, but I have done some … stuff.'

Above the Wellingtons her bare legs were long, shapely, and smoothly tanned, dusted with golden hairs. 'Like what?' he demanded savagely and thwacked the sodden mop into the bucket once again.

'Like, um … well … watering flowers!' she said triumphantly.

'Oh yeah, I can see that you're an expert on watering. But for everything else I bet you have some Mexican maid who goes around cleaning up after you.'

'She is not Mexican! She is from Venezuela.'

Ed opened his mouth, then snapped his teeth shut with a click. He couldn't think of a riposte worth of this inanity.

Instead, he snorted derisively, and wrung out the mop one last time. The floor was almost dry.

'Now look,' she said, changing tack. 'I'm sorry about the flood. It was my fault. That was stupid of me, I know. I apologise. I'll pay for any damage caused.'

'You certainly will,' Ed warned grimly.

'I made a mistake, OK? I'm very tired. I've just come back from a weekend in the country ...'

'Poor you.' He upended the bucket into the sink. 'No doubt you were visiting some millionaire's mansion, with flunkeys at your beck and call.'

'Well, I ... I understand why you're so upset.'

'No you don't,' he exploded. 'You don't understand a bloody thing about what it's like to save and struggle and sacrifice to build something, and then have some empty-headed spoilt rich girl come and ruin it. You can't possibly understand that.'

'I am not an empty-headed spoilt rich girl! I am a fine woman actor. With an Oscar. And I've been working *very hard*.' She stuck her fists on her hips, a gesture that made her robe gape open. Jesus Christ, she was naked underneath. He had time to see the milky skin and opulent swelling of her breasts before she clutched the robe tight to her neck. Now he could see the outline of her nipples through the thin material. His mouth was dry. He turned to pick up the mop and drove it furiously into the empty bucket...

'Working? You call that working?'

'Actually, I do, yes. I suspect that you don't know much at all about the kind of work I do.'

'If you mean that I haven't wasted much time watching filmic dross, you're right.' He pumped the mop up and down.

'There's no need to be offensive.'

'Oh, isn't there? I suppose that back in California, people are just delighted when water comes cascading through their ceilings, if the famous *Paige Carson* was responsible.'

She stamped one Wellington boot. 'Quit being so snotty! I'm not asking you to treat me like a movie star – just like a normal human being.'

'Then start behaving like one.'

They glared at one another.

'You know,' said Paige loftily, 'it's lucky you aren't the only Englishman I've met; otherwise I'd have a very poor impression. Fortunately, I've met one, at least, who knows the meaning of good manners.'

'Bully for you. I hope you'll be very happy.' His fingers tightened on the handle of the mop.

She shook her head sorrowfully, causing her towel-turban to slip sideways. 'You have a problem with me, don't you?'

'I have no interest in you whatsoever. If I have a problem, it's with the know-nothing culture you represent. You can't even be trusted to turn off a tap!'

'A what?'

'A tap, for God's sake!'

'You mean a fawcett?'

'Oh Jesus, she can't even speak English. To think, she's coming over here to act Shakespeare!'

'As a matter of fact, in many ways American English is much closer to seventeenth-century English than English English.'

She was right, annoyingly.

'Well, Yankee doodle. How much do you know about seventeenth-century England, I wonder? Who was Oliver Cromwell?'

'He – I – oh, go to hell.'

'I think that is my cue to leave,' he said, picking up the mop and the bucket.

'So soon?' She raised an eyebrow and stood aside to let him pass.

Ed paused, and looked at her sharply. He had the feeling that she was almost enjoying this. And so was he, in a strange way. He smiled. 'Do you know, I think that's the nicest thing you've said to me this evening?'

'It most certainly is not.' She glared at him, arms folded.

He reached for her elbow and swung her round so that they could both see themselves in the hall mirror, visible through the open kitchen door: himself in stained running kit lightly sprinkled with plaster, mop in hand, wet hair standing up in spikes; Paige Carson in a dishevelled robe and wellies, with her towel-turban leaning at a drunken angle. He watched her lift her chin and try to look unconcerned. Then their eyes met in the mirror, and they both burst out laughing.

'Don't think this means I've forgiven you,' he told her.

'I wouldn't dream of it.'

CHAPTER 18

'And here, of course, are the flamingos.' Tudor pointed to a pool where half a dozen pink birds floated nonchalantly under a spot-lit weeping willow.

'Of course.' Paige laughed. 'What else would you expect to see right in the middle of London?'

In fact, nothing about this evening was quite what she'd expected. When Tudor had invited her to a 'birthday bash', she'd imagined that it would be held in a private house, not a noisy nightclub. She'd kept her eyes on the ground when they entered the building, feeling exposed as she always did in public places, and clung to his velvet-jacketed arm as he escorted her into the elevator. It was a shock to be hit with salsa music and a roar of voices when the elevator doors opened again. She had a vague impression of pink banquettes, a silvery bar and funky chandeliers adorned with feathers. Various people greeted Tudor, but he just smiled and waved them aside, devoting himself to her. Then suddenly they were outdoors again, in a rooftop garden lit by hanging lanterns and warmed by patio heaters. Her nerves gradually subsided as they strolled together through vine-covered walkways, past statues, potted palm trees and secret benches. A hundred feet below, London spread out around them in a sea of sparkling lights. Tudor pointed out the golden tower of Big Ben, dwarfed by the silvery wheel of the London Eye, and a distant dome which he told her was

St Paul's Cathedral. 'And this' – he gestured at the immediate neighbourhood – 'is Kensington.' Paige was enchanted. Here at last was the real London.

And Tudor was a real Englishman: refined and respectful. He had picked her up from the apartment right on time, complimented her on her appearance (the Balenciaga cocktail dress and shoes with crystal heels), and driven her here himself in an adorable vintage sports car. In the elevator he'd murmured, 'Don't worry, they don't let the wrong sort in *here*.' Now he whipped a couple of glasses off a passing tray, carried by a Zorro lookalike (the party's theme appeared to be vaguely South American), and handed her a rum punch. Paige raised her eyes to his as she sipped. He smiled back at her, slightly nervous, as if he could hardly believe his luck. That was so sweet. He looked very handsome in his open-necked cream silk shirt. According to Davina, his family owned a castle in Scotland.

Suddenly he staggered forward, reeling from a thump on the back. 'Turdface!' shouted a raucous voice.

'Stewpot!' Tudor responded cheerfully. 'Where've you been hiding, you little squirt? Sorry, Paige. Allow me to introduce you to my thuggish brother Stuart, the black sheep of the family.'

Paige saw a tubby, flushed-faced man with blond hair messily thatched over his forehead and ears.

'Super to meet you.' Stuart thrust a moist hand into hers. 'Thrilled you could come. Total fan, of course. Everyone's dying to meet you.'

'Everyone?' Paige felt alarmed.

'Old chums, family, that sort of thing.' Tudor placed a soothing hand on her back. 'Go on, you run along with Stuart, and I'll catch up with you later. There are a few people I need to speak to.'

Paige pictured him dutifully making the rounds of elderly relatives. 'OK,' she said. 'But don't be too long.'

'Terrifically keen on you, my bro,' Stuart told her as he

steered her back inside. 'Got out all your DVDs before meeting you last weekend. Even looked you up on the net.'

Paige found this faintly disconcerting, then told herself that it was a good sign that Tudor wanted to find out about her career and interests. It showed what a considerate person he was.

She was introduced to a number of people in rapid succession. 'Paige? Americans have such peculiar names!' roared a chubby young man called Rufus Hornyold-Sporran. Everyone seemed to be a cousin of everyone else, and all the men to have been 'at school' together. When Paige, trying to make conversation, remarked on this coincidence, the group she was with burst out laughing. 'School means Eton, you see,' explained a woman who been introduced as the Honourable Tacita Bryze-Norton but whom the others called Ticky. 'I suppose that, being American, you wouldn't know that.' They all laughed again.

Paige had an uncomfortable sense that she was being paraded around like a trophy. The conversations were mainly about who had met whom at which party, and how 'hammered' they had got (this seemed to mean drunk). Everyone seemed to agree that Stuart had done 'awfully well' and was 'awfully clever', though she never found out why. 'Is it *your* birthday, then?' she asked at one point. 'Oh, yah. Sort of,' he'd replied, with an embarrassed grin, mussing up his haystack hair. People she met were either sycophantic or determined not to be impressed. Some of the women cold-shouldered her, as if her very existence were somehow both threatening and offensive. The men were boisterous and rather silly. Either they leered, or went on talking to each other in their own private language as if she were invisible. 'Dropped half a bar last week,' one man announced to another over her head.

Paige looked around desperately. Where was Tudor?

An older woman whom Stuart had introduced as 'Flip' seemed rather nicer than the rest. 'That's a relief,' remarked

Paige after they had been introduced. 'Most of the women I've met here have such complicated names ending in "a", like Laetitia and Prunella and Sybilla.'

The woman smiled kindly. 'I'm sorry to disappoint you,' she said, 'but Flip is short for Philippa.'

'Oh dear,' exclaimed Paige. 'I've goofed, haven't I?'

'Don't give it a second thought,' said Flip. 'I've always hated the name Philippa anyway. Didn't I read that you are playing Rosalind?'

At last someone with a brain, thought Paige. 'Yes, that's right.'

'How are you finding it?'

'I'm enjoying it, but I can't pretend it's easy. Live theatre is very different from film.'

'No Jackson Rolfe, for starters,' commented Flip. 'I'm so looking forward to seeing him in *Arthur the King*. What's he like to work with?'

Paige felt suddenly uneasy. She decided to play it safe. 'It's a privilege to work with such a great artist.'

'Such a great arsehole is what I've been told.'

Paige tried not to laugh. 'We pronounce it asshole in America.'

'Hallo, Flip,' drawled a handsome, square-jawed man who kissed her on both cheeks. 'Up to your old tricks, I see.' Paige noticed his expensively-tailored clothes: a dandy, she decided. On his arm was a busty blonde falling out of a hideous pink dress that ended about mid-thigh in layered flounces.

Flip gave a quick smile and then turned towards Paige. 'Miss Carson, this is Simon Fin, the feared critic, and this is Cosima Gussett.'

Paige shook hands with them both. 'Courageous of you to venture into this menagerie,' said Fin. 'I must say that I'm slightly surprised to see you here without armed guards. I hope you haven't been telling this vulture any secrets.'

'Simon, you're making trouble, as usual,' interrupted Flip. 'Will I see you at Badminton this year?' she asked.

'No, I think not,' answered Fin. 'I've given up field sports. I can't *stand* the people. And if I'm out of London for too long I come up in a beastly rash.' He looked round helplessly at Paige.

'I love your dress,' enthused the blonde woman. 'It's Balenciaga, isn't it? I'm a fashion designer, you see.'

'Oh, right. I like your dress too,' she added lamely.

'Where's the fag corner?' Fin demanded suddenly, taking out a pack of cigarettes and sticking one in his mouth. 'Outside, I suppose. *Vile* nanny state.'

'Ooh, me too.' Flip's eyes lit up, and the three of them simply turned away and left Paige standing.

She was immediately pounced on by two women in their mid-thirties who'd been gazing at her with frank curiosity.

'You're Paige Carson, aren't you?' said the tall, dark-haired one, attractive in a sharp-featured way. 'I'm India Fitzdare, and this is my friend Angelica Dropmore-Trews.' She gestured at her more mousy friend, swathed in printed silk. 'I'm utterly riveted to hear from Tudor that you're living upstairs from Edward Hawkshead.'

'Oh, do you know him?' Paige was slightly surprised that Ed would know anyone at this party.

'Used to, back in the Dark Ages. We were at Oxford together, only he was in the year above. He was an absolute dish back then. I suppose he's fat and bald now.'

'No, he's ... He's not,' said Paige.

'And he had the *sweetest* Northern accent. Yorkshire, I think – or was it Geordie? Do you remember, Licky, how he used to talk about "poonting" instead of punting?'

'*Such* a hoot.'

Paige, who had no idea what they were talking about, said she hadn't noticed any particular accent.

'Well, you wouldn't,' trilled Angelica, 'being an American.'

'We were madly in love.' India Fitzdare sighed nostalgically. 'He was so romantic – always buying me presents he couldn't afford, poor lamb. And do you remember those poems he wrote me, Licks?'

'God, yes. You used to read them out to us. Had us all in fits!'

'So what happened?' asked Paige.

'Well, it was a bit awkward.' India gave a tinkly laugh. 'He wanted us to get *married* – can you believe it?' She puckered up her face and put on a strange accent. "I doon't want to wayest time, India. Ma Farther died young, and I want to get on with ma leaf." The other woman yelped with laughter. 'Of course, it was impossible. We were far too young, and he didn't have any money. Still living in a *basement,* from what I hear. And anyway he was NoC.'

'Enno what?' asked Paige. She definitely didn't like this woman.

'Oh, sorry, you're American, of course you don't understand. NoC means "Not our Class". I mean, he was lovely, but just not the sort of person one could marry. Any more than ...' – she looked around the room for inspiration – 'than Tudor could marry someone who doesn't hunt. It's just impossible, don't you see?'

'I'm beginning to,' said Paige grimly.

'How are you getting on, darling?' Tudor had appeared at her side. 'Ah, I see you've met India. She's married to one of my cousins, you know.'

Paige turned to him with relief, ignoring India's request to 'say "hi" to Ed from me'.

'Come and have a look at what Stuart's been up to,' he said, guiding her across the room. His voice was suave, but Paige detected an inner tension. What was worrying him?

On a table beside his brother was a display of several smart rosewood boxes in various sizes, each inlaid with an onyx device. Stuart picked up one about the size of a laptop computer and handed it to her. 'What do you think?' Paige admired it politely. 'Go on, open it up.' She pressed the brass button on the front which released the top, and was surprised to find a row of banded cigars inside, with a dial like the face of a pocket watch set into the lid. 'It's a humidor, you see.' She offered the box back to him, but while she was still holding it a camera flashed nearby.

'Can I get one of the two of you together?' asked a voice, and Stuart slid his arm around her waist. She squirmed at his touch through the thin material of her dress. 'That's nice. Good. Smile, please.'

'No!' Paige twisted out of Stuart's grip, holding up a protective hand. 'No photographs.'

'Oh, come on, Paige, don't be a spoilsport,' pleaded Tudor.

But Paige banged the humidor back on the table, then pushed through the crowd and out into the garden, Tudor at her heels. She rounded on him, furious. 'What the hell was all that about?'

'Nothing sinister. Calm down. It's Stuart's new business venture: importing luxury humidors from Vietnam. In fact, he's sort of launching it tonight.'

'You told me this was a private party.'

'Did I?' He gave her the slow smile she'd found so charming; now it just looked false. 'It does happen to be Stuart's birthday, and most people here are chums. But, well, he thought he'd celebrate his birthday and launch the business at the same time.'

'And you said you'd help him out with the publicity by bringing me along?'

'Just a few snaps, that's all. What's the problem?'

'He set me up with that woman Flipper or whatever her name is. She's from the press, isn't she?'

'Only *Tatler*,' confessed Tudor.

'That's the only reason you invited me out, isn't it? It was a publicity stunt.'

'Of course not.' But his sheepish expression gave him away.

'I bet you never saw *Angel in the Dirt*.'

'I'd *like* to ...'

'For all I know you could be married – probably to some cousin called the Honourable Britannia Hunting-Boot. God, I've been stupid! I'm going home now.'

'If you're absolutely sure.' His tone was cool. 'I'll call you a cab. Obviously I must stay and support my brother.'

He wasn't even going to escort her back!

'I'll call my own cab.' Outraged, Paige strode back into the club, where everyone was listening to Stuart, who stood on a chair giving a speech. 'We're so delighted that Paige Carson was able to join us tonight,' he was saying, 'all the way from Hollywood. I'm sure we all remember her in *Biker Boys*, eh?' Paige pushed through the chortling crowd. 'Are you leaving so soon, Paige?' he bayed after her. 'Byee!'

As she collected her coat from the cloakroom, Paige realised that she had no money, because she'd been expecting Tudor to take her back after the party, and no one to call for help. How far was Islington from Kensington?

As she stepped into the street outside several things seemed to happen at once. She heard a shout of 'over here, Paige,' and looked up, to be blinded by the flash of a camera. She'd been set up. She spun away, and saw that a miracle was speeding towards her in the shape of an available taxi. Putting a thumb and finger in her mouth she emitted an expert, unladylike whistle. The cab glided to a halt beside her. Paige yanked open the door as another flash-gun popped, and scrambled into the back. 'Islington!' she ordered as the cab sped away from the kerb.

'Blimey, what was all that about?' asked the driver. 'You famous or something?'

'I'm Paige Carson,' she announced.

'Means nothing to me, I'm afraid.'

Normally she might be peeved not to be recognised, but this was a relief. She leaned forward, addressing the back of his head. 'I'm a movie actress.'

'Oh well, that explains it. I don't watch films or TV. Load

o' rubbish, innit? I prefer the theatre. In fact, I'm a bit of an actor myself.'

'Really?'

'A lot of people have told me I should go professional.'

'Is that so?' Paige raised her eyebrows in the darkness.

'But it's no life, is it? Out of work, most of the time. Driving a cab I'm my own boss, see. I can tread the boards whenever I fancy. Shakespeare, mainly.'

'No kidding?'

'There's a cabbies' Shakespeare circle, you know. Small but select.'

'Do you know *As You Like It*?'

The driver cleared his throat. '"All the world's a stage, And all the men and women merely players; They have their exits and their entrances, And one man in his time plays many parts …"'

'"His acts being seven ages",' continued Paige, laughing. 'This is so weird! I'm playing Rosalind, starting in two weeks' time.'

'Smashing part, that. I played Orlando once. Course, I was younger then, but I'll always remember the time …'

He talked about himself non-stop. It was rather soothing. Paige was beginning to relax when the driver interrupted his monologue. 'We're being followed!' he exclaimed in disgust. 'See that motorbike? Unless I'm a total wally, which I'm not, that bloke on the back is the photographer. Paparazzi, they call themselves.'

Paige turned her head and peered into the darkness. There was a bike carrying two men a few yards behind. She hunched low in her seat and turned up the collar of her coat, remembering Davina's warning: the British paps were the worst in the world.

When the cab turned into her street the motorbike followed, its single headlight glaring through the cab's rear window, its throaty roar audible above the softer chug of the taxi engine. Rummaging in her bag, Paige found her house key and held it ready in one hand. She told the driver where to stop and slid forward to place her other hand on the door-handle of the cab, poised for a speedy escape. However, she had reckoned without the cab's locking system. Only after squeezing the handle several times did it finally click and release, by which time the photographer was already in position. When the cab door swung open she caught a momentary glimpse of him before being blinded by a series of flashes. The sleazebag was actually lying on the sidewalk, practically at her feet, with his camera tilted for an upskirt shot. She lurched awkwardly from the cab, trying to keep her knees together, one arm flung up to shield her face.

The camera shutter whirred. Bright spots danced before her eyes. Suddenly a figure loomed from nowhere, right in her path. Paige screamed, even as she recognised Ed emerging onto the street carrying a garbage sack.

'What the hell is going on?' he demanded.

'Oi, my fare!' yelled the cab driver.

'Give us a smile, darling.'

In a panic Paige ran up her steps, caught her heel and tripped so heavily that the shoe was wrenched off her foot. Scrambling upright, she aimed her key at the lock and pushed it home. Shit! It wouldn't turn. The cab horn was blasting. The motorbike engine growled. There was a clash of angry voices at her back – all male, all shouting.

'Leave me *alone*!' she screeched. Then the lock turned, and the door fell open. She stumbled inside and slammed it shut.

CHAPTER 19

Ed opened his front door and blinked. Sunshine was streaming down into the basement well. He could feel it warm his back as he locked up and jammed the keys into his jeans pocket. Invigorated, he bounded up the steps two at a time, grabbed a railing at the top and swung himself out into the street. It was lateish on Saturday morning. Maddy and Lilly were coming to lunch and the cupboard was bare, so he was off to Chapel Street market. He clapped a palm to his chest, feeling the reassuring wodge of folded banknotes in his shirt pocket, and slid his sunglasses into place.

The curtains and shutters of the upstairs flat were open. He glanced in through the kitchen window as he passed, but there was no sign of his tenant. He wondered if she'd calmed down after last night's little drama. It was a bit much when one couldn't even put out the rubbish without finding photographers snapping away, motorbikes roaring, and people shouting. She'd even shouted at *him* – when he'd been trying to help! Next time he wouldn't bother. And he'd learned his lesson: don't rent to famous people.

But the image of her fleeing up the steps like a hunted deer, all long legs and frightened eyes, lingered uncomfortably in his mind. No woman should be chased like that. She'd been in such a panic that she'd even lost a shoe. He'd retrieved it from the gutter and placed it on his desk, ready to return to her. All morning, while he was tidying the flat, it kept catching his eye, making him wonder where she'd gone last night, and who with, and what had happened to make her dash home alone – and how anyone could walk in such flimsy and fantastical footgear – until he'd had to hide the wretched thing behind an armchair so he could get on with his chores.

Ed paused at a pedestrian crossing and absently pushed the button. Paige Carson was none of his business. She lived in a completely different world. He could have nothing in common with someone whose best friend was Davina (Maddy had shown him a gossip item about Paige and Davina playing darts – darts! – in some Wiltshire pub). And yet he felt involved, even vaguely responsible. After all, she was a foreigner, and a guest (albeit paying) in his house. In her terms, it had probably been quite brave to come to London alone and live in an ordinary flat, without the apparatus of protection she was used to. He wouldn't want her to get the wrong idea about England and the English. Her jibe about there being '*some* Englishmen with good manners' rankled. Perhaps he had not been an absolute model of courtesy. Of course, it was perfectly reasonable to be angry about the flood – who wouldn't be? But to be fair, she'd put a handwritten note through his letter-box the next day, apologising for the damage and insisting that the repair bills be sent to her. The note had been surprisingly well-phrased, without a single spelling mistake. She was at least trying. It would be churlish not to meet her halfway – if the occasion arose. Which it probably wouldn't. Thank God.

Ah, asparagus, the first of the season. He had now arrived at the top end of Chapel Street, which was closed to traffic on market days and packed instead with stalls selling fruit and veg, fresh fish, jellied eels, bolts of cloth, African carvings, hippie-style dresses, cheap shoes, and the best apple fritters in the world, cooked on the spot in a vat of oil before being tossed in sugar and placed, steaming, in a paper bag. Ed could already smell them. He headed for the stall, pausing to examine prices and produce while concocting his lunchtime menu. Lilly, having been forced from an early age to eat what Maddy was eating or starve, was a reasonably adventurous eater. He might try her on asparagus, to be dipped into a buttery-lemony sauce and eaten with fingers, followed by sea-bass steamed with ginger and lemongrass, accompanied by crispy sauteed potatoes. Any failures would, he hoped, be redeemed by a chocolate and hazelnut torte, purchased from the Italian deli.

Ed enjoyed cooking, when he had the time and someone to cook for, and he found the selection of ingredients almost as pleasurable. As a boy he'd often had to shop and prepare food for his mother, especially after she was widowed and working so hard to establish her teaching career. It made him smile now to remember her lavish praise when he had presented her with his first attempt at supper: overcooked chicken drumsticks, lumpy mashed potato and watery peas, plus a sticky trail of destruction in the kitchen. His mother was on his mind. The next school term would be her last, and though she joked about becoming a lady of leisure, and kept telling Ed how much she would enjoy seeing more theatre and attending literary festivals – perhaps even join the National Trust at its special OAP rate – he knew her too well to be taken in. But it was not until this morning, when he had rung to suggest that he visited her over the forthcoming Easter weekend, and heard her voice bounce up an octave, that he had truly appreciated the depth of her unhappiness. He should have gone long before, but the drive took at least five hours in each direction and there always seemed to be something to keep him in London: a deadline, a party, a repair to the flat and, most recently, the Grapevine deal.

This was one reason Maddy was coming over today. It was impossible to discuss the subject in the office. The plan was to have lunch, then park Lilly at a children's workshop in the local puppet theatre so that the two of them could talk in peace. Ed already knew that he wanted to say no. His telephone conversation with Wolfe earlier in the week had not gone well. He had planned to persuade Wolfe to change his stance about Maddy's future, but instead Wolfe had steered the conversation onto the necessity for Hawkshead Barry's films to sell to foreign buyers, particularly of course to the Americans. Ed was damned if he was going to sanitise his work just so that it would appeal to the bloody Yanks. Possibly he had been a bit rude to Wolfe. Well, so what? Ed popped an apple fritter into his mouth and chewed defiantly. He didn't like being told what to do. He liked things as they were: just him and Maddy.

Yes, Maddy was the real reason he didn't like the deal. He wanted to protect her from the knowledge that Grapevine did not want her as part of the sale package. Maddy was important to him. She would never dream of interfering with the creative side of the business. He couldn't imagine working without her. If he succeeded in nudging her towards a negative decision, over a delicious lunch and plenty of wine, he'd never even have to tell her that Grapevine didn't want her. It would be a perfect outcome. He'd keep his independence; she'd keep her job and her self-respect. There'd be no cash, of course, but money wasn't everything. He was prepared to make the sacrifice, for Maddy's sake.

Ed was still busy justifying this course of action to himself as he completed his purchases in the market and then followed a meandering route home through a cobbled pedestrian passage lined with antique shops and chic eateries, which always provided diversion on a sunny Saturday. Sure enough, his eye was caught by a little pantomime being enacted a few yards ahead, where the proprietor of one of the antique shops was ushering a customer from his premises with so much bowing and scraping that it was evident he had just made a spectacular sale – presumably the ludicrous gilded cage with a stuffed bird inside that swung from the customer's hand. Female, of course. In fact – it was Paige

Carson! He stopped dead, paralysed by conflicting emotions: irritation that famous people somehow thought they would 'blend in' if they wore a baseball cap; a shock of pleasure at the way she looked, in white jeans and a stylish leather jacket, wrapped tight at her waist; and anxiety about how he should behave. As well as the cage, she held a cluster of large shopping bags: how was she going to get those home? He stepped forward automatically to help, then remembered her furious demand last night to be left alone, and stopped again. He did not wish to intrude. Anyway, there was no time to dawdle; Maddy and Lilly were due at his flat at any minute. Yet he couldn't simply ignore her. He dodged behind a news-stand and surreptitiously observed her over the blaring headline of the *Daily Mail* ('Is Celeb Culture Degrading Our Morals?').

The antiques proprietor had now re-entered his shop and shut the door with a final leer of deepest gratitude. Ed watched Paige peer uncertainly down the passage one way, then the other, hesitate, then set off purposefully in the exact opposite direction to the house. Birdbrain! Idiot! The carrier bags were banging against her knees. She was clearly struggling. Serve her right for buying up half of London. And yet … Apprehension showed in her face as passers-by turned to stare. She put her nose in the air and strode straight towards him. What if she looked up and saw him gawping like one of her mindless 'fans'? Absurdly, his heart was hammering. At the last moment, he stepped smoothly into her oncoming path. 'Doctor Livingstone, I presume.'

Shopping! There was nothing like it to give you a high, thought Paige, or to restore your self-esteem when life kicked you in the teeth. Tudor had turned out to be as much of a jerk as Calvin. She wasn't having much luck with her quest for a man. On waking this morning she had considered spending the entire weekend hidden behind closed shutters, wallowing in misery. But, hell, why should she? This was her free time. The sun was shining, and when she tentatively opened a window a warm breeze flowed in, bringing with it the chatter of people in the street and the buzz of a big city out to enjoy itself.

Apparently there were lots of cool stores in Islington, as Fizz had made abundantly clear when Paige had asked how long it would take to get to Harrods. ('What do you want to go there for? Nothing but chavs and tourists.' Paige hadn't quite grasped what a 'chav' was: possibly the urban equivalent of a 'grockle', but she had registered that it wasn't good.) No, Islington was the place to shop. As well as the street stalls where you could buy rip-off Chanel bags for ten dollars, there were designer boutiques, galleries and an antiques market that operated on Saturdays, practically on her doorstep. Paige accordingly armed herself with credit cards, travellers' cheques and map, put on her usual street disguise, and set out to explore.

After two weeks of walking to and from rehearsals she was becoming more confident about going out in public. In an attempt to avoid people she had found her own route to rehearsals, which took her through quiet backstreets and across a churchyard, shaded by trees that grew greener and lusher with each passing day. Certain faces were becoming familiar: the people who worked at the health food store, the woman who walked her Highland terrier every morning, even the tramp who had so terrified her on the first day of rehearsals. He had not been talking to himself about a shoe, Paige had discovered, but trying to sell her a magazine called *The Big Issue*. According to Fizz, this had been set up to help homeless people, who could buy the magazine at half its cover price and make themselves a profit by selling copies on the street. Paige thought this sounded better than Welfare, and had daringly bought a copy the next time she saw the guy, who turned out to be perfectly harmless and now gave her a friendly greeting whenever she passed. He seemed to know all about the Old Fire Station

Theatre and why Paige was in London, but treated her like a neighbourhood customer rather than a star. It still seemed peculiar, though, that very rich and very poor people lived side-by-side in the same part of town. For it had gradually dawned on her that Islington was not the crummy slum she had first perceived, a realisation driven home by the startling property prices advertised in realtors' windows (or estate agents, as the British quaintly called them). She'd seen plenty of old run-down homes on sale for five million dollars and more – and they didn't even have swimming-pools!

England was not cheap, that was for sure. But this morning she was having a ball, as the money drained from her bank account and the shopping bags mounted up. She could even tell herself that this was 'ethical' shopping: antiques were a form of recycling, right? The network of cobbled streets and arcades was a treasure-trove of old furniture, glass, paintings, porcelain, toys, vintage clothing and jewellery. She bought a fabulous Spode tea service for Mom, which was being shipped home, as were the two original movie posters she'd found for Nathan, who collected such things. For Gaby she'd picked out a vintage Dior three-quarter-length coat, white of course, that would be perfect for chilly Californian evenings. The best part was that she'd be able to give it to her personally, since Gaby was flying over for the opening night of *As You Like It*. In between these lavish purchases Paige had picked up a few minor items for herself, but it was the music-box store that was her downfall.

She'd been attracted inside by the sound of birdsong, and was enchanted to find that it came from a mechanical bird perched on a branch of fake apple-blossom within a gold cage. There were at least a dozen similar cages dotted around the shop. It was hard to say why she was so smitten, except that the birds were charming and cheery and she was lonely. Noticing her interest, the proprietor explained that they were nineteenth-century and French, and pointed out the exquisite workmanship in the feathering of the birds and the perfection of the mechanism. Prices started at four thousand dollars. Paige hummed and hawed for at least an hour before settling on the most beautiful cage, with a gorgeous red bird that would sing all day if you wanted, and a porcelain panel set into the base, depicting a pair of lovers. No, she didn't want it delivered or wrapped, she would take it home now, just as it was.

This was easier said than done. The cage was heavy, and she was already laden with her other packages. She'd forgotten to pull her sunglasses down from her head before loading herself up and had no hands free to do so, which made her feel vulnerable. And now she'd gotten all turned around and was not absolutely sure which way led home. To make everything worse, the bad-tempered man from downstairs suddenly stepped right in front of her and made a snotty remark that she didn't get.

'Hello,' she said warily.

'I see you've been hitting the shops.'

Was that a jibe? With several thousand dollars' worth dangling from her hand she could hardly deny the charge. 'Yes, I – I have,' she admitted defiantly.

'Well, do carry on, by all means. But if by any chance you were on your way back to the house, it's that way.' He pointed back in the direction she'd just come.

'Oh.' Now she felt a fool. 'Thank you.'

'Perhaps I could help you with your parcels – if that wouldn't be an intrusion?'

Paige couldn't tell if this was a snide comment or a genuine offer. He appeared to be smiling, but since he was wearing sunglasses she couldn't read his expression. Maybe her hair was sticking out and he was just laughing at her. But her arms ached. It would be silly to reject his help if they were both walking the same way. She held out the birdcage. 'You could carry this for me – if you dare.'

'Why? Does it bite?'

He surprised a smile out of her. 'No. I mean, it's just not very … masculine.'

'I'll survive. And give me that carrier bag as well. You can take this instead.' He plopped a small paper bag into her hand. 'Apple fritters. Help yourself.'

They walked side by side in awkward silence. A tantalising smell rose from the bag, but he made her too nervous to eat.

'I'm sorry about the trouble you had last night,' he said at last.

Paige flushed with embarrassment. No doubt she'd looked ridiculous tripping over her own front steps. 'I apologise for the disturbance.'

'No, it's me that should apologise. It's quite wrong that you should be harassed like that when staying in my house. I told those low-lifes on the motorbike to fuck right off.'

'Yeah, I imagine you'd be pretty good at that.' She shot him a sideways glance to see how he'd take this, and didn't know whether to be pleased or sorry when he looked abashed. 'It's the cab driver I feel bad about,' she hurried on. 'I never paid him. And he was such a nice man, too.'

'Don't you worry, the matter's been dealt with. Careful, there's a car coming,' he added, as she was about to step off the kerb.

'Do you mean *you* paid him?' she asked once they were safely across the street.

'Yeah. It's no problem.'

Paige was disconcerted by this new, polite Ed. 'First I flood your house, now you're paying my cab fares. You must let me reimburse you.'

'I wouldn't dream of it. It's entirely due to our nasty gutter press that you were put in such an unpleasant situation. As an Englishman, I bear some responsibility. I must be allowed to make this small gesture of apology. And we'll forget about the flood, shall we?'

'I will if you will.' She smiled at him, and for the first time he smiled back properly. Maybe he didn't totally despise her after all. He looked a lot more attractive when he wasn't scowling. She liked his shirt, one of those subtly striped affairs, worn casually over slim jeans. She noticed that his sunglasses were an expensive brand. It occurred to her that Ed 'I am an intellectual' Hawkshead might be the teensiest bit vain.

'Oh look,' she said, spying a familiar figure on the street-corner ahead. 'Can we stop for a second?'

'Don't be shy, give it a try!' the *Big Issue* seller called out to passers-by. When he saw Paige he expertly flipped a magazine from the pile under his arm and waited while she reached into her pocket for coins. 'No rehearsals today, then?' he asked. She made some standard reply, noticing that Ed was looking at her with surprise, his eyes speculative. 'Tweet, tweet,' the man added to the bird.

'It only speaks French,' Paige told him, and felt disproportionately pleased when Ed laughed. As they walked on down the street she decided to try one his apple fritters. It was delicious.

'So ... did you have a good time last night?' Ed enquired. 'I mean, prior to the, er, photographer incident. Obviously.'

She shrugged, and waited to swallow her mouthful. 'It was OK.'

'A date, was it?'

She glanced at him, wondering why he was so curious. Should she be on her guard? 'I *thought* it was a date,' she confessed, deciding to trust him, 'but it turned out to be more of a publicity stunt. My mistake.'

'What happened?'

'Oh ... some guy I hardly know invited me to a party. I thought it was private, but he'd tipped off the press. Really, it's no big deal.' Absently she took another bite of fritter.

'Do you mean to say someone set the hounds on you and then left you to escape as best you could?'

'Happens all the time.'

'Not an Englishman, I hope … The one whose manners you compared so unfavourably with my own? Not having much luck, are you?'

'Oh, I don't know,' she countered, licking grains of sugar from her fingers. She wondered whether to mention that she had met India Fitzdare at the party, but had an instinct that this would be a bad move. Better not, she decided. 'People like Paige Carson,' she continued, 'but they don't always like me.'

'How odd. The funny thing is, I quite like you – it's Paige Carson I can't stand.'

Paige's eyes flew wide in protest. It was startling to be spoken to so directly. But she could see from his face that he had simply spoken his thoughts aloud. It was sort of flattering. He 'quite liked' her, did he? Well, maybe she 'quite liked' him, too. He was forthright, but he was honest. She was beginning to catch his sense of humour. Plus he looked damned sexy, even with a gold birdcage.

'Tell me more about your films, Ed,' she said. 'Do you have any on tape that I could borrow?'

He began to tell her about his Bafta-winning *The End of Reason,* and they were deep in an enjoyable argument about whether modern Kabbalah was rubbishy nonsense (Ed) or a powerful tool for activating human potential (Paige – largely quoting Gaby) when the house came in sight. A woman was just emerging from the basement well. 'You bastard!' she called to Ed as she strode towards them. 'We've been waiting for hours.' But she was grinning, and when she was close enough she hooked an arm familiarly round Ed's neck and kissed him.

So that's how it was. Paige felt deflated. The woman was pretty, too – and she had a child. A girl of about six or seven, wearing a red sweater with an appliquéd kitten, had followed her mother as far as the top of the steps, where she stood transfixed, staring at Paige.

'We thought you must have forgotten about us,' the woman said pointedly to Ed.

'Of course I hadn't forgotten, Maddy. I've been out buying your lunch.'

Maddy glanced at the birdcage in his hand.

'It's my fault,' Paige cut in. 'I met Ed on my way back from a shopping splurge and he very kindly offered to help carry my packages. I'm afraid I slowed him down. I'm Paige Carson, by the way.' She held out her hand.

'I know. I'm Maddy, Ed's partner.' The woman eyed her with curiosity. 'I'm glad to see that you two are speaking.'

'Oh – the flood, you mean?'

'Bugger! I've forgotten the lemons,' Ed burst out.

It was agreed that he would race back to the nearest greengrocer, just around the corner, leaving Paige's shopping as well as his own on Paige's doorstep. 'I'll only be a moment,' he added, and dashed off, leaving the two women awkwardly together.

'Is that your bird?' asked a penetrating voice.

Paige saw that the little girl had sidled to her mother's side. Maddy introduced her as Lilly.

Lilly gazed up into Paige's face with round, worshipful eyes. 'You're Miss Lovejoy, aren't you?'

'Well, yes, sort of. I made a kids' movie a couple of years ago,' she explained to Maddy. 'Miss Lovejoy is a schoolteacher with magical powers.'

'I know.' Paige wasn't sure how to read Maddy's noncommittal tone.

'Can I play with your bird? Does it talk?'

'No, you can't, Lilly,' said Maddy. 'It's not a toy. I'm sure it's very valuable.'

'No, that's OK.' Paige was determined to show that she wasn't a standoffish movie star. 'Why don't you come in for a moment and I'll show you how it works?' Without waiting for a reply, she unlocked her door, picked up the bird and led the way into the kitchen. Lilly followed, holding

Maddy's hand. Paige placed the birdcage on the kitchen table and released the ratchet that set the bird singing. The little girl watched, enraptured, then pressed her lips to the bars and sang back. Paige caught Maddy's eye, and they smiled at each other over Lilly's head.

'Mum,' asked Lilly, dragging at Maddy's sleeve, 'can she come to my birthday party? Please please *please* ...'

'I'm sure that Miss Lovejoy is far too busy to come to your party,' said Maddy.

Before Paige could decide how to respond there was a shout from the street. Ed stood outside the window, waving to be let in. He must already have deposited the lemons in his own flat, for there was something else in his hand that caught Paige's attention.

'Here you go, Cinderella,' he said, when she opened her front door to him, and handed her the crystal-heeled shoe she thought she'd lost last night. 'At least, I assume it's yours.' His grey eyes glinted with mischief. 'It says "Marc Jacobs" inside. Perhaps it belongs to a transvestite?'

Paige gave a spluttering laugh. Why had he decided to be charming, just when she'd discovered he wasn't available? 'Marc Jacobs is a brilliant fashion designer,' she told him reprovingly. 'Don't you know anything?'

'Guess what, Ed? Paige is coming to my birthday party,' Lilly announced from the kitchen doorway.

'Are you?' Ed looked at Paige in astonishment. But she also detected a hint of approval. So although she'd never intended doing any such thing she answered, 'Yes, I am.'

CHAPTER 20

'Not "twenny", ducky – *twenty*. Enunciate!'

Paige took a breath and tried the line again. '"Ay, and *twentee* such."'

'No need to overdo it. The words should simply *r-r-ripple* off the tongue. Shouldn't they, Albert?' Paige's dialect coach stroked the obese white cat on her lap, whose unblinking eyes watched Paige with contempt.

This was her third session with the 'brilliant' Joan Gilbert, known as Gilly. Paige couldn't say that she was enjoying the experience. Gilly's flat, where the sessions were held, was situated on the sixth floor of a hideous old red-brick building in Bloomsbury, known as a 'mansion block', though anything less like a mansion would be hard to imagine. From the outside it looked like a maximum-security prison. The inside was old and shabby, and had the tiniest elevator Paige had ever seen, with a folding metal door that you had to shut yourself. It rose so slowly, and with so many groans and clankings, that Paige feared each moment would be her last. The flat smelled of cat and boiled fish. Coaching took place in Gilly's living-room, a theatrical affair of Persian-style carpets, fringed standard lamps, and framed photographs of actors, signed with fulsome tributes. Gilly herself was at least seventy, with iron-grey hair chopped off at jaw-level and a bad hip. She conducted proceedings from a brown corduroy armchair liberally speckled with cat hairs, and had so far proved impossible to please.

The first time Paige had turned up (with a bottle of gin, as advised by Fizz), Gilly's greeting had been discouragingly forthright. 'American, are you? Never mind. In you come.' At her request, Paige had stood by the window and declaimed one of Rosalind's speeches in her best English accent. Gilly had listened with her head thrown back, eyes closed in concentration, and at the end said, 'Lah-di-bloody-dah, darling. I can see we've got our work cut out.'

They began with tongue-twisters. A proper copper coffee-pot. Three grey geese in a green field grazing. Freshly fried fresh flesh. 'Move your lips!' Gilly would bark from her armchair. 'Let us have some precision. Faster! ... And again.' Next, they'd moved on to the rhythm of the language; 'never mind the meaning for now.' Gilly would tap out the beat on her coffee-table with a pencil, and make Paige go over and over the same speech: on the beat, ahead of it, behind. Speaking Shakespeare's lines was like playing jazz, she said. With jazz you knew the tune, you had a basic rhythm; but by themselves these were inert. It was the improvisation of the human artist, musician or actor, which provided the emotional energy that touched the hearts of the audience. Energy, Gilly reminded her dryly, did not mean shouting.

Today they were working on the scene in which Rosalind, pretending to be a boy who is pretending to be Rosalind, flirted and joked with Orlando. It was a key scene but also one of the most difficult, full of puns and lightning changes of mood. No matter what she did, Paige could not seem to get it right. 'Stop bloody acting,' Gilly told her. 'Be natural.' In the hope of striking 'some faint spark of spontaneity', as she put it, Gilly made Paige repeat her lines while standing on a chair, then to sing them, then to dance them.

Paige felt hotter and more inadequate with each passing moment. And she was getting annoyed. She was Paige Carson. People paid millions of dollars for her talent. The fact that she'd accepted peanuts for this particular role did not make her a performing monkey. '"O ... that thou didst know ... how many fathom deep I am in love,"' she trilled, tittupping idiotically round the room and flapping like a swan trying to take off, before coming to a faltering halt in front of the brown corduroy chair, one toe pointed and her arms held ballerina-style above her head.

Gilly closed her eyes as if in pain. 'Gawd, darling, haven't you ever been in love?'

'Of course I have! Lots of times.'

Gilly regarded her sceptically.

'Well, not recently, maybe.' Paige folded her arms across her chest. 'Anyway, so what? It's only a play. It's not real. '

Gilly said nothing, but continued to stare in that irritating manner.

'OK – I haven't had a boyfriend in over a year. Is that what you want to hear? Nobody likes me. They think I'm a spoilt princess. They think I'm stupid. Or else all they want is a piece of my fame. You're right, I'm no good at this stuff.' She grabbed her script from the windowsill and hurled it across the room. 'I can't act. I can't talk properly. I don't know a thing about love.' Paige's eyes filled with tears. She turned her head away. 'I'm sorry ... I'm just tired. I didn't have any breakfast ...' She gave a loud sniff.

'All right, ducky,' Gilly said quietly. 'You have a nice sit-down on the sofa. Albert and I will fetch you a little something from the kitchen.' Pushing the cat off her lap, she heaved herself out of the armchair and limped out of the room.

Paige sat on the edge of the couch, trying to compose herself. What was wrong with her? She felt so alone. There was no one to turn to. No Gaby – or Nathan or Heather or Akira, not even Concepcion. She wasn't talking to Dad, and Mom never listened anyway. Everything and everyone here was strange. Even Davina was different, now that she was married. Paige buried her face in her hands. She'd been crazy to come to England. All that was waiting for her here was another big fat failure.

'Here we go. Choccy biccy and a nice glass of orange juice,' Gilly's voice rasped at her shoulder.

Paige straightened up and shook back her hair. 'Oh ... thanks.' The juice was not freshly squeezed and tasted peculiar, but of course oranges didn't grow in England. The 'biccy' was a cookie covered in forbidden chocolate, which she nibbled out of politeness. It was stale. She washed it down with more juice.

Gilly lowered herself stiffly into her armchair. Paige stared at the gaudily patterned carpet, too embarrassed by her outburst to meet Gilly's eye.

'You think I'm an old tartar, don't you?' said Gilly. 'Well, I am. All my lovely boys and girls have felt just like you.' She gestured at the photos on the wall. 'Every one of them has wanted to throw something at me, and plenty of them have. But I know what I'm doing, and I get results. You're going to have to trust me.'

'OK,' Paige said slowly. She set down her empty glass, then bent to pick her script off the floor and smoothed its crumpled pages.

'There's really nothing complicated about Rosalind,' continued Gilly. 'She's just a larky girl who's fallen in love. Clever old Shakespeare contrived a plot whereby Orlando can discover that she's not a virtuous goddess on a pedestal (silly chump) but a real person, with thoughts and desires of her own. Dressed as a man, she can let herself go as a woman. As soon as you do the same, you'll be home and dry. Find love, and you'll find the key to the part.'

Paige frowned as she digested this. 'Are you saying I should get myself a lover?'

'It's an idea.'

'Are you crazy? We open in ten days' time. I'm working day and night. How would I even find anyone?'

'I daresay there's somebody handy lying about. It shouldn't be difficult for a pretty girl like you.'

'You'd be surprised.' Paige glowered.

'Well, it's up to you, of course. But to my mind you'd do a lot better to stop thinking about acting and accents, and start feeling like a woman. Nothing like a bit of sex to give you some oomph.'

'I'll bear that in mind.'

'Good girl. Feeling better now? Ready to continue?'

'Er, yes. Sure. Actually, I'm feeling a lot better.'

'Thought you might. Albert and I put a little drop of gin in your juice.'

The morning session was just finishing by the time a cab dropped Paige back at the rehearsal studio. As she pushed open the front door, she met Orlando wheeling his bicycle towards her down the hallway, pursued by Fizz who was shouting something about Health and Safety regulations. Paige held the door open for him, and he gave her a wink as he made his escape.

'Honestly, Paige, you shouldn't help him.' Fizz regarded her balefully. 'I've told him a million times he can't keep his bike in here.'

'Oops,' said Paige unapologetically. Fizz rolled her eyes.

'Anyway, how did the rehearsal go?' Paige asked. 'Who's here? Did anyone miss me?'

'I did,' drawled a voice, as the door to the rehearsal room opened and Harry Keenan's eel-like frame slithered through. 'Julian's been absolutely bloody. He's threatening to sack me if I don't learn my lines.'

'You liar!' Fizz laughed. 'He picked you up on one tiny slip. Harry was fantastic,' she added to Paige. 'Really good.'

'Harry's always fantastic.'

'Well, I'm feeling very hurt.' Harry wriggled his shoulders moodily. 'I need a drink.'

Fizz and Paige exchanged glances. Harry always needed a drink.

'Who's coming to the pub?' Hands in pockets, he swivelled from one to the other.

'Not me,' Fizz sighed. 'I'm on phone duty. Oh! Fantastic news, Paige. Bryan Candy wants you on his show next week. The publicity's really hotting up. Ticket sales are going like a bomb.'

Paige felt a punch of panic. 'Who's Bryan Candy?' she asked

'A complete pillock.'

'Shut up, Harry. *Bryan Candy Live* is *the* big TV chat show over here, Paige. I'll run it past your publicist first, of course, but I'm sure she'll be up for it.'

'Well ...' At this moment the idea of going on television and having to 'be marvellous' made Paige feel sick.

'Darling one, are we going to the pub or not?' Harry demanded.

'Sure. Let's go.' Paige suddenly felt eager to escape. 'You've got some catching up to do,' she added. 'I've spent the entire morning drinking gin.'

The pub, on a quiet side-street a block or two away, was exactly Paige's idea of what an English pub should be: old, covered in ivy, with panelled rooms, a fireplace and a friendly barman who called her 'love'. She felt safe walking there beside Harry. They attracted a few glances, but no one bothered them. She might even have dispensed with her sunglasses – except that the day was actually sunny, for once. Although she hardly ever drank alcohol at lunchtime – and never spirits – somehow she let Harry buy her another gin to go with her spinach and goat's cheese pie, or 'ghastly vegetarian muck', as he called it. It was, she acknowledged, a gruesome combination, but she was so absorbed in talking to Harry that she hardly noticed.

She'd gone to the pub with him before, but always in company, usually with his little fat friend, Sid. Together the two men were a hilarious double-act of non-stop jokes, reminiscences of theatrical disasters, and wild tales of girls pursued, persuaded, evaded and lost. Being alone with Harry was quite different: more intense, more intimate. Despite his age, he was a very attractive man, and a terrific flirt. They sat opposite one another at a small corner table, gossiping about other members of the cast. Eventually she plucked up the courage to ask him how he thought she was doing. 'The nearer I get to opening night, the more scared I feel. I guess you've gotten over that, with all the stage work you've done, but—'

'Gotten over it?' Harry interrupted, eyebrows rocketing. 'Are you out of your tiny mind? There is nothing on earth more frightening than opening a play. My knees knock, my bowels are tied in triple knots, my tongue feels like a flannel. I hear nasty voices in my head: *Over-reached yourself this time, haven't you, matey? ... Such a pity you never actually learned to act ... Dear oh dear, and I thought this was supposed to be a comedy...*'

'Really? You feel that way too?' Paige was shocked.

'Every time.'

'It must get better.'

'It gets worse.'

They stared at each other, locked in silent contemplation of this terrible truth.

'Well, thanks,' Paige told him. 'That's really pepped me up.'

'What we need is another drink.' Harry started to straighten from his gloomy slump, like a collapsed marionette jerking into life.

'No, it's my turn.'

Paige stood at the bar and ordered a pint of best bitter for Harry. It might help if he was a little softened by alcohol before she made her move. Her pulse quickened. Was she doing the right thing? Fleetingly she thought of Ed. But she pushed the image of his amused grey eyes and sardonic smile from her mind. He wasn't free. Harry, on the other hand, was fair game.

'Guess what Gilly told me this morning,' she said to Harry, setting his pint glass on the table.

'Terrifying woman.' Harry shuddered. 'Breathes fire. Is that beastly cat thing of hers still alive?'

Paige sat down, leaned her elbows on the table and fixed her eyes on Harry's face. 'She told me that I didn't know enough about love, and I wouldn't be able to play Rosalind until I did.'

'Interfering old bat.'

'She thinks I need a lover.'

'Does she indeed?'

'I think she could be right.' Paige looked at him steadily. 'What do you say, Harry?'

For a long time he said nothing. His long fingers twitched, as if summoning up words. 'My darling girl,' he sighed. 'I'm a thousand years old. I drink too much. And I love my wife.'

'Your *wife*?' Paige recoiled in shock.

'We're not married, in actual fact. I only call her my wife to annoy her. But we've been together for a hundred and seventeen years, or whatever it is. More or less. On and off. Fairly on, at present.'

'But I thought – Sid said –' She didn't know where to look. How could she be so stupid?

'Ah yes, Sid. We go back a long way. He knows I haven't always been a good ... "partner".' Harry released the word in a gust of disapproval. 'In fact I've been a bit of a bastard – well, not so much a bit as a ruddy great chunk. But that's all in my shameful past.'

'Of course. Absolutely. I totally understand.' Paige twisted from side to side on her chair, grabbing vaguely at her jacket that was slung on the back, and trying to stand up.

'Hang on a mo.' He reached over for her hand and held it until she was still, and had raised her eyes to his. 'Don't misunderstand me. I am *immensely* flattered. But you really must raise your sights a little higher. You're a beautiful young woman—'

Paige protested and tried to pull her hand free.

'No. Listen to me. I mean it. You should value yourself a bit more. What you deserve is a beautiful young man, not a half-shot, dotty old poseur like me.'

She looked back bleakly. Her mouth twisted. 'So you say. But where is he?'

CHAPTER 21

'No, it's not cat sick, Gracie, it's lovely houmous. Yum yum.'

'I want more jelly!'

'Jelly, jelly in your belly.'

'Mummy, Joshua said a rude word.'

'Belly, belly, belly, belly—'

'Yes, thank you, Joshua. Now, who's ready for cake?' Maddy pushed the hair back from her flushed face, turned to Paige and let out a throttled scream. 'God, this is exhausting. I can't believe we asked you to Lilly's party.'

'No, no, it's great to see them all having such a good time,' Paige assured her, dodging a flying carrot stick.

Truthfully, she could hardly believe that she had accepted. It was Ed's fault. If she hadn't been so determined to show him that she was not a stuck-up movie star, she would not be standing here, in the smallest, messiest kitchen she had ever seen, while eight children dressed as princesses or pirates sat round a small table screaming, punching each other, cramming food into their mouths, popping balloons, and knocking over their drinks every five seconds. Back home, the adults attending a birthday party were usually seated together in a secluded part of the house or yard where they could view the children from a safe distance. Refreshments would be served by the catering staff. There would be an entertainment: the hosts might, for example, hire some dancers from the Cirque du Soleil, or maybe an elephant to give the kids rides. Sometimes they'd show a pre-release movie in the screening room. At the appropriate moments you would present your gift and admire the cake – a professional creation in the shape of a fairy castle, say, or a surf-board. In LA the guests often included a camera man, who might video the proceedings and then edit it down to a ten-minute mini-movie in the style of Laurel and Hardy, or Tarantino, to be sent out afterwards to guests as a cute memento. There were always plenty of nannies and so forth to keep things running smoothly.

But this was England, so obviously there would be differences, maybe even some quaint rituals which it would be interesting to observe. She was also conscious of her own role as a guest of honour. Since Lilly was such a big fan, Paige thought that she owed it to her to play fairy godmother and sprinkle a little magic dust on her special day. Accordingly she had bought several presents and had them gift-wrapped, plus a giant azalea in a pot for Maddy. It had been very satisfying to watch her driver load these into the stretch limo she'd hired, ready for the trip to Acton. (Wasn't that the place where they had the fancy horse-races?) She'd half-hoped that Ed might emerge from his basement and be impressed by her efforts, including her own appearance in a simple Stella McCartney dress – chosen after much thought, so as not to stand out from Maddy and the other mothers. (He, apparently, had no intention of going to the party himself – in fact, he had looked at her as if she were deranged when she'd suggested that she might see him there.) But although she spent quite a while on the sidewalk, giving the driver instructions in her stage voice, he did not appear.

Maybe he had gone out of town for the holiday weekend. Just about every other Londoner seemed to be on the road, creating interminable tail-backs and snarl-ups which meant that she arrived late at the party. It became obvious that this was not the horse-racing place. Paige was surprised and a little shocked to find that Acton was a drab and not very upscale residential area, carved up by railroad tracks. Maddy's street was so narrow that the limo could barely fit between the rows of parked cars on either side, and completely blocked it when they stopped in front of the house. Some drivers who'd found their way barred were ungracious enough to honk, even though Paige herself was standing in full view while supervising the unloading of her gifts. It had been very gratifying, however, when the car-horns had brought Lilly running out of the house, her face alight, followed by a trail of wide-eyed children in their charmingly home-made costumes. England was so different from materialistic America, where the kids' outfits would have been bought brand-new or even specially made by a dress-maker. A somewhat frenzied-looking Maddy, dressed in jeans and a chocolate-smeared apron, appeared behind them, to greet Paige before excusing herself to deal with last-minute preparations. She seemed completely overwhelmed by the azalea.

Paige had allowed herself to be led into the doll-sized house and seated on the couch, with the children vying for a place at her side or sitting at her feet, and bombarding her with questions in their precise English accents.

'Is that your car?'

'Have you got a swimming-pool?'

'Can you do magic?'

It had been fun dispensing the presents: fake-diamond rings and beach sarongs for the girls, remote-controlled helicopters for the boys. Lilly was thrilled with her pink sequinned princess dress and tiara, and had rushed upstairs to put them on. Everyone got an autographed DVD of *Miss Lovejoy's Secret*. Soon the carpet was littered with ripped wrapping paper and circlets of discarded ribbon. As the boys became more rambunctious Paige began to wonder where all the parents were and when the entertainment was going to start. Only when Maddy reappeared with a young foreign girl, introduced as her nanny Verushka, and started pushing back the furniture 'so we can play some lovely games', did Paige realise that they were the only three adults. The parents had dumped their children and disappeared. This party was going to be a lot more hands-on than she had anticipated.

By the time they'd finished Grandmother's Footsteps she had discarded her shoes. After Blind Man's Buff she mentally consigned her dress to the thrift shop and her hairstyle to oblivion. But, weirdly enough, she was enjoying herself. The kids' delight in these simple games was infectious. It was fun making them laugh when she had to do a forfeit. It had been a while since she'd been around kids, apart from brattish movie moppets, and she'd forgotten how forcefully and physically they expressed every emotion. With the real thing in front of her, she was appalled to remember the casual way she'd sometimes considered adopting a baby if the right man didn't turn up in time, and at the same time wondered if it would really be so bad to have a little step-brother or step-sister. It was also strangely bonding to be in this situation with Maddy, who stage-managed the proceedings with enthusiasm and tact. From time to time they caught each other's eye over the heads of the children, and smiled or raised their eyebrows in wordless communication. Paige could see why a man would like Maddy. She was high-spirited and easy to be with.

Nevertheless, both were flagging by the time Verushka announced that tea was ready. The children had stormed into the kitchen to make an assault on pizza, sausages, and white bread smeared with a yucky-looking brown paste called Marmite, ignoring the bowls of healthy veggies and raisins. Paige was now leaning against the counter, nursing a cup of (peculiar English) tea while she observed the mayhem. Whoops! There went another paper cup, knocked across the table by Oscar's rubber pirate hook. Verushka, who was cutting up Amber's pizza, made a guttural exclamation in her own language. 'Maddy, we have spilling. Where is paper towel?' Maddy sighed, abandoned what she was doing, and went to the rescue.

'What can I do?' Paige asked. 'Let me help.'

'Well, you could stick the candles in the cake – if you're sure,' said Maddy. 'Everything's over there by the fridge.'

Paige found herself looking at a lop-sided, unevenly iced cake which at first appeared to be in the shape of a very fat cockerel. No, those pointy bits at the top weren't a coxcomb, but a crown. The round part was a head, the big triangle a dress, and the two stumps at the bottom must be legs. It was a princess – a brown chocolatey princess with 'Happy Birthday Lilly' written in wavering pink icing. Paige picked up seven candles and carefully arranged them, three down each side of the dress – blue, pink, white; blue, pink, white – with a final pink one in the middle of the crown. She straightened to admire her handiwork.

'Er, Paige, you need to put the candles in the candle-holders first – these plastic things, see? Otherwise the wax drips onto the cake.'

'Oh, God, Maddy, I'm so sorry.' Paige was mortified. 'I've ruined your beautiful cake. I feel terrible.'

Maddy laughed. 'Don't worry, it's a crap cake. I was up until three in the morning finishing the bloody thing and it looks like a drunken dinosaur with a skin disease. A few more holes won't hurt. All Lilly cares about is that I made it myself.' She removed the candles, expertly inserted them into the holders and replaced them. 'Have you never put candles on a birthday cake before?' She gave Paige an amused glance.

'Not really. In fact, not at all. But I'd like to learn. Back home, someone else usually does that kind of thing, I guess.'

'You mean, a cook?'

'Yeah, or a caterer.'

'Ooh, it must be nice to be rich.' Maddy said this in such a straightforward way that Paige couldn't be offended. And it was true. It *was* nice to be rich, but it wasn't everything. When she saw the awed look on Lilly's face as Maddy carried the lighted cake to the table, she doubted whether any commercial cake, however expensive or exquisitely decorated, could have been so rapturously received. Paige volunteered to take pictures – this, at least, she could do. Afterwards, Maddy whispered to her, they could plonk the children in front of *Miss Lovejoy's Secret* until the parents arrived.

But Maddy was wrong. Someone had poured their fizzy drink into the DVD machine and it had shorted out. All the children denied any knowledge of this crime, although Joshua giggled in a suspicious manner, then suggested that Jack's toy parrot might have weed in it. Jack punched him. Joshua doubled up in melodramatic agony and announced that he was going to be sick. Quite suddenly Maddy's sunny temper gave out. 'Verushka!' she yelled. 'Come and do something with these monsters.' The nanny appeared, wearing rubber gloves and protesting that she was doing 'vashinup'. At this point Oscar let off his helicopter, which circled the room and crashed into one of the china figurines on Maddy's mantelpiece, scattering lethal-looking shards across the living-room carpet. 'Nobody move!' Maddy commanded. 'Verushka, get the Hoover!' Lilly started to sob.

Paige looked on, horrified. This was her fault. The party was ruined. Or was it …? She found her bag and pulled out her cell phone.

Five minutes later the children were piling gleefully into the stretch limo, summoned by Paige with the promise of a hundred-pound bonus if the driver took them on a little local tour. Only Joshua had initially resisted. 'Can I drive it?' he asked Paige. 'Absolutely,' she replied, without batting an eyelid. (Mentally she added another fifty pounds of danger money for the driver who would have to tell him otherwise.) Verushka, who had been appointed to accompany them, was now all smiles, as thrilled as the kids by the deep leather seats, TV screen, black-out windows, and mini-bar – from which Maddy hastily removed the alcoholic drinks. 'You are a total star,' she told Paige, cheerfully waving them goodbye. Then she realised what she had said, and laughed. Normally Paige didn't care for the word 'star' – she preferred 'artist' – but she did feel kind of wonderful, so she let it go. They turned back to the house together. Only as they reached the front door did Maddy seem to realise that she was still holding several small bottles in the crook of one arm. 'Pity to waste it,' she said.

Which was how they came to be sitting on the couch, one at each end with their feet tucked under them, drinking champagne and discussing Maddy's job. 'I can't believe I'm rabbiting on like this,' Maddy confessed: 'Your job is so much more glamorous and interesting.'

'Believe me, a lot of the time it really isn't. Tell me more about this offer for your company – well, yours and Ed's. To build something up from scratch and have someone else want to buy it – that's such an achievement! It's really worth getting a good lawyer, you know, to screw these bastards down. They sneak all kinds of stuff into the fine print.' Paige knocked back her drink, only to find that there was none left. England was having a bad effect on her behaviour. Gaby would be shocked. She leaned forward and offered her empty glass so that Maddy could share out the last dribble from the bottle.

'Yeah, well, we've decided not to sell.' Maddy subsided against the arm of the couch.

'Really? Why not?'

'Ed doesn't want things to change. I think he's frightened of this Alex Wolfe character who runs the show. He'd rather keep control than have the money.'

Paige nodded. 'It's hard to let things go. I understand that. But what about you? What do *you* want?'

'Oh, I'd take the money and run. I'm sick of the TV treadmill. I'm sick of being stretched at both ends and paying someone else to spend time with my daughter. Lilly will be off to university before I know it. I want to enjoy her. Don't tell Ed,' she added.

Paige was confused. 'But … you must have told him yourself.'

'All my fat salary does is keep me chained to London, and school fees, and a succession of Verushkas. But if I had a big lump sum, plus the money from this house, I could move to the country and just about get by. I know you'll laugh, but I have a secret ambition to re-train as a psychotherapist.'

'I'm not laughing. One of my best friends is a sort of therapist. But why haven't you said all this to Ed?'

Maddy shook her head in frustration. 'I can't. He relies on me. He needs me. He loves his films, and his little empire. And … I suppose I always do what he wants. Pathetic, isn't it?'

'Not if you love him, I guess. But if he loves you, wouldn't he want to—?'

'Whoa, whoa, whoa!' Maddy jerked upright. 'What's with the love stuff?'

'I'm sorry. I thought – You seemed – Ed said—'

'We're *business* partners. And good friends. That's it.'

'Oh,' said Paige, reproved. She opened her mouth to say something else, but could not seem to formulate any words. 'Oh,' she repeated, with a tiny upward inflection of speculation.

Maddy heard it too, and met her eye with a frank look. 'Yeah, he's free. But he's hard to catch.'

Paige instinctively bridled at this. 'I hardly need to, uh …' She hardly needed to what? And why didn't she? Unable to think of an anwer, she gave a dismissive laugh instead.

Maddy ignored the interruption. 'I've seen the girlfriends come and go. Somehow they've never heated him up. He's charming and polite and interesting – and cool.'

'Huh! You wouldn't have said that if you'd heard him shouting at me about an itty bit of water in his precious apartment.'

'No,' agreed Maddy thoughtfully. 'I have to say I find that rather intriguing. He's been complaining like mad about having a "celebrity" in his house, but I wonder if that isn't all a bluff.'

Paige was prevented from pursuing this enigmatic remark by a sudden burst of noise from the street. First one car-horn tooted, then another, followed by a sustained blast. An alarm siren started up in sympathy, immediately followed by a peremptory rat-tat on the front door. Maddy jumped up to answer it. Paige heard the click of the latch, then a woman's voice boomed, 'You won't believe it, Mads, but some idiot is trying to drive a stretch limo down your road. How's Joshie? Has he been completely vile?'

Paige scrambled for her shoes, smoothed her dress and hair as best she could and stood tensely by the mantelpiece. A large woman in her mid-forties, wearing ill-fitting jeans and one of those sweaters that appeared to have been knitted from oatmeal, surged into the room. 'Oh, hi, you must be Oscar's mum,' she told Paige confidently. 'Aren't boys a menace? You look exhausted.'

More mothers trickled steadily into the room. 'Paige Carson,' she heard one woman hiss to another, nudging her warningly in the ribs, as if Paige were a rattlesnake. As usual in such situations she felt more like a prize sow, but she smiled brightly and tried to say the right things. One particular mother stuck to her like a leech, sucking up every detail of her clothes, make-up, and hairstyle, and wondering aloud if Paige would like her spare ticket to the Chelsea Flower Show next month. It was a relief when the children rushed into the room, full of stories about their limo ride ('Joshua stuck his tongue out at a policeman!'), and were prodded into stilted thanks before being shepherded home. Paige collected her bag, hugged Lilly goodbye, and waited until Maddy was free.

'About the offer for your company,' she said. 'I'm really worrying about this. I know it's none of my business, but

I'm going to say what I think anyway. You have to tell Ed how you feel.'

Maddy's freckly face twisted. 'I know I should. But I can't. And it's too late now. He said no yesterday.'

So that was that. Paige felt an obscure sense of disappointment in Ed. But she'd probably only made Maddy feel worse by raking over the subject, so she shut up. Instead, she made Maddy promise to call her if she wanted any tickets for *As You Like It*. 'And thank you for including me in Lilly's party. I'm so glad I came.'

'Oh, me too,' said Maddy, and spontaneously hugged her. She waited with Paige on the sidewalk until the limo, which had been cruising majestically round and round the block, came into view again and stopped in obedience to Paige's upraised hand.

'Good luck!' Maddy called, as Paige ducked into the car.

'You mean, with the play?'

'With everything.'

On the drive home Paige continued to puzzle over Maddy's strange inability to break free from Ed and their film company. It seemed wrong to her that someone so warm and high-spirited should feel compelled to go on living a life that she had outgrown and wanted to change. Maddy was like the mechanical bird singing away in its cage, except that she was not mechanical but alive, so why didn't she push the door open and fly free? And Ed: what was going on in his mind – apart from great intellectual thoughts? Was he really so self-absorbed that he couldn't see that Maddy wanted out? It was none of her business, but she liked Maddy and she sort of liked Ed, though she couldn't figure him out. She wondered if she'd been right that the two of them had something going – maybe not now, or maybe only in Maddy's head, but she sensed a history there. Maddy had said something about Ed being charming but 'cool': perhaps she had experienced this treatment at first hand. So what made Ed pull back from commitment, whether it was committing himself to women, or committing his company into other hands?

It was early evening by the time her car pulled up outside the house. Over the past week the weather had been getting steadily warmer and more spring-like, and when she stepped onto the sidewalk she paused for a moment to look up and admire the pale turquoise sky streaked with apricot-tinged clouds. Even at this time of day it was so warm that she didn't need a sweater. It was sad, though, that that all the nice sunshine meant that the flowers in her window-boxes had shrivelled to papery wisps.

'Slumming it again, I see.'

She couldn't help feeling a flicker of excitement as she recognised Ed's voice, though as usual his tone was mocking. He stood with one hand jammed into his jeans pocket, hip thrust forward. His shirtsleeves were rolled up, revealing lean, lightly tanned forearms. Paige followed his gaze to the huge limo, now easing away from the kerb. 'I had a lot to carry,' she told him, smoothing her skirt. 'I've been to Lilly's birthday party.'

'What, you actually went?'

'I actually did.'

'No wonder you were raising your eyes to the heavens. Was it a nightmare?'

'As a matter of fact I was looking at your jonquils.'

'My what?' Ed cast a hasty downward look at his clothes, as if she'd made a personal comment.

'The daffodils.' She pointed up to the window-boxes.

'Oh.' He looked relieved.

Impulsively she began to recite: '"I wandered lonely as a cloud that floats on high o'er vales and hills, when all at once I saw a crowd, a host, of golden daffodils."'

He was looking at her the way you'd look at a donkey that suddenly started singing opera.

'That's a poem by William Wordsworth,' she explained.

'Yes. I do know William Wordsworth.'

'No kidding! Is he a friend of yours? … OK, OK, what's so funny?'

'I'm sorry.' Ed was laughing at her, but not in a mean way. His eyes were warm. 'Actually, apart from the fact that Wordsworth died at least a hundred and fifty years ago, you're bang on target. He *is* a friend of mine – his poetry, anyway. He lived in the Lake District, and wrote about it, and that's where I grew up. In fact, I'm driving up there tomorrow to stay with my Mum for a couple of nights.'

'Wow. Isn't the Lake District like in Scotland or something?'

'Not quite. But, yeah, it's a long drive.' He tossed a keyring in his palm. 'I'm just off to get my car out of the garage.'

'And is it really the way the poem says – thousands and thousands of daffodils, just growing wild? That must be an incredible sight.'

'It is.' He hesitated. 'I could show you, if you like.'

Paige stared at him speechlessly. What was he suggesting?

'I mean, I could, you know, give you a lift up there, book you into a hotel – *obviously* – ha ha! – not that you wouldn't be welcome to – it's just that my mother …' He ground to a halt. 'Sorry. Stupid suggestion. You must have a thousand more interesting things to do.'

Paige, whose weekend was booked solid with a VIP tour of London, a day in a spa, and lunch at the Ritz with Davina, heard herself say, 'No, nothing at all. I'd love to get a ride with you.'

They stood gazing at each other in shocked silence, both wondering what the hell they'd done. Then he said, 'Right. I'll be setting off at ten tomorrow morning. Bring your walking-boots.'

CHAPTER 22

'The Red Lion has four legs, so now we're even-steven again.'

'Well done! You're getting the hang of this.'

Paige laughed, and shot a glance at Ed at the wheel beside her. The English were so silly! Ever since they'd left the freeway in search of lunch, the two of them had been playing this ridiculous game called Pub Signs, where you each took turns to spy a pub and then scored points *according to the number of legs on the sign*. How dumb was that? She looked ahead eagerly. These pubs tended to spring out of the rolling countryside without warning. In fact, could that old cottage be one?

'The George,' announced Ed. 'That's two legs, so my score goes to sixteen.'

'Now wait a minute,' objected Paige. 'I didn't see any legs. There was just a head and shoulders, exactly the same as the pub I had a while back which you said scored zero.'

'Ah yes, but that was The King's Head. Obviously a head doesn't have any legs. If you doubt me, consult the rule book, paragraph forty-four B, subsection twelve.'

'Phooey.'

'I do hope you're not going to be a bad sport,' Ed observed piously. 'The trouble with you Americans is that you always have to win. We English take a more mature attitude: "It matters not who won or lost, but how you played the game."'

'For your information, an American called Grantland Rice wrote that, and you're misquoting. "For when the One Great Scorer comes to mark against your name, He writes – not that you won or lost – but how you played the Game."'

'You don't say?' Ed looked taken aback at her correction. But not for long. 'Oh bad luck, The Royal Oak. Please try not to get too upset. Now I need your help. Have you got the map the right way up this time? Congratulations. Can you see a village called Slaughter-in-the-Marsh?'

'I can see it, but I'm still not sure I believe it.'

'Look out for the letters PH.'

'What do they stand for?'

'PH equals public house equals pub. Don't you know anything?'

Paige wrestled with the map, which kept collapsing in concertina folds. The trouble with England was that all the villages were arranged higgledy-piggledy, and linked to each other with a maze of different roads, some of which suddenly veered off in an unexpected direction or terminated in the middle of nowhere. She wasn't absolutely sure whether they were on the brown road or the yellow road, but didn't like to ask in case he thought her stupid. 'I can see something called Dead Woman's Bottom.' She giggled. 'Oh, and a castle!'

'Do try to concentrate.'

'OK, turn left, then there's kind of a funny black dot with a cross on top—'

'A church, we call it.'

'... and then—'

'Ah, The Coach and Horses. Fancy that.' Ed swung into the parking area, sending up a spray of gravel. 'That's, let's see, six times four legs for the horses, um – shall we just agree that I've won?'

'That means you buy the lunch, right?'

'Devious woman.'

'At least I don't cheat.'

Paige was enjoying herself. The drive itself had been unexciting so far – cars and more cars, just like California – but Ed was a fun companion. He hadn't tried to make her feel small by talking about Plato or Einstein's theory of whatever. Instead they'd talked about normal stuff like vacations and their families. Ed was an only child, like her. And he had grown up the only child of a single parent, because his father had died while he was a boy. Paige did not tell him about the little step-brother or step-sister that was about to be foisted on her, but Ed's few words about his father made her reflect that she was lucky to have her dad, baby or no, and to wonder if it wasn't time she got back in touch. She remembered her behaviour at the ranch. Had she been a little bit selfish? She couldn't be Daddy's little girl for ever. Perhaps it was time to grow up.

Without making a big deal of it, Ed found them a secluded table, brought her the menu and ordered the food from the bar himself so that she wouldn't be subjected to the usual stares. Paige couldn't resist the sound of a ploughman's lunch, which was bread, Cheddar cheese and about half a ton of tasteless salad leaves and raw veggies. 'Cheese is my greatest vice,' she admitted to Ed, who seemed to find this very amusing. He wouldn't find it so funny if his own job depended on how fat he was – though irritatingly he seemed to be one of those people on whom calories had no effect, if today's huge platter of fish and chips, followed by treacle tart and thick cream, was a typical meal. He had a rangy, athletic frame without the suspicion of a paunch, or those beefy shoulders she always found really gross. Even on camera, which added ten pounds or more, he'd look pretty good.

'What is it?' He looked up unexpectedly. 'Have I got tartare sauce on my nose?'

'Of course not.' She selected a radish and nibbled at it delicately.

'So how's the play going?' he asked.

Paige felt a jolt of panic. They were opening in five days' time. *Five days!* 'Fine,' she said.

'Meaning that you don't want to talk about it? That's all right.' He smiled. 'I understand. I feel the same way when one of my films is aired. Sorry, I shouldn't have asked.'

This was so English. An American would have gushed that she'd be fabulous. Or maybe it wasn't English; perhaps he was being nice. Perhaps he *was* nice. Either way, suddenly she wanted to confide in him.

'In lots of ways I'm loving it. I like the fact that there isn't a constant emphasis on how you look, the way there is with a film, where people are fiddling with your hair or the lighting every five seconds. I like the intimacy you build up with the other actors, and with your character, over a long rehearsal period. Some movie directors give you no rehearsal time at all, and mostly you're acting to the camera, not to a real person. With stage-acting you can build up this phenomenal energy over the length of the play, instead of releasing it in two- or three-minute bursts just like that.' She snapped her fingers. 'Though if you think that's easy,' she challenged, recalling some of his earlier remarks, 'all I can say is, you try doing it, day after sixteen-hour day, for ten or twenty weeks.'

'No, no, I'm sure—'

'If our jobs were easy, every waitress in LA would be a movie star, and every jerk taking pictures on his cell phone would be a top documentary-maker, right?'

'Er, right.'

She nodded firmly: point conceded. 'The company is great,' she continued, 'all except the actress who plays my cousin Celia, and hates me because she was going to get my part if I said no. She's my understudy, and used to try to give me little tips about my interpretation of the role until I told her where to get off.' She checked to see if Ed was going to register disapproval at this, but he looked impressed and faintly frightened.

'And I love the character I'm playing – at least, I do once I get going. But there's this part at the beginning, where she sees a guy at a wrestling match—'

'Orlando.' He nodded.

'Oh. You know the play?'

'A knowledge of Shakespeare is part of every Englishman's heritage.' Then he grinned. 'Well, to be honest, I had to study it at school for O-level. That's a sort of exam.'

'OK, then. Explain to me how they fall in love at first sight. They barely see each other, they hardly speak, and yet the audience has to believe that this is the real deal.'

Ed considered. 'Well, she's beautiful, of course, and a Duke's daughter.'

'Excuse me, Ed, but we're talking about *her*. Here's this independently minded, privileged woman who meets a complete stranger – totally outside her world – and within a matter of seconds recognises that he is The One. How can I make that work? What's my motivation? She doesn't even know him.'

'And he doesn't know her. Isn't that what the play's about? Them getting to know one another, when they live together in the forest? With her allowing him to get to know her by pretending to be someone else, and him *not* pretending because he sees no reason to conceal his feelings.'

'Wow. You really do know this play. But that doesn't explain how she falls in love right at the beginning. My friend back home – she's this amazing kind of therapist and guru and life-coach all rolled into one, you'd totally love her – says they're probably karmic soulmates. You know, their souls created something in a past life, and they have chosen this lifetime to help each other heal.'

'Bollocks,' Ed snorted, forking a chip. 'You might as well say that their star signs are compatible.'

Paige pressed her lips together. That had been Gaby's other suggestion. To be honest, neither had been very helpful, but she wasn't going to admit this to scornful, sceptical Ed. 'OK, then, since you're so smart, what's your explanation?'

For once he didn't have a glib response. She could see him concentrating, digging deep into his mind and experience. He cocked his head in a way that she was beginning to recognise was characteristic. 'Perhaps you're thinking too hard. Isn't the explanation quite simply that she's *ready* to fall in love; that she's looking for it even before she meets him? She's separated from her father. Her future's uncertain. She's lonely and full of love, with no one to spend it on except her cousin. Then she sees Orlando: brave, handsome, stripped for a fight. He's down on his luck, dispossessed by his brother. What could be more romantic?'

Paige felt the faintest stirring of new understanding. 'She's ready, you say.' She leaned closer to Ed, gazing into his face. 'Is that it? Is that all it takes to fall in love?'

His expression went blank. She felt him withdraw. 'Don't ask me.' He shrugged. 'It's not really something I do. Drink up. It's time we were back on the road.'

It was late afternoon when they turned off the main highway onto a single-track road leading into the mountains. A wind was shaking the trees and puffing small white clouds across the sky. Their shadows raced over moss-green fields separated by low stone walls. According to Ed, these were made without any kind of mortar, but so skilfully that they lasted for decades. Paige hadn't known what to expect of the Lake District, but she had felt anticipation rise when the mountains first came into view – not the crumpled rock and cactus canyons of California, but smooth-shouldered mountains from which blue-green ferns spilled steeply into the sheep-nibbled turf of the valleys. Now that they were off the freeway she felt as if she had entered a different country, an ancient and mysterious kingdom with fairytale cottages of grey stone, gnarled trees, and hump-backed bridges crossing back and forth over tumbling streams.

They were approaching a pass between two foothills when Ed said, 'Right. Close your eyes, and don't open them until I tell you.'

Intrigued, Paige obeyed. She felt the car descending in a long curve, then slowing to a stop. She heard the rasp of the hand-brake. 'You can look now.' She opened her eyes, and gave a cry of delight. In front of them stretched miles of sapphire water, teased by the wind into waves that sparkled in the spring sunshine and frothed into diamond crests. On all sides mountains rose sheer out of the depths. Above and beyond them clouds billowed into sky, as dramatically as in a Biblical screen epic.

'Ullswater,' announced Ed, 'your first English lake. In fact, what you can see now is less than half of it, because what appears to be the far end is only the inside of a dog's leg.'

'It's beautiful,' she breathed. 'Awe-inspiring.'

Ed looked pleased. 'That's what your friend Wordsworth thought. In one of his most famous poems he describes stealing a small boat at sunset when he was a boy, and rowing out on this lake in the moonlight. He was rounding a headland when suddenly a huge black cliff loomed over him, blotting out the stars, and seemed to chase him away.'

'You mean, like a spirit?'

'Exactly. He didn't believe in God, but he was very sensitive to the power of Nature. It was his own kind of morality. He read the mountains and streams, and the people who inhabited them, like his personal, private Bible.'

'And did that make him a good person or a bad person?'

'Good question. A mixture of both, I suppose, like most of us. Now, there's something else I want to show you, further down the lake – unless you want to go straight to your hotel?'

'No way,' Paige protested. She wanted to see more of this stunning scenery – and in particular to see it with him. This was Ed's territory – personal and private, as he'd said – and he wanted to show it to her. She was flattered.

As they drove along the winding road that followed the shoreline, Paige couldn't get over how empty and uncommercialised the landscape was. If this was America there'd be hotels and condos, dancing plastic hot dogs advertising some cheap eaterie, speedboats and jet-skiers criss-crossing the lake. Here there was nothing but the occasional picturesque boat-house or a small farm tucked into a green hill. The lake was empty, aside from ducks. The only people she saw were a couple of hikers.

After a few miles Ed pulled off the road by a belt of trees. 'Time to put on your walking-boots.'

'These *are* my walking-boots,' Paige retorted, showing him one of her ankle-high moccasins with the cute fringes.

'Eh, thoo'll nivver be able ter walk in those silly larl sproits, thoo divvy.'

'Excuse me?'

'I said you couldn't walk in those silly little boots. In Cumbrian.'

'They speak a different language here?' Paige's eyes widened with anxiety. How would she make herself understood at the hotel?

Ed laughed. 'Not really. Not nowadays, anyway. It's mainly the accent that's different, and a few words like 'thoo divvy'.

'Which means?'

'You idiot.'

'Gee, thanks.'

Paige got out of the car and zipped herself into the parka she'd brought, electric pink with fake-fur trim on the hood. She watched while Ed laced up battered hiking-boots and slung on an olive-coloured waxed jacket. This was definitely not the stylish Ed of London. But he looked relaxed, at home, less guarded. There was a new energy in his step as he led the way along a trail into the woods. He gave her outfit a dubious look, but all he said was, 'Mind you don't frighten the ducks.'

'Where are we going? Is it far?' she asked, stretching out her legs to keep up. The air was fresh and invigorating. This was an adventure.

'Not so many questions, Miss Nosy Parker.' He gave her a playful biff on the arm. His eyes sparkled with mischief. Paige was charmed. *He likes me!* she thought.

He began to tell her about Wordsworth – how he'd been born and brought up in the Lake District and had roamed hills and valleys similar to these throughout his early childhood. These experiences would stay with him all his life and inspire his greatest poetry. But his mother had died while he was still a boy, and then his father, when he was still only thirteen. There was no money, and the children were split up and sent to live with different guardians. 'As you can imagine, that had a profound effect. It drove Wordsworth into himself, into his mind and imagination and memory.' He'd studied at Cambridge University, and afterwards travelled in France at the time of the Revolution. (Paige nodded. She was a little hazy on her revolutions, but didn't want to interrupt Ed.) There Wordsworth had fallen in love with a French girl and fathered an illegitimate child, but he was forced to return to England before it was born because England and France were on the brink of war. 'So he didn't meet his daughter until she was almost ten years old.'

Paige was much struck. This was the age she'd been when Dad had come back into her life. 'They must have been so happy to be together.'

'Well, no. By that time Wordsworth had decided to marry another woman, and war was about to resume. He wouldn't see his daughter again until she was a grown woman.'

'But that's so sad! Poor little girl.'

'I know. But he'd been very young when he fell in love with the mother – only twenty-one. You don't always pick the right person at that age ... Anyway, in the meantime he'd set up home with his sister Dorothy. Having been separated as children, they were very close once they were reunited, and lived together for the rest of their lives. Eventually they returned to the Lakes, and were living in a little cottage at a place called Grasmere. That's about a day's walk from the far end of this lake, over the mountain pass. You have to remember that everyone walked in those days, unless they were rich enough to have their own horses and carriages, which Wordsworth wasn't. No stretch limos. I'm not boring you, am I?'

'No, I love hearing this.' It was true, though it was as much Ed's enthusiasm that she liked as what he was saying.

'OK. Well, in 1801 Wordsworth went off to propose to the woman he wanted to marry, leaving Dorothy behind at the home of some friends who lived at the top of the lake, called the Clarksons — maybe you've heard of Thomas Clarkson, the anti-slavery campaigner?'

'No,' she confessed.

'Never mind. The point is that, when he returned, they would walk back to Grasmere together. Of course, when Wordsworth marries this woman, Dorothy's life will be turned upside down: the intimacy that she has shared with the brother she adores will never be the same again. So they are both in a state of high emotion as they walk home along this lake. And what do they see?' Ed paused dramatically.

'I don't know.' Paige looked at him in expectation.

In front of them was a stile over a stone wall. Ed climbed over first, and then reached back a hand to steady her as she stood on the narrow wooden board a couple of feet above the ground. With his other arm he swept a wide arc towards the view ahead. 'Da-da!'

Gripping his hand for balance, Paige looked up and gasped. Thousands and thousands of daffodils dotted the grass for as far as she could see. Their golden petals fluttered in the breeze, making it look as if they were dancing.

'It's just like the poem!' she exclaimed.

'Of course it is.' Ed's face, tilted up at her, mirrored her own delight. 'This is where Wordsworth saw the daffodils, when he was walking back with his sister from the Clarksons'.'

'No kidding? This exact spot?'

'Well, nobody knows for sure,' he conceded, 'but near enough.'

Paige stayed on her perch, drinking in the scene. It was like being inside the poem – inside the poet's skin. The flowers really did seem to twinkle like stars, brilliant yellow in the darker grass. Perhaps Dorothy and William had once stood in the same position as she and Ed were now – holding hands and looking from the daffodils to smile into each other's faces, wanting to remember this special moment. Not that she and Ed were brother and sister. Not at all. She became aware of the warmth of his palm and the way his eyes lingered on hers. She felt a crazy impulse to leap down into his arms and see what would happen. Instead she said, 'I wish I'd brought my camera.'

Instantly his face darkened. 'Forget your bloody camera! This is the real thing. Remember or forget it, as you wish, but at least live the moment.'

Paige flushed, feeling rebuked. Why had she said something so crass – so American, Ed would think? It was impossible to explain her true feelings. She climbed down from the stile. Ed let go her hand. 'I'll remember,' she said fiercely, almost to herself.

They walked on in silence, following a narrow path towards the lake. Ed strode ahead while she followed in his footsteps. What a complicated man he was – one moment open and ardent, the next prickly and unreadable. But what did she expect: a laid-back California surf-bum? Like Wordsworth, he had been shaped by this harsh, majestic landscape, and by the loss of his father. He too had fallen in love young, with the wrong woman, and had written poetry. She pictured the Ed of ten or more years ago, romantic and boyish, pouring out his heart to chilly, silly, superior India

Fitzdare, who had made fun of him with her friends. *Bitch!* Paige was startled by her own vehemence.

They emerged from the trees, and once again the lake spread out before them. Waves slapped at the shore. The breeze tugged at their clothes. Ed stood at the water's edge with his hands dug into his pockets, gazing moodily at the far mountains. What was he thinking? He had retreated from her again. She wanted to call him back. She spread her arms wide and drank in the fresh, clean air. 'Whoo-hoo!' she cried, exhilarated. Her voice carried and echoed across the lake as she recited aloud:

> The waves beside them danced; but they
> Out-did the sparkling waves in glee.
> A poet could not but be gay
> In such a jocund company.

There. He was smiling again. It wasn't so hard. She felt elated when he turned back to her, and said, 'You really do know your Wordsworth. I'm impressed.'

'Don't be,' she told him. 'I know I'm not smart. I didn't even graduate from high school. I'd like you to think that I'm the kind of girl who reads poetry, but I don't want to pretend something that isn't true. Not to you, anyway.'

'I don't understand.'

She scuffed the shingle with her boot. 'When I was little kid, I stuttered. To get me over it, the speech therapist made me learn poems by heart and recite them aloud. That's how I knew about the daffodils ...' She glanced up, prepared to see his expression hardening into scorn. 'I'm sorry to have disappointed you.'

But his eyes were gentle. 'You haven't,' he said.

CHAPTER 22

Ed looked over his shoulder and carefully reversed out of the driveway of his mother's cottage. It was late morning on Easter Monday, and he had consented to collect Paige from her hotel and bring her back for lunch, prior to driving back to London. His mother had been insistent. 'Edward, I sometimes wonder if you have any social skills whatsoever. What will she think of the English? Americans are always so hospitable. You're to ring her up *now* and invite her.'

He put the car into first gear and engaged the clutch, feeling irrationally grumpy. It wasn't that he didn't want to see Paige. He did. Over the last two days he had thought of her maddeningly often. Even while taking his mother out for a swanky Easter lunch or chatting with her by the fireside, images of Paige's wide smile or her green eyes, confiding and direct, would swim without warning into his head, making him momentarily dizzy and distracted. He kept wondering what she was doing, and pictured her reading glossy magazines in the hotel lounge, or making phone calls to that Gaby person she talked so much about. 'My guru', she called her – or rather, 'goo-roo'. (He could certainly believe the 'goo' part.) Consequently, he had kept himself busy by chopping wood, digging over his mother's entire vegetable patch, and fixing all the small things that had gone wrong in the cottage since his last visit. His mother, no fool, guessed that something was bothering him, and asked if he regretted turning down Grapevine's offer for his company, to which he'd given a long and involved answer. Later she'd enquired tactfully if he was 'seeing anyone' at the moment. 'No,' he had replied shortly. Nor did he disclose that he had brought his famous tenant to the Lakes. His mother would only ask questions to which he had no answers.

But he had reckoned without the local grapevine. This morning he had come down to breakfast after a restless night, to find his mother understandably peeved, having received a phone call from some old busybody. 'Apparently, everyone's talking about how you came up here with Paige Carson. I feel a complete fool. Why didn't you tell me?'

'I didn't come *with* her; I simply gave her a lift.'

Now, as he negotiated the outer fringe of Keswick and headed into open countryside, he faced up to the reason for his grumpiness, which was simple social embarrassment.

Paige had been used to luxury all her life. What would she make of his mother's simple cottage – his own boyhood home? He squirmed with anxiety as he visualised her reaction to the worn carpet, the outdated kitchen, the framed picture of a smiling rabbit which he'd drawn, aged four, and dedicated in uneven handwriting to 'the best mumy in the wold' … Oh God! The loo that required a special technique to flush. At the same time he despised himself for such trivial and contemptible anxieties. He let out a groan, and pressed his foot on the accelerator.

Why had he invited Paige in the first place? His impetuous suggestion had only landed him in trouble, starting with his realisation that he would personally have to find her somewhere to stay, and that every decent hotel room in the Lake District would be booked over the Easter weekend. On Friday night, after several fruitless phone calls, he'd remembered that an old mate from school worked at the hotel where he was now headed. The friend had sounded very doubtful until Ed had mentioned who needed the room. No problem! Ed had been quite shocked at this turnaround, imagining how some other poor guest had been relocated to a staff bedroom, or fobbed off with a story of double booking. The experience had given him new insight into Paige's character. What must it be like to have everyone bow down before you? In talking to his friend at the hotel, Ed had of course laid great stress on the fact that this was a private visit: Paige was 'travelling incognito'. The friend had promised to say nowt. Ha!

Here was the hotel up ahead. Ed turned in through an imposing set of gates and sped up the drive, coming to a halt outside the main entrance. Having expected that Paige, accustomed to making people wait for her, would still be packing or doing something with her hair, he was surprised to see her emerge almost immediately, wearing long boots and a cream coat that made her look like – well, like a film star. No fewer than five members of the hotel staff followed in her wake, variously thanking her for her visit, carrying her suitcases or just plain hanging around for a tip – which they got. She opened the passenger door and greeted him cheerily, showing him a bunch of daffodils. 'Do you think your mother will like these? I picked them myself.' Unseen hands stowed her luggage in the car boot while Paige, accepting this level of service as automatic, climbed in beside Ed, filling his car with her perfume. She placed the daffodils carefully on the back seat. He was startled by how well she looked, pink-cheeked and bright-eyed, and mumbled something to this effect as they drove away from the hotel.

'Thanks. Must be all the fresh air.'

'You've been for a walk?'

'Not very far this morning: only a couple of miles around the lake. But yesterday I climbed Skiddaw. It was fantastic! From the top you can see Scotland.'

Ed turned to her, to see if she was joking. Skiddaw was the third highest peak in England, and a stiff climb, as he knew only too well. The going was steep, and often difficult when the cloud came down. Sometimes you could see only a few feet in front of you. Paige had no walking-boots. You couldn't climb Skiddaw in a *pink* jacket.

'Careful of that tree,' Paige warned. Ed jerked his head back just in time to see that the car was veering off the driveway, and wrenched at the steering-wheel. While he concentrated on his driving, Paige burbled on enthusiastically about how 'someone' at the hotel had spare walking-boots that fit, and another 'someone' had lent her a jacket and a map. Even so, she confessed, she'd got kind of lost, but had fallen in with 'a darling couple' on the path up the mountain who'd shared their thermos with her, and had no idea who she was. 'They told me there was too much sex and violence in movies nowadays, and they preferred to read Dickens aloud to each other.'

'Stop!' Ed was shaking his head in disbelief. 'I can't take this in.'

Paige folded her hands complacently in her lap. 'You think actresses just look pretty and repeat someone else's lines, don't you? Well, let me tell you that for my last movie I had to train with the Marines. I'm not as fit as I was, but Skiddaw was a breeze compared to running up mountains in ninety-degree temperatures, with weights in my rucksack and a sadist yelling at me.'

'No, no, I'm sure that—'

'And we do lots of research. I bet you don't know the Arabic for "hostage".'

Ed admitted that he didn't. Nor that an asp – 'you know, the thing that killed Cleopatra' – was a cobra.

'And can you name me the countries that border Lebanon?' she demanded, getting into her stride.

'Let's see. Israel, Syria and ... Guatemala?'

'Now you're teasing me.' But she was unruffled. Suddenly Ed felt wildly happy. He liked this girl. He had missed her.

His social anxieties returned when they reached the cottage. Initially, neither Paige nor his mother appeared to their best advantage. His mother, more flustered than she would have admitted, took refuge in ponderous formality ('Edward, why don't you ask our guest what she would like to drink?'), and sent him to fetch the 'proper' napkins and 'good' serving spoons. Paige would think her small-minded and dull. Meanwhile Paige, trying to be an appreciative guest, over-rhapsodised about the cottage, Ullswater, England. Ed winced when she said she had totally fallen in love with the Lake District and was thinking of buying a house there. It transpired that she already had 'a little place' in Hawaii as well as a ski lodge in Utah. His mother would think her a brainless, spoilt American movie star.

Under the influence of food and drink everyone began to relax. Paige told a funny story about auditioning for the part of a cheerleader. 'The casting director asked me to do a toe-touch, but I didn't really know what that was, so I just jumped around and smiled a lot. They gave me the part of "the goofy one".' Under sympathetic questioning Ed's mother ('please, Paige, call me Katherine') opened up about her teaching career and its imminent, abrupt ending.

'One thing that can be really helpful,' offered Paige, 'is to find a stone – you know, like an ordinary … stone, and kind of pour all your troubles and hurt feelings into it. Then you throw it away, as far as you can. Outdoors, I mean.'

There was a silence as Ed and his mother exchanged brief, appalled glances. 'I think I'd rather join the National Trust,' she said.

But then Paige redeemed herself by making some really rather good suggestions about holding classes for adults who'd missed out on a good education and had a thirst to learn – 'like me, for example. You're a teacher, Katherine. That's what you're good at, so that's what you should do. You just need to find a way.' At the end of the meal she insisted on putting on an apron and 'doing the dishes', though all she did was faff about vaguely with soap bubbles. ('Don't worry,' Ed's mother whispered to him, 'I'll do it properly later').

In these familiar, domestic surroundings it struck Ed how different Paige's own childhood must have been, and that he should make some allowance for her failings. It was no good expecting her to behave like other girls when she'd been brought up among Hollywood royalty. How much time had she spent with her mother and father, learning to do ordinary things? Not a lot, he would guess, to judge from their case histories. It was much more likely that she'd been alternately petted and neglected, set adrift on a tide of money with no one to guide her except maids and nannies. It was surprising that she wasn't even more spoilt. He remembered the way he'd shouted at her for not knowing how to use a mop, and felt ashamed.

'She's a sweet girl,' his mother pronounced when Paige had gone to 'freshen up' before the long drive back to London. He felt unaccountably pleased until she added, 'But, darling … be careful.'

Instantly he clammed up. 'She's from another planet, Ma. I gave her a lift up here because she wanted to see the Lakes, and now I'm taking her home. End of story.'

'Yes, Edward.'

At the beginning of their journey home Paige chattered happily about the lunch, his mother, her adorable cottage, and how much she had enjoyed the trip. Ed felt comfortable and content. Eventually Paige's comments became more desultory and her responses dwindled to a murmur. By the time they were on the motorway she was asleep, leaving Ed alone with his thoughts. There was a smile on his face as he reviewed the events of the past few days: from his impetuous, stumbling invitation to the look on her face when he'd showed her the daffodils, to the sight of her in his mother's kitchen, inept but delightful. She was like a daffodil herself, he thought, fresh and cheering. He no longer thought of her as 'Paige Carson'.

But perhaps that was a mistake. He frowned. *Be careful,*

his mother had warned. He jerked his shoulders irritably, knowing that she'd been thinking of India Fitzdare. But that had been years ago, when he was young and stupid. Oxford had been full of India Fitzdares, glamorous and confident and utterly out of his reach, usually only seen in the company of braying public-school boys, or spotted on college lawns hosting champagne parties to which he was not invited. He'd told himself that he had no desire to join their ranks, but when he'd met India one bright October morning, having a fag break on the steps of the Radcliffe Camera library, he'd been dazzled.

Everything about her delighted him, from the tumble of her dark hair to her long legs; her careless generosity to her apparent contempt for convention. Having been brought up to be hard-working, respectful of authority and serious about his studies, Ed found it thrilling to be teased by this delicious girl, who called him 'darling' within five minutes of their meeting and had seduced him by teatime. (Making love in the afternoon! This was so decadent.) They had lived together for the rest of his final year at university, in a little flat which she decorated herself in bold colours and filled with extravagant flowers. Every holiday he worked as a labourer on motorways, gruelling but highly paid, so that he could afford to take her out to dinner, dress to please her (including leaving the bottom button of his jacket undone) and, once, as a surprise, to whisk her to Paris. It turned out that she'd been there before, several times, but that didn't matter because he was the man she adored, she told him, and everything they did together was like the first time – special and unique. She was clever, too: knowledgeable about art and architecture, fluent in French and Italian, quick-witted and funny. India was his 'new-found continent', full of exotic riches, as he told her in poems that now gushed from the depths of his romantic soul. At the same time, in his careful, methodical way, he was saving money and planning how to make a future for the two of them. He would marry her, of course.

Ed abruptly pulled out into the fast lane to overtake a lorry. He did not want to remember what had happened next. He could perhaps have borne it if India had considered his proposal seriously, and decided that she was too young to know her own heart. He would have waited. Even if she'd told him she didn't love him enough, or had found someone else, he might finally have accepted this. But to *laugh* ... to ruffle his hair and call him a 'sweet old thing' ... to tell him that he simply wouldn't 'fit in' ...

The car swayed sickeningly in a sudden sideways gust of wind. Paige stirred in her sleep. Ed gripped the steering-wheel and slowed down. What was he doing? The speedometer had been pointing at ninety.

'What's happening?' Paige murmured.

'Nothing. It's fine. Go back to sleep.' He chided himself for being so reckless. *Be careful* ... He glanced at the figure beside him, now still, apparently asleep once more. Paige was not India. There was no comparison – except that they both inhibited quite different worlds to himself. But the thought unsettled him.

He drove on in silence, trying to compose his mind. He would think about work – the *American Empire* idea, for example. But within two minutes, the thought of America had brought him back to Paige again. And she wasn't asleep. He was aware of her straightening up in her seat and turning to look at him.

'Um ... Ed?'

'Yes?'

'You may think that what I'm about to say is none of my business. But there's something I think you ought to know.'

'All right,' he said slowly, wondering what on earth she had in mind.

'It's about your company. Maddy told me all about it. I hear you've decided not to go ahead with the sale.'

'So?' Ed was suddenly defensive.

'Well, I said it was none of my business, but ... did you

know that Maddy really wants to sell? She has this ambition to move to the country and start a new life, only she doesn't feel able to tell you about it.'

Ed was stunned. Was this true? If so, why hadn't Maddy told him? Even as he asked himself the question, he knew the answer. Maddy always did what he said; it was one reason he liked her. It was why he didn't want to sell the company to people who would question him, as Maddy never did. The realisation made him ashamed. But he fought the feeling. Paige must be wrong. How could she, a comparative stranger, know something about Maddy that he didn't? How could a millionnairess have any idea what it was like to start a business from scratch? Why should he trust the judgement of someone who couldn't tell the difference between Goering and Goebbels?

'It's a bit late, now,' he said stiffly. 'We've already rejected the offer.'

'I know that. But maybe you want to re-think the situation. Yeah, I know I'm sticking my nose into your affairs, and I know it's awfully pushy and American of me to do so – but I don't like the thought that you might be missing a big opportunity: an opportunity for you both. There comes a time when you have to let go of things, and move on. This might be it.'

Ed didn't speak. He didn't know what to say.

'OK, I'm going back to sleep now.' She drew her coat around her shoulders and snuggled her cheek against the back of the car seat. 'Good night, Ed.'

Ed stared down the conveyor belt of approaching headlights, his mind awhirl. Was Paige right? Was he selfishly clinging to the status quo simply because he was afraid of a new challenge? Was he a coward?

Yes, he was. The idea of going back to Wolfe, cap in hand, and admitting he'd made a mistake, made him cringe. He couldn't do it! Anyway, it was too late now to put things right … wasn't it? Something Paige had said came back to him, which at the time he had dismissed at the time as guru-speak: if you really want something, you should keep trying, you shouldn't give up until you've given it your best shot. That was the thing about Americans: their optimism, their sense that everything is possible – even climbing Skiddaw, or acting Shakespeare on the London stage.

He glanced at the girl who slept so trustingly beside him. Her beauty struck him as if for the first time. And there was a brain, after all, inside that lovely head. He adjusted his hands to the correct ten-to-two grip on the steering wheel. *I'll look after you,* he promised silently. Her voice echoed in his mind on the long drive home.

CHAPTER 24

'Let me get this straight,' said Wolfe, 'because I'm not entirely certain why I'm here.' He placed his clasped hands on the tablecloth and surveyed Ed steadily.

Ed fingered the knot of his tie. This was going to be sticky. The two men were seated opposite each other in a classy Mayfair restaurant, famously frequented by actors and supermodels, cabinet ministers, bestselling writers and the racier young royals – but never before by Ed. The décor was stylish, the atmosphere casually exclusive, the service impeccable. The bill was going to be huge. It had been Wolfe's suggestion to meet at L'Escapade – a piece of sadism which Ed thought he probably deserved, though this realisation made his discomfort no easier to bear. However much he had rehearsed what he was going to say, now that he was here, with Wolfe's dark-suited bulk looming at him like a thundercloud, his brain and tongue seemed frozen.

'As I recall,' Wolfe continued, 'just over a month ago Grapevine approached you with an offer to buy Hawkshead Barry. It was a good offer, made in good faith, and you were interested enough to pursue various practical and financial implications of the deal, which we did our best to address. Or so I believed.' His dark eyes challenged Ed to disagree.

'Yes. No. You've been very ... ' Ed waved his hands helplessly, trying to conjure up the adjectives that eluded him.

'Nevertheless, last week you formally declined our offer,

in a manner that I took to be conclusive. Frankly, I have to say that I was surprised, and a little bit vexed. My understanding had been that we were ironing out points of detail, not that you were averse to the deal in principle. You will appreciate that we had invested considerable time and effort to reach so advanced a stage.'

'Yes, I do realise that. The thing is ...'

'I accepted your decision, of course. So it was somewhat perplexing to receive your phone call this morning, only a few days later, telling me that you felt you had "made a mistake" and wanted to see me "as a matter of ugency".'

Ed nodded. Telephoning Wolfe was the most nerve-wracking thing he had ever done. In fact, the past twenty-four hours had been fuelled by continuous, stomach-churning anxiety. For the rest of the drive back from the Lakes, and in between fitful snatches of sleep, he had thought about what Paige had said. It had been something of a dark night of the soul as he had confronted his own selfishness in regard to Maddy, and his fear of relinquishing control of Hawkshead Barry. Any rational person would say that selling the company made sense. Yet he, who had always prided himself on his rational thinking, had consistently reacted to the Grapevine deal in a emotional, personal, immature and shamelessly manipulative way. As a result he had kissed goodbye to a million quid, stopped his best friend and partner doing what she wanted, and pissed off one of the most powerful media groups in Britain. He was, in short, a pompous idiot.

The realisation had been painful, but this morning he had gone into the office determined to put things right. After a brave stab at resisting his interrogation, Maddy had burst into tears and confessed that what Paige had told him was true. Ed had sensed that there was quite a lot she wasn't telling him, but what she did say was enough to make him realise that he would have to ring Alex Wolfe and see if the sale could be salvaged. 'You can't!' Maddy had gasped.

'I've got to try,' he told her, 'and not just for your sake,

Mads. This whole place could go down the tubes if we don't get an injection of cash. I've been a fool. I'm sorry.'

It had been a nightmare getting past Wolfe's secretary, who told him crisply that Mr Wolfe's appointments were fully booked and that he was leaving the following day for a two-week business trip in the US. Ed had pleaded, argued and persisted until at length Wolfe's chilly voice had come on the line and eventually, unwillingly, agreed to this 'highly inconvenient' meeting over dinner. Ed was sweating by the time he put down the phone.

'So tell me,' Wolfe now said, spearing an olive with a toothpick, 'what exactly has happened in the last few days to change your mind?'

To explain that he hadn't understood what his partner wanted sounded too feeble, so Ed was forced onto another tack. He began talking once again about the issue of editorial control – though this wasn't what he had intended to say, and he was aware that he wasn't very coherent. Wolfe listened to him patiently, but his expression was sceptical.

'So that's why we weren't confident about taking this further,' Ed concluded lamely. 'Er, but now we are.' There was a pause.

'Edward,' said Wolfe gently, 'Imagine that you are me. Why I should invest in you? As a viewer I admire your programmes, but as an investor it is obvious to me that you need stronger financial management. As you know, I am leaving tomorrow for the United States. The purpose of my trip is to sell our product in the American market. Co-productions with American partners are an essential part of profitable programme-making. Of course there will programmes that don't sell, but these should be the exception rather than the rule. We can't have too many like *The End of Reason*, can we? I think we can confidently describe that project, in the international market at least, as a dead duck.'

'One *canard farci*.' A waiter set a gently steaming plate in front of Wolfe. 'And the battered baby squid.' Ed stared down at an artistic arrangement of pale tentacles nestling in a bed of pimentos and rocket. Had he really ordered that? The waiter bustled about with bowls of vegetables, refilled their glasses, and withdrew.

Wolfe stabbed his meat with a fork and sawed through the crispy skin with his knife. Blood trickled onto the white plate. 'You're telling me now that you're ready to make a deal, but the offer's no longer on the table. You're going to have to convince me that you can be a player within the Grapevine umbrella.'

Ed couldn't help scowling at this mixed metaphor before hurrying into the speech that he and Maddy had prepared, cunningly peppered with Wolfe-speak such as 'synergies', 'excellence' and 'exploit'. But the words seemed dead. Even though Ed believed the essence of what he was saying, he sounded unconvincing, even to himself. He needed to *gush* – but he didn't know how. Wolfe was gazing over his shoulder, his inert body language indicating that the felt that the meeting had been a waste of time. Ed felt sick with failure.

Suddenly, however, Wolfe's whole demeanour was transformed: he sat forward in his seat expectantly, his bored expression replaced by one of delighted imbecility. Ed felt a hand rest on his shoulder as he was enveloped in cloud of familiar perfume.

'Hello, darling. Am I late?'

Ed jerked around in shock. Paige! What was she doing here? My God, that dress! Fire-engine red, halter-necked, and swirly skirted, it revealed a thrilling expanse of silky skin. She looked as glossy and expensive as a race-horse. Were those real diamonds in her ears? The smile she was giving him made his head swim.

Wolfe staggered to his feet, knocking the table so that the wine glasses rocked alarmingly. 'You're Paige Carson!' he gasped.

'And you are the famous Alex Wolfe!' She gave an ecstatic sigh. 'It is *so thrilling* to meet you in person at last.'

The restaurant manager was hovering discreetly. 'May I be permitted to set a third place?' He snapped his fingers at a waiter to bring another chair, and eased it in behind Paige. Within seconds another place had been laid and Paige was perusing the menu. 'Does anything take your fancy?' Wolfe purred into Paige's ear. 'Might I recommend the crispy duck?'

She shot a look at Wolfe of wonder and admiration, as if he had just revealed the secret of a fiendishly difficult puzzle. 'My God, you must be a mind-reader! How did you now that was my absolutely favourite dish?'

Wolfe grinned like a schoolboy. As Paige turned away to give her order, he raised his eyebrows at Ed and muttered, 'You're a dark horse.' It seemed to Ed that there was a new look of respect in his eyes. He opened his mouth to offer an explanation, couldn't think of one, and closed it again.

'So,' said Paige, after the waiter had gone. 'How are you boys getting on?' She beamed at Wolfe. 'I told Ed how lucky he is that Grapevine wants to buy his company.'

'You – you – you've heard of Grapevine?' Wolfe stuttered.

'Well, of course! Al was telling me just the other day – Pacino, I mean – how great it was that he could access one of your programmes on the net. He's researching the background for a part in an upcoming movie. I think it was some science thing ...' Her brow wrinkled deliciously.

'*From Mould to Gold*?' Wolfe was astonished.

'Yes, that's right,' agreed Paige. 'And of course, since I met Ed' – she laid a proprietory hand on his arm – 'he's been talking about you non-stop. You know, Alex – may I call you Alex? – I think the secret of your success is that you seem to have a sixth sense about picking the really top creative people, and let them run with their ideas. I know because I'm a creative artist myself. It makes such a difference when I work with a really intelligent director. I know I do a better job. That means the movie's better – and *that* means that everyone makes more money!' She laughed happily. Wolfe glowed at the comparison with a film director, Ed noticed, especially an intelligent one.

'It's like Ed here,' she went on, as her duck arrived with unprecedented speed and was laid reverently before her. 'Ed is *so* talented. He has a *brilliant* future ahead of him. He needs to be concentrating on making films, not running a company. It's so wonderful that he can call on a top business brain, like yours. That's why this is *such* a smart move.'

Ed said almost nothing as Paige spun a web around her victim. He was still bemused by her sudden appearance, but he had the sense not to question it. The change in Wolfe was miraculous. A few minutes ago the man had seemed as compliant as a granite wall; now he was putty. Paige was irresistible. Ed himself couldn't help grinning like a loon, even though he knew that she was acting her socks off. What he might once have dismissed as ditziness was to a purpose.

She was now shamelessly flattering Wolfe, laying on the charm with a trowel – no, a bloody JCB. 'You know, I suspect that you're a creative person underneath,' she said, shooting him a flirtatious look through her eyelashes. 'I bet you have some great ideas of your own. Am I right?'

'Oh no, I'm just a boring businessman,' simpered Wolfe.

'Boring!' Paige tossed her hair at this obvious absurdity. "Come on, Alex, you can tell me.' She put a hand on Wolfe's arm and leaned towards him, so close that he could have looked right down the front of her dress. In fact, that's just what he was doing, Ed noticed indignantly.

Wolfe blushed. 'Well,' he admitted, 'I did wonder if a history of golf ...'

Paige gasped. 'What a brilliant, *brilliant* idea! We'd love that in America, especially in Hollywood where the whole history of the movie business is tied up with golf. I could ask George if he'd be interested in participating – with your permission, of course. Maybe he could do some of the presenting.'

'C-c-c-?'

'Clooney, yes. He's crazy about golf, and you have to admit that he's got the sexiest voice in the business. Even people who hate golf would tune in to listen to him. And, of course, you'd have the Japanese fighting to buy it – well, probably the whole world.' She let out a ripple of laughter. 'Alex, that's pure genius! Ed, wouldn't you just *love* to make a series on golf? With Alex here as Executive Consultant?'

Ed glanced at her in horror, encountered a fierce, green glare, and managed to croak, 'Absolutely. Marvellous idea.'

'You see!' Paige turned to Wolfe, eyes alight. 'This is going to be such an enriching partnership.'

The waiters had cleared away their plates, and the three of them were now studying their dessert menus. 'I really shouldn't,' announced Paige, in a voice indicating that she'd like to.

'Oh, come on,' urged Wolfe, 'surely a little pudding wouldn't do any harm? You're so slim,' he added, peering down her cleavage once more. Eventually Paige consented to his asking for an extra spoon so that she could taste his Lemon Sabaillon.

'I guess I can't very well say no to Ed's new boss,' she said coquettishly.

There was a small silence. Paige glanced at Wolfe, who was sheepishly regarding the table cloth, then at Ed. 'Oh, Ed.' Her voice was reproachful. 'Don't tell me you've been keeping poor Alex here in suspense.'

'No, not at all. I'm extremely happy to, er, play under the Grapevine umbrella, synergy-wise.'

'Alex, did you hear that?' She gripped Wolfe's hand impulsively. 'Aren't you *thrilled*?'

He gazed besottedly into her expectant face. 'Yes, I am,' he agreed. Then, as if realising what he had said, he tore his eyes away and reached his free hand across the table. 'Welcome aboard, Ed.'

'I think this calls for champagne,' said Paige.

*

Ed pulled the cab door shut and sank into the seat next to Paige, who was blowing a kiss to Alex Wolfe through the window. Wolfe waved back from the pavement. He still looked star-struck. The light from the restaurant's fluorescent sign gleamed on his infatuated smile.

Paige kept her position by the window until Wolfe was safely out of sight, then fell back beside Ed and collapsed into giggles.

'I can't believe it!' he burst out. 'How did you do that? He even paid the bill!'

'I know. Wasn't he sweet?'

'Sweet! The man's about as sweet as a rattlesnake.'

'He just needed a little warming up.'

'Well, you certainly did that.'

'You got the deal, didn't you? Stop complaining.'

'That dress!'

'You don't like my dress?'

'I didn't say I didn't like it.' Ed fell silent for a moment, thinking of how she had lit up the whole restaurant with her beauty and vivacity – how Alex Wolfe had melted into a puddle of vanity. 'You were outrageous,' he told her.

'I was fabulous,' she said complacently.

'Outrageous and shameless.'

He caught the gleam of her smile from the streetlamps as they swung through Berkely Square. 'What's the point in being a movie star if you can't get what you want?'

Ed had to laugh. She was so much more self-aware than he had given her credit for. 'OK. Outrageous, shameless and fabulous. I owe you.'

'You sure do – big time. And I already know what you can do for me in return. I want you to come to my dress rehearsal.'

'You know I've got a ticket for your opening night?'

'You have? That's so nice. But even so, I want you to come and tell me – honestly – if I stink. I know I can rely on *you* to tell me the truth,' she said pointedly.

'Done. I'm honoured. But the rehearsal's not tomorrow, is it? I'm going to be busy nailing down the details of this offer. I don't want to let it slip through my fingers again.'

'That's OK, tomorrow's crazy for me, too: technical rehearsal, then recording the Bryan Candy show. The dress rehearsal is the day after, in the afternoon.'

'Then I'll be there – and if you want, I'll cook you supper afterwards. How does that sound?'

'Sounds wonderful. Can you really cook?' She seemed impressed.

'Come and find out. What do you like to eat?'

'Not red meat, that's for sure. I can hardly believe I ordered that duck thing, just for your sake.'

While they discussed what she did like, Ed thought about how marvellous she was. He was only just taking in the magnitude of what she had done for him. 'How did you know I'd be at L'Escapade?' he demanded suddenly. 'What made you come?'

Paige explained that she had called Maddy earlier in the day, anxious that she had betrayed a confidence. By that time, of course, he and Maddy had already spoken. Maddy knew all about the difficulty of getting hold of Wolfe, his suggestion of a particularly grand and expensive restaurant, and the fact that this was their last chance. She'd even told Ed which tie to wear.

'Oh, I get it.' Ed frowned, uncomfortable at the know-ledge that the two women had been discussing him. 'Maddy thought I'd cock it up.'

'Not at all. She just told me how worried you both were about getting the deal back on track, and that you and Alex hadn't quite hit it off yet. It was my idea to drop by the restaurant. I did kind of hover outside and peek through the window, to check how things were going. Then Jesus saw me – relax, that's the name of the *maitre d'* – and we had a little chat and decided I should come inside.'

'Well, I'm very glad you did.' Ed grinned at her. 'I'll ring

Maddy the minute I get home and give her the good news. She'll be so happy.'

And so was he. The die was cast, the company was sold, an unknown future awaited. After the turmoil of the last few weeks he felt supremely content to be trundling through London at night, with Paige beside him, feeling her shoulder nudge his each time the cab turned a corner, knowing that she had dressed up and turned out for him (and Maddy, of course). From time to time hysteria bubbled up in both of them.

'Your face,' Paige giggled, 'when I said you'd love to make the history of golf!'

'I'll have what you're having, Alex,' Ed mimicked in a simpering falsetto.

'Stop it!'

They were still laughing when the taxi pulled up in front of the house. Ed leaned forward to pay the driver, then opened the door and climbed onto the pavement, before turning back to help Paige out. She virtually stepped into his arms, still smiling – and it seemed entirely natural to pull her close and kiss her.

For a moment he was lost in physical sensation: the incredible softness of her lips, the brush of silky hair against his cheek. His whole body responded instantly to hers. He must have closed his eyes, for when he opened them he saw that Paige's were wide and startled. Self-consciousness drenched him like a bucket of icy water. Holy shit! He'd kissed Paige Carson!

He let go of her and stepped back. 'I'm sorry. I shouldn't have done that.'

'Why not?'

'You're – you're … my tenant,' he finished at last. 'I only wanted to say thank you.'

She eyed him steadily, then gave a small shrug. 'OK. You're welcome, then.' She turned away. 'See you Thursday.'

He heard her front door slam as he was thumping down his basement steps. Bugger, bugger, bugger, bugger, BUGGER!

CHAPTER 25

'"Do you not know I am a woman?"' asked Paige. '"When I think, I must speak."'

Seated alone in the third row of the theatre, Ed stifled a chuckle. He was here on sufferance; as a rule, actors and directors didn't much like strangers to be present at a rehearsal. In a note shoved through his letterbox, Paige had warned him to remain as inconspicuous as possible. Only a handful of seats scattered around the auditorium were occupied. Ed had tried to identify the other watchers: the game old bird with the limp must be the voice coach Paige had told him about. The director sat in the front row with a pencil and pad, stroking his beard and occasionally checking his watch.

Paige's rhetorical question was given an ironic twist by the fact that for much of the play she was dressed as a man, with knee-high boots. She looked disturbingly attractive. There was something intrinsically perverse about the appeal of the pantomime boy played by a beautiful girl. Although the analogy wasn't an exact one: Paige was playing a woman playing a man. She swaggered about the stage like a caricature young male, though betrayed by the occasional feminine gesture. Once she sat down the way girls do, with their legs neatly tucked, then noticed how Orlando was sitting, with knees up and legs splayed, and quickly copied him – a clever, endearing touch.

This was the first dress rehearsal, on the afternoon before tomorrow's opening night, the culmination of weeks of work. So far as possible the play was being performed in real time, without interruptions. There would be no interval. Ed had often enough been to the theatre, but had never before attended a rehearsal of any kind. It was a strange experience to be watching a play when for much of the action there was as many or more people on the stage as there were in the audience – a bit like productions on the Edinburgh Fringe. Ed spotted the odd blemish – a missed cue, a muddled entrance, a wobbly piece of set – but almost from the beginning he was entirely absorbed in the drama unfolding before him. It struck him forcibly that *As You Like It* was all about love – love in all its aspects. Perhaps it was only now that he was open to its message …

He had worried that she wouldn't be any good. Face it: Americans just couldn't do Shakespeare. It wasn't in the blood. But she was astonishing: luminous, witty, scintillating … irresistible. She delivered the verse as well as any English actress, with a perfect, unforced accent and no trace of the dreaded stutter. Even the most carping critic would not be able to withstand her poise and charm. While she was on stage it was impossible to look at anybody else. At least he found it so. When she spoke, it was as if she was speaking to him. Her words went straight to his heart. Lines that would have been innocuous from the lips of another actress seemed to him barbed with meaning. He wondered whether she was conscious of his presence in the audience, or whether her mind was entirely in the part. Who was it standing there, he asked himself – was it Paige, or was it Rosalind? The very fact that he could ask himself such a question was proof of her success. Yet he found this ambiguity tantalising. Ed wanted very much to know what Paige was feeling. The woman on the stage was obviously 'fathoms deep' in love – but who was she? And who was she in love with? He realised that he was actually jealous of Orlando – or the actor playing Orlando. What was going on here?

Automatically he assessed the set and the lighting, both rather Chekhovian, laughed at the very funny Touchstone, and clocked that Harry Keenan was turning in a brilliantly waspish performance as Jacques. But his emotions were entirely engaged with Paige – or was it Rosalind? When she reappeared dressed as a woman once more in the final scene, he felt a lump in his throat. After she had delivered the epilogue, he burst into spontaneous applause, and continued clapping for a moment or two, until he realised that the few other members of the audience were observing him curiously. Then Paige had gone, and the stage was empty. The lights came up. Ed felt dazed. The director rose to his feet, turned and asked for the auditorium to be cleared so that he could speak to the cast. 'We'll be about ten minutes,' he added. 'If any of you would like to wait, please do help yourselves to a cup of coffee in the bar.' Ed made for the exit. He would certainly wait. There was something he very much wanted to say to Paige.

Fifteen minutes later he was at the stage door, bearing a large bunch of newly-purchased flowers. The doorman let him in, and when he hesitated in the warren of passages in the basement a tall man directed him towards Paige's dressing-room. With a slight jolt, Ed recognised the actor who had played Jacques, now dressed like any other arty North Londoner heading home from work. He heard a burst of laughter from somewhere, and a complaining voice: 'I can't think why Julian wants us all back *again,* tomorrow morning.'

Here was her makeshift nameplate: *'Miss Carson'*. Ed knocked urgently. So many emotions swelled in his chest that he could hardly breathe.

'Come in,' she called. He opened the door and saw her wrapped in a dressing-gown, taking off her make-up in front of a mirror.

'Ed!' She spun round in her seat, cheeks flushed and eyes glittering with post-performance euphoria.

She looked so desirable that he wanted to grab her and kiss them both into oblivion. 'I've brought you some flowers,' he said, shoving them awkwardly in front of him.

'Oh, they're gorgeous. Let's see if we can find a vace – or is it a vahze?'

'Never mind that. There's something I want to tell you. In private.' He turned to shut the door, but found that someone else was pushing from the other side.

'Surprise!' trilled a voice.

A petite blonde woman, dressed head to toe in spotless white, swept past him, advanced into the room and held her arms open wide.

'Gaby!' Paige jumped to her feet and stepped into the woman's embrace. 'How wonderful to see you!'

'I know we said we'd meet tomorrow, but my plane landed early and I'm not a bit tired. I just couldn't wait to see you, so I caught a cab over.' The woman cupped a palm to Paige's cheek. 'You look tired, sweetie. Why don't we go for a nice early dinner and get you into bed?'

'Well, I, uh ...' Paige looked distractedly at Ed over the woman's shoulder.

'My, my, is this how the British treat a famous American movie star? I'm so glad I brought you some green tourmaline to amplify your creative energy.' The woman was now glancing disapprovingly round the shabby dressing-room. Her eyes fell on Ed, still holding his flowers. *Ghastly female!* he thought, with her sugary voice and jangly gold jewellery. Paige was having dinner with *him*.

'Ed, this is my friend Gaby Himmelfahrt, whom I've told you so much about. And, Gaby, this is Ed Hawkshead, my landlord.'

'Oh ...' said the woman unenthusiastically. Ed remembered cutting off her phone call during the flood.

'How do you do?' he glowered. Why didn't she go away?

'Actually, Ed and I were planning to eat together,' Paige began. But her voice was hesitant. It wounded him to see the way the confidence and joy she had shown as Rosalind seeped out of her.

'But, darling,' protested the woman, 'there's so much we must catch up on. Don't tell me you're too busy for a little dinner with Gaby, when I've come all this way to see you.' She gave a reproachful pout.

Paige looked from Ed to Gaby, and back again. Her face was strained. 'Ed, would you mind awfully much if we made it another night? Gaby's just flown in, and we haven't seen each other for quite a while.'

'Of course not,' he said brusquely. 'Some other time, perhaps.' There was an awkward silence. 'I'll just leave these here, shall I?' He placed the flowers on the dressing-table. 'Good evening,' he said formally, and left.

'Please welcome PAIGE CARSON!' Slumped in his armchair, an open beer can by his side, the remains of the crayfish he had prepared for Paige on a plate at his feet, Ed thumbed the remote to kill raucous cheers from the studio audience as a brass band, dressed in matching Hawaiian shirts, shorts and sunglasses, played a jazzy fanfare. Paige sashayed down a ramp, looking sensational in a low-cut mermaid-green dress. She flashed her perfect smile – the one she used on everybody. The host, Bryan Candy, stepped forward to greet her with an embrace, kissing her lingeringly on both cheeks, as if they were old friends. He escorted her to an uncomfortable-looking leather sofa, then retreated to his interviewer's chair.

'Fantabulous to have you on the show, Paige,' he simpered in his camp way. 'Wonderful to be here,' she cooed back. Ed grunted sourly. She should be *here*, sitting by candlelight at the table he had laid so carefully, drinking the wine that had been chilling in his fridge, eating the food that he had prepared. He felt an utter fool.

The euphoria he'd felt at Paige's dress rehearsal had evaporated. Only a fantasist would have imagined that a Hollywood film star could want to get involved with someone ordinary like him. He had been swept up by sentiment, confusing theatre with reality. She hadn't been speaking to him this afternoon: she'd been playing a part. *Acting*, stupid! Perhaps Paige liked him – he was almost sure that she did – but she was a realist. They inhabited different worlds. She lived on one side of the screen, and he lived on the other. The minute one of her Hollywood friends had appeared, she'd dropped him dead.

He watched Paige cope with a series of questions about what she was doing here in London. She was very accomplished. He hardly recognised the girl he'd taken to the Lakes. There was a sneering undertone to the interviewing which she deflected expertly. The host seemed to find it hilarious that the star of *Cleopatra* – 'a bit of a stinkerino' – would be playing Shakespeare. Paige conceded smilingly that it was 'a huge personal challenge' and she was 'very privileged'. A part of Ed despised her coming out with this pap. At the same time, remembering what he had witnessed earlier that afternoon, he felt indignant on her behalf.

'Of course, what we're all *dying* to know is this: what do you think of English men?' Bryan Candy leaned forward and leered at Paige. *Stop gazing at her tits, you creep.*

'Great!' enthused Paige. 'Though some are greater than others, if you know what I mean.' She giggled inanely. Several female members of the audience whooped and clapped.

'Because, you know, some nasty foreigners say that Englishmen are no good between the sheets.' *What a sleazebag.*

'I'm sure no one would ever say that about you, Bryan.'

'My wife would.' He turned comically to the audience, who roared their approval. This was successful television, Ed told himself bitterly. He could hardly bear to listen to the meaningless banter, and was relieved when the host thanked

Paige and announced, 'Now it's time to move on and meet my next guest, JACKSON ROLFE!'

The brass band perked up again. Suddenly Jackson appeared. He ran down the ramp to the edge of the stage, ignoring his host. With both hands raised high above his head as a form of greeting to the audience, he bellowed like a footballer who'd just scored a goal. 'Prat,' muttered Ed. Eventually Jackson allowed himself to be ushered towards the sofa where Paige was waiting. She smiled sweetly at him. They did not embrace.

'Super to have you here, Jackson,' Perry continued when the excitement had died down. 'You've just won an Oscar for your role in *The King*, which is hitting our screens next week, am I right?'

'Yeah,' growled Jackson. 'You Poms are always behind everybody else.'

His host chuckled sycophantically. 'And yet you're playing an English king. What attracted you most about this part?'

'Well, in the first place he's Celtic, not English.' For some time Jackson pontificated about the role of a despised outsider who triumphs over an entrenched, snobbish hierarchy. Bryan nodded seriously several times before moving the conversation on to include Paige again.

'Now you two have just finished making a film together, haven't you? It's called *Code Red*, and I believe it's a thriller about the American President who's held hostage in the Middle East. Does that have a metaphorical significance, would you say?'

'Definitely,' said Jackson. 'That's why I agreed to do it. I genuinely believe this movie could have a greater impact on the peace process than all those politicians' summits put together.'

'Well, we've got a clip here, so let's have a look.' For the next few seconds a fast-cut series of images filled Ed's television screen: Paige in uniform, Jackson in a blindfold: both of them soaked to the skin and running for their lives while bullets sprayed up sand. The camera lingered on Paige's nipples projecting through her skimpy T-shirt. Finally, there was a close-up of Jackson and Paige kissing passionately.

'Phew!' Bryan Candy wiped imaginary sweat from his brow, 'No prizes for guessing why you wanted that part, Paige.'

'Sadly not. Jackson's a happily married man. But in a way you're right. It's true that I accepted the role primarily so I could work with such an exceptionally talented artist.' She turned to smile at him shyly, and the audience cooed. They liked her. 'I don't know if you realise this, Bryan, but Jackson's a great Shakespearean actor, too. He's just too modest to say so.'

'Really?' Ed could tell from the panicked way in which Bryan Candy's eyes scanned the autocue that Paige had just veered off-script.

'Well, sure. Just ask him about all the roles he's played.'

Bryan Candy rose to the challenge. 'Hamlet?' he hazarded. 'Er ... Romeo?'

Jackson looked disconcerted. 'Aw, it was just small parts, really. That was right at the beginning of my career, before I—'

'But tell everyone *where* it was,' Paige insisted.

Jackson's lips tightened. His nostrils flared. 'Australia,' he said eventually.

'But not just Australia. In the *bush*. I think that's so wonderful, don't you?' she appealed to the audience. 'I mean, playing Rosalind on the London stage is one thing. But having the dedication to say, "Yes, my Lord" to some bushmen and a couple of kangaroos – now *that's* what I call acting.'

There was dead silence. Bryan Candy's face was stuck in a manic grimace. Jackson Rolfe's was thunderous. The audience gazed sheeplike at the stage, uncertain of what they were supposed to do.

'Let's give him a nice little round of applause?' Paige

suggested. She led the way herself, clapping her hands very prettily and beaming encouragement at Jackson.

'What a great girl,' Bryan Candy told the audience when the applause had died down. 'Star quality, that is.' He seemed genuinely moved.

At the end of the programme Ed zapped the screen. The picture had only just died, and the screen was still crackling with static, when his telephone rang. Ed groped for the portable handset.

'Greetings, Ted. I've just been watching your lodger. What a stunner! Great body! Do you think she and Jackson were, you know ... ?'

'I have no idea, Phil,' Ed replied stiffly.

'Course they were. These film stars fuck everyone, don't they?'

'If you say so.'

'Everyone but you, eh? Come on, you don't expect me to believe that, do you?'

Ed was finding Phil even more offensive than usual. It was hard enough to endure his smutty drivel at the best of times; now, while he was still raw with humiliation and disappointment, it was almost unbearable. 'You know me, Phil. Celebrities don't interest me,' he said in a bored tone.

'Oh, aye? A little bird told me you were spotted having dinner with her.'

Ed sat up in alarm. Whatever feelings he and Paige might have for one another, they were private. 'That was a business meeting.'

'Pull the other one. Come on Ted, you can tell your uncle Phil. Gorgeous girl like Paige Carson, all alone in your house ... You're only human. Thou shalt not covet thy neighbour's ass, eh? Eh?' he repeated with a dirty chuckle.

Ed gripped the phone tightly. He was beginning to get angry. It was essential that he got it into Phil's thick skull that there was no liking, let alone romance, between himself and Paige. 'Look, Phil, try to get this into your one-track mind. I have no interest whatsoever in Paige Carson.'

'And why's that, then?'

In his current state, it was easy to think of reasons. All he had to do was exaggerate and throw in some convincing details. Ed spoke fluently for at least two mintes, at the end of which he put the phone down on Phil with a sense of satisfaction. That should put him off the scent for good.

He had cleared up the debris from the living-room and was on his way to bed when he noticed an envelope on the doormat. Puzzled, he picked it up. There was no stamp, just his own handwritten name. He slit it open, and unfolded the note inside. It was very short.

I'm really sorry about this evening. I made a mess of things. Please give me another chance. X P.

Ed read it again. He stared at the 'X' and then, feeling only a little foolish, kissed the paper.

CHAPTER 26

By eight the next morning Ed was in the office. Having skipped out early yesterday to watch the dress rehearsal, he had a mountain of work to catch up on. Besides, he couldn't sleep. Paige was like a song he couldn't get out of his head. She invaded his dreams at night. By day the thought of her swung him helplessly from euphoria to uncertainty and back again. It was intensely frustrating not to be able to speak to her. He cursed the Gaby woman. He even cursed the play, which today of all days must take priority over his own longing to sweep her into his arms and let the rest of the world go hang. He would see her tonight – but almost certainly only in the presence of hundreds of strangers. Afterwards she was bound to be celebrating with the cast, if not already claimed by the Woman in White. This is what it's like to be in love with a famous actress, he told himself. She'll always be busy, absent, surrounded by cronies, and pawed by handsome actors, and never have time for ME. It was not what he would have chosen. But it felt right.

In fact, everything seemed to be going right in his life. The decision to sell Hawkshead Barry – far from making him fettered and resentful as he had feared – had fuelled him with new energy. Ideas for programmes gushed from his brain. He had already begun to feel what it would be like to have Grapevine's steady hand on the tiller of the little ship which he and Maddy had captained alone for so long, through uncertain seas: a relief, frankly.

Nevertheless, when he'd unlocked the door marked 'Hawkshead Barry' early this morning he'd felt a pang of nostalgia, remembering the excitement with which he and Maddy had moved into this rickety building in a side-street off Charing Cross Road, with little more than hope and a handful of commissions. He loved this place, despite its dusty, uncarpeted stairs, dubious loo, his tiny little private office, and the ill-fitting sash windows which in windy weather emitted ghostly wails and rattled like dead men's bones. It was comforting to hear the familiar sounds of his staff trickling into work, and then to see them through the glass door of his office. First, as always, came the two-steps-at-a-time gallop of his video technician, a bicycle nerd who arrived every morning in a blaze of skin-tight yellow neoprene, exuding sweat and eco-virtue. Next, the twitter of his assistant and the latest office runner, who would chat for England unless Ed gave them a glare. Maddy usually arrived backwards, banging the door open with her bum, being encumbered with briefcase, shopping from the nearby market, a take-away latte, and a mobile phone pressed to one ear. The last to arrive was lounging, laid-back, super-bright Toby, Ed's great white hope (except that he was black), wearing his 'I'M NOT AS THINK AS YOU STONED I AM' T-shirt and reading the paper. Phones began to ring. Emails pinged from the ether. The first crisis hit Ed's desk via a message from the film crew he'd hired for next week, announcing that they'd just had their van and all equipment stolen. Barely was that sorted before John reported from the editing suite in the basement that one of the cables was buggered – most likely, chewed through by rats. Ed reflected that there could be an upside to moving.

By mid-morning he was still only halfway through the report for Wolfe which he had come in early to write. There was his phone again. Ed answered it brusquely, his eyes and brain still focused on his screen.

"allo, am I speaking weev Monsieur 'awk'ead?'

'Ye-es,' Ed answered warily. No genuine Frenchman spoke in such a ludicrous parody of an accent.

'*Ah bon.* I telephone you habout *le Festival de Cannes.* We interest ourselves very much in your *film documentaire, Ze Hend of Weason.*'

Oh, very funny. As if anyone outside North London, let alone the Cannes Film Festival, had even heard of *The End of Reason.* Ed sighed irritably. 'Phil, you dickbrain, is that you?'

'*Pardon?*'

'Look, bugger off, will you? I haven't time for your pathetic jokes.'

The voice at the other end began to huff and puff. But this was no joke! it protested. The Artistic Director himself was speaking. Monsieur Hawkshead's film had been recommended to him by Bernard Tavernier ...

Tavernier! At the mention of the great film-maker's name Ed stood up, as if in the presence of royalty. Honeyed words poured into his ear: '*superbe*', '*estimable*', '*magnifique*'. His eyes widened. For several seconds he stopped breathing. The courteous voice flowed on – indisputably, authentically French. Phil would have been sniggering by now. 'A gala screening ... great honour ... not in competition, *naturellement,* but—'

'Shush! Go away.' This was said not to the Artistic Director, but to Ed's assistant who had been rapping on the glass of his cubby-hole and now entered his office waving a yellow Post-it note. Ed shooed her away furiously. Couldn't she see that he was busy? She hesitated, then made a dash for his desk, stuck the note next to his keyboard and exited on exaggerated tip-toe. Ed glanced at the note, automatically registering that it contained a couple of lines of text and a phone number under the heading 'URGENT'. But the next moment he had forgotten it. Nothing could be more urgent, more sweetly compelling, than listening to the Artistic

Director of the most prestigious film festival in the world ask him – no, *beg* him – for the privilege of screening his documentary. Of course it would have to be cut to feature length, and the festival was next month. Did Monsieur 'awk'ead feel it might be possible to trim half an hour off the original series? Normally Ed would have thrown a tantrum at the suggested loss of even one minute: now he answered that nothing could be easier. They discussed dates, venues, press conferences, parties. Ed's mind filled with images of palm trees and yachts. At the end of the phone call he collapsed into his chair, with a goofy grin on his face. Cannes! Recognition! He was not a sad, deluded documentary-maker, swimming against the tide of crass commercialism, but – according to the Artistic Director – an *auteur*. He laughed out loud. He, Edward Hawkshead, would be walking up a fucking red carpet! ... God, how terrifying. But it would be OK because Paige would be at his side. She would know what to do. Wait: he was getting ahead of himself. But surely this was a sign. Here was a gift that he could lay at her feet. She would love him. She *must* love him.

For one wild moment he thought of phoning her, but that was impossible. She would be in the final, final rehearsal, preparing for tonight's opening. He must not disturb her concentration. Anyway, the person who most deserved to hear the Cannes news first was right here in the office. He rose from his chair, just as his phone started to ring again. He switched the call to voicemail, opened the glass door and beckoned to Maddy urgently. She frowned at this interruption from her computer screen, though Ed knew perfectly well that she was obsessively trawling the net for country cottages. But when she heard his news she squealed with surprise and delight, and threw her arms around him. 'Ed, that's fantastic! You so deserve it.'

'*We* deserve it.' He smiled at her affectionately. 'You don't think I'd go without the woman who made it all possible, do you?'

'But ... I'm leaving. I've let you down.'

'Come on, Madds, we've been through that. You're moving on. And I know you think Cannes is a scrum, but that's because we've always had to stay in cheapo hell-holes and slog our guts out. This time we shall be *feted*. And you have to come' – he tried to look sober, but failed utterly as images of white-walled luxury and turquoise sea crowded his mind – 'because the Artistic Director has already booked us into the Hôtel du Cap!'

They were both so excited that they sent Ed's assistant out for champagne. Ed paced about his tiny office and tugged at his hair, still trying to take in this dizzying news.

'You know what this means, Maddy?'

'It means that you're a genius' – Maddy had taken over his chair and was spinning herself round – 'and that I'll be staying in the same hotel as George Clooney.' She stopped spinning and gave him a stricken look. 'I'm starting my diet tomorrow.'

'It means,' Ed said, 'that we'll be making *lots* more money.' The Grapevine deal had been structured with an up-front payment plus a so-called 'earnout' payment, which was dependent on their hitting a profit target in a couple of years' time. But it was typical of such deals that the earnout was largely academic, because the profit target was set so high that it was impossible to achieve without a miracle. Now the miracle had happened. If *The End of Reason* was showcased at Cannes, it would almost certainly be picked up for worldwide distribution, including America. It looked very much as if his 'dead duck' had just laid a golden egg. 'Forget cottages,' he told Maddy. 'I think you've just upgraded to a Georgian rectory.'

This set them off on another bout of hilarity, at the end of which Maddy wiped the tears of laughter from her eyes and regarded him soberly.

'Thank God for Paige, eh? We really owe her.'

'I know.' Ed's face softened into an infatuated smile.

'Maddy, I can't tell you how amazing she was with Wolfe.'

'You *have* told me.'

'Oh.'

'Several times.'

'Sorry.'

'In fact, you've hardly stopped talking about Paige since you met her.'

'Well, that's simply because she's – I'm – that is, we—'

'You like her, don't you?'

A dozen different answers sprang to his lips: denials, qualifications, justifications, apologies. 'Yes,' he said simply.

'Good. So do I. I *think* I'll put you in the west wing when you come to visit.'

Ed didn't know what to say. Her generosity overwhelmed him. No teasing, no reproaches: a girl in a million. He was going to miss her like hell. He hoped that somewhere, not too far from the Georgian rectory, a kind, clever, single man was at this very moment waiting for the right woman to walk into his life.

'Oh goody, here comes the champagne.' Maddy stood up and went out to help Ed's assistant, who was struggling with a couple of bulging plastic bags. The rest of his staff looked up with interest as the two women cleared a space on the so-called conference table at one end of the large open-plan room and began unloading bottles and plastic cups. All of them, except the runner, had contributed to *The End of Reason*, often working nights and weekends and putting up with Ed's obsessive drive for perfection. He was smiling as he rehearsed a few phrases with which to announce the celebration. His heart swelled with pride and happiness.

Oh, for heaven's sake. Women never knew how to open champagne. Twist *the bottle*, not the cork. And don't point it straight at the fragile glass of the sash window! He strode out of his office and grabbed the bottle out of his assistant's hands. She shrugged, and answered the phone that had been insistently ringing on her desk. After listening for a moment she sighed and pressed the hold button. 'Ed? It's that journalist guy again.'

'What journalist?'

'I put a note on your desk hours ago,' she told him reproachfully.

Ed frowned. It couldn't be about Cannes already. As for Grapevine, he and Wolfe had agreed to keep a tight lid on the news of the sale until the papers were signed and the press release agreed. The office still didn't know. It would be bad if word leaked out early. 'Ask him what it's about,' he said, giving the bottle another twist.

She returned the phone to her ear, and after a moment looked up. 'He wants to know if you have any comment about the Diary story in the *Evening News*. About you and Paige Carson.'

The champagne cork shot into Ed's hand with a festive *pop!* Maddy caught the first froth in a plastic cup. 'Come on, everyone, it's party time!' she called.

'Tell him, "No comment",' Ed said brusquely. 'And see if anyone's got an *Evening News*. Quickly!' He felt uneasy. It was no surprise that Paige was in the papers, but why would anyone want to talk to him? His scalp prickled. Something was about to go horribly wrong. 'Look, can you take over here?' he murmured to Maddy, handing her the bottle.

'But, Ed—?' Then she saw his face. 'What's the matter?'

'Just do it, Maddy. Please.'

His assistant had found him a paper. He snatched it from her hands and took it into his office, sweeping the door shut behind him. The pages tore as he wrestled it open and hunted for the Diary page. The picture caught his eye first, a still from *Cleopatra* that showed Paige wearing a very small bikini top and a very large snake. Underneath was the headline: 'Hollywood Hottie Leaves Me Cold'.

Ed subsided slowly into his chair as he read the opening sentences.

*

Once again our home-grown actresses have been up-staged by a Hollywood celeb hoping to kick-start an ailing career. Tonight Paige Carson, winner of this year's Golden Raspberry Worst Actress Award, opens in *As You Like It* at the super-chic Old Fire Station. *Le tout* London is agog to know how Carson, 29, will measure up to the Bard – and who better to ask than the man who's been sharing his house with her for the last month? 'It's a freak show. People won't be coming to see Shakespeare, but to gape at a film star. Soon we'll be seeing Tom Cruise as Hamlet,' quips TV producer Edward Hawkshead. That seems to put the kibosh on the interesting rumour that Carson and Hawkshead, spotted dining tête-a-tête at L'Escapade, are more than tenant and landlord. 'You must be joking,' insists Cambridge-educated Hawkshead. 'She may be easy on the eye, but her IQ's barely into double figures.'

It got worse. Much worse. Ed cried out in protest. He could hardly bear to read to the end. The piece wasn't signed, of course. But every line dripped with the poisonous malice of Jessika Diamond. It curdled his stomach. Phil, he thought: oafish, cretinous, clever Phil, goading him into saying the exact opposite of everything he felt, with Jessika lapping it all up and spewing it out again in this putrid rubbish. *Why?* How could anyone earn their living by making misery for others? His fingers curled into fists.

There was the sound of wild cheering. His staff began to sing, 'For he's a jolly good fellow.' Ed had just enough self-control to turn round and give them a brief thumbs-up sign. He wasn't a good fellow. The thought of Paige reading this lying garbage – of her lovely, open face closing with hurt – made him feel sick. She wouldn't believe it, of course. She couldn't. But he needed to explain how it had happened – better still, stop her from reading it in the first place. He rang her mobile, but it was switched to answerphone. 'It's Ed. Ring me as soon as you hear this. Please.' He hesitated, wanting to add to this bald message. But it was impossible to say what he wanted to a machine. He cut the call, feeling frustrated.

What about the theatre? Yes, that's where she would be, he realised with relief. That would explain why her phone was switched off. With luck she would have been too busy rehearsing to be aware of the Diary piece yet. He got the number from Directory Enquiries and, while he waited to be connected, racked his brain for the name of that friendly girl who'd rented his flat on Paige's behalf. Another champagne cork popped. Fizz: that was it.

But when she finally came on the line she was far from friendly. 'What the fuck do you want?'

Ah. So she'd seen the piece. 'Look, I can understand why you're angry. Needless to say, that Diary item is a complete distortion of what I said. I was trying to protect Paige—'

'Protect her! What, by portraying her as a Hollywood bimbo who can't act? By making out she wasn't good enough for a poncey TV producer like you? How do you think she felt when she saw what you'd said about her?'

Ed felt as if he'd been punched in the stomach. 'So she's seen it, then.'

'I had to tell her about it. I've had some bloody journalist on the phone all morning, trying to get hold of her for a "comment". Better she found out from me than be caught unprepared. I gave her a watered-down version, of course, and made her promise not to read the real thing.'

He sank his head in his hand. He had to shut his eyes against the picture of Paige reading Jessika's venomous words. *His* words. How could he have been so stupid? 'This is my fault,' he told Fizz. 'I was trying to – oh, never mind. The important thing is Paige. Is she terribly upset? Can I talk to her? I've tried her mobile but it's switched off.'

'I know. I've tried it too.'

'But – but isn't she there, at the theatre? I thought there was some kind of rehearsal.'

'There is. It was supposed to start half an hour ago. She didn't turn up.'

Oh, God. This was getting worse and worse.

'What's more, she isn't going to turn up. I've been informed by that American advisor of hers that – and I quote – "Miss Carson regrets that she has had to quit the play for personal reasons and is returning to California."'

'No!' Ed burst out. 'She can't!'

'We're on red alert here, trying to decide whether to cancel the performance or put in the understudy.'

Ed had stood up and was pacing desperately about his office, oblivious to the curious glances he was receiving from his colleagues through the glass. 'Don't cancel. Set up the understudy if you have to, but please don't cancel. I'm going to find her. She can't do this.'

'It's not my decision, Ed. Anyway, I should think you're the last person she'd want to see.'

'Please, Fizz. Believe it or not, this is even more important to me than it is to you.' He looked at his watch; it was just past noon. 'Give me until six o'clock. I promise to find her. She *will* be on that stage tonight.'

Fizz was silent. There was perhaps one degree less frost in her voice when at length she said, 'You think you know where she is?'

'Yes,' he lied.

'And you can get her here in time?'

'I guarantee it.' Ed was already shrugging himself one-handed into his jacket. He grabbed a pen and scrawled *Maddy – crisis – hold fort – explain later* – on a sheet of A4, and propped it in front of his computer screen.

He was at the door of his office now, fingers grasping the handle, phone still clasped to his ear. He could hear a murmur of voices as Fizz conferred with her colleagues. His staff was now singing the *Marseillaise*. 'Well?' he demanded impatiently of Fizz.

'I must be mental,' she told him. 'Six o'clock or you're dead.'

CHAPTER 27

There was no answer at Paige's door. Ed banged the knocker repeatedly, stepping back each time to see if her face appeared at a window. Nothing. He tried calling her again, but her phone went straight to message. There was nothing else for it: he raced down the steps to fetch the spare keys, and returned to let himself into the hall. 'Paige?' he called tentatively. No answer. Feeling like a burglar, he advanced upwards through the flat: kitchen, sitting-room ... bedroom. Pushing open the door, he was assailed by her scent. Her bed was unmade. A cream nightgown lay in silky folds across a chair. The wardrobe doors gaped wide. Her clothes were still there. Christ! Look at all those shoes. He stepped further into the room, knowing he was intruding but unable to resist. On the bedside table was a jumble of cosmetics jars, an eye-mask, an alarm clock and a fat paperback book. What was she reading? He edged closer. *The Collected Poems of William Wordsworth*: a brand-new edition with the sales slip acting as a bookmark about a quarter of the way through. His legs folded under him and he sank onto the bed, and smoothed his hand back and forth over the sheet where she had lain. 'She was a phantom of delight ...'

He pictured her the first time she'd visited his flat. He'd known then, the minute she'd walked in, that this was his girl. But he couldn't admit it, could he? She was everything he'd taught himself to despise: rich, entitled, out of his league, sure to break his heart – like India. Except that Paige was nothing like India. She was gentle and vulnerable. And he'd hurt her.

With an effort he pulled himself together. *Concentrate.* The guru had issued a statement on Paige's behalf, hadn't she? Find Gaby, and the likelihood was that you'd find Paige. After a not-too-intrusive hunt he discovered Paige's address book in a drawer in the sitting-room. He took it down to the kitchen in case she returned, and started combing through names. Gaby what? But the what wasn't a problem, because Paige had her listed under 'G'. Hmm ... Two of the numbers were clearly Californian, and the third, possibly that of an American cell phone, elicited no more than a drone followed by a disconnecting click. She must be staying somewhere in London, but he had no idea where.

OK, Ed, think. Who else did Paige know? After their first meeting, what next? The flood ... flowers in the sink ... a country weekend ... of course! Davina. He thumbed through the pages to 'D'. There was a formidable array of numbers for Davina that seemed to span the globe. He chose 'Wilshire', which looked like an English number, though Paige's Californian spelling made him smile. But once he'd keyed in the numbers, the enormity of what he was about to do made him hesitate before pressing the call button. *Hi, Davina ...?* Hello, Mrs Lovett ...? How could he cold-call the most successful female singer of all time? A woman he'd only ever seen in photographs, and then usually ninety-nine per cent naked? Ed steeled himself. He must.

For the next ten minutes he was interrogated, transferred, put on hold and obliged to repeat his message that he needed to speak to, er, Mrs Lovett about an emergency concerning Paige Carson. He had almost given up when a husky voice came on the line: 'Hi, Ed, what's the problem?' To his consternation Davina seemed to know all about him ... 'You're the guy who took Paige to the Lake District, right?' she said, by way of clarification. Well, yes, Ed agreed. But his heart sank: he could already guess from her tone that Paige was not with her, and that she knew nothing of the Diary piece. It was excruciating to have to explain what had happened. 'Oh, my God!' she cried out; then 'Poor Paige'; then 'Boy, did you ever screw up.'

Every moment he expected her to slam the phone down on him. Even to his own ears, his justifications sounded pathetic. But he pressed on. 'Never mind what you think of me,' he told her. 'It can't be worse than what I think of myself. The main thing is to find Paige, and to persuade her to do the play. The problem is that I don't know where to start.'

He was hoping that she might have some suggestion to make, however tenuous. Even so, he was astounded when she said decisively, 'You need help, kid. I'm coming right over.'

It transpired that she was not in leafy Wiltshire, as he had imagined, but in London. She had come up especially for Paige's opening night, and was at this moment working out in some gym in St John's Wood. Her chauffeur was outside. She would be with Ed in twenty minutes.

Ed pocketed his phone, feeling dazed, then took it out again to double-check if there were any messages. There weren't. The little screen showed him that it was now almost two o'clock. Only four hours left to find Paige and persuade her to come back. Perhaps he could try calling all the most likely London hotels to ask if Gaby was staying there? It was like looking for a grain of salt on a beach, but at least it would be something to do. The *Yellow Pages* would list all the hotel numbers. But first he needed Gaby's surname. He called one of the Californian numbers for Gaby in Paige's address book and waited for the message: bingo! He began calling hotels. Ten minutes later he had reached the letter 'B' when he heard the rat-tat of the door-knocker.

Davina already? That was quick. He glanced out the window and saw a silver Bentley double-parked outside. Bloody hell.

Still uncertain how to address her, he opened the door. A man of about sixty was standing on the doorstep. Ed's eyes travelled incredulously from outsize sunglasses down to harlequin-patterned snakeskin shoes, via a black leather jacket and indigo jeans, then back up to the single silver earring, nestling in a lock of grey hair.

'Hey, how're you doing?' said the man in a friendly fashion.

Ed said he was doing fine.

'Is Paige home?' The man stepped forward, confident of admittance.

'I'm afraid not.' Ed gripped the door tightly, barring the way.

'That's OK. I can wait. That way I'll really surprise her, huh?' The man's eyebrows rose momentarily above his sunglasses as he bared his teeth in a crazy grin.

Could this lunatic be a friend of Paige's? Ed was wary after what had happened last night, though it was hard to believe that even the most resourceful journalist would dress up like a – a . . .

'C'mon, let me by, feller.' The man pushed casually at the door, and at the same time pulled off his sunglasses to reveal shrivelled, bloodshot, but eerily familiar green eyes.

. . . like an ageing rock star! 'You aren't by any chance Ty Carson?' Ed enquired cautiously.

'That's right. Thank you, thank you,' he added, as if Ed has just told him that Scrap Metal was his favourite band ever.

He ambled into the hallway, stopping to gaze upwards at the plaster ceiling rose. 'Cool,' he said, before veering into the kitchen. 'You got any iced water?'

Ty did not seem at all surprised by the presence of a stranger in his daughter's flat. It dawned on Ed that Paige's father must assume him to be some kind of houseboy or butler. He was just beginning to explain who he was and why he was here when he noticed a black limousine draw up behind the Bentley. Davina stepped out of the back wearing tight white jeans, cowboy boots and a black cowboy hat, an orange poncho and the inevitable dark glasses. Feeling his grip on reality begin to loosen, Ed left Ty and went to open the front door for her.

She'd already taken off her sunglasses. Frank blue eyes raked him up and down. 'Hmm … nice,' she murmured, and strutted past him, down the hall and into the kitchen. He heard Paige's father cry out in surprise: 'Davina!'

'Ty!'

'You look great, babe.'

'I always look great.'

'You doing the Cool Planet gig?'

'Man, I'm headlining.'

Pausing only to bang his forehead once, very hard, against the wall, Ed rejoined them. 'About Paige …' he began.

'She's not home yet,' Ty explained to Davina. 'You want some iced water?'

'Why don't I make us all a cuppa?' Davina smiled brightly.

'No!' insisted Ed, more loudly than he had intended. 'I'm sorry, everyone, but we must find Paige.'

Davina patted him on the cheek. 'Chill, Ed. We're going to figure this thing out.'

'So where is Paige, anyway?' Ty asked.

It was at this point that Ed's respect for Davina began to rise. Slowly and clearly she explained the situation, while making tea for three. It was painful to listen to his own ignoble role being ruthlessly laid bare, through strangely they both seemed to blame the 'media scum' rather than him for Paige's misery.

Wrinkle by wrinkle, Ty Carson's brow cleared. 'I get it! "Where Is Paige Carson?" It's like a detective story, right?'

'That's right, Ty.' Davina gave him an approving pat.

'So what we have to do is, like, recon- recons- reconstr—'

'Reconstruct?' Ed offered.

'Dude!'

'I don't really think ...' Ed began.

But Ty was on a roll. He stood up and began to prowl around the kitchen, teacup in hand. 'OK, this is how I see it. Paige is here in the apartment. Alone. Ready to go to her rehearsal. Suddenly the telephone rings. *Brr, brr.* "Hello?"' Ty raised the teacup to his ear. 'It's the chick from the theatre telling her about the shitty newspaper story. So what does she do?'

'Well, she's upset, naturally.' Ed hated to think about it. 'And angry.'

'Wrong!' Ty arrested him with one finger pointed upwards. 'I'm not asking what she feels – what does she *do*?'

Silence. This was hopeless.

'I'll tell you what I'd do,' Davina said bluntly. 'I'd go right out to the nearest newspaper stand and read the article for myself.'

'Yo!' exclaimed Ty. 'Let's do it! Let's go find the newspaper stand. Maybe the guy who sold her the paper saw where she went next.' He clapped his hands, looking pleased with himself. 'Hey, this is fun.'

Ed wasn't convinced, but they had to do something and he couldn't think of anything better. He hustled his guests out of the house – whereupon they started arguing over which car to take. Trying to contain his irritation, Ed explained that it would be much simpler to walk. The other two seemed astounded by this notion.

'The cars can follow us,' Davina decided after some consideration. 'That way we can always just jump in if we hit a problem with the civilians.'

'Yeah. Like ... follow,' Ty agreed.

This was how it came about that Ed, despiser-in-chief of all things to do with celebrity, found himself walking down his own Islington pavement flanked by two rock icons, while a chauffeur-driven Bentley and a chauffeur-driven limo followed in convoy, purring at their heels like two overfed pets.

Ed explained that the first place where Paige might have bought a paper was the corner shop on Upper Street. Sure enough, the Ethiopian proprietor remembered Paige coming in that morning. She had bought a paper at around eleven. Yes, she was alone. No, he didn't know where she had gone afterwards. 'I love Paige Carson,' he revealed. '*Cleopatra* is my favourite film of all time.' They asked a boy stacking the shelves if he had seen which way she had gone, but with no more success. 'Aren't you Ozzy Osbourne?' he asked Ty.

Ed was briefly elated that someone had at least seen Paige, but they were no further forward. The three of them stood aimlessly on the pavement outside the corner shop, wondering what to do next.

'Don't say no, give it a go. This week's *Big Issue*!'

The chirpy voice at his elbow made Ed spin round. A *Big Issue* seller was holding out a copy of his magazine and smiling at Ed in a familiar fashion – almost as if he knew him. Recognition dawned. Wasn't this the man he'd met with Paige a couple of weekends back?

Davina was getting twitchy. 'I think we'd better get in the car,' she said.

'Wait!' Ed raised a commanding finger. Davina and Ty turned back meekly and listened while Ed interrogated the man about Paige. Yes! He had seen her here this morning, 'though she didn't seem herself at all ... didn't even see me until I'd said "good morning" to her twice. Now that's not like the Paige Carson I know. Lovely girl, she is,' he told Ty ingratiatingly. 'I reckoned it must be first-night nerves. I get a lot of theatrical types round here. Artistic temperament and that. Well, I don't need to tell you, do I?' He winked at Davina. 'I expect that's what made her want to take the cab.'

'What cab?' Ed pounced.

'How do I know what cab? I just flagged it down and popped her inside.'

Ed gripped the *Big Issue* seller's arm. 'Look. This is very,

very important. Did you hear her say where she wanted to go? Do you remember anything – anything at all?'

'What do you think I am – stupid? Course I remember.' He eyed them cannily. 'Tell you what, buy my last three *Big Issues* and I'll tell you where she went.'

'Do you take dollars?' asked Ty.

Ed reached for his wallet, pulled out a note and handed it to the *Big Issue* seller. 'That should cover it. Now where is she?'

''Fraid I haven't got much change.'

'Never mind the change! Where did she go?'

'Thanks, mate. One each, was it?'

'Where?' Ed was ready to throttle him.

'Parkview Hotel, Piccadilly.'

Yes! Ed spun round on the sole of his shoe and spontaneously hugged Davina.

'We can go in my car,' she said, disengaging herself and raising an imperious hand towards the limousine, which was waiting in the bus lane.

'Why not mine?' asked Ty, pointing at the Bentley behind it.

'Mine's bigger.'

'It may be *longer,* but you've got to think of the engine power, babe.'

'For fuck's sake!' Ed was nearly frantic. 'We're going in Ty's car, and we're going now,' he commanded, practically pushing Davina inside. 'Parkview Hotel,' he barked to the driver, as if he'd been ordering chauffeurs about since birth, '... and make it snappy.'

'Way to go, man.' Ty clapped a hand around Ed's shoulder. 'Let's rock and roll!'

CHAPTER 28

Paige stood at the hotel window, gazing out over the park. Fresh green leaves fluttered in the treetops. Birds darted busily in and out of the canopy, building their nests. The sky was a gentle blue scattered with silvery pillows of cloud. Why wasn't it raining, to match her mood? The colours ran together as once again her eyes blurred with tears. 'I wonder if I'll ever see London again,' she sighed.

'Who needs it?' There was a sharp click as Gaby snapped the lock of her suitcase shut. 'The sooner we get out of this nasty little country, the better. Isn't it fortunate that you had your passport with you in your knapsack?'

'I guess,' Paige said listlessly. Gaby had booked them two tickets on the early evening flight back to LA. The car would be here any minute to take them to the airport.

'Once we're home, someone can arrange for your things to be picked up from that awful man's house and shipped over,' Gaby told her. 'Now, is that everything?' Paige heard her moving around the bedroom, opening drawers and cupboards to check that she hadn't left anything behind. She turned round with a wan smile.

'What would I do without you, Gaby?' Her friend seemed so purposeful and determined, while she just felt numb. She hadn't known it was possible to cry as much as she had done today. Gaby had insisted that she drank plenty of Kabbalah water to make sure she didn't get dehydrated.

'Come and sit down,' Gaby urged. 'We still have a few minutes before the airport limousine arrives. Let's see if I can get rid of those tension knots.'

Paige plopped herself down on a damask-covered ottoman and turned back to the window again. Gaby's hands swept her hair aside and began kneading her neck.

'This whole trip has been a bad dream.' Gaby's voice flowed soothingly into her ear. 'You'll see that, once you get back to your real life. Just think: you'll be home *tonight,* California time.'

Tonight! Tonight Paige was supposed to be on stage. The now-familiar faces of the company flitted through her head: Julian, Fizz, Sid, lovely Harry. 'I feel so bad about the play,' she moaned. 'But I can't do it. I just can't walk on to that stage and pretend to be a woman in love when – when –' She bent her head and pressed her fingers to her eyes.

'Of course you can't. No one could possibly expect it of you. Thanks to *that man* you've lost all your emotional energy. I was shocked when I saw what he'd done to your aura. Anyway, didn't you say there was an understudy?'

'Well, yes, but ...' But Rosalind was *her* part. Paige hated to think of the Celia girl pulling on *her* boots, adjusting *her* dress, speaking *her* lines and getting the laughs which belonged to *her*. Paige had loved playing a woman who was so brave and funny and confident – the kind of woman she wanted to be herself. Rosalind wouldn't have fled when the going got tough; Rosalind could stand up to anything and anyone. But then Rosalind had Orlando. He wrote her love poems and hung them from the forest trees for all to read; he didn't pour contempt on her through the pages of a newspaper.

'And really, Paige, what does it matter?' Gaby continued. 'It's only some little British theatre. Hardly anyone would have seen you – nobody who counts in Hollywood. Oh! – by the way, guess who I've just added to my client list?' She mentioned a big director, with an even bigger drink problem.

'Right now he's casting the most exciting new picture and – well, I did just happen to just drop your name into the conversation. It would give me such pleasure to facilitate a meeting between you two. You'd be playing the lead, of course, a beautiful woman attorney defending a man on a rape charge. She herself was abused as a child, but she starts to fall in love with the man and—'

'No!' said Paige, sitting up so sharply that her hair snagged painfully on Gaby's Tree of Life ring. 'I mean, I appreciate it, Gaby, but I'm just not ready for that.'

'Whatever you say, sweetheart.' Gaby pulled her firmly back into position. 'Try to relax.'

But Paige was thinking about Hollywood: all the hustling and the deals, the parties and the gossip. Did she really want to go back? And then there was her reputation for pulling out of projects: wouldn't this make that worse? She stood up abruptly and faced Gaby. 'I think I should stay and do this part.'

Gaby cocked her head and gave Paige an indulgent smile. 'Is that Paige talking? Or is it our old enemy Mr Misplaced Guilt?'

Paige hesitated.

'You don't owe these people anything,' Gaby told her. 'They haven't respected you. I saw that drab little dressing-room. I know what a pittance they're paying. And how you could even contemplate going on stage after that disgusting article ...' She made a face and pointed towards the round breakfast table on which the newspaper still lay open.

Paige's face crumpled. 'Don't!' she begged. The cruel phrases she had tried to put out of her head flooded back. She could take any amount of bitchery and lies from journalists – but *Ed*? How could he have said such terrible things about her? Why? What had she done wrong? Veering away from the offending sight of the newspaper, she hurled herself face-down on the bedspread and burst into tears once more.

'I always said he was no good.' The bed sagged as Gaby

perched herself on the edge and laid a hand on Paige's shoulder. 'I did try to warn you. A man like that could never make Paige Carson happy. He's a little English nobody who thought it would be fun to fool around with a movie star. And so rude! As if any real person would care whether Wordsmith is alive or dead.'

'Words*worth*,' Paige sobbed, and buried her face in the pillow. That was the part of the article she could never forget or forgive. For her, their trip to the Lake District had been magical. He'd shown her his special places. He'd raised the shutters and let her into his life, and she'd done the same. They'd helped each other with their work. He'd *kissed* her, and she'd been sure it was for real. That's how it felt to her. And yet he'd betrayed her with a cruelty she hadn't thought he possessed. *Hawkshead laughed off the rumour of romance with Carson. 'How could I be interested in someone who thinks that William Wordsworth is still alive?'* The press might have made up the rest, but that detail could only have come from Ed himself.

Paige dried her face on the pillow. Gaby was right. Ed was not the man for her. She was finished with him, and finished with England.

There was a rat-tat on the door. 'That'll be the porter. Our limo must have arrived.' Gaby stood up. 'Why don't you run into the bathroom and rinse your face with some nice cold water?'

Moving like a sleep-walker, Paige crossed the Aubusson carpeting to the bathroom. Puffy eyes stared back at her from the mirror. She could never have played Rosalind in this state. Artists were more easily hurt than ordinary people, Gaby had told her. They had thinner skins.

Water gushed into the marble basin, cutting off the murmur of conversation between Gaby and the porter. They were still talking when she turned off the faucet and reached for a towel – and now she could hear raised voices. Maybe there was problem with the car?

'I'm telling you, she's not here!'

Paige was shocked to hear the sharp note in Gaby's voice. What was going on? She walked back into the bedroom. Gaby was gripping the edge of the door and trying to shut it on a tall figure in black.

'Baby!' roared a voice.

'D-D-Dad?'

Her father burst into the room, pushed past Gaby, and held out his arms to Paige. A cry tore out of her. The next moment her cheek was pressed to leather and her eyes squeezed shut as she hugged him tightly around the waist. He felt strong and warm and safe. 'Hey, beautiful,' he murmured.

With a sound halfway between a laugh and a sob she drew away to look up into his face. 'Wh – Why – What are you doing here?'

'I came to see your gig. My girl's going onstage, and I wanna be there.' His expression grew serious. 'You know, you gotta go on. Can't let the fans down.'

'Oh, Dad, if you only knew ...' But her words trailed into silence as she saw past his shoulder. Two other figures were edging past Gaby, who stood by the open door, angry spots of red on both cheeks. First came Davina, who gave Paige an encouraging grin. Behind Davina, looking pale and pent up, stood Ed.

'Go away!' she shouted, lunging towards him.

'Please, Paige.' He put up his hands defensively. 'I'm sorry. It's all my fault. It was a terrible mistake.'

'You bet it is. I never want to see you again.'

'Just listen a minute. I know what you must think of me—'

'Liar! Skunk! Two-faced, snotty, British ...'

'... twit,' supplied Davina.

Paige spun round to the breakfast table and slammed her palm down on the open newspaper. 'Are you going to deny that you said this?'

Ed's jaw clenched as he met her eye. 'No.'

Her hand clawed the top sheet of newspaper into a scrumpled ball and hurled it at his face. It dive-bombed to the floor a short way beyond her toes. His expression altered subtly. Was he laughing at her? She stamped her foot in fury. 'Get out!'

'Er … taxi to the airport for Miss Himmelfahrt?' A pimply young man whose uniform hung off his gangling frame hovered in the doorway. He looked round them with a nervous smile.

'Paige, you can't leave,' pleaded Ed. 'No matter what you think of me, you have to do the play. You'll hate yourself for ever if you don't, and I couldn't bear that.'

'Don't listen to him!' ordered Gaby.

'I'm not asking for myself,' he said. 'I'm asking for you.'

'He's right, you know,' interjected Davina. 'He may have acted like a jerk. But that's no reason to fuck up your career.'

Paige hesitated. If only Ed wasn't looking so handsome, or so troubled. Despite everything, she ached to touch him.

'You may take the luggage,' Gaby told the pimply porter. She turned to the rest of them and announced, 'Paige and I are leaving.'

'Don't listen to her,' begged Ed.

'Paige cannot tolerate this kind of disturbance to her delicate psychic system. I must remove her before any more damage is done. Come on, sweetie. We can do some meditation on the plane.'

'*Remove* her?' Ed was scowling furiously at Gaby. 'She's not a piece of furniture. She'll do what she bloody well likes.'

Gaby drew herself up. 'Please do not use language in my presence. Come, Paige.'

'Man, is that one uptight chick,' Dad murmured audibly to Davina.

Paige had picked up her coat, but now put it down uncertainly. 'You know, Gaby, I'm not sure I want to leave right this minute. I sort of think I should do the play. I mean, Dad's here, and Davina has come specially to see me. Why don't you stay on for a couple more days, like we originally planned? I know how much you wanted to see Madame Tussauds.'

Gaby looked at her sorrowfully. 'It's that man, isn't it? He's completely mesmerised you.'

'He has not! I hate him.' Paige snatched up her coat and marched towards the door.

'Don't, Paige!' Ed stepped forward and caught her arm. 'Can't you see the woman's manipulating you? She doesn't want you to succeed. She likes you dependent. That's how she earns her living. Don't tell me you don't pay for everything – plane fares, this hotel, the privilege of talking to her'

Paige yanked her arm free. 'Gaby's my *friend*. That's something you wouldn't understand.'

Ed blocked her path. 'Walk out on me if you want to, but don't walk out on the best role of your career. Which are you going to choose, William Shakespeare or the the Ashag of Shagpile here?'

He flipped a hand at Gaby, who gasped and squared up to him like a puffed-out dove confronting an eagle. 'I'll have you know that I am a certified member of the American Association of Transpersonal Counselling!'

'Certifiable, more like.'

'Plus a doctorate in Holistic Life Science.'

'Oh yeah? Where's that from – the University of the Astral Plane?'

Gaby gasped, and looked pathetically at Paige. 'Did you hear how he spoke to me?'

Loyally Paige put her arm around Gaby's shoulders. 'Let's go. You do not have to listen to this garbage.'

The porter, who had already picked up Gaby's bag and put it down several times, bent again to grip the handle.

'Just a minute.' Davina, who'd been sitting on the arm

of the couch next to Ty, now rose to her feet and sauntered forward. 'If she's your friend, sweetpea, how come she told the theatre this morning that you'd pulled out of the play for good, when a minute ago you just said you were ready to do it?'

'Did you?' Paige's hand slipped from Gaby's shoulder. 'You never told me that.'

For a moment Gaby looked nonplussed. Then her usual serene expression reasserted itself. 'Trust me, Paige. You don't have the resources to carry this part. Human beings are like waiters in a busy restaurant: we can carry only so many plates of stress at a time. That newspaper article was a great big platter. If it hadn't been for *him* ...' She shot Ed a steely look.

'Did someone say something about food?' asked Ty. 'Mine's a steak, medium rare.'

'If it hadn't been for Ed,' said Davina forcefully, 'you wouldn't have the option of going on stage. They would have cancelled tonight's show if he hadn't stopped them. As it is, they're standing by. If you don't show up some understudy's going to play your part.'

Paige glanced at Ed. Was this true? Then at Davina, who was slapping her cowboy hat impatiently against one knee. Then at Gaby, whose sympathetic gaze seemed to suck her in. 'I don't know what to do,' she moaned.

A babble of voices broke out around her.

'If you stay here I cannot be held responsible for your spiritual health.'

'Don't fuck up, sweetpea.'

'Keep the faith! You gotta show up for your fans.'

'We'll miss that plane if we don't leave *now*.'

'Shut up!' a voice shouted above the hubbub. Everyone turned to stare at Ed, who was standing on a gilt chair – none too steadily, though Paige thought that he still managed to look romantic, in a dishevelled, desperate way. His eyes glowed with passionate intensity.

'Paige, listen to me. Everything in that article is the exact opposite of what I feel, which is that you're clever and brave, and generous and funny – a beautiful girl – a terrific actress ...'

'Keep going,' murmured Davina.

'... and I love you.'

'You do?' There was a tremble in her voice.

'Yes, I do.' A sudden smile lit his face. 'I really do!' He laughed joyously and leapt off the chair. The next moment she was in his arms, while he planted wild kisses on her hair, her ear, her cheek-bone and finally her lips.

'Oh, this is so romantic,' Davina sighed. 'Didn't I always say that English men were the *best*?'

Ty burst into song, accompanying himself on air guitar:

I was on a pinnacle, cynical,
Then you came along like a miracle, lyrical,
My little girl, rockin' my world.
WHAAAAH!
What a surprise, the girl with the grass-green eyes.

'That's great, Ty,' said Davina. 'Maybe you could sing me some more in the car?'

'Huh?'

'We'll see them later, at the play. Right now Ed and Paige need to, you know ...'

'Oh, right. I'm outta here.' He rose to his feet, then frowned. 'What happened to the uptight chick?'

But Gaby had gone. So had her bags. Paige was ashamed to feel relieved. But right now there was something important she had to do. Stepping out of Ed's embrace she touched her father's arm. 'Dad? When you get home, be sure to say "hi" to Lindsay for me, will you? And – and tell her I'm looking forward to coming to the ranch and seeing you – all *three* of you – as soon as I can.'

'You mean it, babe?'

'You bet.'

He gave her a huge, leathery hug, then did the same for Ed. 'If you ever need the jet,' he told him, 'just give me a call.'

'And Davina,' said Paige, 'you saved my life.'

'Not me, honey. Ed did.' She gave him a wink. 'Now shouldn't you call that theatre?'

When they'd gone Ed talked to Fizz on the phone while Paige nestled her cheek against his back and wrapped her arms around him, eyes blissfully closed. Her fingers slid under his jacket and played tantalisingly up and down his ribs, while their combined body temperature soared towards melting point. 'Everything's fine,' he reported, trapping her hand and swinging round to face her. 'They're expecting you in, let's see, a couple of hours' time.'

'Davina's left us her limousine. She's going to ride with Dad.'

'So ... you're not in a hurry.' He was grinning at her.

Paige glanced at the huge canopied bed. Her eyes danced with mischief. 'I'm going to lock that door,' she said.

CHAPTER 29

The dressing-room smelled of stage paint, face powder, and the mustiness of theatrical costumes. Nathan's handwritten note, wishing her success, lay on the table in front of her. The picture Mom had sent of Darcy the dog, apparently saying 'hi', was stuck into the lightbulb-framed mirror. Rosalind's boots were set out next to the chair where she sat, ready for her to step into. For the moment, she was wearing the low-cut dress in which she made her first appearance on stage.

Five minutes to curtain-up. The sounds of the company, as they limbered up for the performance in their own eccentric ways, echoed comfortingly round the steamy basement.

'*Vroom, vroom, vroom!*'

'"And did those feet in ancient time" ...'

'Aaarghgle gargle ...'

'Six Scottish sock-cutters cockily cutting socks. Six sottish cocksuckers – Bleedin' 'ell ...'

She recognised every voice; she shared their nerves. They all depended on her. Rosalind was the sun around whom the other characters revolved.

Paige leaned forward to examine her face in the mirror. There was a speck of lipstick on her teeth. Wasn't that supposed to be lucky?

She heard a light knock, and Harry put his face round the door. 'All right, then?'

'Fine.' She smiled. 'Break a leg.'

He closed the door softly, just as Fizz's voice came over the intercom. 'Beginners, please!'

Paige tensed. This was it. In a few minutes she would sweep onto that simple stage – nothing more fancy than a few raised floorboards and a back curtain – and begin to draw her audience into a comic tale of pretence, misunderstanding, and true love. It was, in Julian's words, 'an enchantment', yet it felt more real to her than anything she had ever done.

The roar of the audience faded to a murmur. Silence fell. The air prickled with expectancy. Then she heard the rumble of Orlando's voice as the play began. There could be no going back now – and she didn't want to. The woman who looked at her from the mirror was poised and confident. A smile lurked in her eyes. When Rosalind fell for Orlando in Scene Two, all Paige had to do was think of Ed. That wasn't too hard. His face floated before her, his words filled her mind. She could still feel his touch on her body. Playing the part of a woman in love was no longer an act.

She glowed with happiness. Ed was passionate and romantic. He was sensitive, intelligent, and loyal – also moody and opinionated, but she could handle that. He told her things she didn't know. He made her feel safe. Best of all, he loved her. He was the man she'd been looking for all her life.

Acknowledgements

Actors, producers, a studio executive, several agents, a publicist, and a brace of screenwriters showed me their Hollywood haunts, divulged their tricks, smuggled me into parties, and regaled me with stories for this book – but only if I promised not to name them. They know who they are, and I want to thank them here for their generosity, candour and good company.

I am particularly grateful to Gary and Jane Krisel, who gave me much advice, hospitality and encouragement, and who read the Hollywood section and returned detailed comments within seven hours of receipt. I'd also like to thank my spy in the London theatre, and the television documentary-maker off whom I bounced my wilder plot lines. Any mistakes or implausibilities are mine.

I lost an initial draft of this book, all my notes and equipment, and my writing space when the building in which I rented an office burned to the ground. (Warning: never leave your back-up disk by your computer while nipping out for a sandwich.) Recovery from this disaster would have been impossible without the patience and loyalty of my unflappable agents, Jonathan Lloyd and Deborah Schneider; and, especially, support far beyond the call of marital duty from my husband, Adam. Thank you, all.